The Parasite

THE HUNGARIAN LIST

THE HUNGARIAN LIST
Series Editor
Ottilie Mulzet

The Parasite

FERENC BARNÁS

Translated by Paul Olchváry

LONDON NEW YORK CALCUTTA

Seagull Books, 2020

Originally published in Hungarian as *Az élősködő* by Kalligram
© Ferenc Barnás, 1997

First published in English translation by Seagull Books, 2020
English translation © Paul Olchváry, 2020

This translation was funded by the National Endowment for the Arts (USA)

Excerpts have appeared in English translation in *Absinthe*: *New European Writing* (Fall 2006) and *turnrow* (Fall 2003)

ISBN 978 0 8574 2 740 3

British Library Cataloguing-in-Publication Data
A catalogue record for this book is available from the British Library.

Typeset by Seagull Books, Calcutta, India
Printed and bound by WordsWorth India, New Delhi, India

The Parasite

Prologue

If I didn't stubbornly believe in the power of the written word, I would never have recorded this patchwork of a confession. Not even my unhappiness could have forced me to do so, and, indeed, perhaps I would have been wiser, instead of lamentably scribbling away and risk becoming a monster in the reader's eyes, to turn to a psychiatrist. But I didn't dare subject myself to therapy, fearing that my doctors would make me even sicker than I already was.

And so I decided to keep a journal. The pages pressing so tightly, quietly against each other, so I hoped, would sooner or later swallow up my depraved thoughts; the written words would show mercy upon the perverse emotions that I kept securely under lock and key and wouldn't have dared share with anyone. By remaining silent I had resigned myself to a continual lie, a lie that in turn built a trap for my cowardice, indiscernibly, so that, after all the years I'd spent trying to escape, it might take me prisoner once and for all. Had I committed a crime, and done so in time, perhaps that would have saved me: a constraint on my external freedom would have forced me into disciplined thinking, and then—so I childishly deluded myself—my illness would not have been able to unfold as it did. As a law-abiding citizen, however, I was undeserving of such simple punishment, so nothing could protect me from myself.

If I didn't talk about my shameful illness even now, I'd surrender once and for all. Like a fool, I am convinced that by the time I record the last of my words, I might breathe easier, and no longer will it be the benevolent narcosis of medications that allows me to accept the unbearable.

PART ONE

1

Perhaps it was all decided at the beginning. It's hard to put a finger on why, but I was always drawn instinctively to illnesses. As a child, for example, I regularly escaped into hospitals with a varying assortment of suspicious complaints, as if I could be secure nowhere else. Hospitals were my world, for no matter how fixedly ordered the outside world purported to be, I felt genuinely free only between those drab olive-green walls. Although after two or three weeks it was invariably determined that there was nothing wrong with me, as I packed my things to go home, I knew without a doubt that, soon enough, I would return. That which children fear, that which makes adults uneasy, was soothing to me.

Above all it wasn't the sundry peculiarities of this or that clinical case that interested me, but the enigmatic aura that illness in general constructs about itself. No sooner would I step into a hospital at my father's side than I would sense it: I had only to notice the tired face of the plump old man slumped behind the little sliding window of the porter's booth by the hospital entrance—a face shuttered by a mixture of boredom and the bureaucratic solemnity porters are expected to display. Surely he was among the most important people here; despite his blank stare he wore his dark-blue hospital-issue overalls with the pride of someone entrusted with authority, well aware that, here, he was not simply a guard carrying out his duty but a breathing crossing-bar at the front, dividing the two worlds. His eyes, glowing sometimes dimly, sometimes almost brightly, seemed to exude an inscrutable light that enveloped all those who entered the hospital. I noticed the difference immediately, as acutely as a virologist senses a sterile laboratory right away while others don't notice a thing. With deep breaths I inhaled this light. Inhaled? Let me clarify what I mean by 'light'; for what little light did seep in through the windows was in fact subdued in its effect by that familiar hospital smell most people find so disagreeable. Perhaps I'm not mistaken in now asserting in words what I then sensed: that this glitter I saw was a materialized extension of the illnesses of those suffering in the hospital present and past. This perception of mine was akin to those rare and fortunate occasions when we manage to see behind another person's smile and notice its supporting pillars—knock those pillars out of place, and what a moment before seemed indestructible is gone, just like that.

I breathed easier on seeing the doctors appear in the hallway. Ah yes, I'm home once again, I thought as my father accompanied me, as usual, to the in-patient receiving office. I was worried only that the doctor who'd been summoned to give me a last-minute look before sending me on to the appropriate ward might reconsider things, and be pleased to inform us that I needn't stay after all. But vigilance saved me. Unfalteringly I followed through on the symptoms I had come up with a week earlier, so that the doctor, after yet another test, would be ready to hand me over to some darling nurse. How could he have suspected that a ten-year-old boy was playing sick? While he racked his brains over the cause of my constant headaches, recurring dizziness and fainting spells, I wanly awaited the verdict, worried that my trickery would be uncovered any minute. The sight of my frightened face, however, could hardly have led him to suspect scheming on my part, especially not the sort at issue: my desire to be in a place everyone else would abandon at once if only they could. But I deceived him. When he notified us that they would have to draw a sample of my spinal fluid for testing, I gave a sigh of relief, as if heartened by the promise of a speedy recovery.

Next I was led into the ward and shown my bed. Rarely would I arrive with pyjamas in hand, so my father would ask the nurse to dig me up some standard, hospital-issue nightclothes. When, a little while later, a rosy-cheeked young woman placed the clothing before me, my reaction was not that of other boys; not a bashful stare but, rather, exhilaration. As if only with this ill-matched, overwashed uniform could I become a fully legitimate denizen of the hospital— in contrast with those patients who wore their own pyjamas and robes, and whom I consequently did not consider full-fledged hospital residents but practically civilians. I may have looked ungainly in those scraps of fabric, but they were now mine as surely as the guile by which I'd succeeded in deceiving everyone around me. Now I only waited to say goodbye to Father. Oh, he tried cheering me up, he did, saying I shouldn't be scared, that they'd pay me a visit in no time. But even as he patted me on the head, I was hoping it would take as long as possible for someone to come along and wrench me from the freedom awaiting me. No sooner did Father step from the ward than I gave yet another sigh of relief; this time, a genuine one. My final link with the outside world had disappeared: no longer would Father's presence disturb my solitude.

In this confinement, the fear I never could have overcome at home or at school began to slowly let up. As if only here—cramped between four walls, separated from the outside world—could I get air. I breathed in what my roommates' sick bodies and frightened expressions exuded, and doing so was as liberating a sensation as a convict must feel on unexpectedly being granted two days of freedom. It was in this atmosphere, bleak and sad to virtually everyone else, that I found my dubious self-identity. Not only was I soothed by the proximity of my fellow patients, but I also drew strength from within them; I nourished myself on their worries, their uncertainties and their pains, not unlike those creatures that cull their food from excrement. I didn't even have to scrutinize the others' faces to discern their palpable vibration, their marquetry of fear. Fear of their illnesses. Perhaps it was a heightened sensitivity to this shadow play, distinguishable from their bodies, that attracted me to the wards to begin with; for there I had the opportunity to observe that the worse off someone was, the more this vibration appeared on him or her as something that separated itself from the material world while remaining in contact with it all the while. Later, when my eyes chanced to cross paths with those of some fellow patient, it was this sort of expression I invariably met with, one that had torn through a veil-like drape. And I couldn't shake the impression that it wasn't even him or her who was watching me, but that in fact the current, the aura, surrounding this face was descending upon me.

It was here, too, that I learnt another thing: silence lays the path for our understanding of those people who, for whatever reason, we deem interesting. For days on end I lay near these wordless bodies, for that was the only way to truly map them. Now, most people believe that we can get to know others best through conversation. My experience on this point differs. A breathing body near us transpires something of singular essence as surely as the blood of the newly executed might suddenly release its still-vital scent on touching freshly fallen snow; one need only note the person-specific 'messages' that emanate from pleasant or unpleasant smells. Perhaps my job was made easier because illness rendered the bodies of my fellow patients vulnerable, having torn away the armour they'd earlier built around themselves through steady practice in the outside world. Here, on the hospital beds, bodies touched as imperceptibly as the individual flavours of vegetables and sauces commingling on a dinner plate served up by a master chef.

Not even if he'd told me in words could I have grasped the dreadful powerlessness emanating from the man in the bed next to mine. His body seemed bound to the mattress with invisible ropes, and before I knew it I too had been sapped of strength. Through the arm's length of space between us I accepted this man's immobility into myself, and soon enough, whatever had slowed his blood pressure had done the same to me. Let's just say I'd wormed my way to the heart of the life force that held his system intact: suddenly I was overcome by a warmth of unknown origin. Why shouldn't I assume that the human body, this skin-draped mass of breathing flesh, this vessel stuffed with cells and tissues, this receptacle filled with fluids at or about 98.6°, would submit under given circumstances to a wholly different gravitational force than the one we're used to? For instance, to the magnetism that fuses two bodies without their ever touching? When we are under the influence of this force, we perceive things in much the same way as those dogs that, even from a great distance, seem capable of sensing that their masters are in danger.

Had I paid attention only to the words of grievance uttered by this or that roommate of mine, never could I have understood the gloom written all over their blank faces and folded hands, the self-resignation woven into every detail of their bearings. Simply by observing how the man across from me was lying on his bed, for example, I could discern his thinking as regards his illness. When he buried his head in the pillow or clasped his hands around the nape of his neck, I knew that he was back to worrying himself silly over the next day's operation, although only a moment before, each of us in turn had told him just how groundless his fears were.

Having listened to all of our encouraging words, all at once he seemed as tired as could be. But there was no deceiving me. Only now was he truly distressed. I saw this plainly from how he clasped his hands. When, after a while, he'd had enough of his solitary fears and got to talking once again, how different an effect his sentences had! It wasn't the meaning of the words as they struck my ears one after another that I now found myself interpreting, but, rather, the mysterious relationship that accommodated his words to the back of his hand, the way he held his head and his ever-changing expressions. He seemed indeed to be involuntarily breathing in reverse, in order to first introduce to his body the sounds he was so busy formulating, and in so doing to give news of his distress. His words consequently brought to the surface the broken fragments of fear lurking in his cells and tissues. Perhaps I perceived the workings of this exceptional process only because I'd already spent days silently studying the body this man inhabited.

Surely this impression of mine was due partly to the fact that when people are confined together in a tight space for a very long time, their minds sometimes take faint presentiments about what the other minds (as well as their own) are up to, and turn them into torrential certainties. At any rate, it can safely be said that illness sweeps us into a radically new if temporary paradigm of being. What happens is this: our internal sense of time overwhelms our usual perception of the clock on the wall, of the world outside us. Oddest of all, while we hardly even noticed this mental bellwether of ours before, within moments we are on the most intimate of terms. Unknown yet familiar, it severs us indiscernibly from the outside world. This is, I believe, a force equal in potency to intelligence, and one whose presence is revealed by illness. If only for seconds, it can return us to a unity that, we thought, wrongly, we had forever lost.

Most people loathe hospital smells. Their stomachs turn, and if possible they open a window. This was not me. I breathed in these obnoxious odours with rapture. If a fellow patient received a hideous shot in the arm or had a bandage reapplied before bedtime, for example, and the bloody swab of cotton or wound-soaked gauze was left atop a nightstand to stink up the room, my nostrils would flare. Many patients managed to talk their way out of their daily baths, but was I troubled by the putrefied smell of their bodies? No, I simply ascribed the stench as rightly belonging to the store of hospital scents, and accepted it as an integral part of life within these walls.

Every day I took long walks around the building. My favourite place was the waiting area outside the operating room, where I invariably encountered wheelchairs and rolling beds. Lustfully I breathed in the smells escaping through the door of the operating room, like someone already so familiar with the fragrances of the most diverse flowers that he would much prefer to finally *taste* a petal instead. Then I walked over to the outpatient receiving area, to those freshly arrived people who, only minutes before, had been going about the city. The odour of petrol exuded from their coats along with a wide range of other smells that had settled upon them in minute particles: the stench of the city. These conspicuously 'civilian' scents were strange compared to the hospital air I'd got used to. So it was all for naught, was it—that invisible filter which, so I was convinced, hung in the air by the porter's booth? Those recalcitrant smells had been able to slip in here nonetheless! I could only hope that they, too, would soon be soaked up by the dominant odour. And, sure enough, soon I found myself imagining that the very colour of the outpatients' breaths had changed: unsuspecting strangers are just as subject as anyone to the hospital's unspoken, unwritten, unchangeable laws. No, I am not referring to measurable conditions brought on by humidity, air pressure or even some malodorous mixture of bacteria, but to that which might be called the hospital's 'actual psychic climate'; or, it might be said, its psychic space free of material influences. Only the initiated are privy to this knowledge. Priests and sacristans understand this full well as their flocks depart the house of worship, and sensitive cantors may also perceive it to a degree.

Sometimes I would leave the outpatients behind and head off towards those former patients who, a few days before, might have been walking about these same hallways. It was entirely by chance that I first happened upon a hospital morgue. I couldn't even recall how I wound up in the basement, but all at once I'd left the building, and found myself there after a short walk. Unable to get in, I could determine only roughly what deodorizers were used by the paid servants of death to make their jobs bearable. The elusive stench of newly rotting flesh also managed to waft its way to my nose somewhat, but it had to overcome various obstacles: walls, doors and the pumping mechanisms of the air-conditioning system. Yet I couldn't indulge in such reveries for long, as I was regularly shooed away from there.

Unlike my roommates, I didn't mind the hospital food. When, as happened each day around noon, the food cart rolled into the room, they conspicuously sneered, as if looking upon swill. By contrast my mouth began watering at once, and before the food ever touched me, my tongue perceived the flavour of the oversalted chicken or beef broth and the vaguely milky, stewed spinach or cabbage the other patients turned up their noses at. Sometimes my fellow patients completely avoided the meals they were served, instead unwrapping the fried pork or breaded chicken that family or friends had brought in during visiting hours. Their fussiness suited me well:

after finishing my own portion, I eagerly fell upon their untouched plates. Ah, the life! I felt like a veritable gentleman.

Although I would have preferred not to notice my roommates' stares on such occasions, I knew full well they were watching me as if I were some hog let loose in the ward. All the same, I didn't raise my head. Instead I stared fixedly into my plate, reflecting upon those fellow patients who found the hospital food so disagreeable that they'd been literally starving for days. As for myself, I'd already had five cups of sugary tea that morning, and I called out to the nurse as she went away: Couldn't I have just one more cup? I said this without looking up. Although I was all but certain I wouldn't have discovered genuine ill-will in my fellow patients' searching glances, I did fear their stares. But there was no avoiding humiliation. I brought it upon myself; for I had a guilty conscience knowing that others remained hungry even as I ate. As soon as I stopped eating I slowly raised my head and even cast a stealthy glance at this or that roommate. All at once I felt light. The shame I'd felt directed towards myself from my observers' stares only moments before had now disappeared without a trace. Though without exception they left the room after lunch, I wasn't left alone. No, all around me I heard the muffled heartbeats of illusory strangers who'd some way or other wormed their way into my bed. So then, this protracted, torturous meal had some significance after all, I thought while wrapping their pliable bodies around myself as I lay there on the mattress. Oh yes, we were a happy, satiated bunch— satiated not by fried chicken and the like, but by the sweet-and-sour scent of our limbs and genitals nestling up against each other.

I moved about these hospitals feeling just as much at home as some woman who, after many years, happens upon the brothel where she was born and raised; for that brothel was, after all, home to her, no matter what it signifies to the world at large. For me, even the most neglected, unkempt hospital promised freedom; once inside, I could look out upon the world without being accused of having done anything wrong. At most, people would feel sorry for me, and since pity is indelibly bound up with the purer sensation of love, my awareness of being pitied was comforting. And yet it wasn't this, but the world of opportunity that would have been unavailable to me on the outside, which really fed my desire to be hospitalized. To observe the sick. A hospital was a laboratory of the soul, where I could glean information available almost nowhere else.

On some days I got my neighbours to talk, not through silence on my part, but by asking them directly to tell me about their illnesses. (From the age of fourteen I was no longer sent to the children's ward, but was placed among the men.) The expertise with which one middle-aged man in particular related his troubles to me would have befitted a doctor. It was very nearly with devotion that he told me the story of his haemorrhoids. He began by recounting the difficulties of defecation—an act that, he observed, most people think about as casually they perform it. But if only some such person were to take his place, he said, hatefully glinting his tiny eyes at me, he would understand at once what tortures the supposedly carefree act of expelling one's excrement can hold in store. Initially even he had regarded his predicament with humour. After all, while sitting fruitlessly on the toilet he could read his favourite newspapers from beginning to end, that mischievous tickling from inside his buttocks occasionally prompting him to chuckle. But when, one day, he found himself waiting in vain for half an hour for something to happen, he became outright annoyed. Only later did he realize that, compared with the discomforts still to come, his patience had yet to be tested.

Here he paused briefly, as if afraid that recalling these events might cause him to relive the pain. But no doubt he quickly managed to convince himself that, after his apparently successful operation, he had no cause for concern. And so he resumed his presentation. 'If you're unlucky,' he said, ominously raising his voice, 'then by God you're at the mercy of your excrement, especially if it's as stubbornly rock hard as mine has been in recent months.' As he'd told his wife more than once, shit is the master of man. This thought had occurred to him when he once spent an entire night on the toilet. Finally he pumped the lousy little sausage out through the thick web of veins around his anus. Sure enough, what emerged was bloody as all hell, just like the textbooks say. Only later did he look up the relevant chapter in the medical reference encyclopedia.

Had I read Nietzsche by the time I was fourteen, surely I would have interjected, 'Sir, you are absolutely right. After all, this German gentleman declared long ago that man would have a far easier time of it imagining himself as a god if he didn't have a hole on his bottom half.' Since I was so young, however, my fellow patient had to be content with sympathetic nodding on my part, which took some doing to accomplish tactfully, I might add, as fits of laughter occasionally came surging up into my throat.

The previous week, continued the haemorrhoid patient, he couldn't postpone the operation any longer, and had no choice but to check in to the hospital. He'd expected a routine incision. But when they lay him on his belly the next day on the operating table, and the shovel-handed doctor began poking about inside his buttocks, his head spun. He was angry with himself, too, for not having taken note of the doctor's hands the day before—hands that, he insisted, looked more like a common labourer's than a surgeon's. But this wasn't what he wanted to talk about just now, after all, but about that particular posture. He'd lived through a thing or two in his day, to be sure, but never, ever had he found himself in such an excruciatingly awkward situation. 'Imagine,' he said, lowering his voice, 'There you are, stark naked and whimpering on the table, on your belly. Your legs are spread apart, your bottom half is propped up, and there's this sandpapery hand the size of a garden shovel fiddling around your sphincter, which it sometimes stretches out, as if bent on directing the scalpel there, only *there*.' He felt as though all his secrets had been exposed to the world. This is not to mention the discreet bursts of wind that warmed not only his behind from time to time, but also doctor's rummaging fingers. Of course, he tried to smooth things over with profuse apologies, but the sympathetic humming of the young female nurse only heightened his shame. 'Believe me,' he said, 'if I was a philosopher type, this little operation would at least have made me see the world differently.' But my fellow patient had to cut short his philosophizing, for a nurse presently arrived to tell him it was time to re-bandage his wound. I had enjoyed his presentation. Indeed, how illuminating it would be if certain men of intellect would undertake to verify their discoveries while in this particular delicate position.

On the brink of adolescence my predilection towards hospitals underwent a decisive change. Previously I'd been satisfied with any department, enjoying medical wards every bit as much as ear-nose-and-throat clinics. After all, the whole point had been to get admitted to any healthcare institution that bore some resemblance to a military barracks. From the age of sixteen, however, I developed a decided preference for psychiatric wards, as I felt it below me to spend those one or two weeks I'd taken such pains to secure for myself among those patients with run-of-the-mill ailments such as circulatory or respiratory diseases. Another factor in my new specialization was, of course, that in these wards I could more easily fool the appropriate people into believing in my supposed illnesses. Yes, it was there that my talent for conjuring up all manner of symptoms really proved itself. If the examining doctor wasn't prone to take my headaches or inexplicable nausea seriously, I turned to shrewder tactics. I was particularly fond of recounting those everyday musings that in normal circumstances I would have kept silent about, if for no other reason that I imagined I wasn't the only person with an active albeit strange imagination. Gaining admittance to a psychiatric ward, however, required a deliberate approach. Effusively I related the most tantalizing among my recurring fantasies. For example, while sitting in the third-floor box at the opera, I often found myself wondering: What would happen if, at the dramatic climax, I was to leap onto those unsuspecting people seated below? During the intermissions I would pick out my victims. Occasionally I considered bounding up to the stage and yanking at the lead tenor's beard while he was busy sounding a high C. Naturally I'd scrap the idea at once, though soon enough my mind was off in another shocking direction: taking advantage of the deep-cut décolletage of the full-bosomed, middle-aged lady sitting beside, in one deft motion I'd slip my hand underneath her blouse. Then I would turn to her husband and ask, politely: Was your wife's breast this warm even before leaving for the opera? Sometimes I told the doctor, I had an overwhelming urge to smack a policeman walking opposite me in the light of day, although I'd always feared those in uniform.

From the suspicion with which my doctor watched me, I knew even midway into my confession that I'd assured myself a spot in the psychiatric ward for at least two weeks. And in fact he was already busy dictating some preliminary diagnosis in Latin to his assistant, while to me he said only, 'Don't you worry, lad, they'll look you over good.'

Having occupied the designated bed with all the usual smugness I assumed after such success, I waited with enthusiasm to see what wounded personalities chance had now brought me into contact with. In this ward, I suspected, it wouldn't be some lyrical yet reflective, objective presentation on haemorrhoids that would make my stay worth its every moment, but, for example, someone's picturesque account of a fairly minor nervous breakdown.

My roommates were mostly middle-aged and older men. Here I was, it seemed to me at first, virtually alone in having earned at such a young age the deference that patients in the psychiatric ward always enjoy within the hospital. As I was soon to discover, though, there is just as much room in this deference for pity as there is for disdain; indeed, in no time I read disapproval on the faces of outside patients who strayed into our territory, stares that unambiguously branded me as someone not to be trusted. And so I was compelled to acknowledge that there are respectable and unrespectable illnesses, but even the most innocent form of neurosis is relegated to the latter category, like a mild case of gonorrhea. Still, it must be said that individual attitudes can shift somewhat over time; for often those very persons who least suspect themselves, their and relatives and friends prone to psychiatric troubles eventually come to know these wards quite well. Perhaps it is the vague awareness of this possibility in the hospital population at large that served to explain that contradictory attitude which, after all, still assured the residents of the psychiatric ward a touch of respect.

I for one placed the psychiatric ward at the top of the hospital hierarchy. My sensitivity and instinctive attraction to disease had evolved to the point where the meaning of my frequent flights into hospitals in the preceding years now crystallized before me as but preparation for the real adventure—that which awaited me in the outside world. Finally I understood that by coming to know the wretched fate of the sick, I would be able justify the course of my own existence. As if I'd sensed in advance that someday I, too, would end up this way. This is what it must be like for a man of the world—in spirit but not yet in wealth, that is—who is led for the first time into an illustrious and glittering assemblage of high society folk. By observing the stirrings of the unattainable, he understands that his only talent lies in the acquisition of this ostentatious wealth and elegance, for, try as he may, never can he live any other way.

One of the men in the ward resembled a friend of mine who'd escaped from an occupational therapy clinic in the provinces. I always did like that ever-smiling wino. After absconding from that teetotalling institution, he took to hanging out at a train station, where his fellow imbibers would sometimes help him towards the public restroom to keep him from wetting his pants even more than he already had. One time I noticed him grinning knowingly at his half-witted chums, who, having been summoned to the train cars for a bit of hard labour to earn their bread or wine, were busily carrying dreadfully heavy sacks full of who-knows-what back and forth for some no doubt noble purpose. No, he wasn't such a fool after all. While the others toiled away, he went about not so discreetly sampling fruit brandy he'd acquired for a modest sum from someone's illicit distillery.

But the countenance of this particular patient in the psychiatric ward did not speak of alcoholism. His alarmingly gaunt face looked as if it had been pressed in with a blunt object. Conspicuously long eyelashes shaded deep-set goggled eyes. It seemed he couldn't even see out, even if he did happen to raise his head on occasion as if he was looking us over. At such times he'd break into a meaningful yet unnerving smile. Unnerving on two counts: only while eating did he insert his dentures, besides, there was something menacing in

21

that smile not at all unlike my friend's knowing grin. I had to take care to ensure that this fellow patient wouldn't catch my probing eyes at such moments even by chance, for perhaps he was able to see out of them all the same. In any case, I did manage to determine that this smile eclipsed even the final traces of meaning discernible on his face. At first I wondered why he wasn't being treated in a mental institution instead; for the other patients in this ward, judging from appearances, at least, did not exactly count as serious cases. Later I understood that his was rather some sort of inherent physiognomic trait; one that, unfortunately, his less than rosy psychological condition only accentuated during his stay here. Indeed, the doctors who dropped in regularly to check up on us devoted not a bit more time to him than to the rest of us. And surely it would be unreasonable to surmise that this reflected slipshod work on the part of specialists. In the final analysis, those people with certain unappealing, innate facial characteristics that, luckily, are normally obscured should be wary of neurosis, and worse; for the singular atmosphere of such wards, coupled with the effects of the medication, can expose our hidden, none-too-attractive lineaments for all the world to see.

Aside from myself and the goggle-eyed fellow with the disquieting smile, there were several others in the room. A balding gentleman played the role of amateur psychologist, offering us bits of expert advice. Perhaps he soliloquized so assiduously only because his asymmetrical mouth spurred him to constant talking, as if frequent drawing of breath and excited sentences were his only hope that his crooked lip would ever slip back in place. His suicide attempt the previous week explained his presence among us in the ward, a place he claimed to know better than others knew their own homes. He didn't even bother denying that he spent at least three to four months a year up here. He'd have to be really nuts, he insisted, to work himself silly like folks out there in the big wide world when life up here was incomparably more pleasant. 'Think of it,' he exhorted us with remarkable eloquence as his glistening eyes darted about and he gestured with disdain at the window, 'how can that dismal rat race out there even be compared with the intimacy, the warmth *in here*? Why, those folks might as well be robots—programmed to be "responsible citizens" who run about all day long not knowing left from right, while those of use in here can chit-chat to our heart's content. And while we're at it, we can feel perfectly free to ogle the nurses' thighs. Damn those thighs, the way they sometimes open wide without realizing it, or happen to rub up against each other!' Momentarily he paused. 'Gentlemen,' he now said, raising his voice, as if for an important announcement, 'let us consider once and for all what freedom this place offers us if we can spend hours considering all possible aspects of a nurse's thigh. We are, after all, privileged—terrorized neither by time nor by the distracting images of the outside world. For hours on end we can bathe our retinas on this most glorious part of a woman's body, which is supposedly designed for changing locations, and meanwhile we are at liberty to reflect upon this and that.'

All this now encouraged me to throw in some observations of my own on the topic at hand. 'Yes,' I began, in a tone that, considering my age, must have sounded surprisingly relaxed and authoritative. But I had read—and heard—plenty. 'For example,' I began like some professor giving a lecture to medical students, 'we might wonder if the husband or lover of the nurse who is the subject of our studious attention has noticed the pale streak at the bend of her knees—a streak that says at least as much as a scar on the face. This ever so faint line, which others would pass their eyes over without a second glance, can in fact help us get to the bottom of such delicate matters as the springiness of the nurse's steps or, say, her body's overall poise, which we cannot hope to decipher solely from the way she moves. Indeed, this streak can reinforce or else cast doubt on whatever we may have presumed about this nurse before we chanced to notice it. Naturally, we might also ponder why our nurse doesn't wear pantyhose. But we'd do well to be wary as regards the most obvious explanation; for, indeed, how foolish we'd be to explain away these naked legs by pointing to the hospital's ever-present excessive heat.' Here I cast a knowing glance at the man with the asymmetrical mouth. 'A far more probable explanation is that these legs desire bareness—that they yearn to confess their nakedness! Let us observe as the nurse sits down by the table beside the coat rack and crosses her legs. At this moment her commingling thighs would hardly tolerate some external fabric, some material foreign to the body, not even the finest silk. Not only would pantyhose of any sort set those thighs apart, but worse yet, it would stretch a net over the freely breathing pores of her skin—a dangerous condition indeed. As someone once told me, the soul lies hidden in the skin. Believe me, gentlemen, a woman wearing clothes is constantly at risk of suffocation.'

Several of my roommates burst out laughing at my last sentence, but having found no reason to take offence, I continued my presentation. 'Or let's look at the nurse more closely as she steps about by our beds. This is not mere walking, but . . . but—paddling! Yes, the air is practically surging like water near some ladies' thighs. Let's not fool ourselves into thinking that the thighs, those esteemed warm pincers, touch merely germs and the dust-laden air. We, who indeed have so much time . . . ' With unabashed affection I now echoed the pronouncement the man with the asymmetrical mouth had made not long before, at which he broke into a knowing smile. I added, 'No, we cannot be content with this amateurish finding of fact. Indeed, the floating effect in the nurse's walk arises precisely because the energy, the force, the accompanying movement, which so often vanishes immediately in the case of other women, here hovers in place, as it were. Yes, some inexplicable magnetism causes that . . . that force to remain between her legs. So the entire leg, or at least the thigh, also rubs against the unverifiable vibrations generated by the knees and the ankles. This may be the secret of this or that particular woman: such magical moments hit *them* most unexpectedly of all, and, gentlemen, the result is unfathomable excitement.'

I used the example of scent to clarify the ambiguous matter of energy escape. 'As we know quite well,' I said, taking a deep breath, 'some people's bodies seem to have no smell whatsoever. While it is not impossible that mad scientists stealthily fumigate these poor souls each and every night, almost certainly such people are, quite simply, riddled with holes. It needn't be a wind or a draft—even a word uttered just loud enough can suck the scent right out of them. Only those can be deceived in this matter who are uninformed, who associate the body's elusive universe of scents with various perfumes and oils. Now, we become exceedingly lightheaded around some ladies, so strong are the scents they exude. One might even venture to say that these aren't scents at all, no, for they have no weight but, rather, the various manifestations of the gravity-free flow of love, capable of checking the effects of even those bodily by-products often held in disrepute, such as perspiration. Those bodies incapable of countering such undesirable smells have, we imagine, been overcome by substances composed of unfamiliar molecules, and have . . . putrefied.'

As my roommates saw it, good fortune had brought them into contact with the city's most refined authority on women. While letting them believe what they would, I kept glancing appreciatively at the man with the asymmetrical mouth, who'd in fact made possible the presentation of my fantasies. How would I, ever hiding away, have revealed that imagination was my only joy? Had I done so, I would also have had to confess what I was doing there among them at all.

My spontaneous discourses concerned not merely the nurses' thighs or the fragrance of the women I supposedly knew so well. The lighting effects in the room likewise excited me, as did the musical possibilities of the snatches of hallway conversation that drifted into the room. The week after my arrival during one of my hospital stays, by which time my roommates regarded me as part of the family, I finally presented my pet theory, which I'd been mulling over for some time—a technique to acquire a knowledge of personality. I wish now to briefly sum up my method.

A composer with a faultless sense of pitch would be commissioned to 'compose' a neurotic who volunteers for the experiment—and to do so not only by transcribing the patient's words but all sounds the subject generates in the course of his activity. The task would not be simple in the least, for this composer would not be content with recording simply the musical equivalent of the sounds produced by speech. It would be all too easy to substitute an exclamation with a high F, or a cool pronouncement with a scale-opening C. If polyphony can be expected anywhere at all, here it must. So, too, the body's subtler sounds must be incorporated into the score. When a sigh slips from an almost pure G to a G flat, for example, the composer must immediately note the glissando, and stand at the ready to ascertain whether the next sigh generates the same shift in tone; for a sound can only become the element of a musical composition if it occurs repeatedly, as does the slide in this case. Chance nonetheless remains a factor, and it is advisable to consider this during the final arrangement of the score. It may take some work, but determining the key is possible. Incessant talking offers countless reference points. Perhaps it is here that the composer of 'personality music' encounters his easiest task. It is child's play to determine, based on the chords that pop up more than once in the course of a sentence, in which direction to nudge those sounds that fall on the border—whether towards a major or minor key, that is. Alas, this artifice can no more be avoided than the need for our composer to decide which among the countless available notes to accord privileged treatment by inserting them into the composition. Notwithstanding, an opus is born whose material was provided by the musical transcription of our patient's speech, yawns, ear scratching or, say, his indiscreet movements transposed as a series of sounds.

Once the piece is complete, the patient would be transferred to the musical therapy ward. There he would be confronted with an acoustic arrangement virtually identical to himself! 'Yes,' he might say to his therapist with flippancy or pride, 'I'll just put myself on the record player, so go ahead and listen while I step out to the toilet.'

Or else the patient—let us call him by an everyday name, Lajos Balogh—wouldn't be sent to the musical therapy ward in those first weeks at all, only his composition would. The specialist would be handed the Lajos Balogh Sonata for Piano and Violin in D Minor and wouldn't even have an appointment with the patient until ascertaining the appropriate clues to the harmony of Lajos Balogh. It can hardly be doubted that the interpretation of personality music is the thorniest matter of all; indeed, the most reassuring scenario would see the psychiatrist himself compose the score. We can't make such demands of those who specialize in mental and nervous disorders, however, so we must settle for the superlative knowledge of musical theory that characterizes our doctor—namely, the musical therapist.

The possibilities inherent in understanding personality through music, even if limited, are a given. Why, the very tonality of a 'piece' says so much! Obviously it wasn't by chance that our composer rejected atonality. One would naively believe that nervous system disorders readily tend towards chordless musical compositions, which reject harmony. Not so. While composing the Lajos Balogh Sonata the composer must have felt all the while that the setting of this personality to music expressly requires that referential centre of notes and chords: a tonic. That is to say, he recorded only that from the nervous system, from behaviour, from the sounds characterizing the personality, which could be seized at all—the 'gravitation', so to speak, whose musical equivalent is the tonic. A general diagnosis can readily be established using this point of evidence. Lajos Balogh may have weighty problems, but his case is not hopeless. Among other indications, the minor key supports this presumption. The caressing strains of a quartet or even a somewhat more frisky sextet demonstrates that his personality is still holding itself in check. However, it would be a mistake to simply take these undeniably encouraging signs at face value. Indeed, this is what serves to distinguish a real specialist from a charlatan: the former will form a suspicion over this very point. In other words, perhaps it is in this very tenderness, this hyperharmony, that the reasons for the thus far obscure illness must be sought. Perhaps Lajos Balogh is in fact *too* delicate, and so a treatment of 'sensitivity for sensitivity' might be ineffective, for it will necessarily lead to a breakdown! Perhaps the specialist has thus found the clue to solving this riddle?

The time has come for experimentation. Having arranged a personal session with the patient, our doctor first plays him the Lajos Balogh Sonata for Piano and Violin in D Minor. Observing his reactions, the doctor soon realizes that Lajos, entirely transfixed by the nauseatingly sweet melodies, is like some obese diabetic who'd devour all the chocolate and pastries he could lay his hands on until dropping dead. Our musical psychiatrist has already formulated his plan. First he allows Lajos to listen to the piece from beginning to end, letting him scoop out even the last drop of the opiate, and then, initially digging up a Mozart serenade—something melodious enough, that is, to ensure that our patient isn't alarmed from the outset—he gradually switches over to those 'foreign' pieces that, via evermore dissonant tones, compel the patient to confront a very different world. Finally he might lure him into the realm of atonality, where the degree of the patient's aversion to this world of sounds generally regarded more as noise than as music, becomes clear. If the selection of pieces is fortunate, then perhaps it is precisely this frightening music that can touch the patient's own inner chaos—namely, the chaos that in his case was, in fact, borne of a desire for harmony. The doctor can now establish a diagnosis. Namely, this personality disorder can be treated only with an even greater degree of chaos! After a fairly precise mapping of the symptoms, the doctor may send the patient back to the psychiatric ward, for the matter now rests with the good doctors there.

My roommates drifted off now and again during my presentation of this wild scheme, and only in the glances of the man with the menacing smile did I occasionally notice something akin to comprehension.

The real excitement, however, awaited me in the lounge. There I met those women who sought refuge after weekend family brawls, attention-seeking suicide attempts and minor nervous breakdowns. Studying them was the highlight of my stay. In those first few days I occupied myself by classifying them, wanting as I did to establish certain points of regularity. And indeed, I discerned an unequivocal correlation between the singularity of a woman's face and her type of illness. A wholly different type of beauty characterized ladies inclined towards hysteria than, say, those suffering depression. When observing the former I saw an open map of tempers and instincts, albeit deciphering this map was anything but easy. While scrutinizing the latter, however, I increasingly felt that the faces had succumbed to so ruinous a force that they were collapsing inward, as it were; or, rather, that they had turned into something akin to drenched plaster that might at any moment come peeling off the wall.

Different comparisons were in order those faces that were obviously the most serious cases. Only on the basis of the eyes, for example, could I properly study a certain middle-aged woman who appeared in the lounge every day at three to take her usual seat. There she sat motionless, staring straight ahead, until early evening. It seemed those eyes were assiduously burning away the entire surface of the face around them. They were indeed all I really saw— those eyes, by turns radiating nervousness or fearsomeness. In her case it would be more precise to speak not of the beauty of her face but that of her eyes, eyes that frightened me every bit as much as they fascinated me. Her plainly manic disposition was augmented by a schizophrenic stare. In spite of or perhaps because of this, hers was a beauty more potent than that of the most perfectly proportioned faces I'd seen. Still, it took me days to understand why no one dared sit down beside her even though, by all appearances, she seemed quite harmless: it wasn't some menacing outburst they feared but, quite simply, those disquieting eyes.

An alarmingly thin girl of around twenty likewise merited special attention. Her chalky white skin seemed to have been pasted right onto her skeleton. It was a wonder that she could even get out of bed and walk to the lounge. She seemed on the verge of dying from old age. Afraid of her shame, of serving as an unwitting mirror to her deformity, I didn't dare look her in the eyes. What I really mean to say, however, is that this girl's beauty was to be found precisely in her dogged refusal to be much bothered by the whole business of shame. Nature ridiculed this girl's body in vain, for by venturing out among us she knowingly risked humiliation, unintentional though it was.

The plainly alcoholic women formed the most clear-cut group. Their bloated, discoloured faces seemed padded with rags that, if tapped when most swollen, would surely have yielded eighty-proof pus. It was more than apparent that these women hadn't reconciled themselves to compulsory abstinence, although medications did assure them a sort of innocent stupor. Nature is so unfair to women! Alcohol never quite manages to ravage men's faces as mercilessly as it does theirs. It renders women's faces sexless. This is striking precisely because the observer cannot escape a paradoxical impression: despite alcohol's success in twisting once-delicate lineaments out of shape, in the final analysis, not even devastated dimples, sagging skin, baggy eyes or clammy, outward-turning lower lips can extirpate from such faces that eerie, ever-lingering mien of femininity-turned-memory. While assigning such facial decay a definitive niche in the spectrum of beauty would have been going too far, when observing such faces I did sometimes imagine that these patchworks of bluish-red welts and swollen knots of flesh and skin nonetheless still harboured some elusive but vital ingredient of beauty.

Having completed my high-handed classifications, it was time for a reckoning. Had someone asked me which group of these women were most to my liking, I would surely have said those suffering depression. Their gloom fired my imagination; which is to say, the disintegration underway on their faces allowed me to imagine that I might put their personalities back together again. While I remained convinced that these faces had succumbed to some ruinous force, it would be more exact to say that what I perceived on and about them was a sort of motion. The anxiety plainly in their eyes seemed to radiate slowly, in shadow-like waves, upon the face around them, which in turn sponged up this anxiety. Blunt fear came undone over the furrows between the eyebrows, entrenching itself in the creases of the skin and drawing barely perceptible vertical lines across the otherwise tender cut of the given woman's mouth. Surely the eyes determined the exact dynamics of fear and anxiety discernable on a face: as if the ever-changing contours of a face were in fact a series of photographs being taken by the eyes, or, rather, by the relentlessly sad stares issuing from therein. And so the exactingly precise lens of the eyes brought into sharp focus both the zigzagging, bitter lines about the mouth and the trench-deep clefts of an incurably bad mood.

As dubious as my assertions may seem, it must be admitted that in extreme cases, at least, the resulting 'softness' of a countenance is plain as day. Gloom saturates a face over a period of months, rendering the muscles flabby, dissolving facial tissue and releasing chemicals that wash away nerve endings. Hit such a face, and its owner won't even wince.

The real challenge of my physiognomic research was yet to come: that of solving the essential problem, replete as it was with so many variables. I had to create a personality from the symptoms I'd assessed. Back then I kept my distance from extreme cases, observing women who showed signs of schizophrenia from as far away as I did psychotics. That said, I would gladly have given myself over to women suffering melancholy. Why? Perhaps because their woe, while deliciously inscrutable, seemed restrained. Its sufferers hadn't yet lived to see out-and-out despair. I was galvanized by their proximity, and was beginning to imagine I'd come upon a precise explanation for my flights into hospitals, the origin of my questionable attraction to illness.

So I'd fallen in love with sadness before even knowing what it was. I began to realize this only now, as I noticed an unmistakable 'gravitation' on and around the face of a girl around twenty seated across from me; this force seemed to be a reflection of my own ever-so-vague sense of self. As if I'd unconsciously engraved this girl's face years before, only so that it might satiate the emptiness inside me on this day. Like stepping before the Lord on Judgement Day and having Him see Himself in us. The sheer force of the woe I saw on this girl's face branded me with my own image, as it were. On realizing this, I felt as wounded as those who are sensitive to words are prone to injury by a perfidious sentence. I shuddered, as if sensing in advance the sort of women's faces I'd be swept towards in the years to come.

It is an irony of fate, as I see it, that the woman who robbed me of my innocence, in the night-duty nurses' room at that, was twenty years my senior and not a bit melancholic. She caught my attention from the very first day. Poising her tall, slender body provocatively as she moved about the hallways, she seemed to have forgotten altogether that this was a hospital and not some fashion show. Her long black hair, which she wore let down, flowed ostentatiously over her silk gown. On stepping into the lounge, she looked us over with a stare bordering on contempt. Then, as if wanting to ensure her superiority, she took a seat amid us creatures of lower standing. Doing so must have calmed her, for soon enough, she flashed her white teeth our way. The message was clear: starting now she was willing to suspend her aloofness. What else would she have begun to talk about but men? And so she did. As she explained it, she'd fled into the hospital only to escape from her 'damn' husband—so she began to explain without ado, as if everyone had been waiting for her confession. The fellow had been tormenting her with jealousy for years.

At first he had no reason to be jealous. Through many long years she asserted her innocence, but when sins she hadn't even committed flew back in her face, she thought it best to identify with the image he'd formed of her. There are no two ways about it, she quipped, some women are branded as whores no matter what. They can have a heap of children or hide away in a cloister, but absolutely nothing will erase the impression of coquetry.

This was my chance to observe this woman more closely. She spoke without self-pity, but her face underwent a decisive transformation. All traces of the vanity so conspicuous just before had vanished; she might have been a teenage girl in despair. She was still strikingly beautiful: not a wrinkle on her high forehead or below the eyes. Nor did she seem at risk of the flaccidity characteristic of the faces of middle-aged women, which nestles up against slackened facial muscles like some invisible membrane. The skin on her face was as taut as a high-school girl's. Sometimes she spontaneously moistened her proportionately wide lips, perhaps the same way she once had after frequent kisses. While watching her I understood that as long as I didn't look into her eyes, I'd desire only this type of woman. But I couldn't forget her gaze, which spread hopeless disillusionment over this otherwise flawless face. As for the taut skin, a closer look revealed that it had embarked on a course of more insidious decay than even that of the bloated, crumpled, wrinkle-strewn skin of the alcoholics. People tend to characterize faces such as hers with the term 'cold beauty', little suspecting the abounding self-loathing that scorches these faces day by day. Only now did I understand this woman's awe-inspiring arrogance: she'd assumed this role in order to flee the emptiness inside her. I even respected her for not reaching for the so-easily-mastered handholds of undisguised neurosis.

Suddenly she broke her monologue. This hit me almost as unexpectedly as had her first sentence. Once again her face was consumed by apparent contempt towards those around her. As if she could change her expression by simply turning some invisible switch on and off. Then she stood, and walked out of the lounge with her usual provocative gait, not forgetting, of course, to cast a withering glance or two at us as she went.

It happened precisely the evening before my scheduled departure. I'd been walking restlessly about the hallway, consumed by the disquietude that always hit me when being expelled from my chosen home. The ward was oddly silent, as if the on-duty doctor had ordered all the patients to bed early, a directive I'd apparently managed to wriggle out of. While passing by the women's ward, I noticed the door to Room 29 open up. Out she stepped. Surely not by chance. I was nervous. Perhaps she'd been watching me for days, I thought, and now she sensed that this was the last chance to get to know me. She came straight at me, as if hurrying to a prearranged meeting. When she then stepped before me, blocking my path, and caressed my face with claw-like fingers, I reacted as naturally as I had a few days earlier on seeing her disdainful stare. Perhaps her husband had been right after all: this beauty was indeed a raging tramp, and it was now easy to imagine that she specialized in corrupting minors. Or was she, too, among those neurotics whose illness is accompanied by overheated sensuality? I didn't have time to think; she led me straight into the night-duty nurses' room, where, to my amazement, there was not a soul. So she'd colluded with the nurses more than once in recent days. How else was her confidence to be explained? I really couldn't complain. Even cats adept at mating in the cellars of urban apartment buildings don't bond as we surely did in that tiny, dimly lit room. The torrid

self-abandon lasted half an hour, perhaps, at which point she suddenly threw on her dark silk gown and announced that we must
leave the room immediately. On stepping out into the hallway I
noticed only that I was alone once more. No doubt I should have
taken it as an omen that my passage to manhood occurred in the
neurological ward of the city hospital, but just then, my exulting
body dispelled all doubts.

On stepping out of the hospital the next morning, what did I
find in my pocket but my initiator's address? I shuddered with
excitement at the thought that the next embrace might come to pass
as well. However, when I looked up the given apartment some two
weeks later and rang the bell repeatedly in vain, someone stepped
out of a neighbouring apartment to inform me that the woman had
apparently fled to Sweden with a wanted man.

I was left alone. But the half-hour intermezzo that composed
this unexpected bliss didn't pass without a trace after all, for I
vowed to myself in the weeks after leaving the ward to bring an
end to my hospital shams. From this point on, I would not go about
pilfering bliss for myself in the lounges and rooms of neurological
wards but, I decided, from girls. By now it wasn't only my sense of
security and of freedom that I had hospitals to thank for, but my
newfound manhood. Like so many people, I, too, had fallen victim
to a false presumption in planning my future, that what had happened to me in that tiny room reserved for the night-duty nurses
had forever changed something fundamental in me—that the part
of myself which had prompted my deliberate withdrawals into hospitals over the years had been soaked up and away by the torrid
heat of our bodies as they bonded, by the desire that followed our
separation . . . by the desire that, as my initiator had left me without
a word, I now resolved to quench by loving other women.

Of course, how would I have understood at sixteen that the force which had lured me into hospitals early on, when I was yet a child, would accompany me throughout my life? Years passed before I understood that my true initiation had been brought on by the hospital milieu—no, not by those wild embraces, which in fact had only set the seal on things, consecrating the place in the depths of my psyche.

So then, my real seduction was to be found in my gradually expanding self-consciousness—which had, by now, established my attunement to illness as synonymous with my fundamental character. It may seem absurd, yet I sometimes think my 'civilian' endeavours in the coming years came to pass only so I might, even if subconsciously, collect evidence to validate the self-identity I'd sensed as a teenager.

2

Or did it begin on the train? That day when, at the age of seventeen, not long after my years of eager escapades in hospitals drew to a close, I found myself on the Budapest-bound express clutching the photograph of a resplendently blond Polish girl from Warsaw I'd met only two days earlier at the Krakow railway station? Standing there in the cold, drafty aisle, I experienced for the first time the consequences of loving a woman. I whispered an inexplicable vow: I love this girl, her and her alone. I may not look upon another. If my eyes linger elsewhere nonetheless, that will mean my love for this Polish girl is in doubt.

That ID-size photo—or, rather, the sixteen-year-old face it depicted—now subtly realigned its lineaments into a sterner expression befitting my self-imposed taboo. As if to indicate that it would henceforth stand guard over my wilful bondage. There was no fooling it. Like an attendant foisted upon me, it lurked constantly in my pocket. But how could I possibly have kept my oath from minute to minute, hour to hour? Sometimes my eyes involuntarily settled upon a woman's face. There was no avoiding this, and so I began to observe myself observing, as if this remained my only option. One minute this other woman's lineaments appeared inert, but then, as if prompted by some invisible summons, the corners of her mouth rose just so. *Perhaps she's smiling to herself*, I thought while following the slender, sickle-like arch formed by her lips.

Almost imperceptibly she crumpled her nose, and a faint depression appeared atop the bridge—the headboard of her smile—ruffling the perfectly smooth skin ever so slightly. Which was when my vow came to mind. I was stricken with shame. Punishment was in order. Like someone undeserving of true love, I was just about ready to give up my Polish girl altogether when it struck me that this would in fact amount to an easy escape—not the punishment that must invariably be mine.

The authority that snapshot wielded over me became truly oppressive only once its scope of activity expanded. For example, the photo entrusted the seductive gestures of other women to test my devotion. On certain days this was so unbearable that I buried the picture away somewhere in my room and headed outside thinking I'd slipped out from under its strict supervision. Yet this unrelenting snapshot second-guessed me, for at such times it had me watched by even shrewder means. If, say, while riding the tram I saw a girl who happened to be letting down her hair, caressing that copious glittering crown of hers, I would think: this woman is putting me to the test. 'Look upon me, yes, go ahead and imagine what it would be like to smell, to stroke my lovely hair! See how, as I lean my head to the side, my hair unfurls, exposing its mass of silky inviting strands . . . ' I understood that the photo had seeped its way into this girl's hand motions as she let down her hair, for try as that gesture did to disguise itself with a veil of seductiveness, it wasn't hard to discern the true instigator, the photograph, machinating . . . watching over me, gauging my fidelity. Finally I turned away my head in vain. In reviewing the scene, my latent seduction weighed heavily upon me. At this moment it hardly mattered any more whether I'd tripped up only in thought. I had to suffer for my sins; indeed, the image before me had already accomplished this, having palpably eroded my sense of security.

No going outside for a week, came the verdict. Thus I might manage to avoid becoming a repeat offender, to avoid killing again. Ensconced in my room, I fished the photo out of its hiding place and promised it that from now on I wouldn't allow my eyes to rest on other women's faces; or, if I did, I'd see them as lifeless objects worthy of contempt. Better to walk the streets with my head down, eyes fixed to the ground. I would loathe all women, and in so doing relentlessly divest them of their claim to beauty; for only my photograph, only my love, could be beautiful.

I ascribed my subordination vis-à-vis the photo to the Polish girl's presumed jealousy. Shouldering the burden of this jealousy was my duty, for only thus could I free her from the agony it caused her. I had liberated her from suffering, bearing its brunt in a way that she could not have possibly known about—all this to verify that only she existed within me. If this proved impossible, I would see to changing the rules of the game. My madness would be the worthiest gift for a love that, being unrealizable in the day-to-day world, was a perfect love.

My wilful bondage lasted half a year. The photograph kept an eye on my every move and thought. It skulked about in my hand, my desk, my nerves.

Then one rainy summer day I travelled to Warsaw. There, a message was waiting for me from my love. She asked that I meet up with her in a lowbrow motel way up north in Gdansk, as she'd had to go to that coastal city due on some urgent business. The next evening I was waiting for her in the designated motel when a mutual acquaintance, a portrait painter who hawked his wares on the street, stepped with a broad grin into my room. Slapping me on the shoulder, he pulled a bottle of vodka from his pocket and extended it to me. 'Have a swig, mate!' he said, casting me a commiserating look. 'I've come from the rail workers' hostel, where your gal is snogging her new beau, a painter chum of mine. So . . . how about us going down for a dip in the sea?' 'Maybe later,' came my strained reply, 'I think I'll take a little walk first.' Crumpling the photograph in my hip pocket, I left the painter behind.

So the angel-faced bitch from Warsaw had dumped me like that! While I had safeguarded our love with pathological fear, she'd consoled herself with a two-bit painter. I had only his perpetually drunk colleague to thank for my discovering the chicanery. All the same, *Polak weger dwa bratanki.* Poles and Hungarians are two friends. . . . Of course, I was well aware that my devotion had been somewhat exaggerated; after all, she could hardly have suspected the nature of my love. In any case, I now passed up a singular opportunity. Instead of unravelling, nay, ripping apart the mysterious threads that bound me to that photograph—that is, by throwing away that piece of crumpled piece of paper and the face it portrayed—I broke only with the model it represented. What I did, and hastily at that, was to board a train and seek distraction away from the coast, in central Poland. By the next day I was sucking away at the lips of a lovely black-haired girl. Never had I known such kissing. Her saliva flowed as if her larynx had malfunctioned and she was unable to keep that silky, salty fluid in her throat. I drank, eagerly so.

I first kissed a girl in a dream. Her dirty brown hair fell straight down on both sides of her head, tenuously defining a face that otherwise seemed on the verge of disintegration; a face whose thick fleshy lips offered the only sure grip. I don't recall how we began, but there we were, kissing madly. Suddenly a viscous, bitter fluid— a yellowish discharge that did not seem to be her saliva—poured from her mouth into my throat. Disconcerted and disgusted, I nonetheless sucked on her lips even harder, afraid of going down in failure before the person most important to me just then. Perhaps, had I drawn the girl completely into myself, swallowed her whole in one gulp without a second thought, as if downing some vile-tasting medicine, I would have conquered my revulsion; I would have stepped beyond something every person who seeks communion with another must transcend. Yet I only continued allowing the pulpy mass into myself without any end in sight—her almost nonexistent face, her squashy lips, and her perspiring body still pressed against me rather than dissolving once and for all into a bitter fluid I might simply have swallowed, only to throw it up promptly after our parting. And so I went on holding her in my arms, my throat still full of the acrid discharge. The memory of that taste has lingered in me ever since.

I thought it best to end my little jaunt to Poland. On the way back home to Hungary I stepped off yet again, now in Katowice, to drop in on a school-teacher friend of mine. Although I was eager to alleviate my coastal frustration with an act of consummation, there I learnt that this friend had found herself a husband in the months since I'd first met her; this, despite the fact that at the drama festival where we'd first laid eyes on one another, she had promised repeatedly to give me her most precious treasure if only I made her my wife. She'd realized that waiting for me would have been point-less. How times change. Whatever happened to all that talk of Polish sluts I'd grown up hearing? Ah yes, Catholicism was spreading like wildfire once again.

Only on getting home did I reach for the photograph once again. No longer did I regret not having torn it up then and there, on the coast. Not as if I could have proven her infidelity. No, that would have meant catching her sixteen-year-old visage on that pho-tograph red-handed—say, as she stole from my nightstand to the bookshelf to assume a carnal position with the large gold-framed picture of my brother, who enjoyed an exceedingly good reputation with the ladies. Why, she didn't try slipping away; true, every iota of her vigilance was devoted to my watchful eyes. All the same, I had to admit that, in the wake of all that had passed, no longer could I delay clearing the slate of our relationship once and for all.

Far from coming to loathe the photograph—and this surprised me most of all—somehow I felt as if the Polish girl's fling at the rail workers' hostel had left it every bit as vulnerable as it had rendered me. An absurd and fleeting thought even passed through me as I stared upon that snapshot lying there in my perspiring palm: it was trying to cheer me up.

I had to break the silence, and so I said aloud to myself what the photo would surely have said, articulating with painstaking precision: 'Look here, it's not really that girl on the platform in the Krakow station that you fell in love with, you know, but the picture she just happened to give you, and which happens to depict her face. Yes, it was *me* who seduced you on that train, me and my suggestive smile, my dubious youth—and perhaps this can be forgiven, if you consider that I was born at the age of sixteen; me and my sad eyes, which render my glance so restive. *I* am the true face. The other, that creature of flesh and blood you rushed off to Warsaw to visit, and then so anxiously went on to Gdansk to follow, she is a mere likeness of me. You foolishly believed that her warm body would be grateful for the love you felt not in fact for her, but for *me*. It was me you lived with, not her; it was *my* glance you so mindfully watched owing to your secret fear that one morning the magic would disappear, that instead of my cherished face a stranger already seeming to fade from your mind would be staring back. Of course I am not calling into question whether, had you been luckier, you could have truly loved her too. Surely an affair in which you can count on conquering both aspects of a single woman is even more exciting; but perhaps I'm not far off in suspecting that you derive more excitement from *my* kind. If I'm not mistaken, you now intend to settle your score with me. Well, go right ahead. It's high time. Yes, physical obliteration can do its part to expunge an unpleasant memory. But wait! Come to think of it, in your shoes I wouldn't be so quick to throw away this crumpled piece of paper I've become. No, instead I'd slip it away between your dusty papers in a desk drawer. Yes, perhaps someday I can still come in handy.'

I wasn't about to let this talk disconcert me, especially since I no longer regretted all that had happened. How did I manage to forget those six months of anxiety and fear, those months during which I'd allowed that photograph to rule over me like some despot? By now telling myself that the Warsaw girl's infidelity was just what I'd needed! Yes, I digested my first break-up by not worrying any further about resistance on the part of the photo; not even *it* could deny that in this case there did, after all, exist a relationship of sorts, albeit hard to define, between picture and flesh-and-blood person. It was just tough luck that, though innocent, the photo had gotten the short end of the deal.

I breathed easier. From now on my photograph could not demand my attention. The hierarchical relationship was over. I could now walk the streets freely and gaze upon women's faces without a guilty conscience, no longer having to fear the shame of being caught in the act, of having the picture take my unintentional infidelity to task on sensing a glance-in-the-making. True, it was I who'd commissioned it with this task of policing me in the first place; I, who had raised it to its inquisitional chair. It had exercised its power with my consent, as if what was really going on here was that I, born into servility, could live only when held tight in a despot's grip.

When I slipped my forsaken photograph between the pages of a tattered spiral notebook at the age of seventeen, I suspect that I escaped only from a picture of the Polish girl—not from the impulse to seek a sense of security in forces outside myself. Among other things, this goes to explain my dread of freedom. I was always most agitated when someone or something did not take me by the shoulders; when the unsuspecting attendant I happened to have chosen on any given occasion left me alone. Indeed, at such times I reasoned that my unforeseen independence could only be due to some irreversible mistake of mine; that it was I who'd heavy-handedly broken the alliance I'd earlier tied with my superior. Freedom left me feeling unprotected, dreadfully weightless, yearning that a stern authority would come along and force me to account for my actions.

Surely I seem to have overstepped the bounds of reason, trying as I am to explain the development of my obsessions, of my illness, by way of absurd theories surrounding a plain old photo. Yet I am not about to be misled by the reader's patronizing smile. The more time I devote to understanding my love for the photo, the more convinced I am the one who cannot be prudent enough when accepting certain gifts. Had I not pocketed that photo on the platform that day at the Krakow train station, after all, perhaps everything would have turned out differently.

3

So it was in vain that I tried leading a respectable life. It fast became clear that if I searched for love in the so-called healthy world outside the hospital, I was doomed to failure. How much more confident I would have been, had that middle-aged woman who'd escaped to Sweden led me past the final trials of my teenage years! But that wily dame had sailed north, leaving me behind to lust after her body. Nonetheless, I continued my experimentation. Not long after breaking up with the photograph, I fell in with a genuine girl who was by contrast so real that she spent her free time lifting weights: she aimed to break the national record, in the men's category. By the by, she was a cellist in her final-year at the conservatory—a pursuit that, as she put it, she'd begun only because she deemed it an imperative step towards mysticism. Indeed, the occult was her real passion, and she'd declared even at our first meeting that should she fail to make a discovery with international reverberations in this dauntless discipline by the age of thirty, she'd commit suicide. Her proclivity for transcendentalism was pronounced, to say the least, and was accompanied by an athletic frame. It was chance that had brought me together with this wrestler who was every bit as excited by the liberal arts as by the matches in the upcoming tournament. Her unmistakably intelligent face nonetheless spared her from looking ridiculous. Her gaze, at least as dauntless as her biceps, fixed itself upon me as if to protect me from some danger. If it were possible to splice parts of the human body, I'd graft her head to the body of my neurotic courtesan; this would have left not me, but the world, in wonderment. Whenever my glance fell to those parts of her underneath the neck, I thought at once of her annual work-out plan, and so I tried looking upon her at eye level to the extent possible. In doing so, however, I didn't forget the danger that a possibly closer relationship would have meant to me. In any case, I tried assuring myself that this intimacy would come to pass later rather than sooner.

My selfish stance was absolved by the chummy nature of our relationship. G. must have been as happy about my arrival on the scene as I was about hers. No doubt she determined in moments that she'd happened upon a subject who would follow even her strictest directions, as long as he didn't have to embrace her. Far from being embarrassed by my finicky taste, she was instead consumed with her plans; for example, how to guide me into the mysteries of ascetics. She regarded strict self-discipline as a fundamental condition of the road to mysticism. And so she was pleased as could be to see that I was willing to wake up at 3 a.m. so we could meditate together. To her, this joint silence of ours must have been comparable to the lovemaking we'd failed to enact the evening before; indeed, I suspect that she even achieved a sort of climax from this duet of repose. Around 5 a.m. she judged that we were ready for the next step. And so she brought forth her cello and plucked the D string: we were to contemplate this sound. In a hushed voice she implored me to immerse my thoughts in the murkiness of this note in the middle octave. For my part, I tried fulfilling such requests of hers, if only because she would otherwise have come forward with demands of an entirely different stripe. For this gal was rather a passionate sort, which she did not hide from me. Indeed, not once, when I dropped in on her without notice, I'd surprised her in the company of two or even three men, and there was no misunderstanding *that*.

It was on just such an occasion that she explained her notion of love, which as she saw it very much dovetailed with her asceticism. It all comes down to the conscious regulation of energy—so she commenced her scholarly presentation—and that we must come to terms with our desires. She'd long before resolved this question for herself. In point of fact, this is why she was in the habit of summoning men to her flat: their varying degrees of potency ensured that her body was kept in order. Were she to forsake her tried-and-tested order out of pure curiosity and enjoy the services of some stranger, surely that would throw her off balance. 'You are the one exception,' she said, casting me a roguish smile, 'but with you, as with some incurable whisperer of sweet nothings, my aims are completely different. But then again . . . ' And now she ran a hand across my face in a stroke that might easily have passed for a threat: she'd be willing to change her strategy at any moment.

She loved the sun. From spring to fall she kept to a rigorous weekly schedule of catching the rays. She soaked them in as if embracing the energy of a man with an inexhaustible supply of energy. In fact, more than once she remarked that the pulsating sensation the sun's light and heat stirred in her body brought to mind some fellow whose loins she would know in the near future. Not that this hypersensuality of hers precluded her from pursuing her esoteric research. I even had the impression that she approached even the lovemaking sessions she left for the late-night hours as part of her scholarly experiments. For example, she had a relationship with a fifty-something biochemist, whose lover she became with an utmost sense of purpose; after a few weeks of his acquaintance she and the scientist fell to mixing business with pleasure in his laboratory; for as G. saw it, some sort of medication could no doubt be contrived from the fluids generated by their bliss. Her liaisons with astronomers and astrologers had an entirely different end. She liked to get her information first-hand; for example, what constellation she found herself in at the moment of orgasm. Of course, the ordinary particulars of astronomy, with which even she was somewhat familiar, didn't really do the trick. What she really awaited was the opinion of an expert with a good grasp of cosmobiology; specifically as to what sort of cosmic forces might have figured in the bliss she'd felt a moment before.

I wasn't the least bit surprised by her predilection for weight-lifters. The heavier boys' division in her larger retinue of regulars comprised three or four gentlemen who each weighed in at almost 220 pounds alone, and she was especially proud of them. I assume that not even in their company did G. forsake her scientific side, and that she managed to work at least a bit of her fitness training into these rendezvous, perhaps with a spontaneous bout of wrestling or, say, with arm-wrestling, which she was especially passionate about.

It would be unfair to suggest that she meanwhile neglected me. To the contrary, every day she devoted more and more time to me. Every afternoon she expected me to drop by, and on such occasions, which had a certain air of interrogation about them, I filled her in on my progress that day. Some days earlier she'd assigned me to study human faces, and naturally she told me what to look for, as she wouldn't have been satisfied with me spouting out nothing but generalities. It was my task to characterize facial expressions relative to the distinctive traits of the shape of the head, and to the proportions of the entire body. The wrinkled countenance of a tall, wiry man, explained G., will render an effect completely different from those of his stocky counterpart, especially if the head of the former is longish to boot. At the same time, she warned, I shouldn't even think of spurting out clichés like 'inviting eyes', 'sidelong glance', and 'bland expression'. What she sought was a precise mapping of the unique lineaments distinguishing each and every individual, and so she advised me to put my eyes to work and stare hard. She found my animal metaphors to be most presentable of all. If, in the course of my little presentation, I told her that in the morning a man came opposite me whose face was 'as nervous as a mouse disturbed while mating', she praised me and proceeded to inquire as to the particulars of the gentleman's hair, skin and facial hair; and as if she only wanting to corner me, she then went about grilling me about whether I'd noticed anything odd about the man's clothes.

One day she gave me the task of observing the people passing by in front of her apartment building. For a while now, she'd noticed a certain unease about her that she could explain only with a change in the aura of the street. For days on end I spied on the pedestrians, especially those who for some reason or other paused in front the building. But I was unable to notice anything out of the ordinary. Everyone was proceeding at their own pace, at least I thought so. After a few days G. came to be of a completely different opinion, and so she thought it more advisable that we conduct the surveillance together. She wanted by all means to bring the case to a close. For hours we stood watch, waiting to nail the culprit whom I, the amateur, had thus far allowed to escape. Every half-hour or so G. said something by way of reassurance, as if to convey the danger we were in, and of course I only smiled at this. Nonetheless, I curiously awaited the developments.

It must have been eleven in the morning when there approached a middle-aged man wearing a hat. Wrenching my arm, G. whispered, 'He'll be the one, you just watch.' When the man reached us, she stepped up to him and asked if he was in the habit of passing by this place several times a day. Surprised though he was, the man replied in the affirmative. G. became visibly excited, as if close to solving a secret she'd long suspected the answer to. With solemn politeness she asked the gentleman if he'd do her the favour of waiting in front of the building while she went up to her apartment. The unsuspecting man agreed. G. scurried up the stairwell, and in a few minutes she reappeared in the doorway with a triumphant expression. Approaching the patiently loitering fellow, whom I hadn't dared tell what this was all about, she said, 'Sir, I am sorry to inform you that you radiate something that's not quite right. I really don't mean to be indiscreet, but you have two options to choose from. Either you approach your destination on another street, or you allow me to examine you.' G. was fortunate, because the man, realizing he'd been taken for a ride, simply stormed off in a rage.

I couldn't get out of it so easily. For hours I got an earful about what a klutz I'd been for letting him go right by under my nose from the very first day on. Needless to say, she wasn't satisfied with a mere rebuke. Instead, that same day she came up with a couple of concentration exercises for me, for she believed as deeply in the possibility of developing hidden aptitudes as schemers do in maliciousness. I wish to mention one of G.'s concentration-enhancement techniques. While standing in front of the mirror I had to count the number of times I blinked in the course of an hour. Of course, she meant that only as a means of warming up for such a more complex task as, say, when she had me compare the frequency of my blinking to the dripping of water from the bathtub faucet. Only once I'd proven a certain adeptness at the former operations could the most delicate test ensue: finally I could devote attention to my own pulse and to the beating of my heart.

The application of such methods new to me naturally did not mean that G. had given up traditional methods of instruction. Sometimes she recommended certain books—or, more precisely, certain sentences of certain books; for she regarded it as an unforgivable sin for someone to read a book from cover to cover. She herself was rather cautious when it came to written works. Though she had a formidable library, never would she take more than one book off the shelf, and she kept the rest of the books locked away inside a long row of closets. Even seeing the titles of books on a shelf was quite enough to excite her beyond measure, she explained. After her daybreak meditations she'd read a line or two, which she would then proceed to ponder for the whole of an hour before finally completing that day's contemplation—as if all too aware of the dangers inherent in absorbing too deeply an idea formulated outside of her own self. If the words at issue occurred to her even once during the day, she'd penalize herself; meaning either that she wouldn't be allowed to read anything at all for a few weeks, or else she would force herself to study works generally regarded as unbearable.

With me she was careful indeed, as it was Nietzsche's *The Will to Power* that she pressed into my hand—in the original German, of course, which she justified only in part due to her concerns over translation. Almost immediately she realized I didn't know a word of German, but at least she could rest assured that I would abide by her method of reading just a sentence. If, by chance, I were to not understand something, she stood ready and willing to help, because she had enduring faith in my development. She exercised similar prudence in selecting musical works that she considered worthy of use in my instruction. While reading Nietzsche, she insisted, one can listen only to Wagner's opuses. Which is why she ordered me to get my hands on *The Ring of the Nibelung* all the sooner. Not that I was to commit the error of listening to all the records comprising this tetralogy right away. No, she cautioned me with wisdom befitting a teacher—this too can be done only gradually. Besides, I was not even to get down to work until I bought the scores; for what is listening to music worth at all without the simultaneous study of the notes that appear on paper? Around two weeks later I dropped by her place with the first record and, yes, the score. Though I thought we'd get right to the task at hand, instead she spent the next few days holding presentations on Wagnerian complexes, on psychological inhibitions, of which I understood virtually nothing. Besides—and this I remember clearly—every other sentence of hers was this: 'We can never be cautious enough when it comes to those Germans.' By the end I was outright begging her to play at least one overture, but she was unbending, saying repeatedly that the road to an understanding of art is a knowledge of method.

Having already got used to such matters in hospitals and in the neurology ward, I wasn't in the least repulsed by G.'s behaviour and ideas. It wasn't at all by chance that I was enjoying the friendship of a gal similar to me; one who, alongside her peculiarities, had something of the pathological about her—a gal who held my gradual preparation for the mystical among her most innermost concerns.

Within the bounds of my talent, I was advancing steadily along the most promising path to an understanding of the secret sciences, when one fine day G. made an unexpected announcement. She was in a fix, because she was supposed to have painted her room but she didn't have the money. As her faithful student I immediately offered my services, as I had a bit of experience in painting work. *That's that*, I thought, *case closed*. But she insisted on signing a statement of intent she'd formulated, which set forth that since she was short on cash, she would remunerate the agreed-upon sum in kind. Refusing to sign was not an option for me, as G. would have been offended to no end.

It was the first evening of work, and I had just finished applying the primer, when G. stood before me and began to undress. Anxiously

I watched her movements, cursing myself for having agreed to the deal. It was unnerving to see her standing there before me with her brawny thighs, her prodigious, imposing bust, her altogether masculine body. In a matter of moments she would crush me, I felt sure. And yet, in the end, almost miraculously I escaped her embrace that evening, after all.

Apparently I'd misjudged the situation. I should have known G. had intended her nakedness only as a preparatory measure, a sort of visual rendezvous. The next morning, when I was just fiddling with the can of paint, she stood before me and said, firmly, 'Take it *off.*'

I protested in vain. There was no eluding her request or, more to the point, her command. As I freed myself of my clothes, G. reflected aloud, and loudly at that, upon the obligation she'd assumed under our contract—an obligation that presently compelled her to develop a better acquaintance with my penis. I had to decide whether to reject her, thereby ending our friendship altogether, or to allow her to bring me pleasure to the tune of a modest five hundred forints; for by her calculation, that was the sum by which she would now reduce the grand total she owed me. After momentary indecision, I opted for the latter. Beyond wanting to abide by our fair-and-square agreement, a purely selfish motive— the excitement promised by the prospect of oral pleasure—also played a part in my choice. But I would not have thought that, within hours, this would bring my downfall.

Citing erotic literature, G. soon proceeded to explain that it was proven that if I were to go about kissing her precious vulva's outer lips, this would bring me at least as much pleasure, as it would her. Indeed—and at this point she quoted specific texts—in some cases this could bring even greater rapture to men, so I should know that she was subtracting another two hundred forints from the total.

It took her some convincing, but finally I assented to taste her rivulet, which, I must say, certainly wasn't a narrow one, as it mightily divided her *mons pubis* in two from underneath. But as I went about quietly sipping from this rather pungent-smelling well— which was fenced in by a wiry, tenacious mass of shrubbery—all at once I belched.

That which is the sign of health in babies, and in good company is a faux pas eliciting a discreet smile, is an unforgivable sin when committed while kissing a proud vagina. At least G. thought so. Most probably it was her sensitive hearing that led her to interpret the acoustics produced by the gases erupting from my belly not as an involuntary signal of natural life functions, but as the unmistakable proof of my intentionally expressed disgust. In vain did I try reassuring her that if she wished, I could even bring her a doctor's note attesting to my hyperacidity; with a scrunched-up face she screamed away to the effect she'd never been humiliated so roundly by anyone. I couldn't have shamed her womanly self-esteem more than I had, she fumed, but I shouldn't even begin to think I'd wriggle out of this with a simple break-up! No, she owed me a measure of responsibility, and so she felt obliged to yank me out of my slough of degeneracy before I'd sink into depravity once and for all.

As the minutes passed G. came up with evermore precise words to characterize my decadence, and as she did so the more even I began to doubt my innocence. Could it be that my hyperacidity wasn't to blame, after all, but the repugnance I'd had from the start for her body—and which this cavernous belch of mine had now so mercilessly laid bare? Unrelentingly G. prevailed upon me the idea of my own debasement, much as not long before she'd presented her latest discoveries or else her teachings about the benevolent spirits around us. Giving in, I admitted the crime I hadn't committed.

But she still wasn't satisfied. No, she deemed my situation too dangerous to simply forgive me. I was 'in league with the most evil forces'—so she summed up the situation. And so, she pronounced, we could not meet for a year. Yes, one year. But, she cautioned me immediately, before I got to thinking that this meant some sort of unwanted holiday that I could spend as I well wished, I'd do well to think again. For one thing, I'd have to promise to be faithful to her, which meant not only my chastity, but that I would continue on my own the studies we'd pursued for months. I'd buy myself a journal, and after twelve months she would consult it to determine whether I'd earned her magnanimity. Besides, the punishment would put my now-dubious character to the test, and so I should behave in this spirit. Then, as if she'd just been bargaining some deal with a scorned little common labourer, she commanded me to finish the painting work without delay.

The next day, I drifted away from G. a broken-hearted fellow, accepting her sentence—a year of penitence—without demur. Never would I have believed that a belch might change a person's life. That's what happened to me, though, because on getting home I arranged my new lifestyle. We had a laundry room not in use that I made habitable with relative ease. That's where I dug myself in.

Not once in the course of those voluntarily months of solitude did I think of escape, though I could have strayed back into the psychiatric wards at any time. It seemed that it was in the civilian life outside of the hospital that I wanted to create the conditions my illness-prone self required. I would be lying were I to insist that back then I was clear on all this, for not even in my relationship with G. did I find anything amiss. Notwithstanding my despair, I regarded it as normal, the dependency that tied me to her even more strongly in the wake of my punishment. After all, I could now experience what I was always susceptible to: dissolving into another person. In those weeks it wasn't my possible innocence I bothered with, but instead I identified solely with the pain I'd caused her, her shame that to my mind seemed almost akin to the aftermath of a rape; I constantly saw before myself her loins warmed up by my belch, and I scorned myself for having sought in those first minutes to deny my obvious depravity.

I awoke at 3 a.m. daily and, walking about the yard, carried out the meditation exercises I'd learnt from G. In my mind's eye I kept afloat the sentence chosen as the subject of contemplation—'I am depraved'—as if everything in the world but this assertion alone was meaningless. As my experiments progressed, from time to time I even felt that I was one and the same with that short sentence, say, which was originally but a thought independent of myself that I'd accepted as my own. My stream of consciousness had shrunk into this complex assertion, ensuring that the memory of my offence would become all the more deeply embedded in my brain. After a while I practically believed that it wasn't even me who'd sought out this sentence, but that it had found me in its effort to identify with myself. Perhaps it is not without grounds that I believe there to be moments when a thought is born not from out of the mind's hard work. At such times the mind surrenders to the gravitational pull of a formation that originates independently of it, as if it is subject to a gravity of sorts just as is matter. So I might say that I wasn't persuading myself of my depravity, but, to the contrary, depravity needed me, which I thought possible despite the dubious deductive reasoning that had led me there.

Over the course of those days, I would have been incapable of gauging the real danger of my self-delusion—that I was paving a path to the development of compulsive thinking. Far from simply accepting the guilt and sinking no deeper into my morass, I sought out and even created laws I could use to make sense of all that had happened; laws that, of course, had nothing to do with cause and effect. An outsider would say I was in the throes of a teenage psychosis I might easily have shaken off had my constitution been more fortunate. Although I, for one, can't decide if this was indeed the case, I do clearly remember seeking newer and newer bits of evidence to prove my depravity.

Above all, what came to mind was that hateful duality that had always been characteristic of me. How very crude I'd been towards G., whose imagination had fascinated me at least as much as her body had revolted me. I'd suppressed this feeling only so I wouldn't be left alone. By no means had I wanted to lose her, and so I'd become a traitor to our friendship. No wonder she'd said that I was on good terms with 'the most evil forces'! Next I reflected upon that weakness of mine perhaps worthiest of contempt: my chronic inability to defend myself. I'd projected upon myself G.'s loathing towards me even before my innocence could have been brought to light. No, we weren't foes, but allies jointly on the attack against the enemy dwelling within me. We'd believed my gesture of irredeemable self-surrender to be sincerity, whereas it really wasn't anything other than self-aggression. With my capitulation we proved that I existed only to the degree by which I was absorbed into a person who, for some reason, had become important to me, as if that person had always been part of myself.

G. had said nothing about self-gratification. As a heathen, she presumably would not have prohibited it, but then again, on certain occasions this may be what love meant to me. So it was that my 365 hushed days of penitence, which were to have been devoted to ritual, were sometimes disturbed by my compulsive masturbations. Yes, I was similar to those priests who teach the Word of Christ by morning and then by night slip into the parish toilet, unable as they are to resist the temptation of this profane pleasure. Of course, they know best of all that there is absolution. And besides, how much easier it is for someone who has himself transgressed to understand the sinner.

The truth is, this cowardly source of pleasure had marked all my teenage years. The fast road to bliss: no need to say a word, no need to share my bleak carnal pleasure with anyone at all, for I made do quite well with myself, thank you. The rest was a matter of the disgust that then unexpectedly but invariably took me in its grip. Again I could despise myself for choosing this pitiful manifestation of the lie I was living. There I stood, alone, and most gladly I would have flushed myself down the can along with my sperm, so this couldn't happen ever again. Yes, this piss-scented love was my due: those seconds of heat between my fingers. This is what my manliness was really all about. I envied animals, which nature had protected from such thoughts.

I am in bed, trying to fall asleep. In vain: after an hour or two of turning about I rise and go out to the john in the yard, as I wouldn't have dared to use the bathroom in the house. The neighbourhood dogs get right to barking, but this comes in handy, for they will serve as a charitable distraction from my solitary shame. I open the outhouse door and carefully lock it behind me, lest someone should disturb me here even by chance. Then I see to my task as naturally as others see to pissing. My lower half is still trembling as I pull up my pyjamas; the draft that gets through the cracks of the outhouse fills my nose with the smell of fresh shit. The situation I find myself in just then, semiconsciously, it seems, is characterized above all by this blend of odours. Then I sneak back into the house like a burglar whose only accomplice other than night itself is his own disgust. Quickly I take off my pyjamas, and I lie down, naked, on the bed. In the low light my eyes pass over my tired body: my chest and belly are coated with a thick mantle of hair; only on my sides, towards my hips, did there remain narrow, hairless passages. Never will I get used to this spectacle. I was only fourteen years old when I shaved it all off, not suspecting that this would only make those hairs grow in even thicker. Examining my broad hips and my underdeveloped chest, I recall an image that invariably makes me smile: I, an embryo, in my mother's womb. The nutrients flowing my way through her veins shape me into a girl; gradually I reach the seventh month, when, owing to some chance occurrence, my female organ undergoes a metamorphosis. I am equipped with a willy resembling a fairy's wand. But this cannot alter the fact that my body began developing as a girl.

At other times it wasn't the modest carnal pleasure my hands managed to wring out that disgusted me, but loneliness. When I find myself alone in the restroom at some local arts-council building, or in the rundown toilet of some train station, the first item on my agenda is to flush the toilet and scrub the bowl, for that calms me somewhat. Never have I really been worried about having the door opened on me. I would stay put only in a stall that locked faultlessly, and no sooner would I sense any danger whatsoever than I'd sneak off and seek another, safer hideaway. Never have I failed to find such a place, which then became untouchable and unapproachable for a matter of minutes; only fear could worm its way closer, and only until my somewhat broken-in disgust allowed it to. I scraped away at the rough stones of my fear until all that remained was a fine, invisible dust, which then descended indiscernibly onto my wretched self. Even as I sat there in this condition I knew full well that I was, for example, ensconced in a decrepit train-station lavatory. And yet, for its part, the intensifying ecstasy—generated by the forbidden motions of my hands, that is—was proclaiming that my cravenness was now straying to a desolate territory which would soon suck me in whole. It was only my self-loathing that kept me from submerging completely. No, I was ashamed not on account of seeking my bliss in a place where others rid themselves of their excrement. The compulsion that drove my repeated acts of masturbation broke me completely free of that cause-and-effect relationship in which toilets have an awkward or embarrassing connotation to them. Perhaps my time there would have been even more unbearable had I not invariably surrendered myself to this wretched act.

My shame, then, in fact derived from my awareness of a stark fact: the bliss I derived from my solitary carnal pleasure was illusory insofar as it deprived me of the very possibility of love—love that, I believed, I deserved as much as anyone. Preposterously I consoled myself with a shit-scented melancholy over the love I'd let slip away or that had slipped out of my grasp. Such kids grow up to be innocent Peeping Toms or, worse, cold-blooded sex killers, for they never forgive women for their constant failures. Over the course of a lifetime they seek revenge for their teenage ineptitude, and God save those who their hatred strikes.

Fear was my only faithful companion in my journeys of escape, though it let up a bit as I stepped in to such public lavatories; for no matter how much my body disgusted me, in the course of those moments it conferred upon me the illusion that even this pathetically developed organism of mine was capable of achieving a sort of semiconscious bliss, which I'd feel ashamed of only after a few seconds had passed. I might even have held myself to be fortunate, for between distress and disgust there emerged a tiny fissure in which, at least for a split second, I could sink my ashen face.

All too often I'd learnt that I, for one, could win women's affection only by chance. And so it was not without reason that I protected myself from situations in which my insignificance would practically be screamed into my face. To avoid outright defeat I went about diligently collecting the evidence of my unhappiness, and in doing so I could at least avoid being openly humiliated by a woman's rejection. Give them up I did, but there was no forgetting my desire: 'Masturbate or die,' I kept telling myself. I was the sole witness to my ignominious surrenders. I'd build myself a maze in which I alone could lose my way. Of course, in the meantime I beguiled myself with the promise of someday becoming the city's most talented lover, at which point it would not be me, eyes shut, jouncing my genitals to kingdom come.

It didn't take much when preparing for my solitary rituals to throw off the image before me of my mother's downcast eyes, in which I saw not only her shame at my appalling sin but also the sparkle of those eyes yet some years before. The sparkle that clung to those eyes while she played the organ in church, on peering above the frayed sheets of her score and glimpsing my long, thin fingers as I, proud little altar boy that I surely was, held out the communion wine to the elderly priest so that once again we could bear witness to Christ's miraculous transubstantiation. I did not fear my own father's rage. This big-natured man had long convinced us that he had nothing to do with any sort of sexuality whatsoever. Of course, he must have been driven by the very conscious aim of protecting us from the devil of the flesh. He could not have reproached me for a thing except, perhaps, for watering strangers' shit with my precious seed rather than transporting respectable girls across the divide, to the far side of pleasure. No, my guilty conscience didn't extend to him. He himself had proven that sexuality did not exist to begin with; and so if I surrendered to my sinful desires, this amounted to nothing more than an error, a ludicrous misreading of the situation.

Could it be that the sense of compulsion that sordidly appropriated my psyche first took shape over the course of these masturbations of mine, which swept me into just the sort of helpless frame of mind that would later characterize my pathological thoughts?

For years I dismissed my surmise. After all, I reasoned, most boys know this innocent transgression like the back of their hands. But now I suspect that my solitude back then, squeezed as it was between those bathroom walls, had something to do with the accursed phantasms that later took hold of me. Even as fiddled with my zipper, I was overcome by the very same sense of desolation that would visit me some years on as I sought to reconstruct the past love life of some sweetheart. And how similar was the later agitation, too! Yes, I always had to be on guard against the joint attack of fear and disgust. Only on account of this possible explanation have I now laid all this forth in such detail. For my despair is greater even than my shame. I'd always been confident that by exposing the charlatan in me who'd believed that his lies could go unpunished, I would see my entire situation more clearly.

All I learnt during those months of penitence was desire. Without a shred of vanity I can declare that I mastered this art with exceptional talent indeed. I call it an art because I toiled daily to perfect the details, only to find evermore evidence of my ineptitude. The method by which I nurtured my secret passion reminds me, above all, of an investigator who tensely observes every move made by the criminals he is charged with pursuing and would rather let them run for it, if by doing so he can gain a deeper understanding of his prey. This investigator makes his way about the city with an inestimable reserve of information at his command, certain that he will yet acquire yet more. Which is why he doesn't strike. Damning evidence leaves him cold, for what excites him is the evildoer's real secret—of which perhaps the fugitive, of all people, knows the least. Excluding the behaviour of the observer, my example is, I admit, a flimsy one but, even if it does so clumsily, at least it partly explains my situation.

And so I remained faithful to G. When venturing out onto the street over the course of those months, I dared to spy only the face of any girl I passed. My eyes mercilessly lopped off the image at the neck, careful to avoid later violating what I'd stolen, for that would have broken the beauty. Severing the face from the body, I carried it off like some stolen treasure. It was up to my imagination to cut this jewel into a genuine precious gem. As always, I kept selecting women with sad faces. Perhaps because I felt they needed my bungling desire, that invisible light with which I lured them unknowingly my way. I was always careful not to be caught. Only by maintaining a distance could I ensure my excitement, which even one unambiguous glance would have disturbed. I appropriated these faces so I could gradually prepare my imagination for that particular expertise in which it could find its fruitless self-identity: the raving phantasms to come.

4

I would have had to endure only two months more; that's how much was left of my punishment. But that was when a well-wisher of mine who'd decided I was on the verge of a nervous breakdown forced me into his car and drove me to a small town in the provinces.

Tired and bleary-eyed I wake up in my new lodging, without a clue as to how long I'll be there. As usual in the morning on waking up, a dull pain fills my jaws. As if my dreams have devoured my teeth. When, years later, I showed the rasped stumps of bone to a specialist, he could hardly believe that it was the result of the grating of teeth. In a semiconscious state I shower, get dressed, head out for a walk. Once out on the street, I take deep breaths of the sultry, small-town air. This makes me feel a bit better. My own brand of incurable syphilis is called melancholy, and this is mine as surely as the fear there is no aborting from my psyche. My muddled, incoherent thinking is but a little plus that's with me just for now only so I'll believe I can perhaps do something with myself, after all. My present loneliness does not lead me to despair. It's as if I'm even happy that I cannot yet return to G. My disciplined, silent madness awaits some external signal.

Moroccan hashish and vodka might still have saved me, back then, but there was no one around to sit me down at their table and press a reefer into one of my hands and a glass into the other.

And so my choice fell to a woman who was, perhaps, even madder than myself.

I pause on the main square of this small town and look around. Grimy pavements that haven't been swept in years; low, filthy old buildings. Dust and despair had long saturated the walls, and would never be scrubbed away. Only by tearing down the buildings could there be a new beginning. The beggarly window displays, guarded by iron-grille shutters, spoke of penury, barrenness, inconsequence. In that minute I nonetheless glimpsed a piece of the world unfolding before me: the unusual, the never-before-seen, the foreign. Of course I know this humble privation well, but I was convinced that I could see it in this arrangement only there. Years later I realized just how decisive this strangeness was for me. The plodding mass of my anxiety could be stirred up to an extent only by the sight of new vistas and towns before my eyes. Arriving in a new town was for me invariably a celebration of sorts. A miracle awaited, and if I didn't find it in the image that unveiled itself unexpectedly before me, I blamed only myself, my inattention, my unpreparedness. But my disillusionment did not lead me astray. I drew strength and impetus from my mistake, my capriciousness: I was certain that in the next town my taut alertness would no longer leave me in the lurch. I was flesh-and-blood proof of Immanuel Kant's rather dubious pronouncement, 'The Self is the world.' So I kept telling myself again and again.

Dismal streets always calm me, which is presumably why I owe such gratitude to neighbourhoods of ill repute. With pleasure I inhale the dubious odours emanating from building walls and the suddenly descending vapours of innocuous sins. The sight of vagabonds, filth and trash makes me feel light, even weightless. I suppose this is because my inner distress meets with an outer one; this is liberating, for in the material world of objects and in the air

I discover that which I am made of, too. Rarely indeed can I experience this ephemeral sense of freedom in the proximity of a human being. The proximity of another person sees me almost snap from the pressure, not that I can say where it afflicts me, really. All I know is that if I can manage it, I flee as soon as possible. Yes, my fear doubles when people are near, and my sense of powerlessness outstrips my lack of confidence. Although I'm unable to catch another person red-handed in the act of casting their own anxiety upon me, I can feel something bunching up in my throat, a gathering of fluids that can't be thrown up. At such times I would prefer to demand that the other person be compelled to pump right out of me the nausea he or she insidiously passed to me for safekeeping. It takes me a long time to leach this foreign fluid out of my throat—and only then do I understand that what I swallowed was the other's imagined fear.

I now headed off from the main square towards the coffeehouse. That is where my well-wisher was to introduce me to the woman in whose presence my dormant illness would really come unto its own. She was like some unknown virus there is no defending against. Even before seeing her, I decided I would fall in love—as if I'd been capable of precisely determining prior to our meeting that this girl was to be the first true love of my life.

If I don't include the neurotic woman who'd fled to Sweden and those one or two Polish teens who diligently protected their virtue even in my presence, why then, until the age of nineteen I'd loved only that particular photograph. As for G., by no means can I include her here, for I would have been repulsed by her body even if my digestive system hadn't pulled one over on me on that unfortunate night.

Suffice it to say that I entered the coffeehouse, and there sat my well-wisher at a table in the company of a thin, blond-haired girl.

The fellow was a crafty one, for no sooner had he introduced me to M. than, citing urgent matters he had to tend to, he left M. and me to our own devices.

There we sat, staring at each other beside cups of coffee that were turning cold, vying to determine which one of us could endure the silence for longer. M. now lowered her head a bit, as if longing to be understood or pitied. Her descending stare cried out for help, waiting for me to lift it up. Her face was shuttered by bitterness that she could have torn away at any moment, but she did not, perhaps because she sensed that this was my specialty. She was the sort of person whose face and stare reveal more about her character, her personality, than do words.

The first surprise was that I felt good with her. Perhaps I'd always longed for these sad eyes before me now, for this frightened expression, which convinced me there was nothing to be scared of. Being near a bundle of misfortune soothes and strengthens me, for I am not focusing on my own anxiety. Another's misery invariably leads to a pause where the other takes a breath, and I exploit this right away, especially if it is a woman facing me.

Something told me that my life had arrived at a turning point, and that M.'s personality was the guarantor. Which was why I could sit there beside her in relative calm. Our meeting was similar to the times in years past when I'd arrived in hospitals, having finally managed to be admitted. How very familiar was this suffocation we both had now sunk into! It seemed we even exchanged glances over this alliance we had yet to even tie. I'd found myself a worthy companion, with whom I could live out my illness to my heart's content. Fate had led me to her. Without her, I might never have understood the nature of the excruciating tension within me.

She offered herself to me. No, not her body. She neither had the courage for that nor, I figure, would she have found such a tactic tasteful. Instead it was her distress that she poured open before me, and this had the effect, in my eyes, of endowing her personality with an exceptional treasure few have the privilege to experience. Who can claim to draw their nobility from that most precious material, suffering? It was the forsaken, defenceless animal in her that clung to me, a creature that figured I'd understand this in a matter of moments, upon which I would be the one who most desired this mating of minds. She figured well. I was happy; for the psyche now stealing its way up close to me was one that, until now, I'd known only as myself. I was almost drunk at the thought of being able to tear up newer wounds, and doing so without having to mask my craving. M.'s attraction to me was the greatest guarantee.

I did not misunderstand our rendezvous. Here was an ailing woman who'd come to me as if by reminder that not even what I was now about to embark upon—my first true love, that is—would allow me to forget my fate. She whom every sound-minded man would have fled at once enticed me with the illusion of bliss, with the notion that, for the first time in my life, I, too, could now experience the self-effacement that comes with genuine love. 'I don't want to live,' she whispered in a veiled voice, touching my hand. 'The only reason I don't dare do *that* is because there are one or two people I love. Do you now understand why you mustn't start carrying on with me?' She'd tempered her voice to keep it from sounding all too harsh and husky, which could undermine the gentleness she'd arrived at after so much searching for just the right tone. Her words had to be rapturous; no, a strong, resolute tone mustn't get in the way of her confession. This woman was consigned to my defence, I understood right away: only my love could save her. *I must cure her*, I thought, *even if it kills me*. Her death wish was all the more justification for my self-effacement. It seemed to me that she was raising the spectre of suicide so as to suggest that I alone could stand in the way, even if she did announce that after this coffeehouse rendezvous of ours, we must never meet again. But I'd already decided! Stubbornly I endured her resistance, demanding another date. Not that I could tell her the truth—that I'd long specialized in those preparing for suicide and that I didn't know any other way to live, as if it was my calling to prove to such people just why it's worth following through. Finally she agreed to meet once again, the next evening.

All night I dreamt of her. The next day I clearly recalled three dreams in particular. In one, I saw her on the platform in a subway station, waiting for the train to arrive. I walked up to her and from behind I took her arm—but not even that was enough to keep her from jumping. The blood splattered into my face. I screamed and screamed until the arriving police led me away. In the next dream-image that flashed through my mind, I was walking on the shore of a lake with houses on it. It must have been dawn, since there was not another soul to be seen. The wind was blowing, and so I stopped to roll down the sleeve of my jacket. That is when I noticed the waves sweep M.'s body ashore. Her face was swollen and, it seemed, smiling. The final dream took place in a hospital. Two tall men led me into a room. One of them pointed at a body lying on a bed and asked, 'It was you who was talking to this girl yesterday in the coffeehouse, wasn't it?' I nodded, upon which the other man told me to follow him. Only in the hallway did I realize that the body was M. So she'd done it all the same, I screamed, starting to run down the hallway. I wanted to get back to the coffeehouse, to that moment the previous afternoon before we'd bid farewell. But I pounded the window of the coffeehouse with my fists in vain: in the dark there was no one to open the door. That's when I awoke. My forehead was soaking wet and my lips were cracked. I sprang up in bed and looked at the clock. It was 4 a.m.

I had to find M.—so I resolved—for she had almost an entire day to fulfil her vow. I ran over to my well-wisher, rang his doorbell and asked him for M.'s address. She didn't live far. In a matter of minutes I was knocking on her door. A moustachioed man opened it, training his piercing, boar-like eyes on me. Just when I thought he'd hit me, M. appeared behind him in a lacy nightgown. I blushed. Usually I can come up with some sort of credible excuse, just like that, and this is what saved me now, too.

As it seemed there was no cause for me to worry just then about M.'s possible suicide, I let them be. The pig-eyed fellow must have been taking good care of her. On such an occasion a normal man drags himself by the tail out to the curb, stumbles into some bar that's open at the crack of dawn and atones for his misunderstanding with at least two or three shots of something strong. But I was already in love with M., and not even the absurd, humiliating scene that had just played out before the door could change this.

The next evening we passed our first night together in her dimly lit bedroom. To me her face was beautiful: a death mask that some-times, quite by chance, gives a sign of life. She seemed anguished, as if she'd suffered a great torment that day. And yet that is precisely what excited me. Only my fear of frightening her kept me from pulling her towards me right away. I had to take care to submerge my neurosis and hers—which each of us wore just then with almost haughtily—in the embrace that awaited us gradually, without any sudden movements. Here I was sitting beside a person like myself, someone vitalized by the awareness of her fragility, her powerless-ness. What was to explain this frailty of hers? Perhaps only the insistence with which she clung to it, as if that alone could account for her sense of self-identity? Perhaps. Maybe she even admitted to herself on occasion that the greatest proof of her frailty was its existence: 'I was born to be beaten down, and this is what gives me my dignity. But is there a treasure more precious than this dignity? Is this not that adornment of self-awareness with which we can rise above ordinary people?' It was precisely this impotent sense of self-satisfaction that I needed, a psyche that had long lost contact with the outside world.

All the same, I then took her hand, which was moist and cold—nervous, fearful of my touch no matter how much she desired my approach. Was it her own body that caused her such anxiety, or mine? Or was she shamed by the fact that my fingers were now discovering the clamminess of her skin? In vain she sought to be natural; her rigid posture and convulsive movements made it clear she was not succeeding. There was no choice but to retreat, I decided, unless I wanted to confuse her once and for all. No sooner did I pull back my hand than she began to speak—as in classic novels, in a solemn, stately tone. 'You know, I may have had several boyfriends up till now, but I've always been alone. You are the first man in my life who, I feel, has touched me. It's as if we've been together for years. Unbelievable? Well, then, listen here! This is how it happens: I'm getting ready for bed. While my boyfriend is waiting *in* bed, I'm in the bathroom feeling as though I'd rather just spit on myself. Again I ask myself that question I've asked all too many times: Why keep it up? Towel dry yourself and then slip into bed beside him, where the two of you will get to fucking right away, because both of you want quick bliss . . . And what will it all add up to? Pathetic straining and despicable shamming, capped off when each of us howl away with so-called pleasure. But again I'll leave the bathroom all the same and do the whole thing from start to finish, because I can't do anything else. For I have someone I can talk to, someone who will hear my words, someone with whom I don't feel as terribly alone as otherwise. The past few days have been unbearable; my boyfriend's thing didn't even stir any more, no matter what I did to rev it up. But I inhaled his shame, yes, I slipped into bed beside him the next evening as well. This lying relationship is what kept me alive. Imagine! Often I didn't step out of this flat for weeks on end. My lonely, sorry life felt invulnerable. And yet by the end of the second week I thought I might go mad. Not that I was able to go outside. The light, the noise, the people—especially the people—were too much to take. Every night I stuffed myself with sleeping pills, but even in my drug-induced daze all I did was stare at the wall, which sometimes closed in on me. How often it crossed my mind to do *that*, too; it did all seem so simple, after all. Two bottles of nitrazepam and a pot of strong coffee, and I'd have fallen asleep nice and slowly. But I am here, you see. Perhaps I saved myself only for you.'

She paused. Turning her ashen face towards the window, she seemed to be watching someone. I'd been conquered. It wasn't the gathering force of her love that now left me powerless—no, it seemed that fate had denied her of the capacity to express love in this manner—but my own schizophrenic condition. Like wax under the heat of a flame, my self had melted off me unnoticed, and by the time she concluded her confession, I had already become *her*. This is exactly what I felt. Yes, I'd taken her place combing my hair in front of the bathroom, vacillating over when to go back out and slip into bed beside my impotent boyfriend. It was *me* who'd been lying for days on end in that room, curtains drawn, staring blankly at the wall. *I* was the one all worried lest some acquaintance should bound right in and, by forcing me to talk, would jolt me out of my stupor, which was more bearable than the presence of another person.

I take the sleeping pill, sit down before the mirror and feel shame while scrutinizing my tight round breasts. Why am I not excited on drawing my fingers over them, and where is the desire when I imagine a man pressing his brawny frame onto me? Combing my straight blond hair over my forehead, I notice that it is parallel to my eyebrows. My thin nose jumps boldly forwards, keeping my longish face in balance. My lips form an almost perfectly straight line, stirring out of place only during rare smiles. Not even my melancholy can erase the lustre of my eyes. My face is my ornament. Can't they see it? And don't they notice my taut belly and alluring hips under my tight-fitting dress? And yet I know they're watching: they turn their heads as I walk past, taking me in with their eyes. But I'm afraid, and my fear is bound up with contempt. All they want is to get between my legs, to masturbate inside me. All at once I am disgusted even by myself. Is this how I'd try wringing out my freedom? I want to scream, but my strength has been sapped by the sleeping pill, which by now has been absorbed by my cells. I lie down, and if I'm lucky I'll even manage to fall asleep. But tomorrow, everything will begin anew. Perhaps I'll go into town, into this goddamn town.

M. could not have known that she had penetrated me, and that in doing so she had indeed taken the reins of my life. I found myself in a labyrinth, with my temptress standing at one of the entrances, as if to throw me a bone of eroticism. And yet my real seductress was not her, but an unnameable being that whispered, with a smile, 'I offer a rapture even more precious than physical gratification. I will give you this person completely, but do know what to do with her.' I accepted the dubious offer. By now I was the one worried about her fear as she passed with free and easy steps along the road and smiled back upon the men whose eyes she met. No longer was it those two nitrozepam pills that ushered her into semi-consciousness every night, but the exhaustion that followed orgasm, while I kept watch a distance away, only to piss her embrace out of me in the wee hours of the morning. No longer was it my story I was living, but hers; or, more precisely, *my* story was *her* story unfolding within me.

On that first night together I do not know which one of us did more to dispossess ourselves of our sexuality. I grew hesitant. Although I no longer desired her, it seemed increasingly inevitable that I would undress her and then do with her what men do at such times. Before touching her, I turned off the light, figuring the darkness would blunt the sharp edge of my act, rendering the whole embrace as if it never happened. As I needed something to cling to and use as a starting point, I pressed my nose to the warm, moist skin of her neck and inhaled. In vain: there was no smell. Then I began caressing her shoulders, but this time it was I who was exposed as a fraud, for my movements were accompanied by pathetic thoughts: 'What I am now undertaking is plainly a lie. I can believe only in the body, and nothing more. Love is born on my fingertips, and there it dies.' Instead I deluded myself, encouraging my fingers to hold fast, because any moment now I might be overcome by that never-before experienced ecstasy in which my consciousness would puncture hers, my newly acquired mania would penetrate her constant suffering. And so our union would be more jolting, more intense than any sort of physical orgasm could be; for how could we compare the rapture of the psyche nearing the brink of madness to some invigorating emission of fluid?

What we sought was the more challenging path of the chosen, which was yet another reason we couldn't trust ourselves to our senses, to these exceedingly unreliable wellsprings of whatever, which pretend to be tools of some higher purpose even as they strive shamelessly to be aims unto themselves. The nipple, for example, wants nothing more than for a dexterous tongue to dance its way around it, securing its borders with a tepid wall of saliva. No, we did not fall headlong into this usual error. It was our task to mollify our neurosis, which was awaiting another sort of gratification. This is why we had to freeze our hands and skin, to undergo the agony of our loins: so the illness we'd already shown ourselves to have would prove to be a virtue before us. We lay there in silence. Eyes shut, M. received my caresses as I toiled diligently to show myself to be a skilful lover.

After a little while I noticed that she was crying. At first her face contorted almost unnoticeably, and then narrow, irregular lines appeared below her eyes, and next around her lips. She kept her lips sealed tight. She tried to control her muscles, all right, but her lineaments consequently tensed up all the more. And she forced down her eyelids all the more—the purplish veins swelled thickly— as if trusting that this would allow her to block her tear ducts. Her face became a seismograph of suffering as everything she wanted to hide spread all at once across it. Her eyes were sinking into the sockets, it seemed, boring their way through the thin bones, from where they started to protrude upward. On reaching those reaches of skin where flesh and cartilage began, they must have gathered strength before breaking through all at once. They filled up the wrinkles, depressions, furrows of her face, whose entire surface now comprised the anxious, glistening light of countless pairs of eyes. Never will I forget their unified glance. It was madness that held them together, madness that struck me as inconceivably distant and yet ever familiar. Somehow I had to define this look of hers, which is in fact why I called it madness, but surely I would have been more precise to identify my discovery with the two servants of this unanticipated psychosis: dread, and the distress that comes from feeling nothingness. Today I am practically certain that I was in fact seeing the reflection of my own stupor, and that M. played only the role of the intermediary.

Our lovemaking was to be defined by M.'s continued tears. It was our fear, not our bodies, that embraced, leaving behind us what had now seemed a weightless realm of sorrow that had only just scraped the outer skin of our existence. Wanting to step beyond this, we conspired to annihilate both our own and the other's being, reaching that certain borderland where pleasure is superseded by pain, satisfaction by suffering. Here it was that we aimed to explore that rarely experienced rapture of the chosen, perhaps only so we could prove that mind is governed by laws entirely different than those of body. Rather than sadomasochism, though, our path towards these secrets was not one of tormenting the flesh. Instead, starting off from the opposite shore, we began making our way over an untouched land, the unexplored landscapes of the psyche, where conquering even the tiniest bit of territory carries severe punishment. We did not fear the fact that our bodies would not give their blessing to all this, no, for we imagined that we could enter the new dominion even without the help of wretched sensuality.

Observing M.'s face, which by now had contorted nearly to the point of being unrecognizable, I was hard put to decide whether it was subdivided by pleasure only masquerading as rapture or else by an insidious pain. At that moment I would have been glad to take on the role of the most contemptible analyst.

Two women are led into the experimentation room, a man accompanying each. The task of one of the men—who has an unrivalled reputation as a lover, as does the woman he's been assigned to—is to embrace; that of the other, to torture his victim with the most varied tools imaginable. All five of us have voluntarily accepted our examiner's mandate: to undertake the test he has devised, by which I am to compare and contrast the physical symptoms of pleasure on the one hand, and suffering on the other.

The first of the questionnaires before me contains a catalogue of body parts. On a given signal, the couples fall to their respective tasks, and I begin to observe them. First, the eyes: how the colours change, how the pupils contract and dilate. How to explain the eyes' half-open state? Is a wide-open, bulging eyeball the result of heightened pleasure or perhaps of fear, nay, of pain? Next I focus on the changing shades of skin: suddenly pale, or else turning from light blue to a purplish hue, only to take on the colour of blood at the next punch or kick. By the same token, I pay all due attention to the sometimes barely perceptible shades of transition. At times the complexions shift for a moment only, as if phosphorescent materials of varied colours have been implanted into the pores, so they might flash in a different hue at a blow or a caress. The facial muscles demand all my powers of judgement, and more. With taut attention I follow every little twitch as it changes the surface of the skin, from wrinkled little hillocks to plateaus stretched tight, from disciplined smoothness to the subdivided surface, which sometimes knot up skin that hadn't so much as quivered only a moment before.

My analysis extends equally to the upper and lower lips. Attentively I must observe how they interlock to determine whether any shift from this position is the result of a joint effort or, perhaps, commands independent of each other. Nor can I be satisfied simply to interpret all the gasps and screams streaming into my ears; I must listen for the resonance of the body as a whole. For example, from the waving motions of the thighs of the woman making love, I am able to conclude that this heated-up knot of flesh is also partaking of that unarticulated cry that erupted from the woman's throat only a moment before. At the same time, I cannot afford to lose my way on this shaky ground. I fit the tone and strength of the voice to the most characteristic movement of the moment, paying special attention to the nuances, which we can never be sure of. As the overseer has cautioned me, the voice will not necessarily be higher on account of blows to the flesh, nor will it be deeper due to newer waves of pleasure; for physiological laws can play tricks on us at any given moment. And so I am able to pass judgement only after meticulous observation.

The second phase of the examination aims to elucidate the similarities between the physical manifestations of anguish and pleasure. In my capacity as analyst, I would presently cite just one example, not forgetting those pitfalls that threaten the experiment throughout. As regards the lovemaking couple, pain must accompany pleasure, and both the man and the woman must be satisfied with this. But the other two subjects can hardly be expected to experience this singular melding of pleasure and pain. She who has subjected herself to torture is not a masochist; her pain is genuine physical torment, which can in no way transmute into some sort of psychological satisfaction. The same goes for the torturer. In any case, by our overseer's dictate they have to switch roles after a while, for only thus can they become equals.

That is to say, demonstrating the possible physical similarities of pleasure and pain occurs on the basis of a rather arbitrary perspective; for it can easily happen that I project the signs of suffering exhibited by the subject who happens to be undergoing torture onto the woman who is making love, whose face now contorts beyond recognition—perhaps because in his desire the man thrusts more and more in an attempt to wring another orgasm out of her, one she does not want.

And yet I would cite one delicate point of similarity. Contracted muscles shatter the face's pale hue, and the lips part, breaking the areas around the mouth into pallid knots of flesh. Certain arches flank furrows, while the barricades of unbroken skin are reminiscent of corrosion. This abruptly born landscape is virtually impossible to put in order. But it seems that the upper part of the face does not obey the invisible order to arrange itself. It seems almost smooth: only the furrows, the crooks under the eyes, speak of a relation to the ravaged points of the face. The expanse from the mound of the cheekbone to the corner of the eye is unalterable, but it's precisely this oasis that is so calming, especially the shadows of the gap between the eyebrows, owing to the plummeting beams of the irregularly shaped wrinkles clogged up on the forehead. The eyes would perhaps fall forward, were it not for the fact that the dilated pupils didn't serve to rebalance their focus indiscernibly inward.

I see this momentary freeze-frame on the face of the woman in the throes of torture just the same as on that of the one making love, whose lineaments are subdivided by a wholly different sort of distress.

But I could not analyse M.'s face, for she'd buried her head into the pillow and started crying again. Besides, how could I have even compared our bodies' agony to any sort of lovemaking? We had prostituted ourselves to the consciousness inside each of our heads, which winked at the exceptional experience even as we barricaded ourselves from the pleasure. Had I been a healthy man, I might even have cautioned her: 'Listen here, my dear, you know what your problem is? You are frigid, plain and simple. You don't know your own body; you've given up on getting pleasure for yourself and for the other. You think your neurosis can coax some carnal pleasure from your lap. In vain I run my fingers along your milky skin, for when I touch your hip, this is what you think: "He's touched my hip, so now a tingle should come over me, but I wait in vain." Only now do I understand just how hopelessly meaningless the term "frigid" is, because if you were simply cold and unfeeling, believe me, it would be much easier! But the barrenness of your calculated thinking debauches the garden of instincts; you wish to give orders to that which works well on its own. And what did you get in return? Cowardly suffering, which thrusts you deeper and deeper into self-torment. Your proud will has also been broken; it is no longer you who are in charge but the suffering itself, which craves both to commit and undergo newer and newer forms of torture. Your freedom lies only in choosing artful tools. You think you can fulfil the aim of existence, by which you can arrive at a middle ground. Compared with that, everything is pleasure: a harmless orgasm is just as suspicious as love that seems so cheap; for it deludes, it strays you from your path. When your face is contorted and you are gasping, you believe you can tear yet another secret out of suffering, cross-examining the Great Tormenter, with whom, after this, your relationship will be even more equivocal than before.'

But how could I have said anything of this sort to her at all, seeing as how she'd already inhaled me into herself, not to mention that I had identified with her, like so many compounds mixing on a chemist's table?

This disciplined madness had already lasted more than three months when, one night, I paid a visit to G. It seemed right to tell her in person that she shouldn't wait for my punishment to be fulfilled. Sheepishly I explained how things stood, though she didn't exactly want to accept it. She was dejected to learn that from now on I would no longer require her services, nor was she capable of understanding it. Just as I was stepping out the door, all at once she clutched me and asked that at least I give her a kiss. I resisted in vain: she pulled my mouth to her lips and began sucking frantically, as if she could only get air from me alone. I mention this harmless incident only because it was this that later decided my fate. A week later I got a letter from G. in which she analysed our farewell with her usual scientific precision, not neglecting to mention, of course, everything she felt when kissing me before I left. As it didn't even occur to me that these lines could be dangerous to me, I slipped the letter into the inside pocket of my coat and didn't give it a second thought.

By that time I was already living in a tiny flat with M., who, a few days later, found the letter. On first glimpsing her face when I got home from my usual morning walk, I knew at once that something had happened. But I asked her in vain: for an entire week she didn't say a word to me. The simplest solution would have been for me to pack up and leave. But I could not. As I saw it, she was still dependent on my protection; it was up to me to cure her. What had I done to deserve all this? I dreaded finding out. If only she'd just set upon me! But no. Instead she chose a much crueller tool: that particular strain of silence that puts the deranged out of their misery.

When, on the eighth day, she pressed the letter into my hand without a word, I understood that my trial was over. She branded me with that infidelity from under which no protection at all could have found me innocent. All the less, because I was her, and so a few seconds later it was rather I who was shocked to learn that M. had been cheated on. I had, after all, touched another body, I'd accepted another woman's kiss, allowing the tongue to worm its way between my teeth, shattering the magic that until now could be sustained only by our embraces! Were M. to kiss me once again, she would taste the unfamiliar in the flesh of my mouth, sense a stranger's distinctive odour; and even if she didn't, she would certainly think all this. She would stand watch, waiting to finally catch me red-handed.

And so I had to bleed to death on a bed of ludicrously banal nails indeed, it seemed. First there was that belch, and now this childish kiss. Perhaps it would have been more fitting this time for me to seal my fate with an unequivocal fart—say, emitted while making love, my behind somehow ending up above M.'s face.

Finally I managed to pacify M. Although she soon calmed down, I for one could not forget my unfaithfulness. Constantly before me was the image of G.'s mouth zeroing in on my face and clamping onto my lips, biting my tongue, bathing my gums in her copious drool. My mouth disgusted me to the point where I could hardly get down mouthfuls of food, and for weeks I didn't so much as touch M. If I didn't figure some way out of this, I knew I would come completely undone.

First I settled my account with G. Had I known my way around the magic of casting the evil eye, I would no doubt have killed her, but the tools at my disposal would have been insufficient even for the doings of a mediocre sorcerer. To think how pleased I would have been to prepare the ritual using the photo she'd given me the first time we parted! Through a complex series of steps I would have begun by turning it into a fetish, only to strike down upon it when least expected, to mercilessly exterminate it. Not having such secret powers, however, I made do with fantasizing. First I tore off her face, and then her thick, ever-moist lips; on yet another occasion I proved to myself that she didn't even exist, or that, if she did, I'd never met her. At times of peril I substituted her image with that of other women I knew whose persons I could not possibly associate with a fact as dubious as the memory of a kiss. My mother was my best bet in this respect, and if for some reason I couldn't conjure up her image, I was forced to adopt more depraved methods, such as turning G.'s mouth into a truly repugnant piece of flesh.

Next came that neurotic woman whose lover had helped her flee to Sweden. In my mind's eye I set fire to the night-duty nurses' room, where she'd initiated my body into that most ancient of mysteries. Nor was I allowed memories of carnal pleasure. Instead I had to bury them with darkness; my newfound fidelity demanded this. I came to hate this woman for having made me unfaithful to M. even before I'd met her. Indeed, my exulting body had cheated on my love even then. Instead of accepting my inevitable seduction with indifference and impassiveness, my instincts had led me astray, into the realm of spellbound satisfaction. It was by way of this false-hood, this meaningless act of self-delusion, that I tried to emasculate my past as well, trusting that I might thus make myself forget my fresh sin. The simplest resolution would naturally have been to get admitted to a psychiatric clinic, and there have myself subjected to some marvellous new sort of electric shock therapy—say, one that would ensure 150 volts for several days rather than the usual 120. I would even have signed a special agreement, under which the clinic could keep up the therapy until, having passed through the stage of partial memory lapses, I would achieve a state of complete oblivion. At that point I would walk out of the clinic and learn to live life anew. But since I did not have the courage for this alterna-tive, I had to study other techniques of forgetting.

Developing a false consciousness demands at least as much self-discipline as toiling to achieve the opposite. Indeed, it requires a greater degree of alacrity to turn our inner truths upside down, for we must lure not only our surroundings into a noose, but also our-selves. Only those who can understand the art of lying are ready to completely lose their way, for aside from the thrill of self-delusion, this is what he gets in return.

Weeks passed before I calmed down somewhat. I was on the verge of convincing myself that by secretly, fancifully murdering faces and facets of my past, and sterilizing their remains, I might ease M.'s jealousy. Not as though I said a word of all this to her, no, bringing it up again would not only have doubled the effect of my infidelity but also of the shame I'd felt since the revelation of G.'s kiss. I call it jealousy, the silent loathing with which M. tortured me, branding me with the unforgivable nature of my act. Not that it was hard for me to identify with this loathing of hers. After all, *her* Self was *my* Self; indeed, I had willingly built the bridges of sameness binding her and me. And that is what allowed me to really come to despise myself, which I alone might never have been capable of doing.

But then a newer obsession undermined my relative security—namely, the notion that my sick desire to eradicate all traces of my past love life from my imagination had suddenly and unexpectedly left me in the lurch allowed something even stronger to jostle into its place. It was as if I wanted to make up for the aggression I'd committed against myself; for having, in essence, hung a scarlet letter A to my chest. What I now needed was self-justification to convince myself that not only *I* had served up cause for jealousy but *M.*, too; and for this I found the evidence in her past. And so I began examining her bygone love life with the same intensity as I had my own. It was now that I could really reap the dividends of the intermittent sameness of our Selves, that sensation which sometimes brought me such pleasure. This cross-examination was like forcing a confession on myself.

The pig-eyed fellow was the first one I caught her with. So M. had cheated on me the very first night we met, I concluded. Even as I'd been consumed by visions of her suicide, she'd been tumbling about with that moustachioed boar. Not even the fact that I'd been the one who'd insisted on meeting her the next day was now enough to soothe my sudden rage. Nor did my simultaneous awareness of my contradictory conduct serve in the least to lessen the effect as I evoked the image of their lovemaking; or, say, cast doubt on whether their embrace had occurred at all. The first image that flashed before my mind's eye as I went about this fanciful cross-examination was M.'s white body lying motionless on the bed. Perhaps she'd slipped her hand down her belly in the hope of wheedling some sort of pleasure out of her loins for once. Then I glimpsed Pig-Eye's hand in the act of caressing M.'s breast. After a few seconds the image began turning hazy, but I took care to stay alert. I cast the scene as a freeze-frame before it might have vanished forever, and waited for my weary imagination to regain strength. Soon M.'s screwed-up face appeared before me, from which it was apparent that they were probably just about done copulating. Observing her anguished countenance with cool repose, I was over-come with hatred, which until now I'd felt only towards myself. Had I been able to, I would have torn the breathing cross-sections of pleasure right off her face and covered the fresh wounds with my loathing. Not even the most depraved torture would have sat-isfied my thirst for revenge just then.

Imperceptibly I stepped beyond such not exactly harmless visions of jealousy. By now I wasn't content simply to clarify the dubious role of the pig-eyed fellow; I required newer evidence to expose M. for what she was. Suspending the logic of cause and effect, my passion broadened the avenue of time to allow anything and everything to have happened within it. I experienced events that occurred some months or even years ago as if they were happening in the present—events that I might consequently even have inter-vened in. I could choose freely from among the infinite planes of time, depending what my despotic whims required at any given moment. Whenever I so wished, I'd walk effortlessly right back into the past like someone going back home to get keys left behind. I would imagine myself choosing some man who seemed a reasonable match for M., sitting down beside the two of them, and bidding them to start making love. Having been freshly appointed by Eroticism as the master of ceremonies, I would stay on into their lovemaking to issue commands at appropriate moments. At other times I would drag the scene into the present along a path unfamiliar even to me; that is, since M. had perhaps not yet been fully prepared on the first occasion, I would have them repeat the embrace. My imagination would now smooth over their earlier fiasco and bestow the lovers, who not long ago had been inept, with true pleasure. As an invisible observer, I could assiduously compare the two scenes, taking pains, of course, to note the differences.

On certain days I arranged to have M.'s infidelity occur in the future. If, for example, on getting home I didn't step from the stairwell straight into the flat, I would wait for the imagined lovers to finish their frisking about, and only then did I open the door halfway, so that I might at least have something to back up my suspicion. I would not allow myself to be deceived by the sight of M. washing dishes in the kitchen or curled up in the armchair, immersed in some book. No, I would not fall for such blatant trickery. At such times I didn't even touch her, for doing so would have obscured the traces of the embrace she'd engaged in only moments before.

Why my visions focused solely on the physical, I am embarrassed to say I do not know. That certain kiss might, of course, serve as a convenient explanation. Although it initially had nothing to do with sensuality, I discovered the symbol of my sin in my transgressing lips, which had fused with G. And so this particular body part invariably took centre stage; it had exposed me to attack, very nearly tearing me from my love. Perhaps to balance the account, my despotism then dragged M. into my penance as well, moronically turning on its head the up-to-then more or less rational logic of my thinking about our relationship.

This gets me thinking. I suspect that, quite simply, M. injected me with the poison that finally allowed my illness to come full bloom. How familiar even the jealousy was on taking hold of me! I'd filched from M. the hatred she'd felt towards me, secretly reversing our roles to make things easier for her. But, after the cheating, it was in vain that I tried stealing back into her that which had originally been part of her. No, her jealousy was now mine.

Like some demon that penetrates the soul, the need to compare myself with others had therefore already taken shape in me; all I had to do was find the territory where I could satisfy its hunger. No, it wasn't through free choice that the erotic became the subject of my visions; instead I was giving in to the demands of my gradually strengthening demon, which seemed outright happy that I'd finally met up with a woman who could maintain her presence inside me. This really struck me only when, one fine day, my dubious moments of time travel unexpectedly took on a life of their own. No longer was it *me* deciding how to pay amends for my own infidelity or, say, for M.'s jealousy. My imagination, which until now had ensured my relative freedom, now turned insidiously against me, and with that I lost my sole support. My imagination had undeniably operated erratically, but at least it had been mine. From now on I could expect not even this: I had to subject myself to compulsive thoughts that, not long before, I myself had contrived. Perhaps I was following my demon's shrewd commands, for I would never have believed that my perverse fabrications were dangerous. However, when the obscene images that took shape in my mind began recurring independent of my will, I understood that I was paying a heavy price for my naivety. All at once I'd become a slave to my visions.

That is when I thought of the man M. had talked about the second time we met. Perhaps he could save me: If only I could convince myself that their love was more exceptional than ours, I would have set the path towards my freedom. It didn't take much to convince myself that, for some reason, M. had kept me from learning of this love, maybe because she sensed that I could never accept the notion of playing second fiddle to her heart. In painting my imaginary portrait of my rival, I built on my inferiority complex. This man could not possibly have loathed himself as much as I. Surely he was among those fortunate souls, I thought, who proudly and confidently bear their own bodies, which are unequivocally beautiful. How self-evidently, effortlessly they must undress! No, they don't understand the sort of shame that seeing my own body causes me. Indifferently or perhaps flamboyantly they show each other their muscles and hairless chests, and they needn't tense up when their lover's hand reaches for the lower reaches of their taut bellies. These bodies did not flee to cowardly masturbation from before the prospect of sexual education in their teenage years, for their self-confidence guaranteed the success of the revelations that awaited. My rival could not possibly have comprehended or bothered about M.'s repressed neurosis, if only because he could hardly have been hoodwinked by the possibility of asexual excitement between two bodies. My realization that his invulnerable manliness did not tie a compromise in the interest of love made me jealous. I began craving his strength—the strength with which he safeguarded his sensuality, that pawn of our existence without which we lose our sole certain handhold. Hence my sense of loss must have been the main reason my visions hinged on the physical. Was it through aberration that I protested my eunuchhood? By now I couldn't bring myself to believe in that man's supposed impotence. No, I could have sworn that M. had lied to me.

No longer was I travelling through time to conjure up visions of jealousy; instead I'd found a man who, in the course of my comparison, had unnoticeably got the upper hand over me, and whom I constantly had to take into consideration when I was with M., even when she just came to mind. This man became her accessory; he belonged to her as surely as the lack of satisfaction did to our embraces. I could have sooner forgotten M. than the memory I'd contrived of this man, which awakened me to my new shame.

It was the man's presence during our lovemaking that frightened me most of all. His whimsical appearances were indeed impossible to prevent. On certain nights he observed my exertions with a derisive smile—a smile that spoke of a cruel confidence that would gladly have yanked me right out of M.'s bed. At other times he seemed to cheer me up, which left me even more embittered. On such occasions I was tempted to shove M. away from me and confront her about her complicity. But I felt his presence even when he wanted to go easy on me. Not that I could make out his nebulous form in the dark, but I knew he was there hiding by our bed, waiting for the right moment to give me a wink.

For a few anxious weeks I endured these visitations. And then they plunged upon me all at once, these creatures I'd shaped for myself with such frantic precision the past few months—freezeframes plucked from past and future that had taken lives of their own; visions that had become obsessions; the stealthily reinforced need to compare myself with others; and the jealousy I'd consciously shaped from the start, which by now I associated with my pitiful comparisons to M.'s former lover.

But, with that, the cup was full. My demons, with my smirking rival at the pinnacle, surrounded me and passed me among each other at their fancy. No sooner did I scratch off my eye one image of M. making love than another pathological sensation would drill into me; for example, the notion of making M.'s past my own. Through my weakening self-control I gauged the strength of my attackers; for by then, I was unable to clearly grasp that I was the one who, back then, owing to my maniacal desire to conform, had dispossessed myself of my own past using a foreign despot; and that the expropriation now underway was merely the same thing, but in reverse. With my independence gone, no longer could I distinguish between that which I'd created and that which had arisen on its own. Owing to my enemies' alien nature and cold cruelty, I was increasingly certain that the latter was the case.

Not even then did I dare say a thing to M. Surely I could deal with the visions on my own, for it seemed but a temporary crisis I'd get through with requisite self-control. Nor did I want to let her in on my secret, because I feared both being vulnerable and that by airing my dirty laundry before her, we would grow distant from each other.

Disappointment was my due. My obsessions took shape and took root indelibly within my mind until it seemed they'd always been there. How could I have imagined that, as time passed, they would dig in their claws even deeper?

M. could not have suspected what I'd been struggling with for months on end. My hushed madness taught me how to behave so discreetly that I didn't even have to try hard to outwit her. Besides, she'd already gotten used to my melancholy, and so she wasn't terribly surprised by those bad moods that conspicuously took hold of me during our most intimate hours. Yes, if there was any subject I might have been questioned on by a demanding committee of examiners, it would surely have been subterfuge. It would have been even harder for her to notice that for some time now, I hadn't been living with her but, rather, with my maniacally recurring thoughts. When she spoke to me, I heard her words as a distant, echoing pronouncement whose meaning I often didn't even grasp. During our more important conversations I often had to tell her to repeat her questions so I'd be able to answer at all. As for delicate matters, I read those on her face, her eyes. At such times I gathered what will I had, and tried blockading that dull current in my consciousness which regularly supplanted the conspicuous bouts of torture. Never had we been chatty, which was yet another reason why my faltering sentences and incomprehension-suffused replies could not give me away.

For me it was reason to celebrate if my visitor did not appear during my nightly embrace with M. But the prospect of breathing easy generally faded as fast as it had emerged; for I was already spying M.'s face with suspicion, waiting for the appearance of the lineaments I knew so well from her imagined acts of lovemaking. Soon the vision was before me; all I now had to do now was slip it onto her face. If, say, one of the doggedly recurring images was slow in coming, then I saw to rearranging her expression, just as my demon demanded. Meanwhile I caressed her body as if my hand was, in fact, my rival's. What had become of the disciplined lunacy of the first time we'd made love? When, through the agony of our physical senses, it had essayed to get closer to the soul's supposed sensuality?! At least we'd been flirting with a sort of eroticism; dubious though it was, we believed it might be ours someday through patient searching. As I then drew my moist finger along her neck, I thought to myself that I was already long beyond this fiasco of ours and that we were approaching the final appraisal, in which it would be pointless for us to decide which one of us was the real loser.

I was on the point of hallucination. Although I was aware of still possessing my own body, when I again touched M. after a short pause I felt it wasn't *my* hand on her but my rival's, demanding his due share. No, it wasn't *I* who'd contrived this absurd fusing into each other but the dissembling despot within me, he who maintained this duality, which was imperceptible to M. from start to finish, when our lovemaking ended.

And so I came up with all sorts of excuses to avoid frequent lovemaking. The ensuing lonely nights I intended as a means of gathering strength, for I continued to trust that one day I could free myself from my persistent visions. But dragging out this game of hide and seek for all too long only served to impress me, like some heavy seal branded into my skin, with the hopelessness of my situation. That is when I decided that, albeit carefully, I would talk to her.

Back then I was the object of all the unconditional love M. had in her. Almost certainly she ascribed no particular importance to that weeklong jealousy-induced terror she'd imposed upon me. True, after the punishment, which she must surely have thought justified, she still went about her business with a pained expression worthy of a martyr. But the intensity of that look of hers seemed to be abating, as if she had good reason to expect more conciliation. My dread during her reign of terror had clearly calmed her, as if it had validated her own importance; for she had had me in her hands more securely than perhaps she'd ever held anything before. M. had achieved a sense of authority akin to that of a merchant who pays his agent—the slave trader—and then receives the goods. She must have felt outright magnanimous for, as she saw it, having practically overlooked my transgression. Why, M. even observed that she would not have shown such mercy upon anyone else.

Yes, I'd received special treatment, and no doubt I would have regained my self-respect as well, had I meanwhile not been swallowed whole by my absurd vows vindicating M.'s reactions. And then there were the compulsive visions this engendered, which insidiously annihilated my own feelings. How consequentially this story of ours unfolded! One fine day I awoke to realize that it was no longer M. who excited me, but my obsessions associated with her. Initially I'd fallen in love with her due to her illness, thinking I could cure her. Instead, she took slow gulps of the poison along with me, for which it would be unjust of me to condemn her, as an outside observer could have told us as much on our first night together.

I'd overestimated my abilities. I had believed that my predilection to illness would be enough for me to defeat the dangers that lay waiting. But, in fact, my immune system only weakened as the dangers gathered force. So it was that I could no longer grasp M.'s increasingly obvious love for me, for my visions drew a net between us in which every word and every movement had a secondary meaning, too, one that seemed directed not at me alone. When she whispered, 'I love you,' I was certain that she was addressing at least one other man as well. When she broke into a smile, I looked around, wondering whom she'd sent this unequivocal message to. When we were out, I didn't even dare look at her, practically certain as I was that she was now using the situation to her advantage to discover among the strangers *that* man with whom I could then compare myself. And my fear was not unfounded, for among my random comparisons, in no time I imagined my rival standing there among two sniggering fellows as he commenced upon yet another witty presentation. One time I snuck into the school where she taught, and went about scrutinizing the group photos on the hall-way walls to determine which of her colleagues she could count on scoring with. I began digging through her belongings, wanting to find at least one letter or photo to finally confront her with every-thing I'd imagined. How insidiously jealousy overpowered me! Although at first I was satisfied with incriminating facts conjured up by my imagination, I now needed physical evidence.

Most despairing of all was the fact that I didn't even love M. any more. One would think jealousy is reserved for lovers. Maybe this is so, but my experience on this point differs. And perhaps this was instrumental in my uttering the sentence that would decide my relationship with M. At first I dared speak only about my rival. In a dissembling tone of uncertainty that must have come out sounding apologetic, I explained that for days now I'd been thinking of the man she'd mentioned before the first time we'd made love. Probing though they were, my questions also had to convey indifference, as if all I wanted was to clarify an unexplainable, unsettling phenomenon. By disguising my disquietude as harmless, I hoped to easily get answers with her help. As if sensing that this ostensibly trivial matter might lead to something less than harmless, however, M. stayed silent. But then she stepped into my trap all the same. Albeit reluctantly, she admitted that this man had been the only one she'd been in love with before me. For a moment she even faltered, as if she'd been caught lying, but then she got through the deadlock deftly indeed, commencing an improvised presentation on my intuition.

So I hadn't been imagining things about my rival for no good reason! If M. had revealed this much, I thought, surely I could wheedle more secrets out of her; I was caught in the grips of that numbing pain which spies must feel on being smuggled behind enemy lines for the first time. Her sincerity definitely eased my situation, for I could now link a confession of my compulsive visions with newer questions about the man—questions she would no longer be able to evade. One night, while making love, I turned suddenly glum and pretended that, for some momentous reason, I was unable to resume our embrace. Buried in silence, I waited for her to ask what I was thinking. When she did then pose her question, I slyly cautioned her that I was privy to a secret that I could reveal to *her* least of all. I took her increasing unease as an encouraging sign, and I was already certain she would wring a confession out of me. I was not to be disappointed. After a little while, she flat out demanded an explanation. I then asked for a guarantee that I would suffer no disadvantageous consequences, such as her getting up and leaving me after I'd put myself at her mercy. Having secured this guarantee, my insidiously choreographed scene authorized me for everything.

I began my story by mentioning the appearance of the man who'd been visiting me even more frequently ever since our conversations began. I wouldn't have brought this up, I told M., if my unknown acquaintance had been satisfied with this much. But he'd been demanding even more, I explained; accompanying me on walks was not enough for him, nor were my afternoon hours of idleness, when he would appear from out of nowhere with an invitation to chat. By now he was even insisting on being present during my most intimate moments with M. No, this was not the first time he'd spied on our lovemaking. Even tonight I'd seen his eyes, I said, giving M. the *coup de grâce*. Dumbfounded, she listened. For a moment I felt sorry for her, and I would surely have put an end to this pathetic comedy when one of my recurring hallucinations struck: M.'s face, contorted with pleasure as she clung tight to my rival's broad shoulders. The scene was all too clear for me to show mercy upon M. All at once the locks opened up, as in the case of a madman who can't be dissuaded from his goal even the by the imminent danger of solitary confinement. I felt that it wasn't even me speaking, but a stranger; one who, for some reason, had commandeered my vocal chords. First I brought up my relationship with my rival, stressing the comparisons that flashed constantly through my mind, ever giving him the advantage. Then I got around to telling her about the dichotomy that had haunted our embraces for months already. All our many hand motions, I explained, insidiously dissolve, for in vain did my hand approach her breast; the moment I touched her, my hand had become the stranger's. Which was why I loathed her smile, too, at such times—so I mumbled, but now to myself—for it was directed not at me but at my rival! A man who could thus partake in the same pleasure as did I. And how shamefully her caress—which I'd gullibly believed was discovering my body alone—ensnared me.

Perhaps it was on account of my excitement, which by now was nearing the point of ecstasy, that I failed to notice immediately: M. had snuggled up to me and was hugging me tight. Although my confession had terrified her—it did, after all, suggest something tantamount to perversion—she started cheering me up at once, telling me not to be afraid, that it would all be over soon. M.'s empathy took me aback; I hadn't expected it one bit. Suddenly the tenderness I'd felt towards her on our first meeting flooded through me once again. Maybe she loved the sick side of me just as I loved hers? The derangement verging on madness that she'd exposed only moments before. Surely she knew that anyone who has such thoughts is no longer good for a thing. By contrast, it was now that M. clung to me with true devotion, as if all the while she'd been waiting for this moment—if only to prove that she, too, was ready for sacrifice. This unconditional devotion moved me, but not even this could stop my recurring flare-ups.

My visions took hold of me ever more insidiously. I could hardly wait for evening, when I would share all this with M., who in the meantime anxiously watched my eyes. Never could she figure out how I would react to her smile, whether spontaneous or consciously assembled; she'd learnt that she could not smile without repercussions, as I might discover something foreign in the lineaments of her face, and then nothing could save me from once again imagining our most intimate moments as not ours alone. I saw the barely stirring arch of her lips as an impulsive call to be seduced, which I immediately interpreted as deriving from a memory of her past flirtations. And that was justification enough for me to go about interrogating M., making her give an account of smiles she'd cast at my rival. Nor from her perspective did the danger pass if, say, I seemed to be looking the other way at the moment her lips stirred suspiciously. Sometimes I mentioned my associations only hours later, although of course I feigned indifference, so as to ensure forthcoming replies.

My madness had reached the point of open cross-examination. And, as so many times before, my desire to flee deceived me even now. At first I intended these interrogations as a way of confronting the facts—facts that could then obliterate my visions. So it was that one fine day, M., albeit ashamed, agreed to my wish. She was to talk about my rival's body. An outsider would have seen terror and self-capitulation in my eyes, for I listened to the details as if a judge were reading out the heaviest sentence I could get; what I heard only added credence to the arbitrary workings of my imagination, giving me reason to keep cooking things up. In point of fact, they gave me strength. The healing magic insidiously turned against me, that is; and so to the extent that this was possible at all, I became even less inhibited. I took to interrupting our lovemaking not only to offer up a thought, but also with my questions. Wretchedly I abused our intimacy, for I chose the moment of interrogation so shamelessly that she couldn't deny me an answer. I presented my curiosity as innocently as could be, as if I'd just thrown a ball in her court that she could easily throw right back. If, for example, at the very moment M. fell into the throes of orgasm I suddenly asked her how things were in bed with my rival, I could almost certainly count on a flattering response. And yet on other occasions I was more stern and ruthless, even though the whole scene revolted me more than her. Still, I couldn't keep myself in check. I just had to listen as she spoke about my rival's penis, his lovemaking habits, or that supposed impotence of his.

In the final weeks, M. broke down. My mania had cornered her once and for all, for I had been torturing her more sordidly than children do flies and frogs. My analogy is, perhaps, imprecise only in that while doing so I never once derived pleasure from what I did. This was, however, no excuse for my depravity. Not even her neurotic past could get her used to my well-honed madness, and she begged me in vain to get professional help. For my part, I was already working out the details of my newest plan. I must split up with her, I concluded one day, figuring that by doing so I would free myself of my visions. After all, in her company I'd traversed a territory of my consciousness that I might never have otherwise gotten to know. And so I deluded myself into believing that distance would grant me a reprieve. I even took the bait of self-pity, consoling myself that the only reason I could have been so cruel to M. was that the visions had tormented me even more unmercifully than what I'd subjected her to. Those who have suffered humiliation must know this feeling well; those who, when the occasion first presents itself, trample weaker souls who get in their way. With maniacal zeal I believed in the success of my decision; I believed at least as much as I had so many times before in the healing power of some scheme of mine.

M. received my verdict with words of muted protest that spoke of resignation.

5

But I was wrong. Because I could escape only M. As for my demon, it remained my faithful companion; its presence alone, so it seemed, could ensure my self-identity. True, immediately after I broke up with M., it slyly retreated, as if hinting that it might just grant my freedom. It was like some daring tactician who, by stepping back in a manner not one bit without danger, gives up territories he has previously acquired, only to strike at the right moment. In those solitary weeks after breaking up it turned out that although I'd ended my relationship with the person who'd given rise to my obsessions, those very obsessions now clung to my consciousness independently of her. Surely this was M.'s revenge for having left her high and dry, I thought. But then I had to reject this assumption, which ran contrary to even a minimum of logic. After all, was it not M. who'd polished the mirror in which I first noticed my leering foes? Even this unquestionable fact was not enough to calm me. It would have been risky, as well as unjust for me to lay all the blame on her for my new circumstances. Perhaps it would be more precise to gauge the danger lurking over my shoulders if I surmised that M. was merely a tool in the hands of someone or something, one I could not possibly have avoided. My demon must have held her to be the most suitable temptress of all. With her I really did manage to step outside my self; so fully, in fact, that the servants of some tyrannical force were able to shove their way into its place: by now obsessions had filled the void that my self, deprived of its will, had left in its wake. I understood that even breaking up with M. was the product of yet another compulsive decision—one by which I wound up even further from what was perhaps my only way out: confronting my demon head on.

After breaking up with M., I had ten years at my disposal to regain some measure of what had always been a rather questionable state of health. Instead, I perfected the method of my phantasms. When lying in bed with a girlfriend—at times of unease I switched lovers weekly, but more often, every two months or so—all I could think about was that not long before me she'd been romping about with someone else. While the words 'not long before me' would seem to reflect my awareness of the passing of time, what really oppressed me was whatever image happened to be floating before my eyes in the present: say, the sweaty intermeshed bodies of some stranger and whoever my girlfriend appeared to be just then. To me, it mattered not one bit whether this vision was borne of an embrace that had happened two years ago, two months ago, or as little as two days ago, for even the most distant past was condensed in the unbearable grip of the present. How else could I otherwise have explained those visions in which, for example, penises appeared on the ceiling?

It was invariably the intermediary who turned the presumed events of the past into the present, in effect guaranteeing that the past didn't even exist. Those compelled to study time can experience that which *has* happened only in the 'now,' for they have long cast aside the shield so often raised between past and present—memory—as a cheap hand-me-down. Perhaps what has in fact happened is that memory has come of its own, deprived of its merciful ability to distinguish between two points in time—having become the experience itself.

At this moment the present is but a riverbed, a shore holding together the process of the past, even though my self is already passing the time elsewhere: say, beside a phallus dancing on the ceiling, which in no time I'll escort to our bed. I shut my eyes, but on looking up once again I see a man falling headlong over a three years younger version of my present lover's body. After undressing, I take out my well-honed knife and slice into my flesh so that it begins to bleed in fine bands; for this is how I wish to mark the lovers' bodies. I do not feel physical pain, which is yet another reason it's so easy cutting the veins on my limbs. The weaker I become, the more certain I am that not even the most painful cut would make me faint. As soon as I hit upon that border between vacillation and resolve where conditions are optimal, with a decisive move I cut off my penis. Using the knife, I slice my manhood into thin slices before turning back to the lovers and smearing it all over their steaming hot bodies. Still I feel no physical pain; indeed, my anguish seems to slacken. When the lovers then emit inarticulate cries out of carnal pleasure, I cut off both my ears. As soon as they open their eyes and, gasping away, stare upon each other, I poke out my eyes. Now they speak, whispering sweet nothings to each other in stifled voices: I cut out my throat. I am almost happy, for I do not hear their groans, I cannot see their interlocked bodies, and the numbed pain has dulled my brain. But this lasts for a moment only; now, if possible at all, their bodies become even more distinct before me. But I have prepared for this contingency as well. Dragging myself over to a pane of glass I set up in advance, I run my fingers over it to locate the sharpest edge, and then with all my might I slam my head against it. For a little while I lose consciousness, but when I come to, I find myself escorting yet another phallus to the bed, where my love is undressing. I take out my knife, slice into my flesh, and then turn to the bodies that, by now, are already making love.

Even until then I'd known full well that I could not keep imagining things with impunity. But, try as I did now, I still wasn't capable of keeping my recurring vertigo from rearing its head. My life became a movie screen, onto which these moments cunningly projected pictures they chose at random. This was a subordinate-dominant relationship in which my whimsical torturer took care only to be sure that the visions hit me in a more or less prepared state of mind. Perhaps this also serves to explain why it maintained one of torture's most important conditions: that the lever be turned gradually upward.

That must be why, on certain days, the images harassed me more circumspectly. At such times I didn't immediately attach a man's body to a woman's hand appearing before me, but, rather, I examined the hand as an object unto itself. For hours on end I would observe it with what objectivity I could muster as it grew practically into a pillar, until finally I had to admit that it was not responsible for its own actions. So it wasn't so much the hand I was jealous about—no, I wanted to grab hold of the fraud lurking within me and get it to stop such nonsense—but instead that certain something that is capable of remembering a caress, a scratch . . . that collects one-time instances of pleasure. After all, only this something had the power to summon the sort of images that afflicted me! Could it not be that the mind guards its wealth innocently indeed, that only my mania obliges it to a confession, because my half-witted desires can achieve momentary calm only by way of this secret interrogation?

The next day I was even more at the mercy of my madness as I commenced my prohibited stratagems, for the newly acquired details demanded further clarification. The girlfriend who happened to be sitting across from me knew nothing about any of this, of course; she must simply have thought it no less advisable to disturb my silence than at other times. Slipping her delicate fingers over the back of my hand, she broke into a suggestive smile. We'd known each other for only three or four days; she had every reason yet to see me as an enigmatic male whom, with patience, she might make her own.

But even in the first hour of our acquaintance I might well have asked her, 'Tell me, please, what number am I? Among your lovers, that is?' Right from the start I would have found my way to the clutches by which I might have more quickly figured out how my next potential victim would conjure up my visions. But I never dared do so. Besides, getting to know someone always carried with it the illusion of a deadening of the senses, as if a holiday had just begun. I call it an illusion because on one of the next few days I already had my mind on the girl's presumed past. I directed within myself her most recent break-up to the finest detail, not forgoing of course the farewell lovemaking that my imagination could not do without. I wasn't flustered by the obvious contradiction in the fact that I could fantasize about this in the first place only because that break-up had occurred. By now I was just awaiting the right occasion. Of course my girlfriend could not have suspected what consequences awaited if she answered the question I posed so coolly, and so she opened up. My relative calm lasted only that long. Again beset by my old anxiety, I knew that in a few days I would again force yet another confession upon her.

What she had to do was to stir her onetime lovemaking up out of the ashes, her blissful or mundane embraces, and I didn't let up the pressure until she didn't tell me what she felt and thought from the first touch to the final caress of the love play that followed the orgasm. Helplessly I listened, with the numbness that precedes mad raving, and hatred overcame me, a rarely felt hatred that gradually gave way to disgust. And yet most disheartening was the fact that not even these images I'd wrung out with such depravity could weaken the force of my hallucinations. It wasn't even the face of my humiliated girlfriend I saw, no, only the conjured-up vision now held my attention, a vision that by now was threatening to erupt into the open. But my insidious tormentor saved me from this, for it must have been well aware indeed that making a public spectacle of this illness would deprive it of further pleasures. At such times I wanted nothing more than to puke. How often I'd thought that there would come a day when I, by throwing up the food I'd digested, I could also rid myself of everything that makes me nauseous to begin with, thereby freeing myself of my pathological thoughts! But that's not how it happened. The phantasms kept me in their grip, that insidious numbing came over me ever more often, and I didn't even get the opportunity to prepare for the assaults. Now and then, after a round of fantasizing that seemed like a seizure, I told myself by way of consolation that perhaps it was best if I kept this feeling of nausea, yes, perhaps I had to keep enduring the vertigo, because maybe one day, before squeezing me to smithereens once and for all, I could nonetheless slip out from under this fiction that was, for me, crueller than anything reality could muster.

Although I compared my condition to a seizure, it is true that that sensation came over me only when my visions reached their apex. Until reaching that point, however, I had to pass through various stages of fear that were sometimes difficult to tell apart. While on my own I had endured the anguish that grown onto me quite tolerably, but as soon as I got to know my newest victim, I immediately lost my confidence. At first all that happened was that some obsession of mine would flash before my eyes, as if it wanted only to test my tolerance. If I endured a moderate level of pain with relative ease, then the compulsion to compare would confront me with a somewhat more difficult trial. The sensitivity of the situation was determined by my feelings for the victim at the time, for if perchance I was in love, then I received this final step as a sort of blow under the belt, which I had to avenge.

This was the moment when the anguish I'd somehow managed to more or less tolerate was subsumed by a sudden fit of nerves, which I then strove to free myself from through my compulsive interrogation of the victim, which of course put me even more on edge. By then all I needed was the girl's confession, which before long I got out of her, too, for no matter how anxious I was about her laying bare her past, I had no choice but to fire away with my inquisition, for I would not have been I, had I done things differently. My pathological excitement was now swallowed by a helpless rage. As if my dark passion had stolen away what remained of my sobriety, over the course of those minutes not even I understood my muddled words. By the time I regained my self-control, however, it was hatred and disgust that possessed me. Invariably I could endure this pressure for a short time only, which is maybe why I was fenced in by that sound; a sound that most resembled a muted buzzing, a sound I perceived simultaneously in my mind and outside my mind. I began turning numb. But then along came a sudden aggression that yanked me out of this semiconscious state. At first I wanted to obliterate the image conjured up by the confession I'd heard, but as this proved futile, I attacked the intermediary—that is, my girlfriend. I shuddered at the liberating effect of this nearly murderous state. From experience, I knew that should I end the relationship immediately, I would achieve a temporary repose. Only after the break-up would I be myself again. But then there was my punishment: a fresh store of memories that I knew, I would never be able to forget.

It was not only the helpless desire to destroy that induced me to such devastation, but also the pitiful consolation that, while alone, I could suffer, at most, from loneliness. It seemed that without intermediaries, the images could not find their way into my consciousness, or if they did, they were colourless and harmless. They needed my living relationships to thrive; only with them in hand could they exercise their control over me. Indeed, they went so far as to treat each of my relationships differently. In some cases they hardly tormented me at all. Had I been a bit shrewder, I would have chosen only women whom my enemies deemed unworthy of being intermediaries. But how could I have duped my torturers when I knew better than anyone that the very reason those girls hadn't stirred my enemies' interest was only on account of their inconsequentiality? Of course, this wanton observation of mine reveals only the absence of love, for which complete insensitivity was my due. It was through the presence and power of my masters that I could validate my love: the crueller they were, the more certain I could be in the importance to me of the girl I'd happened to choose. There developed a triangular relationship that, as muddled as it was, had easily definable contours: three of us vied for the lead role—my self; my love, who'd unwittingly become the intermediary; and my compulsive fantasies. But then it would become clear, again and again, that in this battle which was unfair to begin with, only the last of these three players could count on victory. If for no other reason, why then, this had to be the case simply because love, which for me had always meant losing my sense of self, guaranteed ideal conditions for its free movement.

How easily I commanded what were presumably the more or less harmless conscious musings of the girls so close to me into the realm of erotic memories! No longer was it just me who, during our intimate hours together, was meanwhile thinking about her onetime embraces, but, I imagined, so were they. By now the two of us were jointly validating the impossibility of caressing each other with abandon; for two estranged observers had compared what had once happened with the present moment. Naturally it was I who silently saw to doubling the compulsion to memory. I'd projected my own obsession onto her imagination, and once convinced that the transfer did not meet with resistance, I perceived my thoughts as her own fantasies, as if she'd been the one who'd now dragged me into this loathsome game. Sometimes my enraged mind would construct a situation even more absurd—such as concluding that it was solely the girl who happened to be embracing me who was beset by hallucinations, which I'd realize on account of some unmistakable movement on her part. Making such a discovery was, of course, simplicity itself. Soon I even discerned those signals that goaded me to resume my less-than-innocent interrogations.

I sought to make order of my thoughts and feelings, so as to avoid the perversion, the near feeble-mindedness, implicit in my fantasies; for it wasn't some abnormal proclivity that led me on my path, but the demon of compulsive remembering, which denied me that so very delicate condition of tranquillity. If only I could have been a spotless pervert, a peeping tom incarnate, the whole affair would have been so much more bearable! There I'd be, sitting in front of the VCR, my eyes locked on obscene images, on masterpieces of pornography, gratifying myself with the spectacle before me. But no. I loathed such pictures; they left me cold, all of them, even the Hamburg Club's hard-porn show, where for 200 marks one could see live acts of coitus from start to finish. Or perhaps I simply didn't have the sort of courage that a certain female friend of mine could call her own? The gal in question was about nineteen years old when, one night, a girlfriend of hers invited her to go up to her flat. A man was waiting for them there. By the wee hours of the morning they were all drunk. At first my female friend made love with her girlfriend, and then with the man, but by then it was self-gratification that was on her mind. Edging out from underneath the man, she walked over to the sofa, where she wrung out yet another bit of bliss. That is when she noticed there was also a dog in the room. It took some doing, but having singled out the creature for the finale, she copulated with him as well. At first I thought she was just pulling my leg. The whole story became more believable only when she herself couldn't decide for sure where on that drunken morning this had happened to her at all.

My perversion, if any, was this: it was precisely the men conjured up by my imagination to whom I ascribed the genuine power of love. A psychologist would of course easily have explained my situation: I was tormented by an inferiority complex that, on penetrating the field of love and the erotic, destroys. But how would this expert have explained my accursed neurosis? Perhaps by citing a form of paranoia verifiably particular to myself; namely, that I'd swept the unresolved problems of my teenage years into a fantasy world. And what might he have come up with, had I mentioned the constant aggression I directed towards myself? Even through others, I wanted only to hurt myself, for that is what my masters demanded of me. Would this, too, have been explained with my innate perversity?

To me, it seemed, the foremost law did not apply. To plummet with another body into the darkness before the dawn of time, into that semiconscious miracle in which bodies cling to each other unreservedly, convulsively, indulgently or perchance disconsolately, so as to fulfil their only command: to *love*, to make love. Whether with abandonment or with an intense searching gaze, happily or unhappily, but by all means, love and make love! Because, after all, perhaps it is true that everyone and everything yearns for pleasure.

If only I'd had the strength to endure this rhythm, that of the natural pulse of existence! If I could have felt that my girlfriend's body was one among a million bodies, a body that my own body draws to itself, so that in this breathless pulsation there might emerge a momentary sliver of ephemeral bliss. Or if I could have possessed the instinct of a girl who lures into her bed some man who happens to be passing by, an instinct similar to that of a she-cat that never loses her bearings—a she-cat that, on freeing herself from one exhausted tom, gets right down to mating with yet another male. It was this condition, free of memory and conscious-ness, that I yearned for, but it seemed that, for the time being, it was to remain beyond my reach.

My hands held and embraced this body, and my eyelashes touched it, so it seemed, but in fact cowardice kept the other from my reach. Fear wormed its way between our cohering bodies, clog-ging the breathing pores of moist skin as it dug itself in beside drops of sweat. My consciousness subdivided into inscrutable segments until it wasn't even my hand that was touching the girl's taut skin but, rather, my memory had settled upon her presumed memory. And sooner will fire unite with water than two memories with each other, for they are so belligerent that even at the moment of peace-making they'd just as soon draw swords. No understanding what-soever can bridge their hopelessly absolute divide.

Throbbing, rhythmic motions, swinging along an indeterminate arc. To keep from feeling my body, I held convulsively to self-hatred. Perhaps that's why I'd always been drawn to music, to material beyond the realm of matter; for there I could temporarily forget those particular, ruthless laws of life I'd been cast into by high-handed chance. Sometimes I thought I was capable of freeing myself, of conjuring my way out of these unavoidable truths. At such times I thought of an image I had so much to thank for, an image my mind had fine-tuned again and again: I am attending Mass in the slaughterhouse of the mind, my consciousness tasked with the butchering. It turns its blade towards me, well aware that only in the event of perfect slaughter can I count on escape; for I'd already become inured to torment. I am dressed in a light, ankle-length silk gown, and I need only enough room in which to breathe easily. After only a few steps forward, I arrive at a coat hanger with just a single hook, but one that holds the masks of all my loves to date. Unperturbed, I stand before that packed-full hanger. All that can be heard is my light breathing. Giving way to an unfamiliar gravitational field, the space around me collapses here and there with my every breath, and each time, one of the masks on the hanger vanishes into the newly formed recess. By the time all the masks have been swallowed up, there appears an unrecognizable being that proceeds to cut off my arms with a cutting implement resembling a knife, and then hangs them on the coat-hook. Next it does the same with my legs, my torso, my head. At the moment, all that's visible of my hanging body parts is my face; the other parts have been absorbed by that singular gravitational field accompanying my breaths. Surely my consciousness should disappear, but the recesses in the space around me do not absorb it.

So then, not even now did the ritual succeed, I realize in a flash. Both the masks and my own body have disappeared somewhere else altogether. Perhaps I just forgot where they are. I must continue getting by on assumptions; for example, that in the next game, my consciousness will be swallowed up after the masks, the hands, my face. And yet I suspect that, in this opening, there won't be a need for any sort of explanation.

6

The woman who was to render precise the contours of my illness came into my life a decade after I broke up with M. I saw her first in a bar. Those dawdling about inside the barely lit place were mostly young—each of them fleeing from something or someone, so it seemed. The music was blaring, so I could hardly hear what the fellow prancing about behind the counter and serving drinks was shouting my way, a man who for his part finally grasped that I wanted a beer and a shot of Unicum. I downed the herbal bitter at once, and an airy warmth flowed through my limbs, as if tepid irons were caressing my insides. Since the bar itself wasn't all that interesting, I took to staring at the ceiling, following the zigzagging of the flies that had remained here from during the day, as they did their well-practised calisthenics along the quivering strips of light rendered by the fan. The air pressure didn't even make them stir. That is when I noticed that the bar had a loft, too, one whose shape—which was reminiscent of a border fortress—did not exactly jibe with the otherwise deliberately planned, leisurely atmosphere of the place.

My gaze was broken by a young woman who was sitting at a table by the edge of the loft and talking with a man a bit older than her. Her very short hair revealed a proportionally shaped, rather longish head that was reminiscent of silver amphoras the ancient Greeks used to store oil. Her smooth, high forehead was supported from below by boldly arched eyebrows, perhaps only to highlight all the more the disquieting effect of her oriental eyes. Her pupils, which practically melted into strikingly dark irises, seemed unwilling to contract. These eyes, when open, swallowed the world. The cats that once upon a time walked about the bedrooms of the pharaohs as those human gods made love must have looked like this. Her elongated eyelashes must by turns have served as a fan, and as a secret curtain to hide from before strangers that which only the possessor of these eyes may see. The most irregular part of her face was the nose: The long, vaguely Japanese arch of the bridge culminated with fairly large nostrils. And yet, on the whole, the contours of this nose seemed from afar as sharp as the dagger of a desert bandit. Her neck seemed to exist independent of her head or trunk. Its almost disproportionate length was redeemed by an iridescent green necklace, which however only served to emphasize all the more the whiteness of this breathing pillar.

I'd just lit a cigarette when I saw her get up and step over to the railing. At full height she towered above me, leaning up against the edge of the loft. I wasn't mistaken: a young feline stood tall before me, one that seemed calm enough on the outside, but as she jerked back her head or ran her long fingers across her face, she displayed a certain anxiety, a torment hardly possible to conceal. Her full breasts were in stark contrast to her almost scrawny frame. In proportion with her upper body were her long arms, which ended in narrow hands that slid by turns over her neck and playfully over the gnarled surface of the railing, as if to erase the unevenness of the wood.

I now knew more about this young woman than one should, I thought. What would I talk to her about, if she opened up so much even without words? And would she even be capable of calling out in words from this corporeal truth, or would her sentences mock this exquisitely executed, soundless language? I ordered one more shot of Unicum and downed it, like that, whereupon I decided to go to the john before joining her up there. As soon as I stepped in the narrow door I was greeted by an image typical for the circumstances but that now held my attention nonetheless: a young man on the grimy floor, liquid dripping in viscous drops from his face into the toilet bowl. Not that I was revolted by the sight. No, the man's position seemed outright natural. In an indifferent tone of voice I asked if I could give him a hand with anything, at which he looked up with a smile that spoke volumes. As he did so the suspicious fluid now began cooling the nape of his neck. I nodded, and took my place beside the other respectable urinators. This boorish scene is noteworthy only because it served to distract my attention from that which awaited me and which, just then, I did not suspect.

On closing the door behind me on the way out, I took a deep breath and then stepped onto the first of what would be thirty-two steps to the loft: precisely the same number as in a flawless human jaw. The wood of the staircase, which was littered with cigarette butts, snapped away under my feet along like the piercing glissando produced by a prepared piano. My ascent was neither fast nor exactly slow, but more reminiscent of the steady, even motions of a work horse in a coal mine, even though this wasn't otherwise characteristic of my gait. On reaching the top I felt the young woman's gaze on my forehead, which now burned more intensely than my insides from the alcohol I'd downed so quickly. Or was I just imagining her stare? I didn't dare look at her. No, I feared she would uncover the desire in my eyes; for I knew full well I'd love her as firmly, as indelibly as the roots of ancient trees know nothing but thousands of years of darkness.

The customary monotony of the pop music was now broken by spirited Arab tunes. Even as my blood pulsed in thick waves against the walls of my veins, I noticed the drawn-out sounds of the string passages, which I'd always believed to be the unmistakable acoustics of seduction. Images passed before me: Nymphets cupping balms and healing oils in their outstretched hands stepped from a tranquil sea and danced their way towards a naked man lying on the beach. The sun daubed the almost motionless water, as well as their dresses, the colour of blood. All at once the man raised his head and pressed it against the cold sand. That is when the percussion instruments—congas and other drums, as well as cymbals—joined in. The rhythm had an even, repetitive beat, hushed and yet unyielding: a tiger stalking its prey. The youngest nymphet now stepped from the group, leant down over the naked man and, using her fingers, began rubbing his body with balm. Finally a song erupted, a rattle of flesh from the direction of the loins. At this point the man stood up, stepped away from the nymphet and over to the water, and submerged.

The music was still playing when I reached the young woman's table. They were talking again—just now, engaged in a comparison of Dostoevsky and Thomas Mann. Although my attempts at introducing myself to women were invariably accompanied by anguish, just now I was surprised to notice that, quite to the contrary, I was overwhelmed by the familiar, pathological tension of intellectual fervour. We're in the same space, then, you young feline, you, I thought: So it's not just the night that deceives with the proximity of flesh, but that enigmatic Russian and the hero of German intellectualism also have their corrupting ways. Smoke drifted towards me in erratic circles from the depths of the room. Meanwhile the Arabic tunes had fallen silent, leaving in their wake the stupor of Eastern fragrances.

The subject of conversation made things easier for me; for by devoting my first sentence to an observation likewise comparing the two writers at issue, I imagined that I was only returning to the ongoing debate—a debate I would now depart from only on account of some pressing matter. Although the man was presumably of a different opinion, it wasn't him, but her, whom I was concerned with. And, judging from appearances, she wasn't disturbed by my unusually confident debut. Indeed, she seemed delighted at the opportunity to charge forth in her role as disciplined analyst and explain things not only to him but also to me.

She spoke with a striking intelligence I'd previously seen only in bland, homely girls. Her sentences were bound up conspiratorially with her body; so much so, that it didn't even seem to be her speaking, but her body. Perhaps I wouldn't have even understood the meaning of her words, had I not simultaneously been interpreting her physique, which didn't so much as complement all that she was saying as it did practically, wholly explain it. How could that mass of predicates have competed with those gestures aimed at rendering them more precise—gestures that called attention precisely to the limited possibilities of her words? No matter how clearly she expressed herself, she seemed always to feel the need to authenticate the words streaming from her mouth with her hand motions. She used this extended speaking tool called her 'hand' with a degree of self-evidence I'd seen before only in the mute, who are compelled to learn this noiseless grammar. If she raised her voice midway through some clause, sure enough her thin hands shot up right away into the air, as if it was there, in that invisible spot, that she'd found the meaning she'd been seeking in vain with those attributive constructions of hers. She would hold her fingers there for a little while, and only then, with an almost excruciating slowness, did she lower her voice, as if guiding to herself a thought that she'd pinched by the ears right out of the air.

The longer I paid attention to her, the less I was able to free myself from my newest discovery. The girl's provocative expression was the product not of a conscious coquetry but, rather, of an involuntary openness that exposed her sensuality, which perhaps she wished to conceal. No, not even the shrewdest flirt could have finagled these inscrutable hieroglyphics of seduction onto her face. It was as if her expression had taken shape from continuous waves emanating from her loins! Yes, it seemed to me that this young woman was making love even when, with apparent delight, she was sharing with me her admiration for Thomas Mann.

My spying was broken the moment the bouncers called upon us to leave. As we deemed it better to shamble away rather than resist, I suggested that we find refuge in some all-night bar. After brief consultation, they accepted my proposal. We were at the edge of downtown, in a neighbourhood of now all but empty streets whose silence was broken only by the discreet sounds—cursing, pissing or blustering—emitted by the occasional drunk who chanced to cross our path. One such gentleman even staggered over to us, wound himself around a light pole, and commenced to pose us riddles: 'How much you folks think the capital's top pigeon gets an hour for shitting on cars downtown?' he grunted before disappearing in exchange for a hundred forints. I always was fond of the Budapest cityscape that, at this hour, resembled a roofless, endless bar. It was in this milieu that we now happened upon a smaller place.

In the corner by the bar was a worn-out piano, and behind it, bent over the keys, a silver-haired pianist in dark-framed glasses. As is often the case in certain places of entertainment, he played with passion despite being out of tune. He pounded away at the most important chords with resolve, thus coaxing out the main melody; as for all those other little notes, he didn't much bother with them. Grandiosely he flung one note atop another as his mood dictated at any given moment. So it was that his unquestionable talent was rounded out by his whims, which grew along with the number of empty glasses on the piano. But this is precisely what is so moving about the art of certain bar musicians: that for them, music is but a means to what's really at stake—that unassailable *ars poetica* of *feeling* for the sake of *feeling*! Besides us and the waiters, there were only three people in the bar, two middle-aged men and a visibly older woman. No doubt they'd already got drunk several times over the course of the day, and they intended this latest stop for sobering up with coffee and orange juice. The flaccid skin and blank expressions that defined their faces made them seem rather like statues. Eagerly they soaked in the maudlin tunes: to them, this served as rest as they stored up new energy for their next round of drunkenness. Perhaps one of them even fell asleep, but it was hard to tell.

We ordered coffee with Unicum, and just to be sure of things, two bottles of cold beer. The young woman sat quietly at the table, and I now found her lineaments even more beautiful. It was my task to break the almost embarrassing silence, I knew; after all, I was the one who'd dragged them into this. And so, like someone wanting to make amends for his obvious roguishness, I began telling some convoluted story. The irregular elegance of my sentences must clearly have come across as clumsy, and so I soon had to admit to myself that, at most, I could count on the young woman's conspiratorial understanding. And I wasn't disappointed, either. Right away she sensed the desire I was trying clumsily to keep under wraps, a desire that corrected the excesses of my nervous chattering with considerable precision. She liked this. At the same time, I caught her in the act, for by chance I noticed a certain glance flit across her face—a glance after which she would not have been able to deny that, for all intents and purposes, we'd passed beyond the first caress. She accepted that she was fated to that particular situation which, on rare occasions, casts unto each other two bodies, smiles, or, as the case may be, shy retiring glances. I shuddered at the thought that, with her glance a moment earlier, she had exposed herself once and for all.

The other man, having had enough of our newfound acquaintance, now feigned a yawn, downed the rest of his espresso and departed with an air of quiet resignation. No matter how confident I'd been of our fated roles in this play of ours, I would gladly have averted this moment. I'd been relying on his presence, as if he alone could have guaranteed that I would no longer be in anguish; indeed, without his presence a few hours earlier, I wouldn't have even dared go near this girl. I feared being alone with her, believing as I did that one of my accursed visions was lurking somewhere in my midst, waiting for the right moment to pounce. But my enemies were merciful on this occasion. Not a single pathological thought disturbed my thinking as I swam through the deep current of excitement, following the silent commands of the moment. I don't so much as remember how we ended up, by dawn, in my rented flat.

It was as if I'd never made love in my life—that's how it was. This girl bestowed me the gift of healing oblivion. Not a single penis reared its head above me, nor did panting women pass before my eyes, opening their smouldering ovaries, and no burning wombs collided with my face, as did the scent of smoked ham in my childhood, when I used to sneak up to the attic to filch some of the sausage hanging from the rafters.

Over the course of those days I became convinced that someone, somewhere, wanted to have mercy upon me. I breathed freely at last: my body had found its way back to the spring whence it came before it might have dried up once and for all. Yes, someone or something had suspended the indivisibility of present and past, for when I embraced my love, my accursed, pathological relationship with time did not violate the staggering beauty I so often discovered on her face. It seemed as if, in reward for not surrendering to the sufferings of the past decade, my fate had now bestowed me the gift of this love. At the same time, the possibility occurred to me that through my illness, fate had rendered me among the chosen; for how else could I have met with this girl who was more than ten years younger than me?! It would be a lie for me to claim that I was no longer afflicted with my perverse thoughts; these thoughts belonged to me as surely as the blood on a murder's dagger even after a good scrub. Perhaps they'd already run their new courses in my nervous system. They were still present, after all. But ever since I'd come to know this girl, they did not torture me. Someone or something had deprived them of their power. It was as if this girl's body had pro-duced an antidote I'd been stealthily injected with. My merciless foes had given themselves up in the face of a demon even stronger than they—the passion of love. And so I found myself believing that not only was my torment over, but even the yearning for my illness had been erased from my mind. I'd fallen in love not with a being who likewise displayed pathological symptoms, and who could consequently have been my accomplice in my self-aggression, but, rather, with a woman whose flawless instincts had rendered me a disciple of pleasure alone. In those days I would have sworn that, in her presence, not even my mania could have possibly summoned forth in me a passion of such force as her body yanked me headlong into. I'd come face to face with the incomprehensible. Never could I have imagined that there was a power more absolute than desire of the destructive sort! When I looked upon her face, I saw not the contours of her past pleasures, inscribed by a man unknown to me, but *love*, which verily incinerated my compulsion to make such comparisons. I'd plummeted into a darkness before time as surely as the newly dead do into utter silence, and all I was capable of remembering was the sensation of that unconscious heat of passion immortalized by our clinging bodies. When drawing her wound-up hips against my own, I felt that never had I ever been afraid; or, if I had, then it must have been some mistake, for I was more entitled to belong to this deluge of sensations than memory was to con-sciousness.

My eyes lit up; for the deluge of passion had wiped away the bitterness that had gathered in folds over the years on my corneas as invisible ramparts—bitterness that not even my lowered eyelids could mask from before others. It had scratched out of me my old-est companion, sadness, as a hawk-eyed oncologist might extricate the first cancerous cells after discovering them on time. And to keep me from remaining empty, the passion had pressed molecules of pleasure in their place. When her slender fingers touched my face, far from scraping forth the shame I'd long felt about my body, they opened up pores that had still been sealed off by fear not so long ago, liberating from within them the timeless reward of all who are borne of carnal pleasure—ecstasy—which then spread all over my face. Her devoted body seemed to compensate me for everything my teenage years and the ten years that followed had denied me: that craven illness and those loves squandered on account of that even more cowardly fear. How could I have even compared this meeting of instincts with that abominable agony in which M. and I had sold off and betrayed visceral love? After all, my newfound experience told me it was precisely our intertwined bodies that gave rise within us and outside of us to that corpus which—even with the smell of sweat accompanying it—was alone entitled to be called transcendental; for when yet another moment of ecstasy led this newly discovered girl of mine unconsciously to dig her fingernails into my neck, she was led by the same hopeless desire as was I when, in her absence, I tried making sense of the love I felt for her. The deeper sensual passion swept me, the more incomprehensible the chemistry of our touches and caresses became.

Often I had the impression that she made love with her eyes— as if a river had opened up from her loins to her face, a river whose mouth was hollowed out neither by her own half-parted lips nor by her knit brows or her darkening eyes but, rather, by that unnameable gaze cast upon all of this; a gaze that bore more boldly into me than nails pounded into the palms of the Thieves on their respective crosses. The ecstasy of our weightless bodies seemed like one thing alone—a return to the original state of being, in which bliss is not so much a gift as it is a circumstance that maintains existence. At such times, the very notion that effect follows cause collapses as surely as two bodies, two entities of consciousness, lose their distinctiveness; for in the only possible moment of parity, that in which bodies are fused in ecstasy, cause is exposed as effect, and effect as cause. It is not touching and caressing that causes the newest wave of rapture to suffuse our bodies, but, rather, it is the pleasure possessing our entire being that demands the repeated motions—and we mistakenly believe this to be the source of our happiness. However, our unconscious state of mind, having fallen back into unity, meets not only with this imperceptible transformation, but also with that delusion accompanying our ecstasy by which, it seems, we can mutually perceive the yet incomprehensible. On our lover's face, contorted from desire or rapture, we discover that particular gravitational pull which rips an expression from the eyes, and which detaches pleasure-born pain from clenched lips; and no longer can we decide whether amid this gravitation it is in fact two bodies that attract each other, or whether what really fuses together are the magnetic fields of the sensations that descend upon the face, the loins, the spine—that is, the invisible particles of love.

Before we might break under the stress of splitting in two, and the sensation of emptiness that follows, our constant separation temporarily ceases. We plunge into orgasm so that our bodies, which we'd believed to be our personal servants, should immerse in the lava of millions of years of expanding time. Perhaps this is why we lose our sense of consciousness at such times: because only our bodies can endure this awareness. This is yet another reason we can trust in the body's capacity to remember; for this is what prepares us for the hour of our death. When carnal pleasure spurts through our cells it not only buries our conscious mind but also re-establishes within us that state of being which vanquishes the fear of death without so much as a struggle. As if your body, from head to toe, becomes one whole, unconscious self, a transition during which it might come to suspect this truth: As it approaches the condition called 'death', the body in fact reverts to a dimension similar to the orgasm it just experienced—one where even the rubbing, caressing and kissing of body parts will no longer be necessary to achieve this unconscious state.

I was on the point of believing I'd recovered once and for all, when one day, two months after we met, she felt obliged to make a confession: 'When we met, I'd been living in promiscuity for almost a year.' She pronounced the sentence as casually as if she'd just told me that she'd been caught the week before without a ticket on the tram. While trying to comprehend her sentence, to assemble the words into meaning, I felt something pressing me, banishing me back to the past from where I'd been fleeing for ten years, from which the past two months had wrenched me from. This single sentence struck me a blow as strong as, some weeks earlier, the happiness I'd no longer hoped for had. Pale and crushed I stood before her, as if completely certain that this was the moment love had come to an end. I suspected that the enemies prowling around me had been waiting for this very moment; that they'd had quite enough of seeing a passion stronger than themselves dispossess them of their power over me.

In vain had I kept secret my onetime psychosis from before her, then; she was the one who'd just unwittingly wrenched me back into its throes. I'd forbidden myself from reaching for those depraved tools by which I might have coaxed out of her the details of her past love life, and now it was her who compelled me to do so. At first I thought that by posing some clarifying questions I might interrupt my plunge. But when she repeated, in a tone even more nonchalant, that over the course of that one year, she'd slept with a different man every day, I knew I'd lost once and for all. How could she have known that this almost boastful pronouncement of hers would, in a matter of moments, become a tool of the most vile black magic of all? As if it wasn't even she who'd spoken but, rather, my demon— a demon that, with this one sentence of hers, had taken revenge for my unforgivable good faith in supposing that I was now healthy. Of course I didn't betray myself, but acted like the model lover accepting as self-evident his companion's awkward revelation; what is more, a model lover who, by pronouncing an elegant closing sentence, suggests that the matter is settled.

How could I have told her of my hallucinations and pathological relationship with time—of the visions that had afflicted me for years?

How could I have made her understand that the only aspect of my own life I could compare to her year of promiscuity was my illness, which I was ever more given to thinking of as a transcendental deficiency?

The more I put off the moment in which I might account for the reason behind my incomprehensible silence, the more relentless the weight of her diabolical sentence became. This only served to remind me of all the time squandered owing to my illness, and that from now on I would be even more at the mercy of my demon. My despondent loathing allowed me to measure the degree of my lunacy, which was many times stronger than that which I'd experienced while with M. For months on end I restrained myself. As a specialist in mild-mannered mania, I took capsules of a slowly killing poison, for I didn't want to lose her.

She persisted in believing that even after all this, she could continue to raise her nervous slender fingers before her face without consequences; for example, when lighting up. And yet she couldn't outwit my vigilance. I understood at once that this particular way she had of showing her hands went beyond a usual sort of narcissism; and one fine day, the image turned mercilessly sharp. In the pores of her epidermis I discovered the traces of strangers still lying hidden: the fine layers their onetime caresses pressed tight like leaves in a book. They could be distinguished. Discerning the thin brushstrokes of my own touches was no more difficult than seeing the traces of strokes from some months earlier. What caused me more of a headache were those virtually merged 'love fossils'—this was the ludicrous term I was compelled to come up with—that lurked deep within the barely visible furrows of her skin. On one occasion I noticed that one impatient love fossil wanted to escape its captivity. Having bored its way through so many other layers left behind by strangers, it seemed almost to have broken free, when all at once those other layers blocked its way. As unbelievable as it seemed, one of its 'fellow sufferers' ordered it back to its place. L. meanwhile went on smoking, of course, not suspecting the drama that had just unfolded on the back of her hand.

While I somehow managed to keep these images under control, my task was far more difficult if her hand moved in a subtly suspicious arch towards some object; say, when she reached for her glass of wine. The space between the glass and her fingers kept troubling me until I realized, finally, that she'd cheated on me. So it was with this glass that she sought to lead me astray: No, it wasn't a glass receptacle filled with wine that she now stroked with her fingers, but another's hand, face or, perhaps, body. What exposed her was the shadow of her hand projected onto the table! No longer could I misunderstand the caresses that she proceeded to reward the glass with. My only task was to render the situation clear. And, indeed, within a few seconds I'd already slipped a man's hand to where the glass had been—a hand that obediently let L.'s fingers run their course. She could not hide from me the traces of her previous love-making, for they were absorbed by the cracks in her skin, by barely perceptible fissures in the epidermal tissue. Her hand was at the mercy of her past. How absurd, the notion that everything is unequivocally transitory! Only a fool can seriously believe that a woman's hip can ever really free itself of even a single memory of early morning caresses. That hip preserves those memories to the end of its life, bestowing them to the earth, maggots or fire only when greater powers call upon it to do so. Perhaps this also accounts for why, in those places on earth that have seen the most lovemaking, the ground is more fertile.

Of course, in some respects we seem able to easily free ourselves of such marks of love. By using special creams and whitening or skin-coloured powders, we render our necks, shoulders and other suspect body parts seemingly innocent. But few people stop to think that never can you evaporate the aroma of past kisses from muscle fibres—that's how hopelessly soaked through they have long become. There are some lovers whose muscles outright atrophy in the absence of such kisses, a condition that doctors naturally explain away by citing an illness of unknown origin. If, one lonely afternoon, a woman's body begins unaccountably to tingle, perhaps what she is feeling is precisely the flow of these kiss molecules, the indelible hand-waving of bygone acts of lovemaking. And who would dare claim that the sounds of excited whispers and uncontrollable screams can be filtered or scraped out of those reaches of the body they have long soaked into—the villi of the lungs, the roof of a mouth and a respiratory tract—with any more certainty than every last vestige of a pregnancy can be extirpated from the wall of a womb? This atonal music of a happy or unhappy love—with its hundreds of upbeats, its thousands of sharps, the highhanded key signature of a libido that lives by the law of lawlessness—vibrates in the body even decades later. In old age it can, at most, soothe the pain of calcifying bones.

It's pleasant to think that our consciousness can, of course, protect us from those of our experiences we once believed to be harmless but turn out not to be. This was not to be the case for me. No sooner did I glance at L.'s hand toying with that glass of wine than I understood: *nothing* passes. I simply couldn't rid myself of this supposition, and the longer I spied upon her hand or the fine arch of her neck, those love fossils took shape before my eyes with evermore fearsome precision—as did, with time, strangers' mouths and embracing arms, as if only now had they really taken possession of L.'s body.

One night the week after her confession, what I feared the most came to pass. We happened to be in the middle of lovemaking, I think, when I felt that there was someone besides us in the room. After undoing L.'s grip, I got up and searched the room but didn't find a soul. L. watched in confusion, having no idea what I was looking for. I managed to convince her that I'd heard strange noises a moment before. By the time I lay back down beside her, I already knew that my haunting visions had returned. Precisely recalling the unmistakable anxiety that almost always took hold of me before visitations from my foe, I was ready for the worst. And, indeed, as soon as I next passed my eyes over the room, they met with the naked body of an unfamiliar man who could have been one person only: L.'s lover. In terror I tried obliterating the image, but the harder I shut my eyes, the more despairingly I pressed my head to L.'s face, the sharper the contours of his nakedness became. About a half-hour later, once the vision had passed, I tried explaining away my incomprehensible behaviour by citing my accursed melancholy, which struck me down like a last shot of liquor does a drunk man. But I knew full well, this would not be enough to allay L.'s suspicion.

From night to night, the visions grew evermore insidious. This time it wasn't just one foe's presence I had to contend with, but one after another. It was precisely L.'s confession that lent credence to my fear that I would meet each and every man who'd partaken in her promiscuity. And so I pledged not to make love with her for weeks. With discipline I would await the moment when my desire would finally conquer my visions, I told myself; and then, taking L. into my arms would again be as it was the first time: powerful, undisturbed, unimpaired. My strict self-restraint would help ensure that my licentious imagination would not project L.'s past onto her.

During these weeks of self-imposed celibacy I breathed a bit easier. The visions disappeared, and my obsessions didn't torment me as much. As if they'd become more merciful, they attacked me less often in packs, and even when they did, they were satisfied with a moderate blow.

Of course, I was able to secure my relative calm only by diminishing the importance of L. in my mind; I had only the temporary suppression of my mad love for L. to thank for my weakened mania. No, my foes gave nothing for free. Indeed, they insidiously misled me, and for this I had to pay an even heavier price. Wickedly they led me to believe that I could get back on my feet. But when, after about a month and a half, I decided the moment had come to put myself to the test, I realized that in fact it wasn't I but they who had grown stronger. With brazen spryness they laughed at me from behind the fortifications they'd slyly built themselves.

All at once an unbearable silence descended upon me. I should have run straight for clattering streetcars and rumbling engine-rooms to pull through this hour. Imperceptibly a current stole its way into my psyche—shifty, sneaky, silent. Unfathomable. A stampede of sorts, but muffled to the point where it was, if anything, only a constant buzz. It would have been much more tolerable had it instead rattled, hammered, kicked about inside me. But no matter how much I tried paying attention, I noticed not a thing. It outwitted me, and as time passed, it threatened to burst open the walls of my veins and plow my bones to loam—and then I would implode once and for all.

L. examined me with wonder. While my wanting to be close to her again must have surprised her, it wasn't so much that which fixed her attention, but more so, the frightening gaze with which I looked upon her face. Somehow I collected myself, and with ungainly motions I commenced to stroke her neck, that skin of hers which I'd admired so often. I thought to myself that if this silence would remain within me any longer, perhaps it wouldn't devour me, but instead it would demolish the images that would soon appear on L.'s face. I imagined that I could support the pillars of my consciousness with this hushed, loathsome flow, and that I would allow nothing into my empty mind—nothing except the pleasure borne on my fingertips, the memory of the excitement that would arise in the wake of a caress.

I touch her as if I've never known her body before. What I discover now will be the only footholds I will allow myself to remember. But, no, I will give up even these, and be content with the

fragmented beauty accompanying my motions, a beauty uncon-
nected to any other moment in time. My constrained pleasure cannot sadden me; for I will be compensated by those fleeting instances
of union I've managed to wring out nonetheless. There will be nothing, not a single memory, that can possibly wedge itself between my
desire and my satisfaction.

True, right after kissing her mouth I forget the moist warmth
of her lips, her gentle bite. But at least the past will disturb not even
those precious moments in which our lips are bound together. No,
my devotion will not be constrained, not in the present. Not like
other times, when fear consumes me; for on her lips I feel the sul-
triness of strangers' kisses. Today on her chapped skin I find delicate
rips formed by my teeth alone. By the time I slip my lips off her
mouth and move on to her shoulders, I will know nothing of the
kiss that has just come to pass. No, I am preparing instead for the
gift to come. I imagine that her entire body is composed of this
skinny, boldly descending slope from mouth to shoulder, and still I
do not fear some idea of mine that could break the magic of the
moment. In the present moment I do not pass judgement on this
shoulder of hers for having given refuge to so many men before me.
I do not hate it for those hours of allowing ecstasy to plough its
way across its flawless surface. I will possess her as objectively as
would a stranger, I decide, and I will not allow anything to foil this
plan of mine. I will behave like someone with a split personality:
Someone who knows neither past nor present, who grasps only
what has just occurred, and whose hapless consciousness is unable
to distinguish between past and present. Someone who, however, is
not so deranged, after all, so as to be unable to decipher the image—
the face, the shoulder—about to come.

But while preparing myself for this healing ritual, all at once
the silence within me was broken. Immediately I understood that

my scheming would be supplanted by my accursed associations. And so it was. Only seconds before, L.'s face had seemed perfectly smooth, but in no time I began to notice almost imperceptible furrows borne of the grimaces that accompanied past embraces. Then there was the sparkle of her smile, which I could delight for only a moment before it was swallowed up by another man's eyes. Yes, the shadow now cast over her smile left me with no doubt that, once again, there lurked some lover of hers. Indeed, when I finally conquered my repugnance and touched L.'s face, it seemed to me that her involuntary shudder was in reaction not to my hesitating caress but to the conspiratorial intervention of a stranger's body. No longer could anything save me. As had happened back then with M., now, too, I imagined that my love was embracing not me, but the man behind those eyes. I felt as if my body had become this stranger's vessel. This also served to explain why my motions were so contradictory. For a moment at a time it seemed that it wasn't *I* who was trying to shake myself free of these perverse associations, but the other, who also went about scratching at my hands, my mouth, my loins. The month and a half of hard-won abstinence I'd forced through with various excuses had now come to an end with complete failure. With unexpected ingenuity my foes thus cautioned me that I must maintain a constant and tight relationship with them. Which is why I repeated the embrace the following night.

I'd known for months that in *his* case, it was completely pointless to talk of prudence, for I myself comprised his personality. He didn't even exist, I kept telling myself. He is what he is solely on account of my imagination, which was predictable at times, uncontrollable at other times. If my madness commanded the strength of the most wicked of all magic, surely I would dispossess him of everything. At the same time, it seemed to me that his way of asserting his equal footing was by causing me pain. It's foolish of me to draw this conclusion, I know, for I come across like some scatterbrained fellow who suddenly pins his hopes of freedom precisely on everything that, to date, he'd blamed for his torment. Except that in my most frenzied moments, I had the sense that were I to give him up, his absence would send me headlong into a listless indifference, and I would plunge right back into that state of mind where I had no footholds at all—namely, the state of mind that was in fact the real hotbed of my imagination.

On this second night, it almost seemed I would pass the obstacles before me undeterred. Not a single, distant lover's memory did I project upon her face, and when her smile contorted from the strains of rapture, instead of being horrified, I ascribed this to the beauty of our embrace. But that is when her eyes began to inexplicably distress me; this, notwithstanding that they were shut, as if she only wanted to give them a rest—which is precisely what scared me. It seemed to me that her eyelids had become shorter, as they drooped only to the bottom reaches of her pupils. The white of her eyes meanwhile shone sharply in a half-arch from below the slightly open lids. Had her eyes become caught on something? She seemed rather like a corpse, except for the fact that her eyelids were still supple. All at once I felt myself to be nothing but a tool; namely, the intermediary that had helped her assume this deathlike pose. Were we to make love again, I thought, then this weirdness, which for once I could not associate with the presence of some lover, would surely vanish from her eyes. But when, after a little while, she embraced me once more, her eyes kept drooping all the same. No, it wasn't *her* clinging to me, it seemed. Instead, that elusive someone was making his presence felt; for he now had L. at his mercy, too. Not that I could have called the barely intelligible, washed out image that had come to possess her face decayed, but I nonetheless had the impression that something on it had begun to decompose. Swept along by an association of ideas, I could only conclude that pleasure had subdivided this face only to lay the ground for decomposition. Was it only to draw this connection that I, too, had partaken of the rapture in the first two months?!

Not even if I'd pushed a mirror in front of her would L. have seen herself. No, she let the apparition possess her completely. I meanwhile spied from behind my pitiful reflexes to see when this frightening duality would vanish from her face.

Of course, even daytime held plenty of dangers in store for me. Whenever we met some man I didn't know, I had to be careful not to give myself away; for I kept dreading a chance encounter with some past lover of hers. Fear took hold of me the moment she began talking with such a stranger. How innocent a situation! Surely no one could imagine the nuances—so I read their thoughts. Elegantly, confidently they stand face to face, saying not a word about that night when, all at once, they found themselves in each other's arms and then did what instinct and curiosity demanded. In the moment of their chance encounter, they need not say a word alluding to all this; all it takes is a complicit albeit barely conscious smile left on a face a moment longer than otherwise would be the case to remind the other of that which cannot be said. Neither can suspect that there is someone in their midst who discovers all this in their cold handshake: a policeman of the emotions who inspects it to a tee.

I imagine it, I see it all. And so it is.

Yes, I whispered under my breath, *you nestled up against that man like paint being brushed on a wall; you clung to him like cells of fat to the walls of a vein. You knew that your seemingly innocent embrace spoke in fact only to that hour spent together. Your meeting was as coincidental as that of two cells fusing on the wall of a womb. A hot current ran through your loins; and something, somewhere seemed to snap along your spine. Yes,* I thought, continuing to fantasize, *anyone who sees as clearly and coldly as you do surely knows that only in sensuality is it possible to find love's true satisfaction. You must have been on such easy terms with bodies as a stuffed sow is with yet another helping of slop plopped down in front of her unexpectedly—slop she doesn't stick her head into, mind you, because she's satisfied with the fatty scent alone. But you felt a warm strength even in the most inconsequential bodies, and if you could manage, you wormed your way close to them, for you could find your self-identity only in the other's body.*

On other occasions, some such chance encounter would teach me a lesson far more nefarious. Sometimes the man's name, when pronounced in the course of the inevitable handshake, sent my imagination flying. Inexplicably I began to fear the first name of the man now sitting beside me, and with time I turned to the most absurd methods imaginable in my effort to escape from out under it. The possessor of this name might, for example, be the very man with whom she first shared her bed. If this were so, the name would, to me, be synonymous with the first time her shy body grew alarmed at the touch of another—with the awkwardness of her unconfident kiss, with her wet labia. But then it would occur to me that, perhaps, she associates this name instead with an unforgettable hand that taught her to feel her own body. Because, before this hand came into her life, no matter who caressed her belly and her loins, she'd remained lamentably subdued, exquisitely insensible, when it came to her own pleasure. In vain did others put into effect the most accomplished embraces of all—wordlessly and coldly she beheld their experimentation. But then there came the hand that discovered the paths of rapture on her restless body, as if all her life she had been preparing for this guide. That is why she is so grateful to this hand, although she has never seen it since that night. And yet she cannot have forgotten the *name*. No, it lives within her ever since, and when she hears it spoken, she feels the same throbbing in her loins that she did then. Next I imagined that it must have been a man by this name who'd proved to her that every love is a colourless, muddled memory compared with an orgasm itself, that only from this radiant plunge can she expect a moment's amends for her failures.

By then, I had come to loathe this name; I would gladly have passed a decree banning its use. Only then will I rest easy, I kept telling myself, if I can be certain that every man has a different name; for this would substantially narrow the number of my dangerous foes, and in this respect, at least, I could then settle my accounts with my wretched obsessions.

My compulsion to look at her askance lasted for a good six months. During all that time, I held stubbornly to the belief that one fine day, the visions would pass me by; that my steadfast bouts of fantasizing would cease; that my persevering silence would bury my fears. But all the lies associated with my self-delusion shaped themselves into a reflex that only led me to an even boggier terrain. Broken, I decided I must speak.

Even now my cowardice opted for a detour. Instead of telling her the story of my more than ten years of illness, I went on the attack and began to question her. She must have been suspicious for some time already. Perhaps for a while already she hadn't bought my regular excuse of depression to explain my ever more hopeless silences, for this interrogation that I now undertook with six months' delay seemed hardly to surprise her at all. Of course she could not have suspected that my more or less understandable restlessness did not stem from my pathological relationship with time, but from that very impotence that finally exposed itself before her. No matter how cleverly I'd disguised my real self until now, no longer could I delay a confrontation. No doubt she was surprised only by my frightened embarrassment, which made me by turns a bundle of unbridled fury and a caricature of subsiding madness. I got down to work with my usual treachery, giving the impression that I wanted only to get to the bottom of a matter yet unclear to me, emphasizing, of course, that I sought simply to clarify certain details. Above all, it was numbers that held me in their grip: Had she in fact made love to a different man every single day? More cautious than before, she barely even nodded this time. And yet I still had the feeling that despite her growing uncertainty she continued to harbour that pride I'd discovered on her during her own confession. But this was not what now held my attention. Hardly could I restrain my nausea. My condition was not unlike that of a patient knocked down by some unknown pathogen. Of course, my body was not under attack by cells tasked with destroying it, but by a single sentence; and not one I processed with my intellect, but with my moist hands, with my ever-colder loins, with my bunched-up oesophagus, with that dull rumbling that demolished the conditions necessary to normal understanding. It was in fact my body substituting for my self that observed. This is the only explanation I can find for that initially dull, then gradually stronger dread that this sentence evoked from me. The words that saturated my cells were free to play havoc as they wished, for nothing could have kept their passion under control.

After a while the usual order must have re-established itself in me once again, for as so many times before, even now it was revulsion that took me in its grip. At first this new sensation seemed to be but an accessory to my overall state compared to the shock I'd just experienced, but then all at once I clung to it as if to some unexpected lifeline. That is when I fell upon L. 'So, which one was the best?' I pronounced with feigned calm even though I would certainly have preferred to shout. 'If you project your orgasms onto a graph, where do I fit in on that particular arch? Or perhaps you don't remember? You, who remember even dreams you had as a child?' To my greatest surprise, L. did not give in. She answered with unsparing frankness, as if well aware that this was the only treatment for my idiotic behaviour. On previous such occasions, with other women, I'd always received some reply along the lines of, 'With others it was all just a sort of massage, really,' or 'Before I met you, I didn't even know my own body.' But L. did not try to calm me down by dishing out such commonplace lies that generally just serves as grease on the fire, but instead fulfilled my curiosity without mercy—as if she understood my unexpected outburst as something not even worthy of being acknowledged. And yet I saw on her a sense of commiseration bordering on pity, which she felt on account of my now being at her mercy. What was most alarming to me was that she simultaneously defended herself and me as well. She chalked up my insidious interrogation not to some sort of perversity but to my illness; for she'd noticed that my sentences, which I'd intended to torment her, had practically punctured my eyes, contorting my countenance almost to the point where it was unrecognizable; and before these sentences might corrode her own sobriety they fell back upon me to ravage my own face even more soundly. She knew full well that anyone tormented so much by his own words must be under the control of a force more insidious than even the sentences that came out of his mouth. And so it was through her reaction that I truly understood my relationship to my demon. Of course, my torment had thus become easier only in one respect: I was able to sense that it had arrived at a new stage—this, in part because there was someone beside me who was at least as strong as my demon, and in part because this person had taught me a more sensible and fruitful means of suffering.

I had to admit that in the case of L., I could rely only in part on my tried and tested tactic: the conscious tormenting of the other in preparation for a break-up that would signify at least an illusory solution. Yet another reason I rejected this method was that I now dreaded newer details. I could not hope for any well-intentioned cheating on her part. At the same time, despite having lost practically all hope of escape, I felt that this was the woman I would not want to leave even after ruining her. Of this, I was virtually certain.

By no means did all this mean that from here on I wasn't compelled to turn to a certain degree of hypocrisy. My despair required information acquired through nefarious means, for in its absence I could not have progressed along my long treaded path.

In the weeks that followed, these conversations of ours repeated themselves, but this newer phase of my compulsive thinking had taken hold of me. There was just one reason I kept trying to gain access to some newer piece of information: so that I might imagine and, yes, reconstruct in my own mind, her year of promiscuity! In fact, it was these vile provocations of mine that I could thank for my fresh discoveries, which six months before, her shocking confession had blurred within me. Only now, as I went about tormenting her in so cowardly a manner—as, even amid my most furious raging, she gave the impression of being forlorn, for I could interpret the understanding she showed in the face of my open madness only as proof of her love—only now did I get it through my head why that confession of hers had opened within me the floodgates of fear and dread. The situation brought to mind my revulsion over corporality—that decade and a half of fiascos, whose foretoken I should have noticed in my pathological obsession with that certain photograph, and which I had then gauged with approximate precision in my era of compulsive masturbations. It was now, too, that it finally occurred to me that the asexual alliance I had entered with M. had opened the door to my downfall.

L.'s one-sentence pronouncement could only have struck me with such force for one reason—because it tore open the wound within me that I'd always subjected to symptomatic treatments. While I'd been fleeing from love in years past with my cowardly masturbations, and with those conspiratorial winks to my nascent illness, all the while she'd been studying the grammar of bodies with strict consistency. That one sentence of hers seemed to declare that my life had not happened at all, for I was already in the throes of my compulsive illness when I began accruing the victims of my jealousy. Yes, I articulated this precisely, for I had long sought *not* love at all, but an escape from my accursed obsessions! L.'s sentence mangled within me the memory of our two months of ecstasy, too; and so nothing remained but despair.

A moment ago I suggested that L.'s confession had served as a reminder of my revulsion to corporality. And yet I could not decide in a reassuring manner whether this anguish was the consequence of the original fear so familiar to me, or else of the power of my obsessions. Or perhaps my demon, too, was simply the creation of this fundamental fear? In any case, I understood that I had squandered my every last possibility of escape. All I could hope for now was to endure the pressure in my throat, the semiconscious plunges into madness as images hovered before me, the despair of my loins. I stood at the starting point of desolation, attempting to take off from there, for I wanted to understand her courage, at least.

No matter how steadfastly and boldly L. defended her positions, at times she, too, lost her patience. At such moments she was perhaps even more at the mercy of our new circumstances than was I. Backed into a corner by my inquisitorial questioning and half-witted explanations, she listened in humiliation, waiting to see what sort of ignominy I had yet to heap upon her. After one such occasion she began to talk about her own, surprisingly recent fears. About the pressure coming down on the nape of her neck, about night-time bouts of dread, and about her need to constantly escape, none of which she would have mentioned at all had I not wrenched her into it. She cautioned me against suspecting that she was up to some cheap manoeuvring. No, she was not just dishing out such facts in an effort to assuage my diabolical understanding of her promiscuity. As for that year in her life . . . she whispered, and then held a long pause, as if she still wasn't certain she could reveal her secret, I shouldn't go envying her for it; for at the age of fourteen she had been raped by a much older man. It took her three years until she was once again able to touch a man's body.

These unexpected details filled me with dread. How pitifully I'd beguiled myself into believing that for the first time in my life, it wasn't the pathological I'd fallen in love with once again! All at once it turned out that while I'd been parasitizing off what I presumed to be her healthy state of mind in an effort to wrest out my own healing, a few years ago she, too, had suffered from a disease of the imagination. For how could I otherwise have understood her talk of this pressure on the nape of her neck, those symptoms reminiscent of a persecution complex, her distressed awakenings? Had I fallen in love with her only because she, too, had been the victim of my own dubious illness—even if in her case it had yielded symptoms wholly different than my own?

Or was this in fact nothing but the scheming of my demon, who flashed the possibility of normality before my eyes, so that this would then cast me into that state of perdition I'd believed to be escape—a condition I would never have voluntarily undertaken? I was practically certain I knew the only reason L. had suffered with me through my hours of anguish and been able to endure my madness: she must have known full well that particular weightlessness of the consciousness and imagination which is a more dangerous burden than any weight can be.

What shocked me most about the revelation L. had just made, however, was that she seemed to harbour an inscrutable strength, one that proved an equal match for her own diseased imagination even at those times when she was most defenceless. This must have been her secret. She'd accompanied me to the precarious edges of my own ruptured consciousness, but I could not pull her over along with me; indeed, she'd been the one who'd kept me from jumping.

My reaction gives me away once again. It was as if I'd deliberately sought a line of reasoning that would validate the hopelessness of my situation. Moreover, knowing that L. had been raped did not ease in me the anguish bordering on revulsion that my memory of that certain year in her life evoked in me. And yet she'd now have been ready to tell me the genuine reasons behind her 'debauchery' of that year, for she saw how muddled my thinking was about this period of her life. I, however, suspected that a questionable effort at consolation was behind this. Besides, I'd already been weaving my newest obsessive plans for weeks! Indeed, I thought that if any sort of relief at all was possible for me, it could come only if I wrote down the history of her promiscuity. Had L. presented her story, she would have deprived me of my newest obsession! I wanted to subdue my diseased imagination with an even more pathological strain of fantasizing, for I believed that, through the magic of words, I could nail my foes on the white post of oblivion.

How much easier it would have been, had someone stepped before me and levelled two punches into my face! Physical pain can make many things clearer. That's what I used to think when, in my childhood, my father ordered me onto the desk and beat the soles of my feet with an electrical cord. I thought I couldn't bear it, but then all the same, when he had me stand in the corner to round out my punishment, I'd never looked him in the eye with more pride. The pain hardened me, and my hatred made my thoughts cold and clear. Never since then have I had such exact and flawless strategies on how to lead my life. Perhaps any longing for freedom at all is hopeless from the outset in the absence of such physical torment? I'd be locked in place along with the exertions of my imagination, and only when my torment finally produced symptoms of physical pain could I count on that certain solution coming along! Maybe, just maybe, while one of my maniacal ideas takes shape before me, my tooth would start throbbing with pain, and no medication would be enough to relieve that pain—only pulling the tooth could do so. Once all my teeth were gone, next would come an earache, which could be ceased for a short time only pricking at the ear. After a certain amount of time I could choose between the various kinds of pain.

How enticing a scenario: to have myself beaten by two moronic mountains of flesh while scribbling my observations on scraps of paper—observations about those hidden associations offered up by simultaneously analysing bodily pain and that other sort of torment, which we perceive as incorporeal. I notice, for instance, that while gasping for air after a precisely targeted punch in the belly, it's as if the vision that was so oppressive just a moment before has become a tad less so. Or else that a deftly delivered kick to my groin forever liquidates some perverse idea of mine. Of course, not even my arbitrarily chosen positions can bestow me with the alertness with which I might ascertain subtler nuances, more cunningly fused associations; for what happens if the fellows hired to beat me silly don't strike their blows right away, one after another, but instead keep me off guard by choosing the least expected moment, one in which my body has not had a chance to prepare itself for pain, although only psychological defence is allowed under the rules? Will I not feel the same fear I do when distressed over an imminent assault by one of my pathological notions? Although I am well aware that such examples can undermine my supposition, why shouldn't I have rightly expected these fellows to beat everything out of me—everything I suffer from even more than I do from their blows?

Perhaps I should have placed an ad in the classifieds: 'Seeking someone to beat sordidness of unknown origin out of me, every last bit of it. Perverts need not reply!' Who knows, perhaps I would have happened upon a psychotic prison guard who specialized in exactly my sort of case! Why shouldn't there be people out there who know not only torture inside-out but also psychology? I yearned for an applicant who could discern the nature of my imagination through my body's agony. I would have been able to determine even from his mistakes whether he was really suited to the task. Even as I smiled at this childish escape fantasy of mine, I was virtually certain that people must have once lived who knew just how to go about exorcizing demons.

But I was too cowardly for such experimentation. Which is why I then began writing down L.'s story. Of course, I kept my hare-brained undertaking a secret from her, for which I had but one excuse: I trusted maniacally in a miracle—namely, that by the time I wrote the closing lines of this story I was now poised to fashion, not only would my demon back out of me, but by *making up* her story, I would also come to understand the justification for her offence.

PART TWO

1

Autumn was nigh. A heavy fog had hung over the city for days, covering roads, trees, memories in a thin veil. Most people loathe such weather, for they sense that sooner or later the fog will settle on their feelings and thoughts, much as silence assaults the eardrums of the deaf. L., however, savoured it, and even now she'd boarded the tram only because the biting cold wind had chilled her. As the tram was packed with passengers, it took some doing on her part to carve herself a free spot near the door; even so, the face of the young man standing next to her, one step down, was all but pressed against her body. At other times, L. wouldn't have thought anything of this, but on this occasion she sensed an inviting signal in this nuzzling. Having determined that no one could be watching, L. touched her hand to the man's face, shuddering as her fingers slid softly across his smooth skin.

At the next stop they both got off. In silence they walked beside each other. It seemed that on this very first day she'd hit upon the right person. Before long they arrived in front of a rundown apartment block. The young man touched her arm, signalling that they had arrived. The ninth-floor apartment comprised a confining little room, a dark living room, and a toilet. The room's only piece of furniture was a queen-size bed, opposite which, propped up against a wall, was a frameless, somewhat blurry mirror. A few books were strewn about the floor. *He must live alone*, thought L., but no matter how she tried, she couldn't figure out where he kept his clothes.

She had to go to the toilet. If she didn't see Grandmother in front of her now, everything would be OK. For years she'd been haunted by an apparition. As a little girl she'd once opened the bathroom door without knocking, only to see her grandmother squatting on the toilet, and a few days later, her grandmother died unexpectedly. From then on, whenever L. went to the toilet, she always saw this image before her, and sometimes she saw it even when simply thinking of the toilet. Even now an old woman was whimpering there. L. lost her resolve—not as if she could have said whether it was her grandmother, but L. closed the door just as fast all the same and returned to the room.

The young man had already undressed. His naked body shone sharply above the blanket. She saw this object—which, owing to some exceptional coincidence, formed a whole out of bone, flesh and cartilage—as flawless. It brought to mind a statue she'd recently observed for a long time at a museum exhibit. Only the dour-faced guard had kept her from caressing this plaster body, and so she had to make do with the spectacle. If only she could now get drunk, she could entwine herself around this statue-like body before her. She had to have a drink. L. told the man she was really sorry, but at this time of day, so early in the afternoon, somehow it just wouldn't work without wine. . . . She'd go down and get some, she announced. At least two bottles, she thought to herself: surely she'd need at least that much.

Before long she returned, the bottles under her arm. The man was still lying there, naked. To L. it seemed this fellow had been waiting for her all year just like this. She couldn't fathom how he'd ended up on the tram. After the first bottle she calmed down a bit. No longer was she afraid. Of course she knew full well that she wouldn't get drunk, no, what she really wanted was to simply delay things a bit. Then she got undressed all the same. She was just about to lie down beside the man when she felt her bladder stretch tight. Hoping desperately not to see anyone in there this time on opening the door, she headed to the toilet. It was empty. She sat on the toilet seat and tried urinating, but no matter how painfully the wine wrung her bladder, she could not free herself of the fluid. She knew all too well that such tactics as letting water run from a tap, counting out loud and slyly rendered breaths would do no good for her. Throwing up seemed her only hope, and so stuck a finger down her throat repeatedly. Her weakened body finally gave her the gift she sought: all at once she was able to piss. She washed off her face with cold water, dried herself with a towel and then she went back into the room.

Unruffled, the man's face betrayed neither anger nor incomprehension. He must have been cold, because by the time she got back from the toilet he wasn't over but under the blanket. Suddenly L. felt hatred towards her victim; she was sorry it wasn't him she'd thrown up on, that it wasn't him she'd pissed on. Her eyes glowed with that singular light in which disdain mixes with disgust. She lay down beside him. When, after a little while, the man touched her, L.'s body was already bathed in sweat. She pushed away the hand and laughed hysterically. She saw the man's penis as it rose underneath the blanket. Mostly she just wanted to hit it with a hard object, but she was no longer in the mood. She sprang up out of bed, dressed in a flash and ran off without a word. Down on the street she felt a heavy force come down on the nape of her neck. She knew full well she'd arrived at a crossroads in her life. If she didn't figure out something right away, she'd go mad. Walking out of the room of the experimental subject did no good; no, humiliating the other in this way could not save her. She was seventeen, and for three years she'd been trying to escape the memory of that particular night.

The next evening, in a third-class dive, she was already on her second carafe of wine when a pockmarked, bony-faced man sat down beside her. She didn't even give him enough time to order before taking his arm and pulling him to her. The man broke into a grin and gave a little wave of the hand, as if to signal that as far as he was concerned, they could be on their way. L. knew she was on a path not of her own volition, endeavouring to reach an important stop along the way, and doing so drunk but lucidly all the same. No longer would her honour be stained, she was certain, because from now on this would be her speciality alone. She was partaking of an initiation ritual, one in which her body, her physical sensations were unimportant; the only essential point was that whose thought alone had until now been enough to fill her with disgust now happen to her. She didn't even remember how they reached the man's apartment.

She was semiconscious as she surrendered herself. The only thing on her mind was that grasp on the nape of her neck: the possibility that she might now free herself of it once and for all, that the rhythmic motions might thrust that blunt, insidious pressure right out of her, that this self-defilement would erase her memory of that first embrace. In the morning, when she carefully disentangled herself from the man's arms and tottered out to the kitchen, she felt as if her helplessness, her barren suffering, had been soaked up by a steady round of emotionless mating.

So was this all there is to it? Was it this night that she'd needed to see clearly? She thought back with bitter irony to her rape three years before. Nothing particular happened to her, after all, just what happens to most girls. Perhaps it was pure chance that she, in contrast with the others, went mad over this humiliation, perhaps just because of a misunderstanding. How easy it would be if she could write the whole thing to the account of her ridiculous foolishness!

But no. For her, there was no longer a way back. Hatred and a thirst for vengeance had hardened her too much already for her to avenge herself. The disgust she felt towards the opposite sex belonged to her as surely as did fear to her early morning awakenings. She was too independent-minded, far too selfish, to think of the other humiliated women out there. Nor was she out to set an example about how to humiliate men. She prepared for reprisal in secret, in complete anonymity. Stepping out of the apartment, she headed for the bar she'd been in the previous night, trusting that it was open so early.

A few mildly boozed patrons were already leaning up against the bar. 'Here are my allies,' she thought. 'Their lives are nonstop delirium; from now on, mine is wickedness. We quench the unquenchable with various fluids: they, through their throats; me, between my legs. We keep count of our glasses, we calculate our depravities.' She ordered a small glass of red wine and sat down to the least grimy table. She would have needed resolute images, but even after three years, the genuine experience, the fact of her rape, gripped her with a fear that could not be outwitted, even though a moment before she'd understood the triteness of such thinking. So she couldn't count on this. What remained was wickedness or, more precisely, wanting wickedness. She repeated the word to herself as if she hoped it would offer redemption. 'I will make love to a different man every day.' Her eyes took on that glitter that immediately exposes the insane. From the start she set the strict condition that the daily mating must by no means ever be tied to any particular individual. That would be risky indeed, for she might fall in love with one of them, which would undermine what was, after all, her plan. Her despair had bestowed her with the gift of a strength such that she didn't regard her rigorous expression, 'a different man every day', as impossible at all. Especially now, when she understood that the thoughts which gave precision to her plan were the results of but helpless groping about compared with the hatred that swept her along in its grip. Never had she been more convinced that compared to the intelligence of nature, the human mind was rather the product of a mutation that brought some illness, certainly not the proclaimed proof of evolution. And so she called it reason, that force of ravaging intelligence that held her passions together, and without which she would not be able to take a single step in the months to come.

The everyday murderer either hides from before justice or else surrenders. She, by contrast, was preparing for a three-part killing spree that would be impossible to uncover, much less prove; for in these compulsory embraces she could bring her own suicide face to face with the annihilation of the other, only to submerge herself, at their intersection into the real act of destruction—namely, into that particular shame whose poison she alone could know. Her situation would be similar to those women who are raped, the difference being that she would let males have their way with her through her own free will, but the defilement would still be the same. She knew full well that she wasn't the type for whom the brutality coming from another could, at a certain point, approximate sexual pleasure. She'd heard of such cases, about raped women who recalled the aggression that had sparked such fear and pain in them as moments of extraordinary bodily pleasure. Her plan might have been called willingly accepted self-rape. She, who was so proud of her imaginative prowess, compulsively insisted on tangible reality, on a trauma to be experienced again and again, one that, as she saw it, would have been unimaginable without repeated acts of coitus.

Her condition most resembled that of someone gone mad, for she knew full well that an everyday domesticated orgy would have nothing in common with desire and satisfaction. Exempt from laws, she obeyed one authority alone: revenge. She shuddered from the proximity of demonic freedom, which was thrusting her towards its dangerous bliss. Her hatred now occupied only the realm of feelings associated with sexuality, but she understood that no matter how deep she would end up in this hell, the certainty that her life was now all about living out this passion would make her tougher, more relentless. It was as if she suspected that one day her absurd resolve would step beyond hatred and revenge, and arrive at a point resembling liberation. The time had come to begin. Having paid her bill, she headed off towards the city outskirts, to the one-room flat her parents rented for her.

Exhausted, she tried to sleep, but she only tossed and turned in bed. Maybe reading would help, she told herself. Yes, that would make her sleepy. She picked up de Sade's *Philosophy in the Boudoir*, which she'd bought months earlier but hadn't yet had the courage to tackle. She feared the secret teachings of this notorious work, believing that if she were to understand the sensualist-philosopher's theorems, her situation would become even more hopeless. But now she didn't flinch when taking the paperback into her hands, and voraciously she fell to reading. Soon she had to put it down. She shuddered. It seemed as if it wasn't the marquis's thoughts she was reading, but her own. It even occurred to her that she'd written the book herself, and only through some fraud did the lascivious convict constantly get the credit. With one fact alone, and incontrovertible one, could she prove the opposite—namely, that never could hapless males have such intense experience with sexuality. No, this was the purview of females alone; and this was true even if she was only imagining this. It was her rage that now put an end to her childish fantasies. Was she really so undisciplined? She hadn't even begun her experiment, and already she thought she'd arrived at some unquestionable truth! Besides, how could she have turned to an authority other than her, even if it was as exceptional a specialist as the marquis himself?

Again she tried to fall asleep. But all at once she saw before her an image three years old, her rape. She sat up in bed and lit a cigarette. Could it be that she'd been violated on that very certain night only to force her to seek a sexuality that had become questionable? Had a man unknown to her arranged that sordid initiation, thus emboldening the rebel in her? Or was she just consoling herself?

Her attempt to fall asleep having failed miserably, she now went to the bathroom. The best thing she liked about her otherwise cramped, one-room flat was that the owner had installed a bathtub long enough to lay down inside. Opposite the tub was a full-sized mirror, which she sometimes looked at herself in for hours on end. She shuddered with pleasure. Was her body cautioning her that beginning today, she did not need to hurry, that it was enough if she just followed the commands of her hands, thighs, loins? She turned the faucet, but then didn't get right in the tub, even though for years she'd been letting the hot water run over her while lying on her back. Suddenly her head began to buzz. At first she thought it was because of the splashing water, but then she recalled that this had happened to her before, too, especially when she'd been alone for a long time. Standing there in front of the mirror, she was beset by the ludicrous thought that her nerve cells were perceiving Time itself, immaterial though it was believed to be.

She undressed, and then stood in front of the mirror, naked, and with dilated pupils she began to examine herself. Birthmarks bestowed her olive skin with a darker tone here and there. Under her breast was an oval-shaped mark, two more faced each other on opposite sides of her navel, and yet another shone invitingly on the mound just above her vulva. She was thin, recalling a starved young wolf, and yet her surprisingly full, taut breasts were the marks of mature womanhood thrusting from her chest. The dark nipples were slack, but she sensed that before the break of dawn they would swell much like night-time flowers, perhaps only so that the light warmth of a man's mouth should again kiss them into softness. At first glance, her tight belly seemed bent on resisting any touch whatsoever, but L. knew that even the thought of a stranger's hand could loosen those muscles, restlessly demanding more caresses. Her groin was sheathed thickly with hair. She always had wanted her loins to be as lushly overgrown with vegetation as possible. Her long, thin legs shone sharply. Hardly perceptible, narrow trenches marked the lines where her sinewy thighs met her bottom. She broke into a smile, picturing images of ancient fertility goddesses. She slipped one hand on a breast, the other on her bottom. 'Behold, the daughter of the goddesses!' she whispered. But she could not continue the farce, for the tub had filled up. Lighting another cigarette, she now lowered herself into the steaming hot water.

She had been soaking for perhaps an hour when she slowly started getting cold. After showering off, she towel-dried her body, slipped into her nightgown and returned to the room. Something told her that tonight she'd be awake a good long while, and so she pulled her favourite vodka off the bookcase and poured herself a glass. And she thought these words: 'I must at least plan out the first few days, I can't trust anything to chance.' Just for emphasis she raised the glass to her mouth and drank the vodka in slow, calm gulps. Her blood vessels seemed to be transporting the alcohol to her brain cells at a faster pace than usual. She was overcome by a pleasing numbness. And then she removed her gown, lay down on the bed, but without pulling the duvet over herself, figuring that if she did so, she would be unable to fall asleep. With the same reasoning, she left the night lamp on. As she now stretched out in bed, she turned dizzy. At a uniform pace she seemed to be drifting away from her body, which sank, heavy and lifeless, into the bed. In vain did she try to move, for now the gradually gathering speed of her departure likewise paralysed her. She knew full well that whatever that scurrying something which had ended up outside of her body, no matter how big a distance it had covered, it hadn't left the room. And this oppressed her most of all, for she feared that the pressure now pouring forth from within her body would plummet right back down and crush her.

The whole thing lasted perhaps one or two minutes, and then this departure from within herself ceased unexpectedly before she might have lost consciousness. Pressing her numb hands against her forehead, tried calming herself with long, deep breaths. She thought it best to get up and wash with ice-cold water. When she lay back down in bed afterwards, she plunged immediately into the depths of unconsciousness.

2

She awoke the next day at noon with a headache. Only Quarelin could help her, she thought. Fortunately she'd bought a bottle the week before. Having dug it out of the nightstand, just to be sure she swallowed two, without even water to help them down. Reaching under the blanket, she slipped a hand onto her belly. 'Well then, let's see what the first night will be like. One thing's for sure: The choice will be mine.' The thought of going off with some man only because he found her desirable made her nervous. From now on, she alone could 'take a liking to' someone; indeed, the very expression struck her as being arbitrary to a tee; 'find a suitable person' was somewhat more precise, though even that was still unfortunate, since from a certain perspective it could be easily misunderstood. She was not seeking persons, after all, but suitable male bodies that would also happen to have personalities. But she must not acknowledge this.

Alcohol would have carried the most promise of help, but she knew from experience that no matter how much she drank on certain days, she just couldn't get drunk. Of course it would seem like cheating, were she in such condition when she let the men upon her, for a drunken embrace was like one that never happened. In vain she'd try remembering; at most she'd be able to conjure up unimportant details, and the taste of the alcohol would be stronger on her tongue than the fragrance of her chosen hero. That would make her mad. Of course an ideal instance of trickery could nudge her out of dormancy, but this seemed impossible to carry out. So this is roughly what her muddled plan looked like. Were she to orient herself solely with her instincts, like some animal, she could easily put her partner's self out of sight, and she would see nothing other than a ridiculously defenceless body. Naturally she'd have to direct things in such a way as to maintain her observer's position despite all this; which is to say, not unlike some schizophrenic, by turns she could hide and whip out her own self. When it came down to it, the other's personality would be present only relative to her own, arbitrary reflexes. 'The suitable person,' she thought, summing up this fantasizing of hers, 'would in point of fact be a flesh-and-blood male robot.'

Her headache ended. But she put a coffee on, anyway, and began playing a record she'd heard so very many times, one a friend of hers had brought for her a year before from Paris: Edith Piaf. Listening to this record always made L. sad. For all their lyricism, she still found these hopelessly beautiful chansons hard, rasping, rough. Poor Edith—not even amid her greatest successes, it seemed, could she forget the madame who was always dissatisfied with her; as if even then she felt the woman's stare, anger, ridicule and scorn for her having proven to be such a hopeless prostitute as a skinny young girl.

The coffee had brewed, so L. poured herself a sizeable cupful and, with the requisite cigarette between her fingers, began taking sips.

It was late already by the time she stepped out onto the dimly lit street. All L. knew was that she was headed downtown. Since she didn't see anyone around when first stepping outside of her building, her first instinct was to draw back under the entryway. At least from here she could keep an eye on the neighbourhood, venturing back outside only on seeing a car approach; for perhaps it would be a taxi. A year before, a girlfriend of hers had been raped close by. She'd been on her way to L.'s place when a policeman had stopped her on the empty road to ask for ID. She handed it over, whereupon the man, saying he couldn't properly check the information here, told her to follow him back to the patrol car. The policeman must have known the neighbourhood well, for no one disturbed their scuffling.

Finally L. saw a free taxi approaching from the end of the road; so she stepped out onto the pavement and flagged it down. Better to get in the back seat, she thought while opening the door; for if things got hairy, she could always jump out. But the driver's expression calmed her; this was a man she didn't have to fear. Every time L. got into a cab, she always thought of her friend. She wanted to help her, even though she knew her depression was incurable. L. was the one who'd stopped her first suicide attempt, but six months earlier, after slitting her wrists, she'd almost succeeded.

That's when it occurred to L. that she hadn't said a thing to the cabbie, and she really should tell him where to go. She decided on the Moon Bar. In recent days she'd sat around here more than enough, after all, for it to do. It was frequented mostly by workers, she recalled, men who wordlessly drank their third-rate wine and only got into fights if absolutely necessary. Here she would not meet up with a professional ladies' man, either. L. loathed this sort especially, though she suspected that with time that would also be her lot. As she saw it just now, a working-class atmosphere was least risky. L. was convinced that these average-looking men with their dirty hands, rough lineaments and uncultivated minds were far less dangerous than any counterpart of theirs from another social class; and in her present situation, this was her foremost concern. L., who rejected all hierarchies, now categorized nonetheless, in the interest of the 'task' at hand, precisely according to social station, oddly enough. Somehow this rosy picture of the working class didn't seem quite in order, either, but she didn't have time to clarify matters to herself; for they presently arrived. As it seemed expeditious not to get out right by the entrance, L. told the cabbie to stop before they got quite to the Moon: Those inside might otherwise think a taxi-riding whore had arrived from the nearby women's school—not as if that would normally have mattered to her, but on this night L. did not want to be conspicuous.

There were three men in the bar, each of them with a shot of Unicum beside their beer. They must have been chums. Their blues shone through from behind their wordlessness; for not even being drunk could hide that. At first it seemed that a fourth man had taken a seat among them, but then L. realized that only she thought so. For years she'd believed her visions to be simple hallucinations; and they scared her, too, for she figured it was the result of too much alcohol. Nowadays, however, she increasingly suspected her imagination; which is to say, if she thought of something clearly, it presently appeared before her, too; for example, acquaintances of hers, with whom she sometimes spoke as if they were sitting right across from her, even though she was hopelessly alone. This tendency of thoughts to objectify as images surprised her not only in the case of people, though; for on occasion some emotion or other would also pull one over on her. On days when she tried befriending fear, say, it appeared before her in the form of coloured patterns that came together in pulpy knots that recalled a tangled mass of tree roots. At such times L. thought that perhaps she should play with fear, forcing it into familiar figures and coloured shapes, and not letting go until it assured all those it afflicted of its 'good intentions.'

L. took a seat in the corner at the table where she often sat on boring afternoons. She ordered an orange juice, then took out a notepad and a pencil, and began to draw. The graphite slid across the paper with a fizzy-scratchy sound that L. called line music. She imagined that it wasn't even the graphite that was leaving tracks in its wake, but that the sound waves were coming together in visible points. She tried drawing without lifting the pencil, but the gathering of related lines, which at other times developed into an intriguing depiction of some scene, now struck her as pitiful scribbling indeed. L. ripped the sheet from the pad, crumpled it into a ball, and began from scratch. She would draw an angel from an animal. Is it possible that God's cherubs were once animals? L. smiled at the thought. Just then it seemed more believable to her that if there was such a thing as reincarnation, embodiment as an animal represented a high state of being in the cycle of existence. She for one would have preferred to have been born again as an animal.

A man of around thirty presently stepped up close to her. His tall, thin frame was rendered even loftier by his long black loden coat. He was headed straight for the bar. There he ordered a bottle of red wine, and after a bit of hesitation he planted himself at the table next to L.'s, but without so much as taking off his coat. He seemed troubled by something. His posture was conspicuously stiff, as if an invisible hand had forced him to occupy a hard-to-define space he barely fit into. Perhaps he didn't even get permission to move. Only his hand was exempt from the sentence—that particular hand with which he could pour his wine and then lift the glass to his mouth. Only when the bottle of wine was empty were the invisible stocks that bound him in place unlocked. At that moment, with a barely perceptible smile on the edges of his lips—one that spoke more of yet another furrow borne of torment, and certainly not a sign of relief—he took a deep breath and leant back in his chair. Raising his head, he looked about the bar with apparent indifference. He'd just about sunk back into his stiff posture of a moment before when, all at once, his glance met L.'s fingers drawing away.

She felt his stare. Though she stopped drawing, L. kept her hand above the paper, leaving him unable to decide whether she would resume the task after giving her fingers a rest. Suspecting that something was about to happen, L. waited patiently. In fact, the man now got up and without taking his eyes off her hand, sat down at L.'s table. She thought: 'Either he's a madman or obsessed with staring.' Not that his approach felt intrusive. Somehow she even thought it natural, though she did have an opinion about his method of taking a seat. Only on determining that the man still hadn't raised his head did L. feel flustered. Had he not sat down for her but for her hands?! The thought enraged her. How did this character dare to divide her up with such brazen partiality, as if she was made of nothing other than hands and nails! As the seconds passed, though, she was compelled to admit to herself that it wasn't so much her wounded pride that nettled her, but more so the strangeness the man brought with him to her table.

The more coldly she thought through the possible motivations of the attention being devoted to her hand, the calmer she became. Indeed, soon this examination into a stare directed at a single body part turned outright exciting. But she did in any case determine right away that this new sensation of hers had nothing to do with desire. Since the man still wasn't looking at her face, she made as if he wasn't even there. A dog laying down by her feet would have perturbed her more than this stranger, who, it seemed, wanted nothing from her except for this unusual observational position, which, albeit in a highhanded manner, he'd won for himself.

By now L. didn't find this strange at all—as if she'd acknowledged that the separation of the hand from the rest of the body was somehow quite natural indeed. Of course, in certain circumstances she'd reject this aggressive partitioning of herself. She sought to conjure up examples but didn't find them. Those victims of auto accidents she'd seen didn't count, for in their cases the collision had mangled their entire bodies. Amputation seemed somewhat more suitable to the situation, but then she rejected this as well, for the pains taken by the doctor to interfere in the natural order of things seemed to have removed itself from the possible comparisons. Then she thought of a newspaper headline in big letters: 'DISMEMBERED VICTIM, PUT IN SUITCASE AND HIDDEN IN TRASH BIN.' Undoubtedly it must be distressing, she thought, to go downstairs to our apartment building's cellar and notice that one of the resident cats has just somehow freed up this very hand, and is presently wrestling away with it. But perhaps it occurs to us at such a moment that certain murderers must unexpectedly turn helpless when facing their victims, and that it is precisely by dismembering them that they wish to get beyond this impasse. All at once it struck L. that, yet again, her mind had gone off the deep end.

It was in fact the man's stare that had thrown her thoughts off balance. He must have had his eyes locked on her for a while already. Had he grown bored of her hands? Did he wish to now pry the depths of her face? She'd have none of that. Indeed, she was about to stand up and leave when she decided to take a good look at him, too. He surely deserved that much for his unwavering observation of her, which, when she now thought of it, was more touching than offensive. Indeed, there had been moments when that persistent stare upon her hand had moved her, and she might even have seen it as reason to celebrate; if, that is, she hadn't feared the sensation of an intensifying weightlessness tightening around her throat.

L. locked eyes with the man. She saw two gaping tunnels, which only minutes ago had been veritable bonfires. It seemed that all the sadness she, too, had just momentarily felt was now issuing from those eyes, eyes that, L. was ever more certain, seemed still bent on observing her.

FERENC BARNÁS

His persistent staring at her hands had in fact conjured up an independent force of observation, so it was that force—issuing from his pupils, from the whole of his expression—which had shone its light upon her hand. Her hand had, in short, been looked at by looking, observed by observation, glanced upon by glancing.

It was this recognition that L. feared most. Could it be that this is what she'd sensed back then—when, as a child, she'd fled from before the pressure coming down on the nape of her neck? Was it the same invisible observer gripping her tight even then? Or had she herself conjured up this eyeless stare? She could not free herself of the impression that a second observer was ceaselessly lurking within her, and determining whether it was in fact her or someone else was impossible. But still, here in the bar, the dread she had then felt over that strange presence now seemed to her more bearable than her present discovery, though not even now was she capable of identifying the hidden observer behind the observing.

L. looked long upon the man's face, but still she saw only eyes. That is when she noticed a brownish spot between his thick eyebrows—his birthmark. The epidermis darkened into a single point between his eyebrows just under his forehead. While this spot unequivocally belonged to his expression, it still had its limits. It only enhanced that sometimes aggressive contrast that served to face off the even-tempered region of the face under the eyes with the disquiet of those reaches stretching upward from the eyes. This must be why that upper region seemed to be in a constant shadow. Parallel furrows defined the contours of his high, broad forehead. It seemed to L. that the eye sockets, those breathing coffins, were heading towards her. Indeed, she would have reached out to caress them, but she feared the motion. The facial muscles stretching out from the cheekbones boldly made their way to his narrow chin. His lips were bordered by a deep furrow on each side, their ends pointing diagonally upward towards the corners of his eyes—as if it was via this secret path that the man's expression sought to keep his mouth in check, subjecting every single word that might come out under strict supervision.

Minutes earlier she'd wanted to get up and leave the man, but now she didn't know what to do. Her hesitation lasted for a few seconds. Having signalled to the waiter to come over to the table, L. paid her bill, whereupon she practically sprang to her feet and headed off to leave the bar. But at the exit she had second thoughts. Why should she have to flee this place? Had the scene that had just unfolded thrown her so off balance? She had, after all, decided in advance that on this night she would choose the 'suitable individual' from among the patrons of the Moon Bar. L. looked around but there wasn't a free table in sight, for the bar had meanwhile become packed without her noticing it. She edged her way up close to the bar and ordered another orange juice. L. knew that if she was unable to forget the man's eyes, her night could be an utter failure. No longer was it even the observing eye left behind on her retina that bothered her, but the ideas she associated with observation. She thought: 'I have one task before me: to find the suitable individual.'

Not so long ago, after considerable practice, L. had developed a breathing exercise by way of which, after brief concentration, she managed to achieve a thought-free state of consciousness. Not even now, in the bar, did her method leave her high and dry. First L. forgot the man's stare, and then her notions about observing were likewise absorbed, perhaps by her nerve endings. Could it be that she'd directed her deep breaths of air precisely onto those bodily tissues engaged in the work of subconscious memory? The thick layers of oxygen must have clamped down like locks onto these centres of mental activity, temporarily disabling their operation. Of course, something continued flowing in her consciousness, but this could not have been anything other than the rhythmic motion of cells, which in contrast with the elliptical throbbing of blood vessels, went on its way haltingly. Perhaps it was by perceiving the difference between the two types of motion that she realized that between thinking and sensation there was something else, something that evoked in her this unspeakably sharp, almost unbearable alertness, and which, strangely enough, nonetheless resembled emptiness more than anything else.

Her thoughts, those uncertain and rambling intermediaries, now fell silent—as if the cells themselves had spoken, giving precise messages. Such her perception must have been in the womb, before she came forth unto the world. As for the 'messages', she comprehended them with her senses, and they did make their way to her nerve centres, but since she'd suspended the superior operations of her nervous system by pressing it tight with air, they couldn't metamorphose into thoughts. The even procession of cells sounded to her like a broken sequence, the friction of protons and neutrons. She'd known this concentrated melody for a long time, but until now she'd always discerned it in sounds from the outside world—above all, in music, which acoustically repeats the order that emerged several million years ago in the life of cells. In music it was precisely the meeting of interior and exterior order that gave her pleasure, and when on occasion it made her sad, this was perhaps only because their intertwining struck her with such unexpected force. At this moment L. heard these vibrations in her body. In addition to giving the impression of a broken sequence, the occasionally recurring, wedged-in pauses were also accompanied by undulating thrusts. Her excitement was tempered by the blood flowing tight against the cells, keeping her condition at the very edge of the tolerable.

The contours of the objects she'd just seen were murkily preserved by her retina for some seconds before slowly fading away only to soon give over their place to darkness. After a little while, sundry spots of light appeared here and there behind her lowered eyelids, illuminating particles of sorts: perhaps the cells' soldiers moved forward. Now they were motionlessly standing guard. Later, paler spots appeared all along the breadth of her inner field of vision, forming an irregular and yet uninterrupted screen. L. looked up. Moving figures in a milky vapour: that is what she saw. She thought she hadn't yet opened her eyes, but when she tried sliding her fingers onto her eyelids, she understood that she was mistaken. Her fear was only enhanced when the silent vibrations arriving from her frontal lobe were suddenly supplanted by a dull murmur, which oppressed her because the buzzing-like noise had no source. It was precisely the man in the black loden coat who wrenched her out of her near-hallucinating trance, for he was presently stepping towards her and he took her hand. All at once all became clear, the time and events preceding her breathing exercise. Smiling at the man, L. apologetically freed her hand. He didn't ask for an explanation; for he understood that in this time and place he was fated to be an intermediary of sorts. He smiled at L., and then turned around and walked out of the bar.

'So then,' thought L., 'we can begin.' Once again she scanned the place. Sitting at the table by the bar she discovered a solitary man who was drinking beer—evidently a lot. 'An auto mechanic,' thought L. 'Comes here twice a week, but then he drinks until they kick him out.' He would be the one, beyond a doubt; she could go searching in vain among the others but wouldn't find a better one anyway. With that, she went to his table and sat down. Her motions were unmistakable: aristocratic ladies of old must have sat down this way when beside their manure-scented peasant lovers. The man really did smell of grease, and it seemed he didn't need to be told to undertake his responsibility. He knew full well what to do. As if he thought of it as self-evident, he didn't seem surprised at all by L.'s advance. He must have been used to these situations. Calmly, without evident embarrassment, he took L.'s hand and began caressing it right away just as naturally as a moment before he'd been fiddling with his mug of beer. Meanwhile he called over to the waiter for two more beers. L. thought: 'I was right: an auto mechanic.' Beyond the pervasive smell of grease, the grimy hands and the black streaks under his fingernails confirmed her supposition. It was in any case encouraging that her intuition had not deceived her.

The man's intended caresses were rough at the edges. His hands likewise grazed her skin, as if she were being scrubbed by a brush made of dried meat. L. suspected that, insofar as this was possible for her, she would love this man for his calloused skin, his cracked and dirty fingernails, and his odour of grease. Had she seen these hands while seated in a compartment on a train, she would have spied them with similar feelings! L. would have liked to light a cigarette, and so she freed one of her hands from the man's fingers. In the bluish smoke rising she sought the other's gaze. To her it looked indifferent and almost resigned, but this didn't surprise her. Irregularly shaped spots sparkled at the edge of the light-brown pellicle surrounding the wide-open pupil. Somewhat oily, dark-brown strands of hair hung down onto his forehead, which was wider than it was tall. He firmly clenched his thin lips together but they still didn't seem stern. 'Will I be able to kiss this short, ruler-lip piece of leather?' she thought, dragging deeply on her cigarette.

L. waited for closing time. She felt calm, poised. She wasn't anxious over the other's naked body, which she saw before her. She would, however, turn off the light. She believed the whiteness of imagined bodies to be more bearable than genuine ones. She trusted that among her senses, that of touch would take control of the situation, distracting her from the sight of his naked skin. Touch would have to dismantle the imagination, and so it would be best if she shut her eyes, too, lest some insignificant detail should disturb her. Of course she was well aware of the dangers of closed eyes. Darkness without a point of support promised only a superficial sense of security, and at any moment it could in fact become a hotbed of uncontrollable associations. But she would do so nonetheless, perhaps because she now trusted more in her powers of concentration than in the prospect that the outside world might distract her—a possibility that, while more innocuous than inner visions, would be more relentless in putting her to the test.

It was the man who snapped L. out of her reverie of planning: he'd already stood up to leave. 'So closing time has come,' thought L. 'The second act can begin.' Besides them, only the employees were still in the bar; they and the cleaning lady, that is, whom L. noticed only now. She couldn't have been a day over forty, and yet she looked to be at least fifty. Thick wrinkles webbed their way over her swollen, yellow face. She was mopping the floor.

He was a quiet sort of drunk, L. determined at home when she went to the kitchen and opened the tap to pour herself a cup of cold water. This would no doubt make things easier for her. She would not have to prepare herself for his aggression, and indeed L. was increasingly certain than what she wanted would happen. They'd hardly said a word to each other until now. She hoped it would stay this way, too; she for one would do her best to ensure this. L. lit a cigarette and turned on the radio. Some foreign station was playing a Beethoven string quartet. L. sighed with relief: it was as if someone had sent her help through the ether. They happened to be in the slow movement. The string-plucking violins formed a counterpoint to the cello's drawn-out softness, and then there came a pause of several seconds, after which the violas kicked in to carry things forward with vigour after the apparent calm.

L. was partial to string quartets. She'd always found the caval-
cade of sounds produced by symphony orchestras suspicious. The
outsized sounds and gathering of instruments seemed to her nothing
but a veil behind which the composers could easily hide. Concertos,
they were outright cunning. The prominence accorded solos, what
with their high-handed-seeming rigor, fools the listener into thinking
for moments at a time that there is solely a single melodic thread,
that the accompaniment is but a helping hand. And yet this is just a
cheap trick of sorts. From the recurring orchestral motif it fast
becomes clear that the leading melody is indeed very much at the
mercy of the background music, which had only seemed secondary.
By contrast, a distinctive part in a quartet cannot flee behind the
blurred sounds of a cleverly composed *tutti*! If, however, the first
violin takes a rest amid a solo, this is not some forced escape but a
long-awaited opportunity to form silence into a musical presence
even more emphatic than the sounds.

L. turned off the radio before the movement ended. The man
must have seen this as an invitation of sorts, for slowly, unhurriedly
he began undressing. L. followed his example. Her calm movements
were accompanied by a quiet satisfaction. Nothing could happen
that she herself would not have wanted. She felt her body to be a
naked object, one whose independence could hardly be endangered
by the man's touch. The slow movement she'd just heard—as if it
couldn't flee outside—could exercise more rights over her than
these over-scrubbed, greasy hands. L. turned off the light and went
to the bed, where the 'suitable individual' was waiting, naked.

The man must have understood that now he'd got permission
for the embrace. He drew L. to him, laid her down on the bed, and
did what he was expected to do, with the same expertise with which
he presumably repaired broken-down motor vehicles. With wide-

open eyes L. gazed upon the body falling headlong upon her—as if only a wet ballast were being lowered, one that by some extraordinary chance was able to move on its own, perhaps only so that it could sometimes press her spine so painfully to the bed. She compared her experience to the coupling of those unimpassioned souls whose pleasure nature has deprived them of by way of punishment. And so L.'s unhappiness was somewhat more bearable, for not even she wanted to achieve satisfaction. She was content with the momentary calm of her consciousness, with the sense of balance that accompanies the successful execution of a set goal. The reason she now loved her submissive body was because it had weakened the power of imagination, which until now had seemed invincible.

L. would have liked to sleep but she couldn't. With half-open eyes she watched the shadows that the approaching dawn painted on the whitewashed wall. With tenderness she thought of the man who slept beside her with even breaths. L. suspected that he loved cars the same as women. Could it be that on going into the garage in the morning, he would feel the same sort of pleasure on seeing a six-cylinder engine as he did just before when he kissed her breasts? At this moment she understood least what had become of the hatred she'd felt on heading out early in the evening. Had this tenderness overcome her on account of this man in the loden coat, or had the string quartet she'd heard just before put her off balance? L. now imagined the following night. Even now she could imagine the man who would presumably note with self-satisfaction how easy it is to slip into the bed of such a young gal. Already she loathed him. Or was she disgusted with herself, with the first day of her promiscuity, from this clear-minded self-rape of hers? No. She assessed her situation too precisely for that. This could only be about the hero she'd meet the following night, whom she would humiliate. If perchance she would overshoot the mark, she could still find another one for herself, someone who, in the interest of romping about, would be ready for just about anything. And yet—so she summarily determined—such are most men.

She must have fallen asleep only near dawn. In her dream she saw herself as a corpse that had already been washed but not yet dressed. The older women who would have put on her final clothes suddenly vanished from the room, perhaps to take the bathing water to the kitchen. She lay naked on the bed where not long before she'd made love with the auto mechanic. Although her body must have turned cold a while ago, the livid marks of death had yet to appear. From somewhere or other a fly landed on her, first sitting about on her belly, and then slowly heading towards her breasts. She wanted to scream but couldn't open her mouth. And then the dream image quite literally split in two. Beside the deathbed, on which her out body was still laid out, strangers' hands were pushing another bed. L. turned her head to look. She saw herself making love with the grease-scented man. Meanwhile the older women returned and, not bothering about what was happening on the other bed, began dressing L. When they finished, they lit candles and fell to hushed prayer. For his part, the man had just finished going about his business with L.'s living double, but as if that wasn't enough for him, he got up and now stepped over to the bed where her body was laid out. The auto mechanic gave a long, blank stare at the corpse, and then, as if the dead body had signalled to him to come, undressed her and did the same thing he just had with L.'s living double. The women went on praying while L., who'd watched both acts of lovemaking, stayed silent. At first she felt that she herself had wished for the dead body's violation, but then she realized there was no difference between the living body and the dead one. For when the man had first touched her, L. was overcome by the same cool, indifferent sensation as when he'd caressed her corpse. But, she thought, perhaps it would be most honest to admit that on neither occasion had she felt a thing.

3

'I should paint.' L. got up off the chair and looked out the window. Thin clouds filtered the rays of late autumn sun. It seemed to her that on this afternoon, luminosity and obscurity were approaching her at once. For a long time she'd wanted to paint a picture comprising shadows alone, although she knew this was technically impossible. For example, she thought, stepping before the canvas, she could force two bodies adhering to each other into an oval spot where grey plays in white and the light background thickens into pale dots regardless of the viewer's perspective. She worked until dusk. Since the outlines turned out to be hopelessly inept, L. tore them up and flung them in the trash. Not that her obvious failure riled her, but she did suspect that after this it would be quite a while before she'd pick up a paintbrush once again.

She got hungry. Since L. had no desire to make supper, she decided to start the evening in a restaurant. As she'd be going to a typically fashionable place, she thought it advisable to dress for the occasion. Her choice fell to that black dress which rendered her well-developed figure provocatively despite her thinness. The relatively low-cut neckline and the soft fabric around it drew attention to her breasts in a way that called out most invitingly to male hands. The dress fit snugly against her bottom, which, though small compared with her tall stature, was shapely nonetheless; and midway down her thighs, the fabric unexpectedly split in two,

exposing the dark-green stockings that concealed her legs, these
ever-distinguished exclamation marks, which—sometimes straight,
sometimes with a bit of a bend—flanked the inscrutable space from
her loins to the soles of her feet. 'My dress will be a dividing line
between the dandies and the real men. . . .'

Hurrying up, L. managed to catch the last scheduled bus of the
day. Besides two girls a bit younger than her, the vehicle was empty.
'Maybe they're heading for dates, yes, they're turning their frightened faces towards the window, as if hoping for encouragement
from the massive old apartment buildings constantly fading into
the distance.' The food was exceptional at the Purple Wisteria, so
L. had heard. Now then was the time to find out for herself. The
name was in any case a promising sign. L. loved the overpowering
fragrance of flowering purple wisterias. All at once she'd smell it
all around her, as if it wasn't even the petrol-permeated stink of the
city she was breathing, but the heavy yet pleasant scent of the wisterias on the banks of the Tisza River.

L. found one free table, though the restaurant was teeming with
patrons who'd come from performances at the neighbourhood theatres. She ordered baked trout, a side of spring vegetables and a
salad with dill dressing. Fish without wine was out of the question,
and so she asked for a small carafe of a light white. L. had always
abided strictly by the fundamental rituals of dining. She determined
that this restaurant exuded a turn-of-the-twentieth-century milieu—
perhaps on account of the dark-brown tables, which had something
of the Biedermeier about them, and which were topped with red-
shaded brass lamps. The circular beams of light served to break the
lurid tyranny of the chandeliers' electric candles, ensuring discreet
light for the party at each table. The walls' cream-coloured drapes
were ornamented with century-old posters and faded photographs:
moving memories of the pre-war theatrical scene. Celebrated tenors,

the proud masters of ceremonies at variety shows, and bowing cabaret performers who'd reached heights unattainable to this day, and who, from but an arm's length away, now looked down upon these modern-day guests who were paying them no heed whatsoever.

An elusive, strange softness suffused the restaurant, as if the walls, floor and ceiling had been padded with the furs of freshly shot predators. Presumably this was why the conversation of those even at the table right beside L.'s was blunt and indistinct by the time it reached her ears, and which the clattering of silverware from even further off rendered even more ethereal. Melodies merry and woeful alike added to the murmuring flow. Immediately behind the tables was an electric piano, behind which a middle-aged woman with sparkling eyes sang as she played. Softly, with just the hint of an echo, she performed her cabaret love-songs and mournful tangos. Perhaps she'd once been a back-up soprano at provincial theatres, always second in line, someone who after decades of this was forced to acknowledge that her incomparable talent could be realized *here*, above all.

This subdued music had become L.'s only certain handhold; it was this that allowed her to determine that she was really sitting in a restaurant and that soon she would be eating fish. Invariably she found herself comparing this place with the yesterday's bar, and behind the seemingly insignificant details of the superficial differences she soon arrived at the point that divided the two worlds from each other: the feminine from the masculine. L. branded this restaurant—its staff, its patrons, its objects—as feminine. The food-scented church of narcissism, that's what it was. Here, L. felt sure, she would find he whom she was looking for.

Finally the baked trout arrived. Two waiters served it. A dark-haired man with piercing eyes stood patiently in place with the plates on his arm as his colleague, whose face had something vaguely voluptuous about it, went about setting the table in order with festive motions—as if these gentlemen had been preparing for this moment all evening. As soon as they finished serving, they took an elegant bow as if to signal that they'd done all they could, and now the ball was in the guest's court.

L. sliced the fish into thin pieces, so she could flavour them one by one with lemon juice. She had always looked with suspicion on those who soak an entire serving of fish right away, only so that they can then focus on eating. For her, the purposeful motions in preparation for that first bite —slicing, twisting the lemon, flavouring the garnish with sauce and spices and the final visual arrangement of the meal—were every bit as important as long, thorough chewing followed by swallowing that was by no means hasty, and which still didn't end the process. No, she took care to follow the progress of the food from where it entered the oesophagus to its arrival in the stomach, even if her ability to do so was naturally limited. And yet all this paled in comparison to the moment when, having just swept a piece of fish or a mildly spiced, buttered slice of carrot onto her fork with her knife, she raised it to her mouth. At this moment L. would momentarily pause, and only after determining that all possible perspectives of the motion at hand had been concentrated in this production, from the smell to the illusion of taste in the imagination, did she receive the food into her mouth. She was of the opinion that taste was strongest just before the taste-buds had actually connected with the fast-approaching nourishment; that is, at the precise instant when there was no turning back. If presently she were not to place on the tip of her tongue the morsel awaiting its fate, why then, it would disintegrate even without her help. L.'s attention would turn instead to the next phase of the production at hand: chewing the morsel, devouring it thoroughly, and finally, swallowing. She was just about to order another small carafe of wine.

L. was about half done with the trout when she was beset by an inexplicable disgust. Pushing away the plate, she somehow or other managed to swallow the morsel in her mouth. She had no doubt that this unexpected nausea had not come over her because she was eating flesh. Some time ago she'd overcome the involuntary, often completely unforeseeable revulsion she experienced when doing so. Sometimes, though, she nonetheless found herself suddenly imagining all manner of things at such times, things she rightly or wrongly thought of as beastly. On certain occasions she wondered: would the patrons notice if, instead of the Wiener schnitzel they'd ordered, the wily chef were to have the unsuspecting waiter serve up a cut of freshly slaughtered human flesh? Perhaps only a few odd souls among the gourmets would note that this meat seemed a bit sweeter than last week's. Lacking a basis of comparison, they could hardly be expected to make the distinction, and as for those who could be expected to give an expert and reliable opinion—for example, people who'd been compelled to cannibalism during wartime penury—well, such patrons are generally not available to make such comparisons. At the same time, theoretically speaking, L. did not regard as justified the premise that eating fish is an inherent human right, whereas eating human beings isn't. Human civilization seemed to demand that animal civilization be held in utter disregard.

Could it be that the muddled ideas L. associated with eating itself undermined her survival instinct, and that these ideas were at this moment stronger than even her hunger? Was it her consciousness that suspended the workings of the nerve cells in her stomach, of her digestive fluids, only so that in the minutes to come, stimuli of unknown origin should protest against the alien matter winding up in her system? Was she similar to hospital patients whose stomachs are led astray by artificially prepared liquids, so as to keep them from immediately throwing up the nourishment forced intravenously into their bodies?

Although it seemed the fastest way of ending the queasiness, L. did not want to leave this place. Running away like that would amount to a helpless surrender. 'I make love to another man every day,' she repeated the oath to herself several times. She was just about to order another small carafe of wine when the waiter with the vaguely voluptuous face came to her table and asked: Did she mind if he had two other patrons sit at her table? L. nodded, whereupon the waiter waved a hand towards the man and woman waiting by the entrance.

The woman looked to be a bit older than L. Her ashen face was framed by vibrant blonde hair parted in the middle. Her deep-set light-blue eyes seemed altogether ill at ease, and immediately after taking her seat, she cast them downward. Maybe she feared her escort, and perhaps not without good reason. The man looked as if he'd walked right out of an advertisement. His shoulder-length jet-black hair was combed straight back and still shone of gel, but not even this stopped him from smoothing it over every couple of minutes. He must have been worried that a few unruly strands of hair would not submit to the fixing agent. He bent his head back a bit, presumably so those seated at other tables could see him in full profile as well. His Roman nose had a slender bridge that extended almost to his lips. His jaw was sheathed by a mindfully groomed coating of bristles, and only on his neck was it truly apparent just how exactingly he secured the border beyond which he showed mercy to not a single stray hair.

If he happened not to be smoothing out his hair, he placed his hands on the table, exploiting all possibilities inherent in the movement that the circumstances granted him; for there, on the table, was an unoccupied flat surface that guaranteed a suitable reception for his hand. Aside from his girlfriend, there was one more woman who could wonder at the setting of this exceptional hand upon the table; indeed, those sitting nearby could thus likewise steal a bit of secret pleasure for themselves.

But most exceptional was his expression. It seemed as if an invisible mirror hung at all times before his face, one with which he could immediately tidy up his look if he happened to find it dissatisfying. If by chance he scrunched up his eyebrows, and then determined that the stern look didn't suit him, using a hand he'd smooth out the wrinkles, whereupon his now wide-open eyes conveyed the image of the intensely thinking man, the effect being that of someone who, in consequence of inner contemplation, has just bestowed himself with yet another stimulating discovery.

It seemed his successful cogitation of a moment before had tired him out. Perhaps this goes to explain why he now conferred his visage with the smile-generating dynamics of a slightly outstretched mouth. He took special care to be sure the tell-tale motion of his mouth should suggest only what it must; for example, the otherwise undetectable fact of a vivid, nay, thrilling inner intellectual life, which didn't let him rest even amid the pleasures of the stomach. The continually changing and yet disciplined grimaces, the tamed soft scowls and the thoroughly planned winces constricted to certain reaches of his face all seemed to be undetachable extensions of his expression. His look was characterized by a dance of shadows built up so craftily that even the most exceptional actor would have envied him for it. And yet it was not in this trickery that his true secret lie. No, if the art of deception promised such a reward, he would have received it for being impossible to catch him in the act.

Only now did he look upon L. The man must have thought that this woman he did not know would be pleased to be chosen as the subject of some sort of inspection. But right away he added to himself that despite this flattering fact, the woman would not misread the situation, and though she might know that it wasn't chance that had directed his attention to her, she would not seek the possible explanation in her beauty, but in he who had jolted her from the depths of her indifference—that is, in him. And yet her surrender could not reach the point where this would endanger his inspection. The man expected that this woman he did not know but who was surely well aware of her own intriguing sort of beauty would handle her wealth with virtuosity; say, by sweeping her beauty under the rug, wrenching it back out only when he so desired. Perhaps not even her beauty was necessary, for in less strictly watched moments this could all hit him unprepared, too. In other words, the ideal situation—so went his scheming thoughts—would be if this woman he did not know would only appear beautiful; for he did not believe that beauty times two was twice as great. No, he feared that one beauty would necessarily vanquish the other.

The man could not have suspected that if L. appeared to give in to the seduction—such was how he took her ambiguous glances, in any case—she was doing this solely because after weighing the circumstances, this is precisely how she sought to outwit him. In point of fact it was the man who helped her in her ploy. L. decided that she must make as if she could not avoid him, as if she, having been overcome, were now obediently accepting his advance. She broke into a roguish smile. First and foremost, she would have to change seats; for until now the man had unequivocally occupied the more advantageous position.

Changing seats was not a particularly challenging task. L. stood up, and as if she suddenly had something to tend to, went to the restroom. Indeed the couple now left on their own at the table might well interpret her departure as a polite gesture, for it gave them an opportunity to settle their affairs. On returning, L. did not take a seat where she had been before, but instead pushed up a chair to the narrower edge of the rectangular table. That is where she settled in, equidistant from the man and woman. Gazing straight outward over the table, she could now observe them both. If the man wanted to continue looking at her, he would only be able to do so under his girlfriend's watchful eye. It was over, that less risky dallying, when she could break off his circumspect assaults, making an ostensibly shy retreat appear as virtue.

With L.'s new position came a change in the roles they had in this silent conversation of theirs. The man went from being an observer to being the observed, the desirable stranger having slipped from his field of view. For her part, the girlfriend pushed her way into the newly vacant space, and only now could she truly read L.'s presence on the man's face, which tried establishing contact with L. again and again. She could eye him undisturbed, waiting for the moment when her boyfriend's obvious clumsiness would entitle her to pass judgement. This galvanized her so much that she now looked less pale than before.

L. decided to wait a bit longer, to let the couple familiarize themselves with the changed circumstances. Only now did she notice that the man had ordered nothing but a vodka and soda. He'd decided against supper. So he was nervous. L. had to begin gauging the situation with the girl. Alongside the seeming ease of this task—so L. thought, lighting a cigarette—doing so would also carry the advantage of excluding the man from the silent conversation. She would at the same time also mislead the girl, for while she and L. were watching each other, the man (for the first time in the evening) could be at ease to rest his eyes on L. But this was not a gift. No, in fact this self-satisfied soul would be given the opportunity to deceive himself. He was presenting his face as a thrillingly beautiful, desirable object, after all, and since he could not allow L. to know just how much he wanted her, he had to make do with the unrequited intensifying of his own desire. He would feel that the ground had been pulled out from under his feet, for not even in a veiled sort of way could he express his attraction for her so it would be noticed. And he would be even more exasperated by his curiosity than by his prickled vanity, for he'd be unable to discern what was being played out between the two of them.

First, then, L. would make the girl her accomplice. By looking her deep in the eyes, she knew, she could force her into a wordless conversation. Her glance would assure the other that she was not a rival, for she'd come here only to have supper, after all. And the girl didn't have a reason for concern, anyway, for L. had seen right through her boyfriend's ridiculous games, which L. wouldn't fall for even if the man had sat down at the table alone. No need to worry, then—so L. would hearten the girl—for she would continue receiving his glances coldly, and if every now and then a gesture of hers would seem deceptive, that was only to fool the man. L. had assessed the situation precisely, for when her eyes met the woman's above the vase on the table, the other even seemed to take L. into her confidence. Yes, this girl's gullibility made her vulnerable enough. But L. smiled upon her, confirming their freshly tied alliance.

The man could not have known whether the woman had conspired against him or if his girlfriend had simply gained a position of advantage over L. and so reminding him of his responsibility; say, by suggesting subtly and yet unequivocally that this other woman had to leave all the sooner, and so that he should make as if she wasn't even here. Of course, nor could he rule out the possibility that his girlfriend, strengthened by the heartening glances of this woman he did not know, would demand of him her own rights.

Everything thus began from scratch, then, but with that not insignificant difference that L.'s plan hit its mark. By superficially rearranging the flow of the silent conversation between the three of them, L. had diverted the focus of attention from herself. The couple—so L. thought, while taking a sip of her wine—would have to content themselves with remembering the everyday experience of those who frequent public places, and which they too know full well: that a bit of excitement woven into such awkwardness was only natural, and that the whole thing wasn't more than pure imagination. 'How, after all, could I have drawn the other woman's attention to myself?'—L. imagined the man saying to himself—'And if perhaps this is in fact what happened, by no means can that change the fact that I am here with my girlfriend, who maybe doesn't look as seductive as this other woman, but at least it's her I'll be leaving with—in contrast with this woman I do not know, who can play out all sorts of things in her mind, but in the end will be leaving alone.' As for his girlfriend, L. reasoned, she had even more cause to accept this hard-to-deny truth of practical wisdom.

L. had known for some time already, that on this night, she would be going home with this dandy. And so she figured it was high time to take the step that would decide the fate of all three of them. That is, she had to once again draw the man's attention to herself, but this time with a sense of urgency from which there would be no turning back. His vanity promised to be her most certain tool to this end. Although L. would have been content to simply let him know that she had noticed the intention behind the suggestive glances he'd cast her way, she also understood the complexity of this sort of vanity, and so she had to consider the prospect of rejection. This particular case justified the use of less refined means to her end, reasoned L.

The crude method would have consisted of emphasizing that obvious difference that stood in all its tension between the girlfriend with her average looks and L.'s alluring body. If the minutes to come would demand it, why then L. would aim a punch below the belt to force the man to think through the opportunity before him: 'Go ahead, don't you have an imagination? Undress both of us, and before letting the man in you stick his head out the window of your instincts, examine us with the expertise of an anatomist!'

And indeed, the man now made a show of sipping the drops of satisfaction that accompanied rejection. He didn't even fail to remind her that she was in a tight corner. With a biting smile he cautioned that she who offers herself to him was a woman lost, for his strength was in acquiring and not in accepting. In case L. hadn't noticed, she was sitting at one table with a conquering personality. L. received this bumptious hypocrisy with cynicism, and awaited the moment when her foe's arrogance would invariably devolve into boredom. Once this occurred, she assumed a look that concentrated the half-heartedness of the past few minutes in a single, tense point. While composing her expression not even L. herself suspected that she would end up in a situation that would be exciting not only for the man but, in addition to the girlfriend, for herself as well.

The seed of the plan that had suddenly occurred to L. was homosexuality. Not even she understood how she realized this. For some reason L. felt sure that only with this could she provoke the man's over-refinement. The fresh energy that she would direct towards the girlfriend—so L. boldly planned—would stir the man's desire. Yes, this suppressed, shrewdly composed eroticism would make its way to him, and only there would it really accumulate. It would unsettle him, for the sensual encounter of the two women (as it would undoubtedly superficially appear) would sweep him to an experience so rare as to overheat even his imagination, which was otherwise used to all sorts of eccentricities. At the same time it would give voice to the latent homosexual in him, forcing him to confront, perhaps for the first time, that which an outside observer has maybe long suspected. How precisely L. had articulated a moment before: the man would have to undress them! No matter how much this imagination-aesthetics of his loved itself, surely it still derived greater pleasure from examining two intertwining women's bodies than anything else. Perhaps L. was not mistaken to assert that this man felt himself to be secure only as an observer. Which is precisely why imagining the two women making love would be so important to him. In the observational position L. would offer up to him, he could meet up with the beauty within him. He would be caught up in the question of how he might bring closer the points of reality and imagination, which had drifted far from one another. That is when he would have to acknowledge that only the acquisition of this woman he did not know presented a solution, for by laying hold of her, he could re-experience the love-making he'd just imagined.

And so he would determine that his earlier behaviour was doomed to failure, reasoned L., and he would walk voluntarily into the trap, where defencelessly he could await his humiliation; for while L. would give him her body, she would flagrantly demolish the exciting details he conceived in the restaurant. At the same time, she would be unequivocal in the manner in which she gave herself. L.'s instinct told her that the man's narcissism went hand in hand indeed with a loathing for his own body. The events now unfolded as L. imagined they would.

For some time now L. had suspected the effect she had on a certain type of woman, though she was not pleased with her discovery. At first she'd thought such women were simply staring at her out of innocent curiosity or admiration. Sometimes she glanced back, while at other times she pretended not to notice a thing. She figured momentary whims accounted for the phenomenon. Only then did she get scared when one night L. caught red-handed the woman watching her. It happened on a bus. L. had been just sitting there, lost in thought, when all at once she sensed that someone had been watching her for a long time. Raising her head, she immediately noticed the pair of eyes locked on her. In her initial surprise L. didn't even see a thing other than the craving eyes embracing her with warmth. She would have sworn that they belonged to a man. But the real shock came when L. broke free of the warmth that had now erupted between them. Sitting directly across from L. was a girl not much older than she. In her embarrassment L. hastily stood up and got off at the next stop. After this incident it became clear indeed to L. that womanly curiosity exploring her face could hardly be innocent. Remarks that came her way from certain woman acquaintances further confirmed that it was not only congeniality that bound them to her but also certain secret feelings that they refrain from speaking about only out of fear of the consequences of a confession. Why shouldn't she try this now also? The man's girlfriend was a suitable means and an even more exceptional victim.

L. chose the girl's lips. She locked her eyes on those reddish knots of flesh, which for now still adhered to each other with the dryness that gives security. Since L.'s unequivocal stare did not expand its focus beyond the mouth, the girl, as if obeying a command, almost imperceptibly parted her lips. With time, though, she had to expand the fissure, and this instinctively stimulated her to touch her mouth with her tongue. When, after a slight pause, the girl's lips closed, L. had the impression that she had kissed herself. The girl then lowered her head, perhaps only so as to hide her mouth from the others at the table. But L. was already planning her next step. In a less delicate situation she would have let things stand at what she'd just witnessed, but out of consideration for the man, she could not stop here. From experience she knew how exciting it is in certain situations for a woman when someone unashamedly looks upon her breasts.

When the girlfriend raised her head after a little while, she did so figuring she was now safe. But she was to be disappointed, for L. staged such a masterfully aloof homoerotic production before her eyes that there really was no defending against it (an outside observer might even have noticed the girl's nipples slowly swelling tight against her blouse after a while); demanding an explanation would have seemed just as ridiculous as indignant protest. The man's relentlessness put an end to what remained of the girl's self-confidence. In vain did she say she was tired—the shrewd male did not give in. Instead, he merely observed perfidiously that she shouldn't be worried, he'd call her the next evening by all means, whereupon the offended girl ran off. As each of them had been sure of this outcome for quite a while already, neither bothered to dredge up an expression of surprise.

With the third party gone, the sparkle immediately faded from L.'s eyes, in essence letting the man know that from now on, she was giving nothing for free. They looked at each other—the man, trying his utmost to conceal his obvious excitement; and L. feigning bewilderment, as if awaiting help. Understanding this wordless message, the hero of the table gestured to the waiter for the bill. They agreed to go to L.'s place. By the time they got to her apartment, L. felt exhausted. Still she forced a confident smile onto her face, for she wished to be face to face only with the man, or, to be precise, with the situation brought about by his presence. She was curious as to the stations they'd pass on the way to closing their account.

Neither the silence nor the girl's shyness flustered the man. He was happy, because after many years he'd finally happened upon an 'experimental subject' who was satisfactory from every point of view; at least this is what the noiseless unfolding of events so far confirmed. And so he required further carefully thought out preparations. He must not think what she's thinking; no, he laid down this condition at once—why would he have given up that which he'd insisted upon in all prior circumstances now, of all times? Namely, that he should force his will upon the other unnoticed. Of course, in the case of certain women, he had to present this as her own will. From this perspective the role of guest he'd now assumed seemed advantageous indeed, for he was the one who'd been invited, and not by just anyone. Fine, then, he would perform his duty, but he'd have a thing or two to say about the details of bringing this about. In point of fact he was now in this flat for this reason alone.

He stepped to the window, and lifted the curtain just enough to see outside. It was almost pitch black, but he made as if he'd seen something extraordinary. Ceremoniously he raised his head so the girl, too, would notice: at this very moment he had hit upon something truly exceptional. Let there be no misunderstanding, in case the other had not yet noticed: here he was, a lyrical soul, musing with fecundity. Having now verified his refined nature by staring out into the heavens, he thought it best to keep standing. Were he to unthinkingly take a seat (the bed was of course out of the question), the other could achieve an advantage that could not be undone. For example, she might suppose that he already wants *that*, whereas at this moment it couldn't be further from his mind. No. And so this standing about suited him best, just like this, so the girl can see him only from behind, if of course she was watching him at all. Perhaps in fact she was attending to herself, becoming familiar with her new situation from her perspective of waiting.

And yet with the passing of time—on mused the man—she would necessarily be jolted out of her relative self-confidence, for it was hardly for this standing about that they were spending their time together here. His patience in standing here with his back to her would soon reap its reward, and then he could show his face, too, accompanied by a smile of praise that would convey something like this to the other: 'Well, well! So you passed the first test. Let's continue, then.' But first he would recall the image in the restaurant when his girlfriend, her head lowered, waited for the danger to pass. He was just about to draw back the curtain when all at once it struck him that this movement would be rash. Calling upon his imagination to get a hold of itself, he went searching for that magical word which could protect him from falling into a fluster: delay. Yes indeed: delay! He must tend to the matter through music.

Composers know full well that the truly daunting task is not that of happening upon a theme but of cleverly unravelling it. The more thoroughly they explore the main melody, the more aware they will be of the illusion they are evoking, which they then try concealing by way of newer devices. For example, they make as if some pleasant-sounding motif that only touches on the theme from afar is in fact an indispensable part of the work. And so they dress it in splendid rhythms, and to lend all the more credence to its indispensable nature, they ornament it with shrewd appoggiaturas preceding the principal notes, and with unsettling trills, so as to emphasize the indelible link between theme and motif. Although those with refined ears cannot be fooled by guile concealed in extravagant technique, they do find yet more proof of their long-held suspicion—namely, that music is in fact not even a division of time. This more or less obscure determination is at most acceptable as an *as if*. Perhaps it would be more precise to say that music seeks to use seemingly autonomous sounds to patch up the void that arises after being bequeathed with a theme, taking pains to tie nothing with something. That certain first determination swaggers over the absurd notion of having pinched time by the ears and then mercifully letting it go only on finding it the suitable tempo and tone. In his struggle with the void, the composer helplessly flees to technique, which imparts freedom of movement upon the theme in an exceedingly suspicious manner. With the help of this ploy, time appears with an after-the-fact illusoriness, and yet it still hasn't given a definitive signal to indicate its presence. Despite it all, it is still reasonable to assert that the value of a musical work can be measured in its delay of an unambiguous (is there such a thing?) reply, where the composer's talent is seen to ride on his meticulous elaboration of seemingly insignificant details. True, accepting this assertion is to yank off the veil of his *as if* music, but it also frees him of the unjust accusation that had been levelled against him a moment before.

Before the man proceeded to apply musical technique to uncovering the inner depths of L., a requirement came to his mind that promised to be interesting indeed. Only then could he turn his head towards the other, when he managed to blend inner and outer time in such a way that the former would take the lead role at the expense of the latter, allowing only as much in the way of concession to external time as absolutely necessary. For example, he had to accept the fact that he was in the girl's flat, which, it would hardly be an overstatement to assert, meant that he perceived this space as time forced between four walls. By the same token, this time was likewise synonymous with this girl he did not know. And that only reinforced his necessary relationship with external time, for the girl had drawn him into her own time, which by now had become matter in all its perceptible form. He had only to look about. Events unfolding here fell as invisible shadows upon the objects, the furniture. Only a carefully planned act of arson could annihilate it all. And so he had to keep his poise in a smart, disciplined way: all he could notice of this all was what he must necessarily draw into his body over the course of a single breath. He hoped that as he drove back external time onto the minimum foundation possible, meanwhile that more delicate substance, the one that created inner time, would get stronger and stronger, relying on the former only by way of support. He knew full well that he could not wait for the two to achieve ideal balance; in part because he could not be certain of his experiment to begin with, and in part because dawn was fast approaching. And he required darkness or, at least, obscurity created by artificial lights.

In one forceful move he drew back the curtain and turned around. The girl was not in the room. He found her in the kitchen, smoking a cigarette and appearing surprisingly calm. He waited until she finished, and then he took her by the hand and led her into the room, to the window with its curtain drawn. Then he bent L.'s head a bit to the side and ran an index finger along her lips, thus gently opening her slightly tense mouth until the part was about the same as the one he'd seen in the restaurant on his girlfriend's lips. Having positioned her to his satisfaction, he signalled to the girl that she should stay just like this, whereupon he walked over to the door. From there he admired his creation. After a little while he determined that there was nothing amiss with the girl, the same could hardly be said of the background and the lighting. She didn't match the greyish-white curtains whatsoever, which is why he now covered the curtains with the brick-red drapes that had been fixed to the edge of the curtain rod. As for the lighting, which he deemed too strong, he resolved that matter by covering the floor lamp with his yellow silk shirt. Then he returned to the door, and knitting his eyebrows he once again began to observe the girl. Now he had to admit that the changed lights and shadows had in fact ruined the altogether successful effect the scene from a minute before.

Far from being annoyed, he seemed even pleased at the new task at hand. In a matter of moments he decided that the gap between the lips had to be expanded so that the glittering teeth would not disturb the quivering light on the slightly moist flesh of the lips. And this made it necessary to suitably reshape the face in such a way that the laws of natural physiology could hardly be realized. Indeed, were he to amateurishly give free reign to the artless—so he thought— then perhaps it would be precisely this that would remind him of the futility of his troublesome work; for even a single unruly mouth muscle could thwart his calculations if it didn't stretch suitably tight under the skin. In other words, he had to mould the now expanded territory above the mouth so cunningly that the details, vying against each other, would enhance the lips. Of course the most exacting task fell to the imagination. Let us only think of that particular adjustment of the face which occurs when, to ensure the contrast of the mouth area, this bit of skin, delicately contorted after thorough preparations, must be practically fixed to the cheekbones, for the girl's expression can be used only in this manner.

After quite a bit of trying, he finally hit upon the most advantageous positioning of the lips. It was by shifting the horizontal walls of flesh a bit obliquely that he discovered that exciting angle by which the face turned suddenly animated. Yes, this was the dynamism he would now have to intensify. He pulled the girl's right hand to her temple with the command that the fingers should pull at the skin, which was perfectly smooth even when calm. Overstraining the right side of the face was by no means an arbitrary measure: Not only did it serve to balance the slight obliqueness that had arisen from the shifting of the lips just before, it also guaranteed the uniformity of the lineaments positioned above the accentuated territory. Although the right side of the face thus became softer, the man meanwhile decided that the hard lineaments had to be counterpoised by slacker, more shadowlike effects. L. patiently bore this adjustment. And yet she quietly noted that this artistic composition, while intended to be erotic, awoke in her not a shred of excitement.

The man stepped over to the bed, which was somewhat further from the door and where the night lamp was. From there he inspected the adjusted face. Together, the newly arranged background and the yellow-filtered light, which seemed like a third inspecting eye, now properly lit up the image. He was perfectly satisfied with himself, convinced that not even the most well-practised filmmaker could have come up with a better set. Were he to step over to the girl and touch her face, all would be ruined. His hand would meet with skin, with bones. His touch would demolish that which he had created through a fortunate collusion of circumstances. He mustn't rub up against that which can only be observed, he thought with excitement—an excitement deriving from his recognition of the middle realm, that intermediate condition, between the face itself and the eroticism emanating from it. The distinction was readily apparent despite the deceptive notion that they belonged together. Only a superficial examiner could believe them inseparable, though the man did acknowledge that desire could blend the two. But the experienced eye discerns their separation at once. Of course he had to admit that without his resourcefulness, he would hardly progress in this area. In keeping with this fact, he concluded that he could count on only two eventualities—which are, in the final analysis, two variations of a single possibility. Under the first scenario he could requisition the 'medium' whom, as the object of his fantasies, he would drag to himself in thought, playing out everything that this furtive relationship would allow. As for the second, he would content himself with the erotic essence separate from the girl's face, which by now lived only in his mind. With this decision before him, he could just as well give up the girl. It seemed as if there had remained in him a single cell that served to remind him of a stage of ontogenesis millions of years in the past, of existence as a self-fertilizing creature.

He could have gone on until morning moulding this face, whose stimulating pliability kept evoking newer possibilities, but the time had come to concentrate on the body. He wanted to reward his discipline to this point, even though he knew that uncovering this beauty would demand at least as much circumspection as he'd devoted to the face. At the same time, he would face a much harder task, for observing the reactions on the face would somewhat weaken the powers of inspection he could focus on the body. And so he had to take possession of the body—he would try even if it was impossible—in such a way that he kept constantly assessing the face, eyes included, but without touching the girl. That, he could do only when fulfilling his duty. His eyes would lock themselves on her wincing face, darkening eyes and the stirrings of her mouth— and by doing so he would be able to measure all the more precisely the airy undulations of the thighs, her erect nipples pressing tight against her black blouse, and the invisible slackening and hardening of her stomach muscles; for he had no doubt that the girl's face would give precise signals indeed. He was indeed convinced that the face was a sort of coastal region separating fluids from one another, the mirror of the invisible workings of the viscera. He took it as self-evident that he'd leave the clothes on the girl; after all, the sight of her naked body would only weaken his imagination. Rash undressing would make him like a composer who would sound the main theme in all its splendour right at the start of a work, voluntarily relinquishing a proper introduction with its potent motifs. Not even as a beginner would he have committed this irremediable error.

He went over to the girl and led her to the bed. For a few seconds he hesitated over whether to lay her on the bed right away, but then he lived up to the demand of progression by degrees by seating her on the edge of the bed. As if wanting only to avoid having the girl become helpless, he asked her to cross her legs. Of course, perhaps he was attracted to the customary image of roadside eroticism. In any event, the image of L. sitting there with her legs crossed seemed to him straight out of some brothel. He even felt a bit ashamed. Could his fantasies be so mechanical?

Now he focused his attention on the slender legs concealed in those green stockings, for this is how he wished to shake off the image that had just beset him. The thighs now warming each other continued beyond the knees as thin calves. Like narrow mountain ridges, the shin bones ran down to the ankles, which were left uncovered by her shoes, perhaps only so that nothing but the translucent silk of her stockings would nestle against them. The top of the feet sloped at a smooth angle down to the tip of the shoes, which were cut deeply, in a sort of half-arc, covering only the toes. The man believed this region, including the toes, to be the most worthy of being touched, for this is where the body is least apt to go shamming. These body parts bashfully act as if their only charge was that of moving the body about—the man knit his brows—and yet they'd have reason to flaunt. It is precisely this humility that fools people, who, thanks to the shallow outlook of superficial aesthetics, confer upon the lower extremities only the most basic recognition. Perhaps the body's spatial arrangement leads them astray. And yet this belittlement, so he thought, ruptures the unity of the beauty of the human body.

He now walked around the bed and stopped behind L. Examining her only from the front would not do. The girl might find his switching of his observational position outright tactful, for he hadn't exploited all the possibilities offered up even by the frontal view; for until now he had marked the border of his field of vision at the start of the thighs. With the exception of the face, which had always counted as a space beyond the territory her body otherwise comprised, he had disregarded the analysis of the zones further up. While from the front his inspection had focused on the legs, while standing behind the girl he set out to discover the surfaces from the hips on up.

The dress nestled tightly against L.'s hips, leaving no doubt as to how boldly her waist grew thin from the point on. But it had to come under thorough judgement; for the hips occupied the deceptive border of thinness resulting from slow growth on the one hand, and slightly girlish yet elegant slimness. As a well-practised examiner, the man could not modify the strict rule requiring him to rigorously abide by every stipulation. That is to say, only objective assessment, which stood above individual taste, could pronounce the final word. After brief reflection, without so much as a qualm of conscience, he opted for the latter, thus clarifying a situation that had been dubious until that moment. His sentence was of course decisively influenced by the girl's proportionally broadening back, which resembled a pressed flower petal and which was split down the middle by a vein-like line of vertebrae. The fabric covering the arch of the neck contrasted sharply with the deep décolletage of the black dress. Her round shoulders comprised a scale calmly supporting the head, sometimes maintaining equilibrium, and at other times counteracting the balance.

Suddenly he remembered the restaurant scene when his girlfriend sat there with her head down, waiting for the danger to pass.

Although he deemed this association of ideas, meant to excite him, as premature, there was no stopping it. But he calmed himself down right away, figuring he'd certainly stuck to the rules. Which is why, as soon as L. now fell back with ease and signalled to him as she lay there looking upward that they'd arrived at the objective of their togetherness, there was no longer a need to adjust her, for they had reached this point after stopping off at the necessary stations. Kneeling up on the bed over L., he ran a hand over her waist from behind. But he did not undress her, no, for he sensed, or thought he sensed, that he would meet with resistance.

All at once the man turned gloomy. The sensual tension of the preparations had insolently left him high and dry. He'd thought this condition would develop in a crescendo-like manner the more time passed and would lose intensity only once their embrace had reached rapture. He'd imagined that the arc of his excitement would resemble that of his drug-induced experiences, in which, the deeper the substance is absorbed, the clearer the hallucinations appear before him. He'd intended the lead-up to this point to be a sort of vaccine. But he'd miscalculated. He did in any case admit to himself that that which he'd strictly insisted upon until now yielded nothing but the promise of the possibility of an exceptional experience. Had he been so deceived by the erotic force that had settled upon the girl's face? Could he satisfy his desire only by making love without touching the other?

L. immediately noticed the change that had come over the man. Listlessly, with an ostentatious enervated expression she began to undress, that very cynicism on her mouth which the other could not misunderstand. Wanting to be done with it all the sooner—not least because in the meantime the image of his girlfriend had left him—the man did not undress completely. L. lay under him motionless and almost stiff, waiting with a mocking smile to see when the man would jump up and leave, but he did not have the courage for that. Obediently he suffered through the act, and then with embarrassment he hastily threw back on what few clothes he'd removed, forced out a courtesy of sorts and faltered away in shame.

Although L. took this meeting as instructive, she nonetheless decided to invite her next victim in the afternoon. By doing so she might spare herself the silence lurking about her at such times. It seemed as if even the hours that had just passed had deluded her! For the silence of the objects all around her had absorbed the usual time, allowing another time to take its place, a time that was perhaps nothing other than the surging of constantly present remembrance. The oblivion sometimes bestowed upon her did not fool her, for in it she suspected the contrivance of methodical torture— as if there were something within her that knew the limits of her endurance, and thus inserted a short rest now and again so as to render the next bout of pressure bearable. In this she sensed a masterfully conceived, murderous game, one in which her sole consolation could be the pitiful hope that after one such pause, everything would resume differently.

4

Perhaps she'd been asleep for two or three hours when she awoke. As if she'd been wrapped in foil, her body was covered with thick beads of sweat. For a few seconds she couldn't help but wonder: Was waking up in fact the continuation of some dream? She became certain of things only when she looked in vain for the narcissistic man beside her. She would not wash the perspiration off, she decided—no, she'd wander through this day like this from start to finish, and it wouldn't bother her even if, after a while, irregularly shaped blotches of salt formed all over her body. Something told her she mustn't hide these signs.

All at once L. was overcome by an inexplicable terror. Sneaking anguish was more bearable than this, for at least in that case she knew she wouldn't figure out its cause, and which, even if it couldn't exactly be caught red-handed, it was high time for—not like this terror, which seemed to have torn her from time itself, to grip her but without revealing where, and to be chasing her towards a place that could never be found. At such times she would have done well to smash apart the place where she happened to be, and while she was at it, herself as well, so she wouldn't be so shamefully at the mercy of this powerlessness! But she didn't want to wind up in that certain building. Which is why all she could do was flee, to run dazed and without direction through the city and its streets, its parks. She knew full well that by thus running amok she could delay the onset of the darkness that sometimes very nearly managed to claw at her. If at such times she could at least just be frightened, no doubt she would have more quickly reached that hiding place built up over the years, and where, if not safety, she could at least hope for a moment's calm; for fear can in such circumstances serve as a life-jacket, it can tear a person away from that pressure which, even as it evokes weightlessness, threatens to break its subject apart. But in these hours she was deprived of even that support, as if to prove to her just how precious a treasure fear in fact was. She pulled on a pair of jeans, a thick sweater and sneakers, and in a semi-stupor, like someone not knowing what she is doing, staggered out of the apartment. If at least she could somehow get out of here! On reaching the street, L. almost broke into a run.

It was as if she were in a city she'd never seen before, one in which everyone was dashing home before it was too late, for a state of emergency had just been declared. Trams rumbled past her, trams teeming with distorted human faces. Yes, L. wasn't mistaken: the sides of the trams were made of enormous plates of glass, and so she could see clearly that all those heads pressed tight against each other were cut off at the neck, as if these people had never had trunks below their heads. Not that this surprised her, but she was curious to see whether the driver had hands. L. stopped so she could get a good look at the next tram coming by. Just to be on the safe side, she waited from underneath of building entranceway; she couldn't be careful enough in this city. When a tram finally made its creaking turn at a nearby intersection before then rolling past her, she was already certain that not even the driver had a trunk.

L. was somewhat relieved at this discovery. She held the consistent workings of her imagination to be the result of discipline—an unexpected brace to cling to. Perhaps this is what she could thank for the fact that when she now stepped out from under the building entranceway and headed towards the intersection, she no longer saw those faces behind the windows of passing trams. Instead, the image before her was one she'd seen a thousand times: weary-looking men and old ladies occupied the window seats so as to cast their uncurious stares upon cars and buildings, over the badly dressed pedestrians, over the layer of grime on shop window displays, over the dogshit-pockmarked pavements. A silver-haired, thick-jawed man seemed even to notice L. momentarily as she passed by the shops, though perhaps he saw only a moving blur, a shadow still evoking a human form, still held together by chance.

L. now recalled that a few miles from the city was a little village surrounded in a semicircle by forested hills. If somehow she could make her way there, surely she could pull through this hour of escape, which still held its dangers; for she did not know when the visions would return, the uncontrollable apparitions, which could bury her at any moment. Even on seemingly innocuous days, L. had to be on guard to beat back the temptation she felt while standing on a subway platform or a railway embankment. But in her present state of helplessness she might not be able to resist a call or, perhaps, an irrecusable command that would no longer give her more respite. 'You've wavered long enough, you must obey! Do you still not understand what beauty I'm holding in store for you?!' the voice in her might say again, and she could not know whether this time she might believe it. L. hated banality, the ridiculous collusion of circumstances. Not even given the opportunity would she have forgiven him for her having fallen victim to such a contemptible error. Such an end would be almost as ludicrous as that of the butcher crushed by a hog that falls from a third-floor balcony. Perhaps she'd seen this in a film. She imagined the friends of the deceased passing along the news with barely disguised smiles: 'Imagine, Joe's kicked the bucket—a 200-pound sow fell on his head. . . .'

She had to leave the city also because of the choking fits. The last time it hit her so suddenly that she didn't have time to prepare. As if some poison was squeezing her throat, helplessly she gasped for air, thinking it would never end. On that occasion a young girl had helped her. Remembering it later, L. imagined that the girl had pulled her tight and kissed her, too.

She flagged down a cab. She knew it was a costly undertaking, but in her present state of mind she was incapable of getting on a bus. Anything could happen to her in a crowd, and then nothing could save her from the mental ward. And she wasn't keen on choosing her next victim from among the patients there. Besides, chance had now brought to her a veritable gentleman: the sixtyish cabbie didn't even lay a claim on the usual questioning. And yet L. still didn't regard his silence as indifference, as disinterest veiled by gentlemanliness. To the contrary, L. was practically certain that the man was thinking about her, but she kept quiet only because he would have felt even the most innocent of questions to be intrusive. And she was all the more reassured by the simple fact that there was someone beside her, for she had to get through a good fifteen minutes before they got there. 'Shall I take you into the centre?' The man slowed down as soon as they reached the village. 'Take me to the end of the village—you know, where the weekend cabins begin.' L. reached into her pocket with some uncertainty, as if not entirely sure she would be able to pay her bill. But as it was, she even had enough for a tip. Then she got out, and headed off on the trail that crossed the road, a trail that led to the forest above the village.

Soon she reached one of her favourite clearings, which she visited at least once a year. She chose the spot that seemed most secure and sat down. The altitude was maybe 700 feet, and yet she felt that over the past hour she'd arrived somewhere impossibly far away. Indeed, at this moment L. didn't even understand completely

how she'd got up here. The calm she'd known so well since childhood, a calm that always followed her repeated flights, now came
over her. Autumn sheathed the ground with a yellowish-brown car-
pet. She leant down and pressed her face against the almost wet
leaves. Her lips trembled. L. thought that she should give herself to
someone who would return her embrace with the same, silent coldness. She wished she could stay here for days on end, if she didn't
have to return to the city, its bars, its beds. From the earth she could
perhaps learn the self-surrender with which she could give her body
to others without expecting anything in return. 'Nonsense.' L.
straightened out with a motion that spoke of shame over her weakness of a moment before. Nonetheless she saw her situation as
hopeless. The colder the expertise with which she carried out her
oath, the more relentlessly her consciousness was struck by her
failure, by the fact that she was capable only of revenge but could
not get even. She might even have exempted herself from her new
law, but she understood at once that this would have brought her
face to face with an even more absurd decision.

She started heading back. With calm, determined steps she
advanced along the trail, which was flanked by pines thickly here,
thinly there, as well as a few odd completely leafless, slightly tot-
tering other trees. She loved the autumn woods; the sight of
denuded trees filled her with tenderness. This is what old people
must look like naked, she thought, the only difference being perhaps
that dried branches of trees are stern, stiff, as if they surrender themselves with determination even to temporary demise. Their contin-
uously fixed position was meanwhile motionless movement, which
imperceptibly sees to maintaining their vertical freedom. Above all
L. admired this imperceptibility, for although she saw in trees examples of time incarnate, in their workings she could not perceive the
threads that tied the here and the beyond.

After hiking to the main road, L. had just caught her breath when she noticed a car approaching from a distance. She waited until it got close enough to see well, and only then did she stretch out her hand. A bright yellow Skoda stopped in front of her. The window rolled down to reveal a blond-haired, smiling man of indeterminate age; it seemed that he was far happier at this unexpected passenger than she was for the ride. Although the smile bent some of the harder lineaments of his face, his sharp features nonetheless remained.

Since even now L. sat in the back, she was able to observe this face almost imperceptibly in the rear-view mirror. It was utterly white and smooth, making it easy to believe that this man never had to bother about bristles, for some abnormality had seen to it that no hair grew on his face. He'd combed his hair straight down onto his high forehead, thus eschewing the seemingly innocuous preening other men engaged in so readily with their hair. The slightly crooked furrows that flanked his taut mouth on both sides seemed to L. to be the marks of carnal pleasure. The longer this man lives, she thought, the deeper these stripes would be, until one day they would hit bottom: bone. She could not catch his eyes, however, for he wore sunglasses. Nonetheless L. was virtually certain that they could hardly be anything but blue, and if by chance she was right, surely they could be only a very dark, almost black, Paris blue. She suspected that this man's eyes resembled those of the dogs whose eyes she'd always feared. She'd seen one recently. Its eyes were bathed more thoroughly in blue than perhaps even people of the most exquisitely Germanic stock could produce, although its enormous body was pitch black. Though riding in the car was moderately electrifying, the man—so she thought with indifference—remained uninteresting to her.

But why couldn't he be next? The conditions seemed promising indeed. Clearly he liked her; he may have been sitting quietly behind the steering wheel, but he was probably just waiting for the right moment to express his attraction. She had to admit that either she would have to make the first move, thereby emboldening the man, or else she would pass up the opportunity, about which she might later be really annoyed with herself. Yes, she would give the first signal—so decided L., not bothering about what the man would think of her as a result.

In recent days L. had in fact pondered this at length before arriving high-handedly at simplistic conclusion that every woman is a whore. Only afterwards did she begin fine-tuning her assertion. The fees charged by bona fide prostitutes left no doubt as to the cost of love. Their bodies have an exact price, and they don't even seek to deny this fact. Not so, with the lyrical whore (L.'s category for most women), who prostitutes her feelings, which she sets forth as pure. She for one must be paid for not with money but with tenderness, devotion and promises, and if a gentleman is unwilling to do so, she breaks the contract right away. Of course, first she makes a scene, issues threats and, citing her ruined life, tries to wring out a final deal, under which their agreement should be tied with even stricter terms than until now. After all, determined L., everyone must make love if they wish to stay sane. And since the winding road that leads there is lined with interests and motivations, women insist on varying conditions before surrendering themselves: some insist on being paid the negotiated sum; others insist on that selfish thing called love; and yet others, on the security promised by family bliss. Of course, she thought, these extreme examples can merge only as feeble analogies into the realm of inscrutable borderline cases. Not that she forgot about the umpteenth eventuality, either: when undisturbed instincts are freed up with the semiconsciousness of animal existence, so that each person can reassure themselves of the fairness of it all; for on noticing the other's face distorted by ecstasy, they can declare that they didn't get their own orgasm for free. Perhaps it was not without grounds that L. believed that everyone experiences this at least once in their lives. She was reminded of de Sade's peasants, whom the master of ceremonies invited to orgies as visual aids, so their desire should be satiated in a brutishly elemental manner.

L. leant back comfortably. Thinking it would be easier for him to say something to her if she did so, she assumed a carefree expression. Never had she understood those women who seek to raise attention to themselves by appearing unapproachable. She suspected that in fact hesitation and helplessness lay behind their customary method rather than clever acting or a display of self-confidence. Of course, L. did acknowledge that in certain cases the forbidden tools were outright compulsory. But those who always crudely applied questionable techniques were committing an irredeemable error. When thinking of women whose eyes exuded aloofness, she grew angry. They were in fact obeying some unwritten rule with shrewd artlessness indeed, as if this was the only way to prove their womanhood, which they later cling to only until they manage to get on top of the man. Naturally the possibility could not be excluded that their seemingly comfortable demeanour, their whipping on masks of innocence and weakness, was in fact a means of gathering strength, that their silence was but careful observation whose dividends they could later cash in. With the ever-present tenderness of those at the receiving end of things they inhale ostensibly solid matter, so that, through persevering work, they can wash it into a liquid substance similar to themselves. But now L. could not leave it to time; even in a best-case scenario she had only a few hours at her disposal, and that wasn't even taking into account the narrow time frame she had for the introductory phase, which would guarantee her a few minutes only to force out a decision favourable to her. Of course she could have made things easier on herself, like this: 'I like you. In the mood to have some fun?' Yes, she could have shown herself to be a common sort indeed. And yet she did not rule out that in the future, she would give this a try as well.

The man may have felt that in the last few minutes the girl had been thinking about him. He removed his sunglasses. L.'s presumption had been on the mark: his eyes really were blue, utterly dark blue at that, though perhaps the black mass of the dilated pupils cast a shadow over the retina. He looked into the rear-view mirror, where he saw L.'s head turned to the side. As with the stronger of two animals engaged in a struggle, whose unfailing instinct intimates that the other will soon fall, he sensed that a change had come over this girl. Before reaching the edge of the city he spoke: 'Shall we have a coffee?' His voice was deep and rasping, as if he had a hangover. L. imagined that this man spoke up only when absolutely necessary, when there was just no avoiding it.

One of her old plans came to mind. She would choose a man she could live with wordlessly for months on end. Only with their eyes and their bodies would they signal to each other, and they would patiently await the moment when their body parts would begin to speak on their own. In the first few weeks they wouldn't even touch each other. They would exhort their passion to maintain strict discipline to ensure that immediate gratification doesn't snuff out that precious energy awoken by the proximity of two craving bodies; for the initial aim is that one organism should come to know the other by tapping at each other without once touching— as if they were newborns again, who, after their experiences up to this point, give up their accustomed mode of becoming acquainted with the outside world. They would be like those air currents that descend upon backwaters in a delicate film in the wee hours on late autumn days and rest there until the morning thaw.

They would touch for the first time when their sensations were in a condition between *before* and *after*; say, at the point where the cold sees the first ripples form on water. But still they can't speak. That is when they enter a new stage, in which their bodies turn towards each other, clutch each other, and in which the man's fingers, preparing to caress, descend upon her body as surely as ice grows thicker and thicker on the surface of water. In the wake of this touching, similar to what had already passed, a film could form on her body, too, a film she might call the substance of love; for something wedges between the before and the after of touching, something that alights even more imperceptibly than drops of mist on a window. How strange, she thought, looking out of the car window, that sadness leaves a palpable, visible mark, one we can wipe away or hide away. As if someone had deliberately wanted to call our attention to it, perhaps like this: 'I'll give a palpable sign of that which is completely certain. For you are sponges that have been dipped in my wellspring, and when touched by the *real* one, you release my warm, salty fluid from your soft tissues.' This fluid should be collected in a test tube, for if the appropriate compound were dripped inside, perhaps there would appear on the surface a film from which the essence of sadness could be distilled! But why couldn't desire also have a fluid that could be cried out or otherwise extracted, and that we could spread all over ourselves? The palpable signs of sexuality were misleading bits of evidence, for how could the degree, the fluctuating intensity, of a man's desire be measured by the density and quantity of his ejaculated sperm cells? Fools could engage in such common experimentation to their heart's content, she thought—let them draw their conclusions with their self-important seriousness. It wasn't the physical side of orgasm in any case that held L.'s attention just now, but the assemblage of moments preceding it, which rips apart the accustomed order of cells, the direction of their flow in a way quite beyond the control of anyone or anything. In short, she was investigating the hidden chemistry of desire.

The man turned onto the shoulder, which after a few yards widened into a rest stop. Right in the middle of the parking lot was a newly built restaurant that had a shaded outdoor seating area off to the side. There they sat down. Standing at the restaurant's main door was a waiter who looked half-asleep. He was clearly unenthused about the new patrons. Presumably he was the sort who is happier to stand about with nothing to do in the late morning hours than about the prospect of a tip. He kept them waiting for perhaps fifteen minutes until, apparently having had enough of idleness, he walked over to their table wearing an indifferent expression. Under normal circumstances they would have taken this behaviour to be outright insolent, but now they let it pass with a roguish wink. Being compelled to wait was to their advantage. Which was yet another reason they broke into a smile when they now finally ordered their coffee.

They remained wordless. Not that this bothered them. Indeed it seemed that the mutual silence descended benevolently upon them both. Without fear L. bore the man's searching eyes. It was as if she was seeing orbs nailed down with coloured plates, which intermittently exuded a different sort of light. Strangest of all was that this stare did not reach her in straight lines—as if the course it took ascended at some point in the space between them, only to form a fine arc as it then descended slowly, softly upon her face.

This was yet another reason L. had always considered 'penetrating glance' to be a slipshod expression, for as she saw it, it captured only the result, without even touching upon the perceptible movement of observation through space, its expansion in time. True, it is easy to draw a line in the sand separating the observed object from the glance itself. But we are constantly ignoring the other components of looking, which is the fault not only of the cheap interest of the outside world but also of internal proportions gone askew—whether a lack of rhythm, rash shifts in tempo, arbitrary changes of direction, unrestrained eye movements, the weariness that necessarily results from inappropriate use of the eyes. It wasn't by chance that she'd thought first of rhythm. L. felt that nature had left this sense high and dry. While it had left it with sufficient instructions, it had stayed inexcusably silent as regards most of those refined, almost artful techniques that it had for example divulged about drawing breaths. In their distress, professional observers are compelled to make up for this omission, and in given cases they may make an attempt, in a manner similar to that of the rhythmic regulation of breathing, to dissect their gazes into readily separable parts.

As a first step, they close their eyes. This could be the equivalent of the pause between breaths. Next, making use of the slippery film between their pupils and eyelids, they carefully slide their eyelids upward until their eyes are open just a crack. They may dilate their pupils only gradually, until the object in their sights is revealed before them in all its manifold completeness. They maintain this position until the eyelashes' playful little pins chafe the field of vision from the pupils to the observed object, that narrowing and expanding corridor they keep arbitrarily stepping into. It would be overly severe to immediately denounce this first manifestation of the 'disturbance'; it would be much preferable to regard it as a warning, a sort of well-intentioned exhortation that in point of fact it's high time to step into the third phase of observation, when the pupils repeatedly contract, shrinking the contours at a calm, certain pace, so as to accompany behind the closing eyelids that which has been seen, where, in the darkness, the image can finally be born. For a few seconds they then stay that way, taking care to keep outside light away from themselves, and only then do they start 'looking' anew if the previous image is safe and sound. With regular practice, after a while they can abandon this circuitous new method of observation, for later the pace of observation takes over the role of dividing the eyelid's various stages.

They must not forget that all this guarantees only the external conditions of observational work! Leaving behind the surface, we arrive at a far more delicate territory. This is the place where we either track our expanding beams of vision or simply ignore them. If however we succeed in perceiving the arches they form, we realize that the observational relationship moves at a two-way intersection. It is in such cases that we can practically feel the other's eyes scratching at us—perhaps precisely because their gaze keeps with certainty not only to that axis which arises between them and the observed object, but also because they extend this line of vision towards inner vision as well. From this is born our impression that a gaze is 'deep', which sometimes seems illusory because we fail to notice that the other is indeed taking care to retain the image culled along the surface of the two-way axis, which he or she will let go of only when continued insistence proves to be nothing but a waste of time. And yet determining this is anything but easy. Which is why the notion that the image is on the surface of the axis seems questionable and, soon enough, imprecise. Perhaps the supposition that reveals the beams of vision comprising a gaze *in flagrante delicto*, in their stark, three-dimensional expansion, is more justified. Why, after all, should we not believe that the structure of that which perceives spatiality is itself like that which it is observing?

Defining more precisely the preconditions of observation presupposes not only greater possibilities but also new demands; for not only does the observer's gaze have a rhythm, a more or less discernible tempo, but so too does the examined face. And so from here on in the observer abides by an unwritten rule in approximating the rhythms of his own watching to that of the face being watched, by no means forgetting, of course, that the aim is not a merging of the two, their dissolving into each other, but simultaneously finding and maintaining a polyrhythm. And yet the divided attention this presumes cannot have a disturbing effect. Quite to the contrary, it is through this two-directional flow that the observer can measure his talent: Is he still capable of separating the independent rhythms in a discerning manner, of making known the new sensations borne by his perception of the differences?

Take the man's smile of a moment ago. If she were to interpret the arch formed by the slightly extended lips as speaking solely to her, she would already be mistaken. She would do better, having set aside personal interests, to take this smile and examine it within herself. It is right to clarify that play of the flesh that is the lips, of those muscles that sometimes just barely stretch tight, is misleading indeed. It is far more likely that she can decipher cause of the smile if she pays attention to the dynamics of the mouth, although just as a firm and fast shift in the arch of the lips does not necessarily signify the smile's revealing spontaneity, neither can one depend on thoroughly prepared shifts. And yet the nature of the rhythm still says the most, especially if the motion also affects the territories above the mouth. In this case it is obviously, or almost imperceptibly, the contrast that develops on the surface of the face from the cheekbone to the inside corner of the eye which accentuates the smile lying low at the edge of the mouth. At such times the slightly accumulating folds of skin also soak the upper part of the face with their darker tone. And yet this still isn't the decisive factor.

Rather, it's the eyes. In fortunate cases it is in the gravitational force of a glance that can explain the cause of the smile; for if the beam of vision merely chafes the arch of the smile remaining on the edge of the lips, it should be clear at once that something is amiss with this smile, for even a superficial observer can see that through-out, their mutual dependency remains a forced relationship. How-ever, if the gaze has absorbed and practically sniffed right in the lineaments that have arisen around the mouth, they will seem insep-arable. Is this the moment when we can't decide whether the mouth or the eyes are smiling? They will be each other's mainstays to such an extent that their power just keeps growing and their moving motionlessness expands over the whole of the face, and so the well-prepared observer will see a vibration of sorts envelop the surface of the face, although in the first minutes of his examination it had seemed that all to be done was to decipher the meaning of an almost innocent motion of the mouth.

The man, before they took the last gulp of coffee from their cups, took L.'s hand, perhaps only to change the direction of the silence. While the initial motion still seemed to be a caress, this was soon supplanted by the relentless grip of a predator, from which L. even hissed in pain. But she did not resist. She left her hand between the claw-like fingers and looked at the man. Those certain lines on both sides of the lips were now even straighter. How precisely she'd articulated it before! Time really had tattooed his manhood beside his lips in flouncing little switches that now fixed their stares on her. She shuddered with fear. Maybe she'd be safer, after all, to keep her distance? If he were this wild now, what would he be like later? Could she trust her body to this burning passion?

No, it wasn't the predator she feared but being at his mercy, of betraying her pride, forgetting her hatred. The man had undeniably got the upper hand, there was no denying that. At the same time, L. felt that it wasn't him she was giving herself to but, rather, to chance. On this morning she must accept the role of the vanquished, for as prey she could perhaps achieve an experience that animals torn to shreds can never know; for in their embrace it wouldn't be the predator gaining nourishment from her, but vice versa, she would suck the power out of this body, and when he lets her on her way, he wouldn't even suspect that his greatest treasure had secretly been stolen from him. She would find that certain territory on the man's body from where she would spoon the stuff out of him like primitive tribes do brains from the skulls of the dead. The waiter turned up once again, and so they paid.

Both of them knew that the tacit agreement had already been born between them, so they were able to avoid discussing the details. They headed off towards the city. With little traffic, they soon arrived in front of a second-class hotel the man must have know well. With a smile that might have been a wink, the clerk handed him the key to room 627, although aside from a polite greeting he said not a word.

L. had suspected correctly. She was being led upstairs by an intelligent predator on two legs but in no particular hurry, as if completely certain his prey would not escape. Indeed, perhaps it had even crossed his mind that it was precisely the prey who sought to hasten her own destruction. As he placed the key in the lock, he was thinking that this girl was like an animal heading voluntarily to the slaughterhouse out of fear that it might be forgotten. The man imagined that he would assist in L.'s self-mutilation, and this scared him, because no one could call him to account for his complicity.

The man did not pause to cajole her. He took L. with such force that she only muttered falteringly amid the waves of orgasmic pleasure crashing into her. L. noticed the lines on the man's face opening up and parting from the skin, descending onto the rest of his body, enmeshing him from head to toe. At first these lines, which assembled into irregular figures, seemed cold, but then they started slowly warming up, and finally they became hot streams of lava inundating her. L. doubled up spasmodically and screamed much like she did in her dreams, except that now it wasn't from fear but from the carnality gushing through her body.

L. woke up with a start to find the man's hand resting on her forehead. She did not open her eyes; the man's expression would have been unbearable to look upon. Yes, she understood, for the length of a scream the hatred had been torn from her heart, and yet she still was not ashamed because of this. Weightless, motionless, she lay there for a while yet. Then she peeled the man's hand off her forehead, got dressed, left room 627 and went down to the street. At the moment she had no idea what she'd do with what she'd just experienced.

5

L. must have been loafing about on the streets for a while when, on approaching that vast neighbourhood housing the university hospital and clinics, she recalled a rendezvous. Some months ago she'd fallen into a conversation with an elegantly dressed gentleman in one of this area's bars. At first glance she'd found him rather obnoxious. Only when he spoke up did her opinion change. L. was amazed at the timbre and tone of his voice, which contrasted sharply with his appearance. (Sometimes L. classified people by the musicality of their voices. For example, she compared those of her girlfriends who had an affected way of gabbling away to whining violins tuned too high, and then there were others she thought of as grunting bassoons. When she got carelessly close to them, their drool sprayed not onto her face but, she noticed, also onto the words they strained to squeeze out. Only rarely did she encounter a voice that addressed her with a cello's evenly descending calm and not at all its ingratiatingly brownish hue. At such times she even overlooked the fact that someone might be talking nonsense. . . . L. loved the human voice as she did music.) Even now she relented for this reason, and so she would gladly have spoken to him. But they'd only just begin their conversation when the man had to go. On leaving, he handed her his business card.

He was a coroner. L. saw signs in everything, so she was certain that this card, produced with mediocre printing technology, had not been pressed into her hand by chance. She knew she would call him, though she had no doubt as to the man's designs.

Not long afterwards L. looked up S. with the request that he let her observe an autopsy. For his part, the doctor tried talking her out of it by hinting that scenes far more exciting could be in store for the two of them, but she remained unbending.

They met on a Monday morning, in the courtyard of the pathology institute. First they stopped in the employees' snack bar, where they each drank a little cup of slop that for some reason was called coffee. Then S. led L. into the building so as to show her the autopsy room. They agreed to meet by the door in an hour—at which S. then asked him to excuse her, and disappeared quickly down the hall. She remained in a waiting room of sorts, where lower-than-usual coat racks in two corners held yellowish-orange gowns. In another corner was a sink, attached to the wall, above which was a much-larger-than-average mirror.

That is when L. noticed that the door of the autopsy room was half open. She stole her way over and peeked inside. Her eyes met the chief coroner's hands, which just then happened to be lifting the brain out of the open skull of a lifeless body sprawled out on one of the tables. Only afterwards did L. realize what she'd seen. She began getting dizzy, but she still didn't dare close her eyes, which now passed over the room. Bright sunshine streamed in through the huge windows, which were at least twelve feet high, even though the thick, frosted glass tempered the rays. Rectangular neon lights hung from thin metal pipes on the ceiling. Though this wasn't necessary, they were lit, presumably on account of some regulation. There were three autopsy tables spaced evenly apart, raised high and covered with wood planks; a corpse rested on each. Suddenly afraid that the chief coroner might notice her, L. turned around and ran back down the hall.

In the waiting room L. happened upon a group of medical students gathered merrily indeed for a practicum. Just then she had more of a stomach even for her queasiness than for the idiotic ease, the casualness replete with forced smiles, with which these neophytes aimed to coax the overbearing indifference of insiders onto their faces. Struggling with her nausea, L. walked up to the second floor. Fixed to the wall along the right side of the wide hallway were glass closets whose shelves held human specimens floating in formaldehyde: three- or four-month-old Siamese twins joined at the head; an embryo, of indeterminate age, with flattened skull; a creature that resembled a sea animal, whose head was cut in two by a plate of bone; body parts collected from various other embryos; and hands and feet that would have passed for bird wings. At the edge of one of the shelves, an insect-like embryo seemed sometimes to move. Her throat tightened, and she felt unusually sharp pains in her abdomen. Suddenly she didn't even understand what she was doing here. But the pains ceased quickly. Only a little while later did she understand the reason behind her unexpected calm: here, standing by the glass closets, she saw proof of one of her continually recurring suppositions—namely, that there is no difference between human and animal specimens, and there cannot be!

This thought had crossed L.'s mind even as a child. One day at school, the cleaning lady had left open the biology storeroom, and L. had stolen into the room like some burglar. For once she didn't hear the rasping voice of the biology teacher talking on and on so cleverly about the arthropods pinned to corkboards, the stuffed birds, the animal hearts floating in formaldehyde. Excitedly L. paced around the room imagining what it would be like if one night she were to take the jars off the shelves and replace them with the hearts of adult human beings, the kidneys of underdeveloped babies and the TB-afflicted lungs. She was only twelve but she felt vile and even wicked for thinking all this, and yet that's not what had frightened her. What she really found exasperating was her awareness that her newfound truth was, deep down, unassailable.

Now, standing there in the second-floor hallway of the pathology institute, L. finally gave herself approval for the act she'd committed so many years before in thought, and which had finally been verified by the fate of these embryos, which had become objects on display. All at once her seemingly wicked idea had become an incomprehensible reality. But in vain had she asserted that it didn't make a difference whether human or animal specimens are kept in formaldehyde; for something—which she'd sensed in the course of her latest examination—struck her as utterly unexplainable.

The pains in her abdomen now returned, along with intense nausea. Again it occurred to her that if she wanted, she could leave all this behind and go outside into the bright sunshine, sit down on one of the benches in the garden among the institute employees sipping their coffee there, smoke a few cigarettes, and then go into some nearby bar and down one or two shots. But no. She'd follow through with this; she'd made the decision in the wee hours of the morning on waking with a start from a dream. With both hands she'd been pounding the chests of dead people, wanting to bring them to life. L. now had ten minutes left before her appointment with S., and so she decided to go back inside and find the ladies' room. She chose the usual method. The vomit was white and watery, as if she hadn't eaten a thing in days.

By the time L. returned to the waiting room, the medical students had already donned their yellowish-orange gowns. They looked a bit more professional this way. L. selected a gown for herself, one that was more deep yellow than orange; and then, after a deep breath, with fierce determination she awaited S., who, as agreed, arrived exactly at ten. With him in the lead, the group entered the autopsy room.

The chief coroner was still working on the same corpse. He was just sewing up the stomach cavity from the chest to the loins with strong, brisk stitches. This reminded L. of the characteristic hand motions of women basket-weavers. The chief coroner was around forty and of medium height, with a muscular frame. His short black hair accentuated his round face. With a stony, indifferent expression he watched the corpse's abdomen, which he finally managed to patch up all the way to the bottom of the chest, where he left a little triangular gap, just big enough to easily slip in both his fists. After the pathology presentation he would stuff the internal organs back in through this little hole; that is, the organs that were lined up on the autopsy table. His gaze was inscrutable, if only because he glanced up from his work only on occasion.

On the table closest to the door was a premature baby of around seven months; in the middle was a man of around sixty with both legs amputated at the upper thighs; and on the last table was a man of indeterminate age. The chief coroner now had only to wash off the body in the middle, for while sewing it up it had become bloody in a few places.

S. stepped to the last table, holding the final hospital report about the patient now lying there. 'Yesterday he was still alive. He went to the hospital a week ago complaining of headaches and dizziness. The attending doctors could not establish the cause of death.' He placed the papers on the little table in the corner and slipped on his gloves. He then picked up a scalpel, with which he proceeded to cut in half the brain placed beside the dead man's head, that irregularly shaped globe, after which he cut thin slices from one of the halves. At this point he replaced his scalpel with a

short, pointy pair of scissors, with which he removed the veins from
the brain's soft pulp and placed them side by side. Again, he picked
up the scalpel and meticulously sliced the veins. He was looking for
blockage. And indeed, in one of the almost paper-thin strands he
found hardly noticeable clots. 'You see, these are what obstructed
the brain's blood flow.' With his scissors he raised up high a dirty
red glob of blood about as big as the head of an insect sawed in
half. Now he placed the scissors back on the table, and with his fingers he began pressing at the grey-white gel of the intact half of the
brain, encouraging those standing around him to give it a try themselves. No one volunteered. L. would have felt it herself but she
didn't have the courage. It wasn't touching the brain that she feared
but the students' glances.

A young woman doctor now stepped into the room. First she
put on her gown and then, with the medical reports in hand, went
over to the middle table, where the amputated man was laid out.
As she was working alone, with no one around her, L. decided it
would be best to leave S. with his medical students and step over
to this woman doctor. Only now did she realize that the dead man's
skull was still open at the back, and that the scalp had been pulled
back over his face all the way to his chin, so that only his beard
was visible. The woman doctor began explaining things. 'You know,
colleagues, the man's legs were amputated while he was still alive.
According to the final report, he died of blood poisoning.' L. gave
an understanding nod, as if she herself had studied the papers. That
is when she noticed a large, reddish internal organ that resembled
a mildewed rag more than anything, covered with black stains large
and small. Since she had no idea what she was looking at, L.
pointed at it and asked, had this gotten mouldy? The woman doctor
pronounced some incomprehensible Latin technical terms, and
then, turning her head to the side, said with amazement, 'I don't

know where this man could have lived, but I've never seen lungs like this.' With that, she pulled the lungs towards herself and, using her fingers, pressed out of it a yellowish-green ooze of phlegm. Little holes appeared in the discoloured surface of the lungs, which, on account of the pressing, were occasionally covered by bubbles. 'What accounts for the edema, I don't know,' said the woman doctor, 'but the discoloration isn't surprising. It's even possible that this man didn't smoke at all.' She cast L. a bewildered look, as if L. were her only hope.

Feeling that she was now ready to touch the brain, L. stepped beside the woman doctor—who was examining the vein walls of the brain—and picked up a small piece of brain that had been set on a little tray. It seemed to her weightless, incorporeal. Was this greyish-white, inscrutably veined pulpy mass the centre of life, this thing now being sliced up in front of her like overripe autumn fruit? She recalled a restaurant scene: she is eating fried cow brains when, with a clumsy move of the knife, the breading separates from the congealed brain. Here in the autopsy room, it struck her that the human brain was a bit drier, less gelatinous, and perhaps even more fibrous; as a point of fact, the convolutions cohere as a compact surface. Gently she pressed her finger into the slice.

The chief coroner's plucky figure appeared by the door. He'd come to check on the tables. Apparently it was his job to cover up any corpse that hadn't been worked on for a while. Since no doctor had arrived to tend to the infant on the first table, he saw to his task. Had it been an adult, no doubt he would simply have covered it, as usual, but he deemed it better to simply lift this foot-long, per-haps two-pound corpse right off the table. Producing a black plastic bag, he then proceeded to place it within. But then, figuring that the doctor might arrive soon anyway, he slid it onto the end of the table. Then he washed his hands and left the autopsy room.

The young woman doctor was by now examining the heart. The cut the veins she'd removed from the aorta, veins that seemed hard and dry. Using her scalpel, she cut one of them lengthwise, and then carefully lifted out the blood clots fixed to the vein walls. L. thought back to pig killings she'd witnessed as a child. She'd always watched from the window the fury with which the men held down the shrieking beast as the butcher then plunged the sparkling knife into its neck. With a quivering stomach she'd let her eyes follow the scene as the pig's hot blood was released into a big blue pot that gave off steam in the freezing morning air. She never ate of the blood and onions, though the family's gourmands considered this to be the highlight of the day. L. saw only the pig's enormous glassy eyes before her. She was certain that if humans instead had found the animal's eyes to be the foremost delicacy, then that is what they'd serve with spices.

Around noon, L. had had enough of the pathology presentations. She said goodbye to the woman doctor, and as for the coroner, she promised to call him. In the waiting room she removed her dark-yellow gown and thoroughly washed her hands while looking long upon herself in the mirror. Her face was sunken and pale, as if she'd been made to stand there after several sleepless nights. It would be best, she thought, if she were to go to the nearby bar and finally have herself a drink.

She would call the coroner: so L. now thought, looking up at the windows of the university hospital. After all, his intentions had always been obvious. She would choose him for the tomorrow night. L. shuddered. Could she be so cruel to herself? Was she forgetting that the hands embracing her are those that every morning examine hearts and convolutions of the brain, that circumspectly spread out vein walls so as to discover hidden obstructions and illnesses of unknown origins? No, she had not forgotten this. But she would choose him nonetheless, for the hands caressing her would be firm and resolute, hands whose fingers exquisitely knew the human physiognomy. Their lovemaking would perhaps resemble an autopsy where the well-practised hands need not open her body. She would have a thing or two to learn from the doctor.

L. went into the same bar she had back *then*, after the pathological presentation. She sat down at the empty bar and ordered a coffee and a mineral water. Only now did she start to understand what had happened to her that very morning in room 627 of the hotel. She thought, *Starting today I can hardly let my daily task pass by unfulfilled; I remember what happened there too clearly for that. I cannot forgot the feeling.* From the bar she called the doctor, who insisted on meeting that evening.

'Have I told you there are more exciting things than autopsies?!' said the man on stepping into L.'s flat that evening, balancing a bouquet of flowers in one hand while leaning over to kiss the woman of the house on the neck. L. thought of the man's lovers. Looking at the coroner, it was clear to her that those girls hardly suspected which branch of medicine their elegantly armoured knight specialized in. For some reason she'd been judged differently.

In any case, it all transpired too fast—though this had its advantages, too; for example, had they instead met the following evening, no doubt she would have had more reason to fear, for the autopsy room would have been on her mind all day long: at ten in the morning he puts on his gown and signals to the medical students to stand around the table. Then he begins his presentation. After a little while he picks up the scalpel and slices delicately into the brain. Meanwhile he'd be thinking of L.: her white belly, her thin arms, her nervously writhing thighs. While later poking his fingers into the lungs laid out beside the corpse, he would break into a smile at the thought of my firm breasts. Surely his own smile would not unsettle him, for he's become used to seeing corpses by now. He must deal with eight or ten corpses a week, of which only the more interesting cases hold his attention; yes, for a while now he has perhaps held it all to be only a sort of butcher's work. Not that she wanted to be unjust, not at all, but for some reason L. suspected something amiss when it came to his style, that of the leading man. Whence the strength, the unassailable hedonism? From the autopsy room? Or was he, too, fleeing from something? Would he be unable to face corpses day in and day out if he didn't console himself every night with the ladies? But perhaps that was why he had several dozen lovers (of this she was absolutely certain): because it was clear indeed to him that this was the only possible protection against decay, from decomposition once and for all, worms and all? As if he sees only his own cold body every morning on the autopsy table, and is repeatedly surprised to find that not even today is it him lying there in front of the medical students preparing for their exams. At such times he breathes a sigh of relief at the thought that his girlfriend of the night will not be waiting for him in vain, after all. Yes, he had a lot to thank these lifeless bodies for; perhaps they serve as a constant reminder that with all the more love, with all the more intense pleasure, he should defy that which brought them down. Maybe it even occurs to him that the dead in fact prefer that the hand working on them is one warmed by women's caresses.

L. could not decide: Was it the man she needed, or the thoughts he unwittingly evoked in her? Only now did L. understand what morbid forces moved her. Yes, on this night she could map even her unexplained desires. If she were to discount her disquiet, which could be seen as natural, why then she had to admit that she felt good in this man's company. In his presence she found a sort of explanation for long-held feelings. For example—it occurred to L. unexpectedly—she had always enjoyed taking strolls in cemeteries.

She was fond of grave-posts leaning to the side and grown in with weeds, and she was overcome by an inexplicable tenderness when reading, at a half-whisper, the names of the dead. Sometimes she slipped her hand onto the grave-posts or stone crosses, as if only touching the faces of the deceased. Ostentatious memorials occasionally enraged her. She regarded these quasi-fortresses as pitiful mistakes, for they paved over the lives of the dead. It was in Denmark that she'd seen the loveliest cemetery to date, one where the dead were free to breathe; not even crosses were stuck in the mounds of earth, which by now belonged forever to their bodies: they had only to bear the insubstantial weight of a single, unmouldable piece of rock.

Never had L. understood what drew her to cemeteries. Perhaps the strangeness of it all? But what sort of strangeness was she carrying about within herself? Was she a wretched exception, who on account of some ludicrous misunderstanding was not conferred with that everyday consciousness with which to convince herself that one day, everyone would decompose, but owing to some odd chance she would be exempted? For who is the poor wretch who does not wake up this way every morning? Was her strangeness synonymous with her having been robbed of an illusion, an experience that reminds her again and again that indeed it wouldn't be she to whom this miracle will happen? She would in any case accept this feeling with less of a heavy heart if it didn't immediately gather force as a sentence of everlasting futility. For if one day she too were devoured by that craven darkness, then what's it all good for? (Of course every now and again she did find this naive question of hers exceedingly dubious.) Or was she simply depraved? Was she incapable of living life? Was that was she rubbed elbows shiftily with mortality? Perhaps that is why she made such fast friends with this feeling early on. If she couldn't subdue it, after all, with time it might strengthen into a worthy partner.

L. held these empty speculations with suspicion. She was more inclined to trust in material truths, which is why she had such a great need for visible signals, for palpable, sniffable reality. Once it occurred to her that she should make a documentary film that chronicles the final days of someone dying of lung cancer. The patient's suffering would validate the film's ruthlessness; for as the person, despite having received the strongest possible doses of morphine, bites his lips in pain and bloodies himself all over with his nails—assuming of course that a whole troop of medical attendants have not lined up beside him to apply their expertise to ensure him trouble-free suffering—the question arises: Why should it not be possible in these moments to record this accursed nonsense in such a way that can be played back repeatedly? After supper anyone could play the film for themselves. Indeed, when the opportunity arises we could prepare our own bodies for their own future presentation. L. suspected that she would not have the courage to make this film, although she thought it would have been instructive indeed if someone finally saw to the task of establishing an entire archive of films that record the stages of the body's final destruction and decay.

It seemed childish to L., that cravenness which seeks to cleanse everyday life of the fact of death—ironically enough, precisely by citing the defence of life. As if only on All Souls' Day can we open the doors of our consciousness to our foe, so as to pay our respects with twenty-four hours of obligatory woe. Yes, perhaps she was depraved, after all; for she believed that the only reputable thing in life was death, which somehow had never let anybody down.

Maybe this, too, was why L. was pleased to have S. so close. The hand poised to draw her in was, in a manner of speaking, a specialist in the ephemeral. True, he too would come to face the unalterable, but at least he maintained constant contact with it. Perhaps she'd imagined it, but when the coroner had pressed his lips against her neck, she sensed the fragrance of dissected corpses. Yes, it was a fragrance, not a smell, as if she could weed out the characteristic, sweetish stink of the dead from the distinctive smell emanating only from individual corpses, which she found impossible not to call a fragrance.

The man hid his impatience. He didn't seem indignant at all; after all, it was he who'd insisted on meeting without delay. And yet he shrewdly suggested that they could go out to dinner. L. gave a nod of approval. Both of them could use this preparatory ritual, she knew. Obviously she had a pro lover on her hands, thought L. while getting on her coat, one who effortlessly hides his excitement behind a carefree manner. He must have understood for a while already that love can truly be celebrated only by sipping slowly of its pleasures and by measuring out portions by degrees. His wisdom must have been ripened by instructive embraces, so that by now he can declare with a roguish grin that only beginners are overhasty. But this waiting came in handy for her, too. She could prepare more calmly for the embraces, she could gauge her courage, and she could soothe her fears, for she still couldn't be sure whether in the last act she might take flight instead. So far, the ideas she'd associated with this man had struck her as fertile indeed, but she could not know how she might handle her possible revulsion immediately before they made love.

A half hour later they were already sitting in a restaurant. Each of them ordered a plate of cheese, and with this, a bottle of dry red wine. The man kept talking but this didn't disturb L.'s thinking. 'I only have to clarify the situation, and everything will be in order. The formula is actually simple indeed. Today's "suitable individual" was almost the same as the others. All I've got to do is slip this dubious word, "almost", in its proper place—and why shouldn't I be able to do that? So we'll have supper, drink down our wine, perhaps drink another bottle, and then go up to S.'s flat. Not that I'm in the mood at all to cheat on anyone, for example, by substituting my elegant coroner even for this morning's stranger. Let's look squarely at the facts. When he starts undressing me, I mustn't turn away my head, no, I should just follow the restrained excitement of the fingers fiddling with my clothes. Yes, this tension is completely different from when we're readying ourselves for an autopsy that promises to be interesting indeed. So he's taken off my clothes—with half-closed eyes he examines my body, and he shudders, for he's looking at a living, animated body! Motionless, he just stares at me in wonderment, as if can't get enough of what he's seeing. For several long minutes he doesn't even touch me, no, he just gapes fixedly, practically without taking a breath. He takes not even a step away from this body; he wants to stay close by, to catch its scent, to drink in its fragrance, so that even if it's impossible, he should get to the bottom of this body's noiseless breathing, its skin, its bones, its flesh. How strange, that the workings of the most perfect structure are soundless! All this will seem to him to be a vision. As if this young body—so it will occur to him, perhaps unexpectedly—was lying lifeless before him just a moment before, waiting to be dissected, and owing to some miracle it had now awoken, and here it lay before him in its faultless beauty. Embrace it, kiss it?! No, instead he'll step behind her and start sniffing, as animals do the other's urine scent: her hair, underarms, loins. He will breathe in the damp warmth of her skin. He believes this hour to be magical, for this transformation is a given to him, not like someone delirious with grief, who screams away as they bury their head into the face of their deceased loved one, unable to accept the unacceptable.

Maybe he'll even turn sad for an instant, but then he'll shrug his shoulders and laugh, forgetting this simple-minded childish joke. To think that this girl's body should remind him of the dead! Why, the moment he steps out of the door of the pathological institute, he leaves it all behind him. Whatever became of those anxious nights in his first years at the job, when he couldn't even open the refrigerator without seeing one of the corpses staring back from inside?'

L. turned angry. Again her thoughts had drifted: she still hadn't put matters in place to her satisfaction. Even though she and the man would be leaving soon for his place. They ordered one more bottle of wine. L. felt she would get drunk, of course due more to tiredness than the alcohol. She admitted to herself that she did not see clearly the man's work-related musings. But this didn't bother her. She had to finally find an answer to her question; which is to say, she had to clarify imprecision that had taken shape around that little word, 'almost'. From now on, she felt, she could pursue her line of thought without digressions.

'We are both preparing for an adventure.' The man had found himself a new lover for at least a night, and as for her, she'd happened upon an individual with whom she could carry out more than just the obligatory act. It is easy to surrender ourselves to a harmless car mechanic or a polished skirt-chaser, but we get scared right away if the hands that touch us are well honed in the ways of death. Not that she could make heads or tails of a territory as exceedingly murky as that, for example, tread by the wife of an executioner. The fine figure of a man comes home from a hanging and yearns for gentleness and love. What must this woman think in the arms of her husband? No, L. decided, she would not fear this mean. She would be outright grateful; for when embracing him, she would be accepting not only his body but also all those lifeless bodies he'd ever performed autopsies on, sometimes with surprise, perhaps occasionally with revulsion, but mostly with no feelings at all, and—maybe most important of all—always with expertise on par with his talent. Through the coroner's hands, his brawny arms, and his longish fingers she would embrace these bodies that had long been buried in the meantime, she would kiss and caress them, and they would know all about this. Several hundred graves across the country would be filled by her hot breath, and the loved ones of the deceased could only wonder: What sort of weather could account for flowers blossoming anew after having been dry for weeks? And what exceptional air current now covered the graves with a colourful mist? L. thought that not even she would be left without a gift, though she would have been unable to say just what that could be. It seemed that's all it took to specify that humble word, 'almost'. She would accept what physical union promised.

Sitting across from her, the man was meanwhile busy tending to more practical matters—namely, paying the bill. After downing their second bottle of wine, L. felt that her slight stupor had now arrived at the edge of inebriation. Now was the time to stop drinking, she knew full well, or else she would be useless. S. noticed this delicate turning point at once, and so he suggested that they leave. On reaching the street, she staggered slightly and had to grab hold of the man's arm. She turned anxious. He must think that she'd drunk out of fear, she thought with annoyance. Which was why she now cracked a bit of cheap wit, thus: 'I hope you're not taking me to your corpses, now.'

Her head cleared completely by the time they reached the coroner's flat. L. even thought back with surprise at her having taken the man's arm not long before. She felt calm and strong. A few days ago she'd still been following her chosen men with anguish! Had she gotten used to this dreamlike procession? She'd aged by years, she knew, although her lineaments gave away practically nothing of this. Perhaps only her expression had become sadder.

L. did not like the word 'sadness'. Invented by cunning cowards, no doubt. What cheap hypocrisy it all amounted to, she often thought, to mask our helplessness with 'sadness', which was ever at the ready!ow How How pitiful that we sweep our obvious bleakness under its convenient rug, and indeed sometimes with the barely concealed aim of beautifying it with emotional pain. 'Bitterness', now that was a tad more tolerable; for it stood more closely to how she would have characterized her own expression. This word was more fortunate also because it evoked in her the possible strategy of her resistance. At such times she felt that if only out of pride, she would not surrender herself to woe, to simpleminded, weary resignation but, rather, she'd become even more determined, more unmerciful and, if necessary, cruel.

Nonetheless—L. added to her line of thought at once—it seemed as if something really wasn't in order with her, as if she had no feelings! At times she suffered terribly at this thought, and on other occasions she even doubted whether this could cause her pain at all. Only from her bouts of despair did she suspect that she wasn't completely lost. These were the moments in which she wanted to learn how to feel. At such times she perhaps envied even the sad, though she was well aware that she sought to perceive a different sort of sadness in herself—maybe the sort a pregnant animal must feel on retreating to its lair so as to bring her little ones unto this world all alone. If she did have feelings, L. wavered at times, why then, they must resemble those of animals more than anything. One thing was certain: she thought of animals with more tenderness than she did of people. She'd long suspected that her defencelessness sprang from her accursed capacity to survive everything, to endure everything.

The coroner sat L. down in the living room while he went to the kitchen to make coffee. Clearly he didn't want their lovemaking to descend into the desire-less nestling of whimsical drunks. Though L. was now sober, she still had to be on guard against turning weak. This evening had cost her too much for her to put it at the mercy of such uncertainty. She'd already learnt that particular art of vigilant balancing in which guaranteeing external conditions was at least as important as the 'task' that would later fall to her.

They were ridiculous, thought L., the extemporizers, the improvisers who hide their lack of lovemaking finesse behind the guise of spontaneity. She saw in them bungling amateurs worthy of pity— people who couldn't get it through their heads that it was the man's responsibility to plan the body-celebration ritual. He who is unwilling to take this exciting detour would be wiser to stick with his tried and tested solitary pleasure; for the woman's capacity to give carnal pleasure must be seduced, it must be heaped with bliss until it reaches the point where it can't receive more pleasure unto itself. The man's domination over the woman lasts until that moment; that is the limit of the authority of the master of ceremonies, the guiding force he has long been identified with, unfortunately enough. But then the roles change. In these minutes the man can experience what it means if the satisfied woman continues the lovemaking; for all the carnal pleasure that until now had contorted the woman's face would now snap his spine, for the woman's pleasure would come descending down upon him. Of course, most men watch with envy as a woman turns pale again and again from bliss, and they manage to forget this only if on occasion their envy is razed by an unexpected orgasm, which the women respond to by plummeting even deeper. Yes, it is this repeatedly doubled pleasure that demarcates the borders between man and woman. He must already have sensed something of this, but—L. thought again—without his supporting ritual all this would become nothing but a pitiful act of copulation.

And so he would bring the girl back in order with coffee, fresh air and conversation—they had plenty of time until dawn, after all. By no means could he allow himself to wink at the other's inebriation and loss of self-control. He had another sort of semiconscious state in the works for her. 'Don't you want some music?' L. wanted silence, unadulterated wordlessness, which would not disturb her preparation. She was virtually certain that the semiconscious rapture she'd experienced that morning, which had squeezed that certain hotness out of her for the first time, would now be absent. And yet she smiled. The man turned towards her with a look of suspicion. 'Are you laughing at me? You're right. Soon I'll have myself believing that we're not even made for each other even for the length of an embrace, though I always did hold all the blustering people do about whether they're made for each other or not made for each other to be the most commonplace error imaginable.' L. broke into another smile. 'You're wrong! You don't even suspect how much we're made for each other.'

'Yes,' thought L., now only to herself, 'we are made for each other. You want my body and I want your corpses, those I see before your face, those I project onto your eyes, those I hide among the hairs on your muscular arms, those I stick to your delicate and yet somehow rough fingers. For I can get really close to them only by being with you. You can call me calculating and perverse, and maybe you're right.' L. drank down her coffee in slow sips. She felt fresh and relaxed. Only now did she become fully aware that it didn't take much on her part to dominate over men—though 'dominate' seemed too strong a word, for all she really did was wait for the chosen individual to show himself. She really couldn't help it that during this time, she imperceptibly became stronger than the other. The man she'd met this morning had been an exception, although their time together—even beyond the silence they'd shared in the garden of that roadside restaurant—had been restricted almost completely to sexual contact, and she might have arranged things differently.

Were they afraid of her? Or should she perhaps seek the cause elsewhere? For example, in the fact that while the men she met were clearly trying to acquire her by all means, she waited with cold curiosity to see when the other would lose his patience. Yes, they couldn't endure her stubborn silence. They get flustered on sensing in her the embitterment without complaints, and with anxious glances they size her up, for what they thought was easy prey cunningly eludes them. And they get scared if they chance to see the bitter lines that appear unexpectedly at the corners of her mouth, the self-ironic *it's all the same* pursing of the lips, and the eyes that adhere all this and burn the question into their faces: 'Well, what are you looking for here at my place? I brought you with me, but do you know why you came?' Gradually she began to understand why these gentlemen become ever more irresolute with time, which oppresses them right up until she gives them the secret signal. And while the wrangling goes on, she can access how discomfiting it is for the other if she were to judge him unsuitable for intimacy. It is the man's sexual desire that is subordinated to her dispassion. That is why it is possible that while she fine-tunes the evening to suit the details she planned out in advance, the men meanwhile increasingly lose their self-respect, only so that that can proudly say that they acquired these goods, too. This would by all means have come to pass. Or did she get the upper hand because her so far desireless will sees them merely as tools? L. neither held herself to be depraved for such a calculating approach, and nor was she filled with pride for doing the same thing as most men.

The coroner was not afraid of her, no, he would simply give up on her, admitting that this time, he'd miscalculated. No doubt he'd solved other fixes before, calming the other with a smile and by saying that it's not necessary to apologize, not even he thought it seriously. Or perhaps he saw her merely as a clinical case. Which is why he is still waiting patiently and isn't fidgeting over the increasingly uncomfortable silence. After all, understanding is part and parcel of his profession; he can hold his desires in check without exertion, for he knows that the patient will open up before him eventually, after all. But it must have been L. who'd dispelled his doubts of just before. He must have been preparing in quiet excitement, using the longer than planned preliminary intermission for sensual reinforcement!

L. did not want to abuse her privileges, for even until now she'd duly employed the man's commiseration, which he'd camouflaged as calm. True, he would have hated her, had she alluded even vaguely to his condition—namely, to the fact that he was maintaining a discreet silence, explaining with his inborn egoism that which he aims to achieve efficiently indeed, with the least possible complications. Nor would she deprive him of this.

The coroner went over to the bedroom and adjusted the bed. On the nightstand was a half-burnt candle, which he lit, because for some reason he sensed that the girl would prefer semidarkness. Only then did L. follow him in. She undressed and lay down on the bed.

The man sat at the end of the bed. He began by caressing the girl's feet. His fingers slid softly along the breathing, olive-hued velvet of her skin. He took care not to greedily hasten his motions, for he was still mapping the territory to be explored. He could get to know this girl only slowly, circumspectly. But it was precisely this consideration that led him to the ankles, the calves! It was in these reaches that he wanted to put his senses to the test: were they what they used to be, or had they weakened to the point where they, too, were inclined to cheap thrills? L.'s taut skin excited him. Decades of experience had told him that this was the ticket to beauty's dominion; for if a woman's skin left him cold, why then, everything was in vain. True, in the first stage of getting acquainted the unavoidable task of exciting the other also fell to him, but not even he could perform miracles.

L.'s skin surpassed all expectations. The man was proud that he didn't rush things—in vain, though, for he'd always insisted that as long as he paid heed to his instincts, he'd get what he wanted; and he could feel free to trust everyday logic to clarify less dangerous questions; as for example was now the case, for it seemed fairly reasonable that after examining the legs, he would become acquainted with the arms and the hands. To fall straightaway to kissing the breasts or, God forbid, the pudenda, would in his estimation have been an unforgivable error. It would have been hardly repairable; for the woman had to wait for that celebration until those reaches of her body demanded it themselves. Otherwise it would not have been the hardened nipples that long to be bathed by the fluids of his mouth, but the woman would *think* that this kiss should feel good, and that can only result in failure. The other cannot in any case figure out when pleasure has intensified to this point, for the woman's body will be grateful only if caught unawares.

The man now nestled up against the girl's upper body, but without so much as touching her belly or her hips. He could attend only to the arms and hands. He took the girl's long, almost scrawny arm and raised it to his mouth. This arm merited more than a simple kiss, he thought; were he to clamp his mouth down upon this appendage reminiscent of a bird feather with a delicate paddle at the end, he would spoil his own growing sensation that seemed increasingly like devotion. His lips would get no closer than a hair's width to the skin of her hand, just close enough to direct his kiss into the pores of her skin. His self-restraint would of course come with a reward: the fragrance of the arm would pour over his face, and he'd be hard put to drink it down. Were his lips tight against the skin, he would feel nothing of this.

But the girl's hands had another sort of celebration in store for him as well. It would be pointless to slide the hand towards the almost unapproachable horizon of beauty by means of secret techniques. The hands can only be seduced; presenting them with the spectacle of beauty in and of itself is a clever but fruitless venture. Specialists know full well that the only possible solution lies in shrewdly misleading the hands; what is more, by convincing them that their true beauty is revealed in its competent caressing of another's body. And so they must be stimulated with glances, kisses and caresses until they feel it practically burdensome. When this moment arrives, we discreetly remind the hands that they can escape their fix only through our bodies. At this time we also offer them a chance to give further evidence of their beauty. The man was thus well aware of the limits of beauty in and of itself, and desired it only until it began endangering his efforts. This was yet another reason he sensed that the time had come for more concrete pleasures.

Above all, he had to find the most sensitive zone on the girl's body. Only laymen can believe that this is easily discovered. Of course, those who only scratch the surface of things can avoid exploration without a guilty conscience, for in most cases not even the women know where on their bodies they would surrender themselves above all. To himself he called these places the inexhaustible wellsprings of pleasure, of which only the always alert and the incessantly seeking can drink. In the course of more fortunate rendezvous that most exciting task fell to him, to unearth his own treasure with the other's complicity. It was in these moments that he felt capable of penetrating the woman's body. If his partner were to prove insensible for a longer time, he would be compelled to reward the efforts of his own fingers—namely, by projecting his senses, like some experienced morphine addict, into the other's body.

If, for example, he ran his fingers along a pudenda, and the woman reacted almost with indifference, he would then repeat the motion, but now he felt as if he'd caressed his own member, although he hadn't even touched it. True, projecting his sensuality into the other's body was something he handled with utter care, for otherwise the method could have degenerated into self-gratification, which he would have been loathe to let happen. When sometimes he did turn to this forgivable method, he invariably noticed that the other's body sensed his roguery, and it seemed as if the floodgates gradually opened before his own sensuality. Never did he abandon such troublesome experimentation, no matter how exhausted the twofold sensations made him; for he knew that if he kept patiently playing this game, the other would not be ungrateful.

Moreover, he had to consider the undeniable fact that in the case of certain girls and women, this zone of sensitivity ran not on the surface of the skin, but somewhere else. Say, underneath the skin. Lovers of questionable talent, that's who they were. They'd earned themselves this singular assessment by being rather capricious in the art of sensuality; for on some nights their skin seems to turn into a sieve, it being practically impossible to differentiate between inside and outside. At such times they are wild, daring, and insatiable. But then, at the sounding of some unexpected alarm or in consequence of inexplicable causes, they close up, locking the capillaries of their delicate skin tightly indeed; at such times they receive their lover's fingers and kisses with a numb indifference. The most hopeless cases, he thought, were those in which he had to speculate on investigating these oversensitive, defenceless territories. But he turned towards this only in exceptional circumstances.

The man now slid his palm onto the girl's abdomen, as if wanting only to map out her viscera. After a little while his fingers sensed the girl's belly start to billow. Yes, this was the point from which he could set off, from where he could proceed to search out those certain wellsprings. But first he must put a brake on this inner dancing of the girl's body. He would see to it that after this lulling, the pans of blood would fill up once again, that the muscles would stretch tight anew; for it is in the irregular billowing rhythm of excitement and slackening that the body can really get to know itself. True, there is the risk that excitement maintained for too long will unexpectedly become dullness. This explains the need for rest breaks. If, afterwards, he touches the body again, no longer will it flee to indifference, but having gained strength, will be capable of receiving newer pleasures. It is precisely the pauses that guarantee the continuity of pleasure, for the cells retain the caresses that occurred before each break. Nor should one forget that with this slowness, a space emerges between the two bodies that fuses them with an elemental force greater than even that of the wildest embraces. We can call this space the materialized field of eroticism, into which we submerge in the moments of timelessness so that our passion, which seems to be waning, can flare up anew.

The time had now come to kiss her breasts. For some reason he thought this was the girl's most sensitive point. But, like some trickster, he focused on but one of the nipples, taking it into his mouth, while leaving the other on its own; for he figured that the incomplete excitement might serve to jostle the girl's sensations. Like an evil magician after a victim has fallen into his hands, he wanted to divide the body into pieces. But before the breasts, the loins, and the thighs might forever go their separate ways, with a well-placed kiss or bite he would put the body parts back together again. And yet it wouldn't be him doing so, after all—it would be the carnal pleasure erupting in the girl, diffusing through her. Yes, that is when the girl would suddenly realize that her body is a knot covered by but one sensory nerve cell! Only in the moment of heaving after orgasm would she really feel that the rapture has dried in fine layers on her bones, her muscles.

Only when they approached her face did L. notice the man's hands. It was this chance occurrence that undid the coroner's magic; for when he raised his hands towards the girl's face, L.'s wide open, motionless eyes froze in terror. At this moment she understood fully what sort of fingers had been caressing her until now. A contorted grimace appeared on her face. Her lineaments stretched tight, as if she were concerned only that an invisible hand would crush her at any moment. The whole thing lasted maybe a few seconds. L. then suddenly broke out laughing. At first the man believed this was the sound of her pleasure about to erupt, but when L. now seized his hands and pulled them to her eyes, he could no longer delude himself.

L. dug her nails into the man's hands; that is how she sought to hold back her vertigo. Images passed before her, by turns with unendurable slowness or in impossible-to-follow flashes. Then she saw herself lying on the table in the autopsy room. She must have been there for some time already when S. appeared above her, poised to commence the procedure. He was just looking at his scalpel when L. grabbed his arm and screamed, 'No, not me! Don't you see I'm alive?' But S. raised the scalpel and cut into the region above her heart.

The coroner freed his hands and tried calming down the girl. 'Hey there, everything's all right, it'll be over soon!' That is when a second vision, which comprised a single freeze-frame, caught L. unawares. She saw the coroner's hand caressing the eyelid of an old man. It seemed to her that S. sought to find, somewhere around that forever closed eye, that which not long before had signified the old man's life.

This image calmed her. She pulled the coroner's hands to her mouth and kissed the fingers all over. L. thought to herself that the invisible pores, the fine cracks in the skin, had filled up with the molecules of this material that can never be known, that they'd become soaked through with the oscillations of the finest substance there is. She knew she was imagining things, that it was all madness; for even if she sniffed corpses through and through, and embraced them, too, not even then could she catch red-handed that certain something called 'death'. And still she couldn't shake her presumption. She was, in any case, practically certain that the coroner's hand had preserved some memory of that which death had left behind— for the living.

Just before, S. had thought he'd interrupt the lovemaking. But the girl's unexpected calm convinced him of the opposite. Yes, he thought, now was the time to kiss her other breast. With that, perhaps he could cajole her back to the simple pleasure of it all. It seemed that he could not pass through all the stations of sensuality with her, for she was among those lovers of questionable talent.

L.'s body contracted with fear as soon as the man began kissing her. Not long ago, she recalled, she'd pressed her own fingers into the sliced up brain of a man she didn't know. Now she wondered: Had she touched not only dead nerve cells on that day, but all the desires and bitterness, too, that the man had amassed in his life? How deceptive nature is! When one day she were to wind up on the autopsy table, not a single doctor would be able to discover the waves of fear that had passed through her brain a moment before. Her brain would be sliced up, too, but it would not occur to a single coroner that where they suspect a blockage, they would in fact have hit upon the path of a onetime fear that had gathered into a convoluted knot!

The coroner was reassured to see that his kisses now did not trouble the girl. He sensed that, for the first time on this night, L.'s body was now opening up. He did not pass up this unexpected opportunity.

No, L. did not reject him, but as she received the man into herself in an almost semiconscious state, she noticed strangers sneaking into the bedroom. So they had come, after all. The figures were blurred. She couldn't make out the face of a single one, and still she was certain that they were smiling. For some reason she thought they were preparing to dance. And, in fact, first they marched past her in pairs, and then, at a secret signal from the first pair, they commenced their ball. The dancers changed partners with almost every move. L. stared fixedly upon this almost impossible-to-follow series of images. So the coroner's deceased had visited her, so as to tell her, through their dancing, how easy it was to be dead.

At first L. thought they were dancing so merrily because they no longer needed to be alive. Only after a few seconds did she realize the real reason: these strangers had intended their dance to serve as a reminder. As if they'd only whispered that it wasn't only death, but also life, that need not be feared. That is when she heard the coroner, as a rattling howl erupted from his throat. No sooner did the man's perspiring body now sink heavily onto her breasts than the dancing figures disappeared.

They must have been lying next to each other for a good long while. L. thought, *I must leave his place now, no matter how exhausted I am.* The man protested in vain. L. got dressed, and ordered a taxi. They went down to the street together. They didn't even have time left to talk, really, for the cab arrived within minutes.

6

That night L. stirred awake several times. In her dreams she saw one of the coroner's deceased specimens knocking again and again at her door, but every time she went out to open the door, the visitor vanished. The last time she woke up, the darkness dissolved into time with excruciating slowness. *Only an hour more to endure*, thought L., *and then dawn will come.* All the same, she got out of bed and went to the door to check the security lock. She had to check, even though she knew she'd turned it several times on getting home. When she lay back down, the dream image unexpectedly sharpened in the darkness under the blanket. The corpse was standing in front of the door. L. sprang up, ran out to the door and opened it wide. She would curse and scream, she decided, if the vision haunted her again. She took a pullover off the coat hanger fixed to the wall and draped it over herself. So surprised was she by her own resolve that it was this, rather than her capricious visitor, that transfixed her in the moments before sleep when, after a few minutes, she got cold, closed the door and went back to bed.

When L. awoke, dazed, in the late morning, she knew that her experimentations had reached a turning point. 'I do not know my body,' came a voice from somewhere inside of her, and it seemed to her a woeful message from her loins. In fact she'd known about this since the lovemaking in hotel room 627. On that morning she'd felt that an extremely narrow conduit opened up along her spine, one that channelled carnal pleasure into a single flow, so as to become a distant memory after an explosive thrust. The rendezvous with the coroner had deceived her. Perhaps it would have been best, after all, if it hadn't been him she'd chosen on the previous night, for his deceased had held her all too much in their grip.

She had to decide. Either she would sacrifice herself to vengeance, and would continue observing 'suitable individuals' with the cool calm of an outsider, knowing that melancholy was the price of keeping her vow, or else she would give up this rather dubious form of revenge, and instead face her own desolation. True, it was precisely her constrained acceptance and passive possession of a different body every night that had helped her achieve this bitter recognition, which she would hardly have been capable of from the start. But now she understood that if she held firmly to her plan, it would consume her also, for her vile detachment could not go unpunished. If her undertaking were still to be accompanied by the memory of that certain rape, then she would have failed irreparably. Never would she have thought that one day she would be subjugated by a passion even stronger than the loathing she'd nurtured towards men—namely, the desire for physical satisfaction. Perhaps this was why she'd yearned for some time now to be in the inscrutable unconscious state of animals, for that strength by which they can maintain an uncertain link to consciousness all the same, and which renders every movement of theirs so seemingly perfect.

Had she pursued bodies so boldly even up to now because she had nothing to lose? Was it not on men, but on herself, that she'd wanted to wreak vengeance? They'd looked upon her at most as a strange bird, one who shares her envied splendour with two hands. Had she come to scorn her body, which others thought beautiful, because it had scandalously deceived her and slyly outwitted her? She'd laid out the warm jewel of her flesh before so many men, after all, but had she been able to steal ecstasy for herself? No. Failure only extends the unmeasurable distance between self-loathing and pride; the more time passes, the more relentlessly, it seems. The more defeats she amassed, the more self-assured she could be in playing the role of illusionist, one who no longer even knows what she herself seeks to make disappear from what. As the champion of nuances she let men loose upon herself, believing that one day she, the observer, could be the high priestess of sensuality. But the more she looked down upon them, the more implacably she came to hate her own role.

Smugly she drew borders around herself that no one could transgress. She would have cut off her own hand before having to admit that she herself was in need of help. To acknowledge this would have been more shameful than even her melancholy. But had this bleakness not called into question from the start the success of her experimentations; for how could a cripple expect to humiliate another? Had it not only been she who'd imagined that she could degrade the 'suitable individuals' by turning them into her tools? That which until now had seemed to be hypocrisy and calculation was now exposed as a demonstrable error. Yes, she'd divided her year not into days but into men. Into pitiful embraces. Instances of lovemaking that grew more tolerable as the body count increased. Caresses that approached a 'solution'. Smells and fragrances that could be distinguished precisely. Impulses that grew stronger or weaker by turns. Classifiable, hierarchical passions. But from now on she could not rely on the rather dubious ruling of a clear-sighted judge who exposes the sometimes blatant, sometimes underhanded planning; for she would have called them to account for that which she, too, desired.

And yet her gravest offence was, as she saw it, that out of pride she did not accept the role of the despised woman. Of course emotional-sensual Machiavellianism thwarted her in this just the same as did that certain frigidity which troubled men, for they either fear that the illness is contagious or else they secretly discern in it a negative assessment of their masculinity. If she had been able to take her due, then she would not have collected merely memories of the bodies, but her hushed loins would safeguard the calm that might be called bliss. She would keep lying to herself as long as she had to keep stitching together the shreds of pleasure amassed from these experiences in her consciousness.

She knew full well that neither cleverness nor indeed the most daring intelligence would help her develop the capacity to experience bliss. She might even use formulas to trace the path that links the start and finish of desire, that searing-hot straight line that prepares its explosion in the flow of cellular fusion and in the tense rhythm of racing blood cells. But even then, the cold onlooker, the wretched observer, would remain; for the hidden centre in her body's depths, this force that could be moved without it moving at all, would exile her from its own dominion. For now she would have to make do with her new resolve; namely, that from now on she could not be satisfied with simply being together with men. She would pick men who know their stuff, for that which she herself and her high-handed nature had denied her, she could acquire only from masterful lovers. No, she had no desire to spend the rest of her life affectedly playing the vengeful role of the unsatisfied woman. She would reject the fertile melancholy of resignation, the unwavering confidence of those who live from their defeats.

In recent days she had at least gotten to the point where she no longer feared human bodies. The experimental subjects, whom it would be fairer from now on to characterize as potential benefactors, could not even have suspected what she was hiding behind her seemingly experience-borne confidence. The men's desire being as easy as it was to rouse, this trick cost L. little exertion. Until now she'd armed herself with indifference, which had protected her even in the most vulnerable situations, but from now on it counted as self-deception; for anyone who arranges their affairs so nastily must fail. She would travel somewhere, L. decided, for perhaps a foreign environment would have a beneficial effect on her increasingly tired body.

L. packed underwear, warm clothes and toiletries into a small travel bag, then gathered up what money she'd saved and headed off. At the railway station she randomly bought a ticket for the first train scheduled to depart, figuring she'd leave things to chance; and anyway, in this case the last stop was her intended destination. After quite a bit of looking, she found an empty compartment, and there she sat down. In this hour she would not gladly have shared her solitude even with silent travellers. She would have found it difficult to wipe the involuntary glances of sympathy from her face, sensing that her own expression was that sad. Now she could not cheat, she could not feed herself the lie that was relentlessness, which amounted to massive unhappiness. No, she was no exception, so L. thought, looking out the window; she, too, would have to tie a separate peace with sadness, ensuring a quiet place within herself. And yet she set a strict condition for her compromise, which could have counted as a failure: that not even in the most muddled circumstances could sadness yank her before it as a shield.

The express train made its first stop at least an hour after heading off. L. happened to be watching the departing passengers and a young man slid open the compartment door and asked, in a deep, somewhat raspy voice if he could take a seat. She nodded, whereupon the other sat down opposite her, by the window, and began reading a half-crumpled newspaper. At the same time, the train started off anew. The man was maybe two or three years older than

L. His short-clipped, dark hair was combed to the side, half covering his boldly jutting forehead, which stood in sharp contrast to his longish face and sunken cheeks. Had he not retreated behind his newspaper, it probably would have been easier to further scrutinize that nervous glitter which L. had noticed in his eyes when he'd first slid open the compartment door. His thinness also conveyed disquiet, as if he'd raised the newspaper in front of him to conceal this fact.

Minutes earlier it wouldn't have occurred to L. that the man's presence might have disturbed her peace, but as time passed she had to admit that for a while now, her thoughts had been focusing on this stranger. Instinctively she glanced at those hands holding the newspaper. She was simply curious to see what he was reading, but since the man had buried himself unsuspectingly behind the paper, L. could persist without risk in her spying. His long, almost femininely thin fingers were curled slightly as they gripped the pages. She could not decide whether these bony branches, which resembled sharply cut skewers, were either exclamation marks of over-refinement, or the elongated claws of a boldly plundering predator. For some reason she felt the latter to be true. If she were now genuinely courageous, without batting an eyelid she would touch one of these hands, not bothering about the consequences. If only she could at least see his face, she would set her mind more calmly on this gesture whose outcome was so uncertain! Why could she not assume the detested role of the rejected woman for once? Was she so at the mercy of her pathological pride? She could easily acknowledge her audaciousness before the man if he were to react with aversion and, perhaps, shock. For example, with barely dis-guised mockery she could apologize. 'I'm really sorry, I lost my head. I promise to keep a better eye on my misbehaving hands from now on.' After assessing the irksome and less unpleasant contingencies of possible fiascos, she began getting acquainted with the more advantageous aspects of her imagined provoking move.

If she'd sized up the man correctly on the basis of his hands, then she had a quiet predator on her hands, one who happened into her compartment perhaps not exactly by chance. It was possible that he'd established his beachhead behind the newspaper pages, and when the time seemed right he would commence his attack from here, for he now knew more about her than she could imagine. Maybe those unbridled hands of his weren't towering before her so innocently, after all? But in that case, he would receive her touch in the most natural way possible, while his eyes would flare up with desire, which until now had worn the guise of indifference, disinterest. Indeed, he would wonder at her audacity for having taken the risk of initiating contact. Perhaps she'd already grown weary of unequal encounters, which only served to insidiously weaken her senses. No, she could not suppress her inborn battle-ready instincts with this dangerous comfort for long, which was why her body would become searing hot the moment she touched him.

The artificial heightening of desire has its own risks. In slyly delaying passion when bequeathed with it, we toil to live out our impulses even more intensely. But only the most talented are really capable of this. They are the ones who stand guard alertly over passion as it tries constantly to run wild, while unsuspecting novices, while endeavouring to perform feats of skill, are dumbstruck to realize that the force which had seemed unquenchable only a moment before has given them a rebuff. This is all the more true in the case of cowardly inaction; postponed, secure embraces cannot compensate for passed-up opportunities offered up by rare moments no matter how impossible it may seem to carry them out.

L. felt with her loins that she would be swept away by the same waves of carnal pleasure she'd once experienced, were she able to make love immediately. It wouldn't bother her even if they were surprised by the conductor stepping into their compartment to ask for their tickets, nor, for that matter, if he were then to call the police at the next station. 'Why couldn't I wait, officer? It would be interesting for me to tell the story of my incurable nymphomania, but you just go ahead and be content with charging me with public indecency.' In vain did she understand that the opportunity for coolly poised, seemingly safe flirting had run out, L. was incapable of touching the man's hand. But by now it was clear to her that she could believe only in passion free of thought, in the inscrutable intelligence of bodies clutching each other.

L. would have misread her situation, had she thought of her feeling of want as akin to emptiness, though there were moments when the two seemed related. The pressure on the nape of her neck had, for example, threatened her with the same collapse as now, when she realized that for years it had been her cheating which had stopped her from coming to pieces. A well-ordered assemblage of healthy cells and bodily tissues only maintained an illusion or, rather, the possibility of concealing our decay from others. We imagine that our final breakdown will occur only once our bodies have given up on us, when our hearts stop. We can be grateful to the matter that makes up our bodies for storing away our lies for decades, a circumstance that one day, given a favourable alignment of the stars, it might even turn to our advantage.

Yet another reason L. could not fill this absence with emptiness was because her present condition had left her feeling satiated, and though thinking this made no sense, she held to the notion all the same. We really can have experience of those things we do not have at our disposal, she thought. Indeed, desire concentrates that particular knowledge which we will demolish in the act.

L. didn't even notice when they reached the last stop. She must have been sitting in the compartment alone for some time already when the conductor stepped in and told her the train wasn't going any further. So then, while she'd been pondering her uncertain plans, the man had vanished from before her very eyes. She took up her bag and got off the train. The silly idea of trying her luck in a small town filled her, if subtly, with a sort of cheer. Above all, she needed a place to stay for the night, she thought while heading for the taxi stand. L. found a free cab, and as usual, she got in the back seat. The cabbie recommended an inexpensive, lowbrow motel right away. L. began by inquiring whether there was by chance a room number 627 to be had. The pockmarked, spectacled clerk stretched out his arms and said with a smile that they had just ten rooms in all, so he could at most give her room number 7. L. nodded. She went upstairs and stretched out on the bed.

It was early evening by the time she staggered to her feet. Well then, she thought, let us see what night in the provinces holds in store. While getting dressed, the man on the train crossed her mind. How foolish she'd been not to have struck up a conversation with him. Had she been braver, then this evening she could have met with him—assuming, of course, that he lived in this town at all. Oh, well—L. stood before the mirror to check her face one more time— why couldn't she cross paths with an even more exciting gentleman? If she didn't trust in chance, she might as well not leave at all.

The motel was close to the downtown. After a short walk, L. found herself on the small town's narrow, pedestrian thoroughfares. All at once she heard snatches of music from a distance. She turned into the side street that led towards its source—a slightly ascending alley of sorts—and quickened her steps. She'd gone maybe a hundred yards when she found herself in front of a dimly lit venue of night-time entertainment. L. stepped into the place, which was crowded indeed, and seemed to have been a restaurant not so long before: a local gem of the socialist catering industry. The row of tables arranged in rectangular form; the thin rug, tattered in places, that covered the flagstone; the lack of a bar—it all added up. At the far end of the room stood a raised platform that had clearly been hurriedly assembled and which resembled a stage: on it played a band, much to the satisfaction of the already somewhat besotted crowd. L. felt sure she wouldn't find a free table when a listless waiter stepped up to her and led her to the table beside the band. She ordered a screwdriver.

The band announced it would now play its last song before a break: 'Where Has Summer Gone, Where Lost Love?' Two tipsy men stood from their tables and led their ageing women towards the stage, on which they began to dance. Perhaps they'd been waiting all night for this song. The couples embraced, and surrendered themselves to the sweet woeful spirit of this song. Yes, this was their time to shine. Beauty and love, which they'd believed to have been lost for ever, had found them once again. In such moments what did it matter that they'd become fat, wrinkled, weary? The melody undid their resignation and drew emotion on to their alcohol-flushed, perspiring faces. (We can't begin to imagine how much beauty mawkish music coaxes out of people!) Having finished this famous song, the music makers took their break. They put down their instruments and sat down at a table beside the stage, where their shots of cheap cognac were already awaiting them.

A man of around forty, with slightly greying hair, stepped over to L.'s table. With drunken determination he asked if she would join him for the next dance. 'No need to be scared of me. I'm not what I once was. And besides, the boys'—he pointed towards the tippling music makers—'prefer slow songs.' L. accepted the invitation and the man walked off in satisfaction. Why shouldn't she dance with this fellow? She gave a little laugh, and took a gulp of her screwdriver. Maybe this tipsy tom would be the 'suitable individual' of the night?

The band got back to playing—kicking things off with a popular tune that was a favourite of such venues as this, a deservedly successful song that began, *Pearl, my dear pearl* . . . L. waited curiously: Would the man indeed return? Late, but looking a bit less drunk, the man soon arrived. 'Shall we go, then?' With a laugh he extended a hand to L. and led her among the dancers. 'Didn't I say these artistes prefer slow songs?' Putting a hand around L.'s waist, he gave another laugh. They were somewhere towards the end of the present song when, above the heads of the other dancers, L. noticed the man she'd shared the train compartment with. He was sitting at a table by the door, sipping a shot of something or other. In her excitement, L. pressed up close to her partner, who must have thought that this unexpected affection was addressed to him. But when the song ended, L. promptly thanked the man for the dance and went back to her table.

She had to figure something out quickly, she knew, or else this now familiar stranger would disappear again. Nervously L. ordered another screwdriver. Perhaps it would be best if she went right over and introduced herself. She could always play the part of the girl who, just about to leave the bar, sees the man she spent a few hours with, as it were, during the day. Or she could confront him with the facts—say, by sitting down beside him and without so much as an introduction, giving an account of the thoughts that had crossed her mind as they rode together in the compartment of that train. Without a word she could settle down beside him and announce that on the basis of a bit of advance research, she did indeed have the right for this intrusive means of introduction. Were he to rebuff her, she could still count on the man she'd just danced with, who looked as if he hadn't been offended in the least by her unexpected retreat. L. signalled to the waiter, told him she was going over to sit down at the table by the door and then, like someone who had nothing to lose, headed off towards the man.

L. sat down with such self-evidence that it seemed this place had been saved for her alone. The man said only that he'd been waiting for her. To L. this scene was like a dream she'd once experienced but that she only now understood. It was as if she'd been sitting here for months already, waiting for the other to say something to her, to tell her why and to what end they were together. But the man, evidently content with his role, kept silent. The silence didn't oppress L. at all, no, she would have grown anxious only if the other had forced her to go explaining things. Not so long ago at all she'd imagined this very episode of becoming acquainted with someone, when two bodies, two memories, two desires approach each other without words and sentences. Perhaps she'd never been so dependent on another. She saw in him help arriving at the last moment, without which she must fail once and for all. L. was certain that at a promising time he would stand up and lead her out of the bar.

L. thought of the last few nights; of the hatred that had filled her so relentlessly. Perhaps her aversion hadn't even been towards the chosen individuals but, rather, masculinity itself, which three years earlier had decided her fate. True, she'd voluntarily insisted on reliving the trauma again and again, on repeatedly humiliating herself and the other, too. In working out her plan she could hardly have anticipated that expectation which the act committed against her made of her. It wasn't the onetime perpetrator L. had to forgive, but herself, for being part of the aggression; for peace can be ours not by punishing our foes, but by accepting the crime that by now exists independently of the perpetrator. In allowing ourselves to be overcome by vengeance we put ourselves at the mercy of forces even more insidious than our foe's original depravity. Improvised wickedness can never be as dangerous as methodically planned and executed revenge. In the case of the latter, we set a trap for our own credulity, for the more refined tools with which we want to avenge wrongs that befall us, the more hopelessly we sink into hatred, which in turn tears us definitively away from ourselves. L. thought she could avenge her rape. From night to night she observed the bodies that crossed her path. Now as an outsider, again and again she evoked the memory, which felt impossible to process, so that one day she would come to understand: *on that night* she was not yet prepared to be humiliated. Her three years of torment, however, not only illuminated the meaning of her having been led astray necessarily (so it now seemed), but also made clear that the memory of the pain could be erased only by an even stronger, more relentless pain. It was her body that led her back to men, whom she no longer called the objects of her revenge.

This realization must have accounted for her present calm. Had she crossed paths with this man earlier, no doubt she would have wanted to subjugate him as well. The man sitting across from her— so thought L., raising the glass to her lips—no doubt saw only chance in this wordless means of getting to know one another. But L. was not fooled; she was convinced that her fate had arranged for this meeting. She looked at the man's hands. This time the long, thin fingers were stretched out straight, resting on the table, as if waiting only for L.'s hands to approach. She knew that even without touching them she would be able to caress these seemingly warm appendages of bone and skin that gathered together the now still disciplined desire in ten separate corridors. The longer she'd delay the first touch, the more beauty and strength would accumulate in them. Their waiting seemed, to her, like that of two animals measuring each other up through sniffs. But her five senses were sharpened in these moments by a sense even more refined than that of smell, a sense that might even be called instinct, the presentiment that through each other's bodies they might recognize each other.

The man slid his hands off the table, maybe into his lap, maybe his thighs; L. in any case could not decide. All she sensed was that they would be leaving soon. The man then asked her if she'd have another drink, but since she shook her head, he called over the waiter and paid. They stood up at once, at which both broke into a smile.

L. would have liked for them to go to the motel. Perhaps because of the memory of that certain room number 627, or maybe because she didn't want to come into contact with the man's personal history. Not that she was afraid of this past, but she did consider it preferable if they could spend the night at her place, as it were. Wordlessly they walked beside each other, as if completely certain they would arrive at the right place. All at once they found themselves standing in front of the motel; L. had no idea how they'd ended up here. Even if she'd been looking for it, she wouldn't have found her way any faster to this building, which she now saw for the second time in her life. In this coincidence that coincided with her earlier wish, she saw the guiding hand of someone or something, and so she asked the man if he'd come up to her room. She had to put this needless question to him even if it meant the end of their time together. But the man took her arm and led her into the motel lobby, where he, too, checked in.

L. didn't dare look at the man, who was already lying naked beside her, even though she knew he was watching her. Now she did not feel shame, though the man's eyes were practically scorching her skin. They were lying here beside each other on the bed much as a body cut in half, she thought, a body that a benevolent spirit would soon join together again. They were continuing the wordless conversation they'd begun in the bar, but that now they were naked. No longer was the man watching L.; he'd relinquished the advantages that come from watching.

L. wanted to discover the man like the blind do an unfamiliar place. But no. For now she could not even touch him or smell him, for to do that would be to transcend the mutually demarcated border and would perhaps prompt them to hurry. She had to wait patiently, until the nakedness lying within a foot of her would slowly descend upon her body. It was as if invisible bridges spanned the space between them, only so the strength freed up from the man's body could find its way more easily to her. From her gradually intensifying excitement she would know when her pores had filled up with these foreign waves.

After a while, unfamiliar currents spread through her. Now she could perhaps draw closer to the man and sniff. She had to lean towards those places, she knew, where she could least expect to encounter smells, and then perhaps she'd be capable of distinguishing various scents. A man's underarm could give off an odour so strong as to suppress and practically obliterate the other, seemingly insignificant scents. Eyes closed, L. sat up in bed. She curved her upper body above the man until she smelt the first foreign scent. The lower she brought her face, the more she felt that the space around the man's body was like a fountain that spurts forth not water but scents, in increasingly strong jets.

L. now chose a point at which to try distinguishing between intermingled scents. She judged the hand to be the most suitable territory. She managed to forget the scents she'd just experienced, for an entirely fresh current of smell now filled her nose. She was virtually certain that she was smelling drops of sweat that had flowed over the back of his hand, which were less salty than those on the underarm, which, if she now touched it with her tongue, would have a sweet-and-sour flavour. She broke the man's desire down into flavours, scents and unnameable aromas, as if she merely wanted to eat a plate of food. Still she held her face from the erogenous zones, for she would have felt it too simple to confront ready-made facts. Besides, she couldn't really trust in her tired nose, for it must have led her astray for a while now, for how could she be certain that the sweet-and-sour, slightly salty scent that hit her just before was in fact issuing from the back of this hand? Perhaps she was simply imagining it in place of an almost dubiously penetrating smell that had set off earlier from the man's loins, only to settle here, on this island with five peninsulas.

The sensations she collected from the man's body seemed to L. to be sufficient handholds so that now she might even accept the dangers that accompany touching. Her initiative was risky, she knew, for the man might misunderstand her gesture, seeing in it an invitation of sorts, and then it would be more difficult for them to avoid that which she wished by all means to delay. Her eyes stayed shut. Tapping her way, as if she were really blind, she found the territories on the man's face under his eyes. Then she carefully slid her fingers upward, counting on her patient lover to perhaps keep his eyes open. But, seconds later, she happened upon the eyelids. She could not determine whether the throbbing vein she could feel so clearly was in her own fingertip or on his eyelid. The eyeball felt like an enormous knot of tissue fluid bunched into an orb, one that would immediately spill in every direction were she to wound it. The secret of this orb was now being discovered not only by the lid, slippery on the inside, but also by her barely moistened fingertips, on which she sensed momentary flashes of light. Yes, perhaps she was just imagining things, but it nonetheless seemed that the man's gaze tore right through the eyelid, penetrating her skin. When she raised her fingers from the lid, she perceived a shadow on the man's forehead, whose memory was preserved by a wrinkle. This furrow was like a horizontal question mark suggesting that which could not be recorded.

She now lowered her hand to the lips like some measuring tin. The slightly swollen, slackly adhering lips seemed conspicuously dry; only in the corners of the mouth did L. feel a mild moisture of sorts. She slid an index finger effortlessly along this hair's-width cleft, taking care to ensure that the motion did not become tickling. Of course this almost-dried-out furrow would be more grateful to her if she touched it with her lips, but if the fluids did not spring forth at her finger's caress, why then, her kiss wouldn't be worth a thing! The man's lips trembled now and again, but then, to keep under control, clenched firmly. Not even if L. had kept her eyes open, would she have been able to track this change more precisely. The thinned mouth must have been seeking footholds, much as the cleft of the lips, which was at the mercy of her highhanded drawing, which could perhaps calm down only if its infinite length was delimited by an occasional vertical stroke. To the man, such an unequivocal gesture must have come when L. now covered his mouth with her palm. The motion could have signified the other's defeat just as easily as it did an invitation whose time had finally come. The whole thing lasted seconds, at most, and then L., as if she herself had been more alarmed than him, snatched her hand away from his mouth.

She had to take a rest, she felt, or she would become exhausted early on. L. lay back down beside the man, and after several long minutes, she opened her eyes—opening her eyelids slowly indeed, for she feared that a sudden change would erase her memory of the images she'd just seen, images that, if hazily, she cherished still. She had to bring the oversensitive light conditions of her inner vision into sync with her outer vision. From experience she knew that images were defined more sharply and shapes took more definitive form in the dark, and one could not be too careful in handling this. Nonetheless she opened her eyes, for if she were to preserve the series of images her senses had just amassed for longer than allowable, why then, they would evaporate in underhanded fashion before they might become memories: outer light was just as necessary as inner darkness.

The man exploited this retreat. He sat up in bed and then rose above L.'s body like some shadow that has been compressed and elongated into an oval shape that radiates heat. As if only gathering strength to subdue the resistance between the two bodies, he waited a few seconds, and only then did he lower himself onto the olive-hued peninsula lying underneath him. Within moments he found the throbbing fissure.

L. screamed from pain. She felt as if an enormous, red-hot bayonet were stretching apart her vagina, which might burst at any moment. But the stinging pain was soon supplanted by waves of pleasure, as if her body had burst into flames in two places at once: in her loins and in the tunnels behind her forehead. After a while the dancing cells must have grown tired of their solitary carousal, for they started off towards each other. Those arriving from the central nervous system must have encountered somewhat less resistance than those endeavouring upward from the loins, for the latter still had to reward the patience of the tissues that had until now been left alone. They let them drink of their fluids before they might have dried up once and for all. Perhaps it was when these cells arriving from different directions met up somewhere underneath her chest that L. screamed. Presumably on account of the secret 'flows' of just before, she could not decide whether her loins or her mind had bequeathed her with the pleasure.

The man must have been lying beside her for some time already when L. recovered her senses. *Yes*, she thought, touching him, *it must surely be gravitation that has been at work here, the very force which seas are also subject to.* Her loins were throbbing still. As if the other's masculinity were still in her body. Perhaps her loins would never again forget this unnameable togetherness? L. imagined that in these minutes it wasn't even her thinking, but her bruised vagina, her exulting clitoris—as if these organs were bringing her the news that there exists two types of consciousness, two realms of memory. The ceaseless flow of one creates in her an abstract, immaterial sense of oneself, while the other on such rare occasions reminds her suddenly of that primal connection which ties her solely to matter. Until now she'd been capable of recognizing this only in physical pain. But she'd considered this negative, for when suffering we seek to deny our bodies altogether. In rapture, however, we become our body's most faithful servants, and we cannot be grateful enough for its existence. It is precisely in these moments that we understand through experience that it is not that particular, primary flow of consciousness which maintains the unity of the body and the self, but this condition akin to a trance.

L.'s rambling thoughts were broken by an image. She saw before her the coroner's caressing hands, and this was accompanied by the sense that her lovemaking of just before would melt into yesterday's experience. So had that lovemaking been so elemental *then* because what up until that point she'd only understood (the inexorable nature of mortality) had suddenly become experience? Had her inexplicable attraction to death transformed into a sensation, similarly to her present rapture, when it was precisely coming to her senses slowly in the wake of unconsciousness that led her to her body's focal point? With the coroner she must have plunged into that particular other focal point—namely, that which preserves the future memory of death. Are we then the helpless servants of desire because only by this crafty means can cells well aware of their own mortality force their selfish will to live upon us? Is it at such times that we turn out to have not only a consciousness of death but also a *sensation* of death? Have we blended the strict fact of immortality with the myth of our will to live forever, even though this can be only be the prerogative of nonexistence? After all, in the moment of death we are accepted into the fold of everlasting existence, which is nothing other than nonexistence.

L. turned towards the man and began looking at his body. She was amazed. At first she thought she was imagining things, but the more attentively she watched the man, the more obvious the resemblance she discerned between their two bodies. Most surprising was his thinness—the same puniness borne of stunted development that she was so ashamed of on herself. Yet still, the man's upper body was proportional; his broad shoulders served as a proud counterpoint to almost puny hips. An outsider might have winked an eye benevolently at the sight of ribs that stuck out here and there, for the round plates that were his taut chest muscles spoke of strength. His belly was hard as a rock. His long thighs, brawny despite their thinness, seemed springy. On his shins, perhaps only the underdeveloped calves left something to be desired. It seemed to L. that she was looking at herself! A rather thin but muscular frame, with exceptionally well-developed sex organs, relatively speaking. So was this why he'd been able to dominate over her from the first minute? Had she been able to surrender herself at once without resistance because the body that had pulled her towards itself was that which she'd always been waiting for? Could she melt away only in a body whose almost sickly thinness was so much like hers? Are we ruled over by laws so implacably strict? Was it not 'us' and, no, not our desires that determines whom we give ourselves to, but our bodies?

They must have been around the middle of their next round of lovemaking when the man began to watch L.'s face. He saw it as a spot of flesh bunched into a single knot, on which the chin and the sharper protrusions of the facial bones bulged out. He now saw the fine arch of the mouth as frills of meat flattened crookedly against each other, with spots of blood showing here and there, not unlike an epileptic who bites her lips during a seizure. On her forehead, though it had been perfectly smooth only moments before, the skin had piled up in inscrutable, frenzied folds. The man knew he could make the breathing stitches of this suddenly erupting pain disappear only by tearing himself out of the girl, for he suspected that this silent suffering sprang from L.'s loins. And so he tried moving ever so softly, as if to overcome the resistance only of the most gentle receptor of all—for example, of water. L. now opened her eyes. She was able to preserve the memory of the pain of a moment before: still lying low within her eyes was the sort of fear that surprises lovers right before orgasm, for they cannot know just where the imminent carnal pleasure will sweep them. This is perhaps the only fear we gladly await.

Even though the wrinkles on her face had meanwhile smoothed out, the man felt L.'s stare to be strange and frighteningly distant. Perhaps it was precisely the tight frame of this unexpected smoothness that enhanced the eyes now riveted on him, which to himself he called the state of unconscious observation preceding consciousness. The borders between observation and sensation in the girl seemed to have perfectly merged. He imagined that in the course of these minutes, the girl was sensing the physical world directly with her mind and observing with her sensory organs—as if something had drastically shortened the body's nerve paths, so that stimuli could reach the tendrils of the central nervous system directly, and physical sensations could become 'meaning' without any mental exertion whatsoever. But most menacing of all was this: as time passed, this muddled mix of sensation and observation gave rise to an order so alarmingly rigid that he would have been unable to endure it, had he not discovered right alongside it something else— namely, gradually intensifying desire. These eyes, so he thought momentarily, might now even kill him. It wasn't the longing that was capable of murdering, but the strangeness that had staked its claim in this girl's eyes and that could not be identical to him. He thought this cold, merciless stare would swallow him whole. He understood that only another spate of carnal pleasure could help free him from its grip. And indeed, when a few minutes later he let out an inarticulate cry, with his own, half-shut eyes he saw that the girl's dilated pupils were now held together by desire alone.

It was in vain that L. heard the cry erupt from the man's throat; an increasingly heavy silence surrounded her—as if the sound had swept this mute current before it, so that soon it would fall headlong upon her in a suffocating way. Perhaps orgasm was nothing other than several seconds of time materialized? The perpetual silence of cells might speak up for a few moments—but only so that after this it might fall back even more deeply into muteness? Do we live through the most elemental union in this semiconscious state only so that oblivion should claw at our precious experience? (To speak to us directly, our creator would surely have chosen the moment of orgasm.) L. began to sink in this corridor of silence, which was so risky because this descent was now accompanied only by the final waves of pleasure, for rapture had meanwhile transformed into memory, bliss. Only with force could she yank herself out of this state. All at once she sat up in bed, took a cigarette from the night-stand and lit up.

An unfamiliar sadness beset her. Was it with such a sense of dejection, close to regret, that we must pay for our passions? Or is this woe the fruit of lovemaking? Perhaps this is when the Great Illusionist is exposed, for he'd tried in vain to deceive us just before, but he can no longer disguise his real nature from before us. Our Lord is sad, which is why he bequeathed us with this very nearly unbearable pleasure. That is when we sense this, in the void after ecstasy. And he also has mercy upon us, because before woe's force of gravity yanks us down into unfamiliar depths, it leads us back to our satisfied bodies. That is the moment of almost perfect equi-librium. The body's hushed pleasure takes possession of our inex-plicable sadness to console us. We couldn't be ashamed of this sort of woe even if we wanted. After all, the distinction ceases between the perceiving self and the body, their borders blurring along the horizon of the sensation of completeness. This is the condition of blissful doubt, when it is superfluous for us to decide whether our body has a soul or our soul has a body. This sadness fertilizes our subdued pleasure, our unassailable calm. Perhaps this force could move the very world from its place. And we wouldn't have to fear that the feeling would turn against us, for it can't live independently. Our bodies stand guard over it! A sense of wonder is born imper-ceptibly from this meeting of sadness and the body, and it spreads through us gradually, until we perceive it as good. The reason we flinch at this time is that not only is our mind the gravitational point of this condition, but also the body; for it is precisely the body, which has become the self, that exudes that strength which we could also call bequeathing love, if our partner lays claim to this love. But that's not what happens. No, our wealth cannot accept the other's gift; we let them waste it on someone else. Perhaps this is why we can say that in the involuntary transformation which follows orgasm, we become each other's secret tools in the interest of achieving goodness.

L. tried raising her head but could only turn it to the side. That's when she noticed that she was surrounded by almost complete darkness. Only the faint light filtering in through the window cast a shadow over the furniture and other objects in the room. Suddenly L. didn't know what had happened to her. She was on the point of thinking this was a dream when a light tingling sensation that came from her abdomen evoked in her the memory of their lovemaking. A calm spread through her and a silence descended upon her, like that which the roots living at the depths of trees must know. Until now silence had been her most unbearable foe. But now this utter quiet, which had practically become a fluid, this pre-birth noiselessness stood guard over her. Without fear or anguish she surrendered herself to this silence, which imperceptibly transformed within her into the experience of accepting everything. She felt herself to be an inviolable force. It did not scare her that this condition very nearly amounted to feeling nothing, for she could be seized only by a power of which she too was a part; for only like objects can mingle.

Perhaps we live for these minutes alone? Do we falter along the borders of beauty and suffering only so we can repeatedly catch red-handed within ourselves this silence that is tantamount to being a force impossible to intimidate? Our solitariness is not, then, loneliness but the instrument by which secret intentions are realized. No, to be alone in this way is not to be without a companion, and perhaps the best proof of this is the onetime decision of He who stands above us, which made us party to his sadness. Just as it does with him, this sadness ties us to other people, too, so we can each be the means to each other's ends.

All at once L. felt so light as to be almost weightless. The silence that had flowed uniformly over her body slowly dissipated. Again she was able to move her limbs. Lifting a hand, she placed it slowly on her face, as if receiving the approach of a stranger's hand. She ran her fingers along her forehead, her closed eyelids, her lips. Previously, whenever she'd caressed her own face, she'd always felt like an orphan. But now she was filled with a pleasant warmth. Next she slid her grateful hands onto her breasts, her belly and her thighs, and finally onto her loins. L. now felt the same sort of tenderness and love towards her own body that she had on that night on seeing the coroner's hands. She passed her eyes over the silently breathing reaches of the pleasure that had assembled on the tissues comprising the surface of the skin. Yes, from now on she must only love this body, for every ounce of strength would rise from within.

L. now noticed that the man was sleeping beside her. She heard his even breaths as the atonal, rising and falling, precisely repeating rhythm of body-music, which was now more strictly subjected to a beat decided in advance. Is it this noiseless pulse that holds together the even more silent working of the body? At this moment the man's body emanated the same silence that L. perceived as coming from the lifeless bodies laid out on the autopsy tables on that particular day. Perhaps the only difference was that she felt this silence to be warm, and yet she knew that this impression derived solely from the fact that this man had been caressing her not long before. Was he dreaming their lovemaking all over again, or was a series of images completely independent of what happened before they went to sleep render his subconsciousness and semiconsciousness so light? L. thought the latter more probable, perhaps because at this moment she believed too strongly in the gravitational force of pleasure. A body that not long before has submerged entirely in pleasure can hardly want to give the lie to his fresh experience with the implausibility of dreams. Not even the most audacious dream images could repeat their fusing of just before, for *then* they plunged deeper than even dream-associations, freed from under the control of consciousness, can reach. Only flesh and blood, inner organs and tissues, can lay a rightful claim on this beauty, which has meanwhile transformed into energy! Which must be why they lock them away right away in their secret capillaries, so as to fortify the body's self-awareness. What does it matter that when this man wakes up in the morning, he will just feel all this but not know it?

L. looked at him. She would have liked to touch him but she did not. No longer would she meet with him, she knew. But she was now sitting up here beside him, until, that is, morning would come with all its certitude. But she would not forget this man's body; she would carry it around within her even after she stopped thinking of him. But no, she wouldn't, after all; for otherwise she would become captive to love. It would have seemed altogether too dangerous to her if she were to identify the pleasure that had possessed her body with a celebration over a long-awaited arrival. At any moment she could lose the reward of her relentless consistency, this fragile freedom, were she to give in to her weakness. Up to now not even disgust could lead her astray from her vow, so why should she be alarmed by the months to come? She felt the same demonic power as she had not so long ago at all in hours of bitterness. And yet its weight was wholly different. It seemed that this present condition of hers had preserved the power of her despair, perhaps only so as to swing her towards a future in which she could tolerate pleasure.

Dawn was breaking. The light descended so softly upon the room as if it wasn't even the windows it was coming through but the walls, drilling its way through the lime-slaked plaster. No longer could she hear the man's breathing, as if this body, too, albeit lying in seemingly calm repose, had submerged into the flood formed at the confluence of darkness and light, a flood that had driven the unnoticeable trenches of time deeply indeed. Until today she'd always waited anxiously for morning, for waking up, which confronted her in advance with the lies and self-justification she'd been forgiven for. From now on she need not fear, however, for this unexpected rendezvous had freed her of the wicked and detestable reckoning. This night had once and for all extinguished her thirst for revenge. Had she known how to fly, she would have compared her new situation to the moment of taking off, the moment she overcomes gravity. Her childhood dream often came to mind: then she'd been flying above the houses, and not once did it occur to her that she might crash. On this night something similar had happened to her. She'd been overcome by the same lightness, the same bodiless sensation, that immateriality which up there, above the rooftops, had once kept a little girl's body in balance. Only now was she able to understand this, now that time had drawn out to sufficient distance.

Then morning came. L. dressed, packed her bag, and then sat back down on the edge of the bed. The man woke up not long after. He saw that L. was ready to go. And so he got hastily out of bed, put on his clothes and signalled that, as far as he was concerned, they could go. Down on the street, in front of the motel, they parted without a word.

A morning fog had descended upon the small town, its thin veil shrouding roads, trees, memories. As much as she loved this weather, L. waved a hand towards an approaching taxi, for she wanted to get to the train station all the sooner.

PART THREE

1

As I wrote L.'s story, we were meanwhile already living with each other. Her continual presence kept awake in me that relentless despair without which I would have been incapable of tracing the origins of my misery. I was undeniably a coward for not having her tell me the story of her yearlong promiscuity, but I have a much easier time bearing pain I cause myself than that which others inflict upon me. At the same time, this cowardice is precisely what saved me—as if my madness had come straight to my rescue! My pathological imagination produced the antidote, one that not even the most talented chemist could have conjured up.

Every day, on finishing my quota for the day, I put down my pencil and went out to join L. in the kitchen, where her story continued in our silence. In the first moments I didn't even dare look upon her face, that's how ashamed I was. Meeting her eyes would have brought me face to face with my depravity. I'd already convinced her that I was working on a novel I'd begun years before, one I could talk about only on completing it. The silence was unbearably loud to my ears, for I heard the sentences I'd written not long before, and indeed some of these hyenas charged with seeing to my torment would take the opportunity to smirk at me. Sometimes I felt that these sentences hadn't even stolen their way to me from those I'd written down, but that they'd burst right out of L.'s body.

If, for example, I gathered the courage to raise my head and look in her eyes, I had the impression that her lineaments had come together from the marquetry of my sentences. I had to turn my head away at once, so relentless was this stare transformed by my adjectives and metaphors. What looked back at me was that which I'd tried that morning to hide away in my fictionalized version of her year. But the face did not settle for simply reflecting what could by no means be called innocence to begin with. It was as if the sentences had outright riveted the skin, deepening the furrows of her smile, dividing the seemingly calm muscles into paragraphs; at the right moment I would realize this all at once, unprepared as they then clutched my throat. This breathing screen projected my compulsive thoughts before me. Until now I'd looked upon this face as one on which I could assess the consequences of the delirious workings of my imagination. But now this face nurtured by my licentious thoughts had become my judge, for it had not only swallowed my sentences but also radiated them back at me. This passing of judgement, which her face wasn't even aware of, must have been like the measures undertaken by the force above us, that force called God, in response to both our wickedness and our goodness. This force amasses every such instance in the centre of its furtive gravitational field, only to look them all over at a suitable time, as soon as we take back that which belongs to us, whether of our own accord or against our will.

How much more frightening and cruel were these sentences that now existed on account of L.'s face! I could not simply cover them up with my palm, as I could in the case of those pages I'd scribbled all over and crumpled up; or, if I could have, the lines would have burnt right through my palm, which would still have been more tolerable, if I consider that after months of this my hands would have surely mouldered away. Nor could I strike out these sentences as I had so often on paper. To do this I would have had to do no less than demolish L.'s face, to irreversibly disfigure it, like some cold-blooded pimp liquidating a bothersome prostitute. Of course, I would not have had to take up a knife or a scalpel; my hatred alone could have effected the destruction, seeing as how even I took flight at the visions I myself had created. At such times it occurred to me that the final judgement would occur in a single, silent fraction of a second, one that we endure only because in that instant we become the equals of Him who has made us our own judge.

The present judgement was cruel. I could not count on help from an unfamiliar force, one that would have guaranteed my equality. It was up to me whether to accept the basic condition that came with staring L. in the eyes—namely, suffering. Until now, whenever the visions had beset me, I'd always wanted to shake them off all the sooner, for it had seemed to me that by doing so, I could cut short the course of fear. It took many long months for me to realize that precisely the opposite happened. Which is why I no longer went about erasing the sentences that appeared one after another on L.'s face, and nor did I shatter the images borne of these sentences; for I knew I had to keep watching the visions until, one day, they would weaken and fade away. I suspected that I could overcome them only with my stare, with the discipline behind my distress. An invisible mirror reflected the wailing wall I'd raised between the visions and my observation.

On noticing on L.'s face the marks of the onetime carnal pleasure my story had sought to precisely articulate, I did not cast down my eyes and, no, I did not run off and seek solace in darkness, which for years had proven to be the most dangerous bunker of all. Instead I allowed beauty to take hold of her face and anxiety to have its way with me. By now I was the one who, while mapping out the chapters of L.'s story, saw to sharpening the images that to this point had always hit me only erratically. With my sentences, which were present simultaneously in her eyes and in my memory, I had rendered unequivocal that which had previously been intermingling uncertainly and developing randomly; as if I was finally able to understand that pain multiplied by two or more could better resist my demons than my earlier, seemingly shrewd games of hide-and-seek, I had in fact doubled my visions.

Not that I could have called these few moments of defiance a rebellion at all. In reality I'd been training myself only for fear, for patience that could be mastered by degrees. I sought a rhythm of torment suitable to my constitution, one that would carry me forward not too fast, no, but by all means more tensely than up until now. When some freeze-frame of a vision I discovered on her face seemed less dangerous for some reason, I kept it prominently in my mind's eye until the light and shadow cohering the image merged. But before this merging took place, my entire body had to swallow and absorb the object of my anguish: a signal of light I'd noticed emanating from the face, a light distinct from the shadow beside it. If only my so-called 'conscious consciousness' had received the message of this vision, I would have come off badly in no time once again. My entire body had to come to terms with the cause of my fear. Never had I believed, after all, that it's solely a lack of understanding that clutches at our throats; that we feel those suffocating, throbbing undulations that scorch our limbs and sweep us into an almost trancelike daze simply on account of our foolishness. Caught in the throes of this feverish pulse, the body seeks to rid itself of the stranger just the same as it would, of poison or unwanted food.

But if we take gradual doses of a given poison, it is possible to raise the toxicity level not only in our bodies but also in our minds without, however, needing to fear a sudden crisis. The mind must surely be subject to a sort of chemical process not unlike that of

matter, of the body, albeit in a more enigmatic, unpredictable manner. I'd experienced this when it came to the 'transferal' of fear;
which is to say, sometimes I had the impression that L. had subconsciously seized the free valences of my fear. This was perhaps possible only because I lacked the courage to live with my own fears.
Only now, while watching L.'s face, was I struck by this, and I
understood at once that this sort of fear-transferal belongs to the
realm of black magic. We can subsist only with own fear, I now
understood. If another person appropriates our fears, even unconsciously, we cannot rest until we get them back. It was in this light
that I understood one of the basic tenets of Christian transcendentalism: Christ may take on our sins, but that doesn't mean he merits
absolution, either.

Once the wordlessness had finally become unbearable, I broke
the silence. L. would not have dared to speak up on her own. In the
weeks following her second confession, as I'd begun to secretly write
her story, she was conspicuously guarded around me. Perhaps she
knew full well that the book I was writing was not in fact that
certain novel I'd begun a while back, but something completely
different. Nonetheless, not once did she ask me what I was really
writing; not that she could have headed off my lies in any case, of
course. I now had to maintain a different sort of duality. My every
word and sentence was the quintessential lie, for even when uttering
the most insignificant statements I was thinking of something else.
Of the duet comprising my comments, only one voice could be
heard; as for the other, involuntarily I whispered it to myself. I could
pay attention only to the latter. I found it impossible to cease wondering, even as I posed L. some commonplace query, such as what
she'd done that day: *What had happened to her in my story?* I stood
on a narrow ridge where the question I'd just asked proved the difference between the genuine and the imagined only acoustically,

and yet was enough merely to ensure that I receive an answer to the question I had not pronounced. I had to take care not to lose my grip in this strict simultaneity. And so I continued to think one half of the doubled question in such a way as to meanwhile react to L.'s replies.

I received these answers even more equivocally, if that was still possible at all. Behind L.'s every sentence I sought a secondary or even tertiary meaning, something I could work into everything I'd imagined onto paper that morning. If she reported having felt sad that morning, right away I suspected either that this sorrow had descended upon her right out of one of the chapters of my fictional story, or vice versa: it had been precisely on account of her condition that morning that I'd been able to capture this feeling in the sentences I'd been about to write! Of course, that got me down the least. I became far more anxious at the thought that her morning sadness might be a memory of onetime despair she still hadn't been able to shake off. My inconsideration enraged me. I had to change course, even if those glances of hers had branded me with the most conspicuous signs of my lies.

At such times I dragged out some conversation we'd previously begun, taking care that the distress I'd shown before would now come across to her as intellectual disquietude. After a while I did in fact manage to deceive her, but the more certain I became of my success, the more disgusted I was with myself. No longer did I feel the mendacity in my sentences alone, but also in my stare, my gestures. Indeed, before long I found myself imagining that the objects in my midst had also been permeated by my prevarications, my deliberate deceptions. Why should I not have believed that the organic and inorganic world around me would be just as much a part of this fraud as was L.?

On certain days I felt certain that I'd hit upon incontrovertible proof of such forces in objects. It is mistaken to think that a chair is defined solely by its shape, its day-to-day comfort, the climate in our apartment or, say, the warmth of our bodies. Naturally we cannot disregard these external considerations, but it would be an error to judge the suitability of a seat, or the role it assumes in our sitting, on this basis. The most important thing to go on is the *quality* of the time spent on the chair. Here I am not thinking of our memory of conspicuously pleasant experiences, but of those many, seemingly uneventful hours in the course of which this object that for some reason we call a 'chair' becomes one and the same as our bodies. This is in point of fact the quintessential moment of 'sitting'—the moment of equilibrium in which we can't decide whether this object is an extension of our bodies or, say, vice versa. Are we an independently moving complement of this object? It is in the vicinity of some uncertain border at such times when we think to ourselves that its substance has lent us the calm we are incapable of producing ourselves.

This adhesion comes into being even when our seat satisfies only a practical need—say, that of rest. At such times our weary body holds the chair to be a sort of refuge, not considering that this object made of wood, metal or plastic could become the body's unnoticed interrogator, if only by chance.

Experience told me all this. Most helpful of all were the chairs I happened upon in coffeehouses. It took days for me to discover the chair that, to me, was unobjectionable, even if I did find all of them comfortable. There was something decidedly disquieting about this or that chair, however; I was practically certain that it was in such chairs that there sat those men and women who would have stirred my suspicions even in my greatest distress. On occasion I sought to verify these presentiments of mine. For example, I observed that an exceptionally obnoxious fellow was in the habit of sprawling out on one particular chair—a chair on which, one afternoon, I was unusually tense. I was tempted to step over to him and call upon him politely to not to be so full of himself when taking his seat, since on busy afternoons at the coffeehouse I too was compelled to sit right there, and more than once I'd already had to confront the consequences of his rather questionable seating style.

Flustered, I adjusted the chair under me and stole a glance at L.: Had she, too, noticed my conspicuous interdependence with the chair, which revealed at least as much about me as my sudden change of tone just before? This chair not only kept my body in balance a couple of feet above the floor, I felt, but my lies as well, my repeated attempts to flee disguised as mere unease—as if the chair's magnetic field had but temporarily absorbed all that which I wanted to conceal from L., only to then radiate it back towards me all the more implacably. With time, of course, I just as readily discerned my deceit in L.'s eyes and on the hand she raised before her face. Our lies invariably find their way to the person sitting across from us. They graze their face, scraping their skin, and settling on their lineaments, even if we know full well that all this is the work of our own duplicity. Only a swindler can see this slyly duplicated image, this double meaning softened by shadows: the consequence of his seemingly cunning machinations. In vain I told myself repeatedly that I alone saw this; I simply could not ignore the traces of evidence of my lies that had descended upon L.'s face. I had to cut short our conversation, for my unmasking, which she hadn't noticed at all, had become outright suffocating to me. My only hope was to find solace in some bar.

Surely the tavern's swarming atmosphere—the blustering of those around us, the blaring of the music and the proximity of strangers—would come to my rescue, but in this expanded space my loneliness only squeezed me tighter. I had mistakenly believed that those in this space were talking solely to lessen that silence from which I'd fled. By then I'd also put L. at the mercy of my loneliness. The same underhanded feebleness now took her down that had held me in its grip for hours; the emptiness that now took hold of her had been borne of my proximity. She'd defended her assertions confidently until then in vain; my distress had swallowed her whole. From this moment on, I knew, she would squeeze the words out of her with force, as if afraid only that they'd injure her mouth and tear her vocal chords. Even more suffocating, however, was this: what had been self-evident just before had now come up against a sort of underhanded resistance. Her sentences had to break through the levee that had been built up from her loins to her throat, which had become increasingly wide as my helplessness took hold.

By maintaining the semblance of a conversation, L. protected us. She covered our mutual shame with her sentences, without which we would have been put on the pillory even more. I was grateful for every word pronounced, clinging to them the same as the girl sitting practically next to me did to her lover's arms, as the alcohol absorbed by my blood did to my cells. Had L. not saved me in such situations, I would have had to give up bars, too: my last refuge, especially when we were together. Of course, I was well aware that some people were watching us. Sometimes I caught a glance as their eyes shamelessly locked in on us. Had I had the strength, I would have sprung right over and told them in no uncertain terms to desist with their spying, to stop playing havoc with us so openly. How shameful, such investigation disguised as a series of involuntary glances, as stares gone astray! Even if they'd deprived us of our clothes, not even then could these eyes flashing at us from a safe distance have stripped us any more naked! I regarded this insidious observation of our despair to be an unforgivable strain of perversion—a wretched voyeurism I held in contempt even though I was well aware that I myself had incited the peeping of those who were, after all, facing us to begin with in this crowded bar.

At such times I was truly sorry not to belong to those peoples among whom being caught red-handed like this counts as an inexcusable provocation, one the perpetrator must bear the penalty for. In a country governed by the rule of law, perhaps we could refine this supposedly primitive custom; say, by pinning a badge upon ourselves in our most vulnerable hours, so as to signal that our faces are under an observation ban. But the real danger came from the waiters, who believed that persistent probing was an indispensable condition of their work. Perhaps certain men and women choose this occupation not for its material advantages, but for the pleasure derived from secretly observing an establishment's patrons. In specific situations waiters come to resemble those psychologists who feel authorized, on account of their doctorates, to go about grilling their patients. Of course, in the course of their work, waiters can get no further than visual interrogation; they cannot transgress the border dividing an elegant if hyena-like comportment from flagrant bad taste. So it was, for example, that the cynical posture of their mouths would turn promptly into an understanding smile the moment our eyes met. What I'd seen a moment before as a sign of compassion, they now sought to exploit for a conspiratorial wink. Their cold, probing stares seemed to me more impudent than even this imaginary pat on the shoulder; for they soon changed their style, as if they realized that behind an unflinching stare, they could recognize our situation more thoroughly.

I could have signalled to L. at any moment that we should be off, and yet I didn't want to leave this increasingly dangerous territory, for I understood that public humiliation was part and parcel of my purification. How could those observing us have suspected that our helplessness was not the usual writhing that follows a failed love, which invariably renders a quick break-up impossible? They must have ascribed our torment to our imminent separation, not suspecting that it was in fact my singular jealousy that had produced these scenes. I was overcome by an unexpected tenderness—perhaps because L.'s face seemed so tortured, even though I was certain that just now she was concerned for me. If clarity of mind would have allowed me, then perhaps I would have also discerned pity in this concern. But as things stood, I happened only upon compassion, and even that, by chance; not wanting to humiliate me, she kept her feelings hidden. Perhaps she, too, suspected that I would not have endured this sort of debasement. I stood at a borderline where I could not lay a claim to compassion. Had I accepted this feeling accompanying her love, I would have had to surrender once and for all.

Only gradually did the hidden meaning of L.'s headstrong resistance become clear to me. She could not protect me from myself, I understood, for by doing so she would cut me off from the path to freedom. Had she relieved me of my torment, she would have succoured my cowardice, which is yet another reason she could not console me. By denying her past, she could have pulled us headlong into yet another lie—one that, of course, I could not have persuaded her of even though I was an expert torturer. Instead, she allowed me to make her an instrument of my rebellion against the illness. Presumably she accepted this designated role on account of the two months during which she'd become convinced of my love for her. In any case, she must have known from experience that help derives not from consolation, not from indulgence disguised as understanding, not from a sanctioning of our weaknesses but from that mercilessness which compels us to judge ourselves. No, L.

couldn't relieve me of my burden, alleviate my suffering. So it wasn't in vain that I loathed her resistance, which seemed so cruel; for this was the force that in certain hours descended upon me with even greater weight than my fears, the force that buried my paths of escape—paths that, until now, I'd always managed to find.

L. must have instinctively understood the meaning of her role. She was the second in the duel I was engaged in against myself: simultaneously observer and observed. Two of us had tasked her with fairly referring the proceedings against me, although originally I had made her the two-legged witness, judge, and condemned of the trial underway within myself. She knew that her greatest sacrifice for me would be to endure my anguish. There is no greater challenge than tolerating this in another. At such times we feel practically useless; this is oppressive not only because we have found ourselves without a point of support, but also because we have become all too accustomed to concealing our own emptiness with the other's solitude.

Around midnight we left the bar. As we stepped outside, L. took my arm, as if wanting to say with her hand that which she'd deliberately kept from saying in sentences—a touch akin to caressing an animal. With this, we both acknowledged my defencelessness. To me, this was more endurable than any encouraging word. We approached the flat like the condemned, who would rather never reach the place where their punishment was to be meted out; for we both knew full well that not even our imminent lovemaking could alter the shame we'd invited upon ourselves in the bar. Each of us would experience the consequences of that shame on our own. Nonetheless, I closed the door behind us a bit more calmly than when we'd left.

From now on it wasn't the memory of some presumed onetime lover that I sought on L.'s body. Instead I saw her as the character

in scenes I'd already written and, indeed, rewritten several times—
a character who now happened to be embracing me. How much
easier it was this way to accept her smile, her embrace! No longer
was L. entitled to these motions simply on account of her own free
will or the love she felt, but also by the good graces of my imagination. She'd had to tread a much longer path than usual over the
byways of my fantasizing. By summoning the character of L. that
I'd created, I also gave my foes a *raison d'être*. When L. now
touched me, she was repeating the unconditional, relentlessly consistent behaviour unfolding in my story—as if she'd stepped out of
one of my clauses, so as to verify my attributives and, with her
proximity, to confirm my assertions. She drew me near along with
the creations of my imagination. The latter no longer had to obey
only grammar but also L.'s love.

My pathological thoughts were thus squeezed tightly by a double lock, even if my aloofness kept the clamp somewhat loose. I
touched L. with the coldness of an outsider, with a detachment
capable only of enduring the facts. But over the course of those minutes, at least, I did not want to deny that which already belonged
to me just the same as to L.'s supposed past. My thoughts now
focused *not* on the scenes of her onetime promiscuity but, rather,
on the truths of her story *as I'd written it* and that was unfolding
within me presently, amid our mutual torment; for I had to create
a truth from out of that distress which was originally the source of
my disgust.

After a while I was unable to distinguish between the bona fide
visions I discovered on L.'s face and body, and the scenes I'd conceived that morning while writing. Sometimes it struck me that I
was scrutinizing L. with the eyes of one of my characters—of the
narcissistic man or, say, of the coroner. This calmed me even amid
the distress associated with my detachment. With their coldness I

tempered my anguish; out of their audacity I stole my courage, without which I would still have been a helpless observer of our lovemaking. I submerged into the lives of my characters as if I'd found my way back to my own past. The safest thing of all was that I had to identify not with an actual man—namely, me—but with fictional persons whom I myself had invented! As such it was easier to convince myself that, for example, the coroner's fearless gaze was in fact mine; all I had to do was get it back from him. I'd proved this in my round of writing that morning, when I'd set him as the example of my own fearlessness. As my hand now approached L.'s face, I was carrying out his gesture—as if this is how I sought to validate a sentence that, on paper, I'd necessarily ended with a period. In these moments I transformed the grammatical subject into a genuine person; the verb, into a genuine action.

I was well aware of the pitfalls of this absurd self-deception. For example, my chosen fictional character could leave me at any moment, leaving me in an even more impossible predicament. This invariably depended on my vigilance. If I was disciplined enough, then one of my newly appointed helpers could hardly flee from me. But if I let some capricious thought of mine take hold of me, why then, I could start it all from scratch. My contradictory assertion requires an explanation.

While writing the story of L., I came to realize that my maniacal thoughts fell into two broad categories. One had caused me anguish for years, while I sought the other one, which I held to be an instrument of healing magic and which, I hoped, would conquer the others. By summoning the character of the coroner, by sponging some energy from him to nurture my present motions and my gaze, I tried driving out of me the obsessions that had long beset me in highhanded fashion. My relaxed breathing, my accepting glances at L.'s body, validated the appropriateness of my dubious method.

At such times I loathed her less. In the fine cracks of her thin mouth, in the furrows of her face, I now discovered not strangers' caresses superimposed upon each other; instead I discerned only the present moment—the moment in which my hand, which had become one and the same with the coroner's hand, descended upon her body. And if by chance I noticed those other marks, after all, I was saddened not by their presence but by the feeling that had struck L. unexpectedly as she made love to the other man. The same anguished tenderness now settled upon me as had settled on L. in my story. These were the minutes when I escaped my demon's grip; neither fear, loathing, nor my accursed thoughts had power over me—as if the story I'd been writing had suddenly opened up and fallen all over me, burying the craters of memory. But one depression was left open: the one that allowed my invented story a comfortable fit.

Had the distress I'd experienced while writing undermined the power of my visions to torment me on such occasions? Sometimes I thought so. Indeed, such a division of suffering seemed even logical. If I'd consistently withstood my deliriums over the course of a day, then my demon would have to be rewarded at night. On certain days I yearned only for numbness, for that precious treasure which the sufferers of insidious physical pain must know when drugged with morphine. But later, when I felt more ready, I reached a compromise even with the presence of fear; a fear formed and shaped—as if I was now able to strangle my foes with the ropes of the anguish freed up in the afternoon. What I really dreaded was when time itself was transposed. Sometimes the unavoidable visions of the previous evening eased my morning hours, but I always accepted this with suspicion, well aware that I would pay for this come night. The energy directing the torture had to free itself, after all.

Which is yet another reason I worked on L.'s story almost like one possessed. If for any reason I had to take a break from writing for a day, right away my demons took hold of me even more audaciously than before. At such times I had the feeling that to them, it didn't matter one bit whether they staked their claim on me or on my sentences; they needed only to have a guaranteed territory in which to dwell. Of course, this supposition, which was tantamount to self-deception, collapsed immediately when I was greeted by certain sentences of mine. Even if I'd wanted, I could not have forgotten the evidence for the delirious workings of my imagination, which made me blush even more than the shame that had led me to formulate L.'s story to begin with. But I was fated precisely for straining beyond the limits! I sometimes lost faith altogether for having taken on all too much ignominy. But I did so in vain: without disproportionate intensification, never could I have squeezed my pathological thoughts into a corner. The power of a perverse idea can be weakened only by one even more perverse. My demon would hardly have recoiled if all I'd done was to draw devils on the wall; to resist, I had to take one more step, one by which I became a monster once and for all. That which others would have kept concealed even from before themselves, I wove into a veil of sentences that could be read, so they would live not only within me but also in a form outside myself. I saw this as a means of building my strength, as the indispensable crutch of a necessary deception that, with time, had to be taught how to walk. In doing this, I was in effect also preserving my obsessions, of course, but compared with the brazen force of the raw images, this paradox was a benevolent force.

2

The real meaning of my venture became clear before me only when, after several months, I finished writing the story. I hadn't yet decided whether to give it to L. First I had to look over what I'd written. This post-analysis shocked me. It seemed as if, with this story of her promiscuity condensed into six days, I hadn't even realized my initial goal. Instead, my plan had indiscernibly gotten the better of me: all at once, amid my words, I discovered a mirror of my own illness.

First the hidden parallels became clear. Instinctively I identified L.'s rape with my own experiences. True, that floozie who'd fled to Sweden had had a surprise of an entirely different sort in store for me in the night-duty nurses' room, but not even that half-hour intermezzo could make me forget the continual aggression I'd experienced as a teenager. The fact that I was not raped by another person is but an illusory distinction. How much more reassuring it would have been, so I now thought, to have been the victim of a single act of aggression. Instead, I'd been bound to fear by the insidious forces dwelling within me. Perhaps that also goes to explain why I became so obsessed devoted with L.'s trauma and built a whole story around it; for in it, I found the firmness of a whole set of cause-and-effect associations to grasp onto, which in my own case I could not rely on. The manifestation of her misery likewise resembled my despair, even if L. had fled to something wholly different. And that is what gave me away: It turned out that the validation of L.'s promiscuity was the story of my desire. The more consistently I defended her actions, the more conscious I became of my cowardice; of the fact that I'd projected onto her that which I was incapable of achieving myself.

I'd always suspected that still lying hidden behind the calm occasionally conferred upon me was the real reason for my fear, which I now saw. While rereading my fictional confession of L., I was stunned to see that my imagination stemmed from that particular sort of envy we tend to call 'jealousy'. Of course, I'd known all about this jealousy up to this point also, but it seemed that only now could I comprehend its meaning. All at once my illness, which I'd believed to be incurable, was exposed as a treacherous fault of character, which I could no longer call an obsessive-compulsive neurosis from any perspective. I came to understand that one of the meanest human character traits of all signified more hope for me than a helpless acceptance of my fate. But I'd deal with this much more easily—so I thought—than I could with those images that had appropriated my will, my mind.

The pathological workings of my imagination had irredeemably twisted my mind; for only a decade after it began could I come face to face with my envy; that is, with the sort of envy that renders some people murders and others, dapper criminals walking freely about in suits. The difference between gentle, seemingly inconsequential aggressors—the grouping I'd assign most people to—and a wanted crook is merely one of style, depending on how shrewdly we manage to hide from before ourselves and others our own feebleness, which we regularly avenge on others. I myself was the type who turn their failures against themselves, for the force borne of mental and physical impotence, which really becomes concentrated in the face of absence, must somehow forge itself a path—ultimately, in self-destruction.

My imaginative journey to precisely define L.'s demon exposed the hidden workings of the images that had been tasked with my torment—visions that had long maintained my lie, that grand deception which had sought to make envy appear like madness. The more audacious the methods I devised for ceasing the comparisons I drew so obsessively, the farther I got from recognizing this. Of course, my personality, ever flirting with illness, played a role as significant in this self-delusion as did my cowardice.

In envy, I had found the common denominator of my sense of loss, which I had earlier called a 'transcendental deficiency'. The memory of L.'s embraces must have hurt so much because she, in contrast with me, prepared herself for revolts with her defeats. True, it was my fiction that had conferred this aptitude upon her, but I was certain that if I'd had the strength to hear her out, she would have told me something similar. Although I knew that no degree of understanding could make up for the ten years I'd lost, I nonetheless believed that by acknowledging my envy, I could at least gain a measure of relief. Yet another reason I trusted this would be the case was because, in the fictional story, choosing L. would also have meant my liberation. By understanding her courage, which seemed demonic, I had not only pilloried my own cowardice, but I'd simultaneously caught red-handed the hidden 'self' within me that not only accepted but also outright glorified L.'s year of promiscuity. The 'L. hiding deep within me' now met up with the person who, until now, had been constructed only in my mind; and it didn't bother me at all that my imagination was just as much to thank for this sharpening of my self-knowledge.

I took L.'s revolt to be a coup against my own feebleness. Hadn't it been me, after all, who'd invested her with a strength that, in reality, she perhaps didn't even possess? The person I'd created lived on my courage, even if only on paper. But that was enough to grant me the transformation I'd never before hoped for. After all, as I'd come to know through experience over the years, that which we imagine can slip into reality at any moment.

My text, divided neatly into chapters, had, it seemed, begun to live a life of its own. Two different L.'s reminded me of my illness every day. One sat across the table from me every night and lay beside me in bed; the other looked back at me from my sentences, to make me increasingly strong, firm and relentless from paragraph to paragraph. I suspect that as I later reread what I'd written, the figures of the two separate persons were by then fused, as if this is how I subconsciously sought to render irrevocable that which I'd already finalized in her story, at any rate. If, in her imagined confession, I'd presented that certain year in her life as her freedom, her libertinism, realized, then I wouldn't have been able to associate the real person with the notion of such freedom. In doing so, I would have neutralized my own efforts. Instead I superimposed the two characters. Sometimes not even I could decide which was real. Only from the fact that my visions were fading from day to day could I deduce that the L. I'd created was gaining strength; that this persona, which was by now partly the same as mine, was radiating onto the woman who could actually be touched, caressed. Not even this proximity frightened me. When I took her hand, I held her warm fingers and, simultaneously, a vision I'd appeased weeks or months before by writing it down now stole its way back out of some chapter of the story. The love that now burnt right out of her hand the loathing I'd felt for months was precisely the love I felt so often while writing.

And yet there were days when I forgot the other L. completely. This amnesia was insidiously one-sided; for rather than swallowing the associated, delirious workings of my imagination, it did quite the opposite, cunningly strengthening them. In vain I waited for the help of some benevolent sentence I'd written; all I saw were the visions proceeding across L.'s face—even when she wasn't with me. Still, this distress was no longer as forlorn a sensation as the sort I'd earlier gotten used to; for the awareness of my envy sapped the strength of my compulsive thoughts. In other words, on noticing the hand of another man, a stranger, on her face, I allowed the anguish to flow through me, and meanwhile, as if out to master the ascetic life through words, I kept quietly repeating to myself: 'You are envious, that's what you are. You want to possess L.'s onetime pleasure; you would ruin that touch which your delirious imagination has made you incapable of.' The more firmly the image fixed itself to her face, the more I focused on these words mean to undo my fear. I tried convincing myself that it wasn't even the vision that was clutching at my throat, but the envy that had suffused every fiber of my body—that almost indiscernible leprosy which first slowly devours the nervous system and, with time, decomposes the entire body. An outsider can notice this only in the eyes and the facial expression; for sound skin, taut muscles and ostensible health serve to mask this inner putrefaction.

Others might not have known my gaze, but L. and I did. She rather sensed it, actually, while I found myself winding up closer and closer to its origins, to the realm where my visions had been born. Even before raising my eyes to L.'s, my glance had already submerged into the decay. I knew full well that the beam radiated by the eyes escapes from the cave called the body and only to returns there. That is why I must have felt my gaze to be even more frightened and vulnerable as I now raised my head and looked upon L. Alongside the barely discernible signs that served as reminders, I also saw my imperceptibly festering tissues and the traces of fermentation bubbling up from the depths of my body. It seemed as if a mirror had formed on L.'s face, a mirror that reflected the decomposition I sensed in my gaze. Lowering my eyes, I led the images back into the open cells behind my forehead, knowing full well that they would then flow down my throat to my chest, and from there, into the inscrutable alleyways of my limbs.

This was yet another reason these images could not have been coincidental! They seemed indeed to be the illustrative tools of this inner decay, the still sound outer fringes of cells that had already begun to decompose within—which by tormenting me, sought to keep from rotting away once and for all. After all, pain that comes in time can, at a certain stage, indicate the patient's possible recovery. The intensity of the torture led me to conclude that I still stood at some uncertain border, one where I could turn the attacks to my advantage. By enduring the telltale signs of the past I'd discovered on L.'s face and body, I'd already taken the first step. It was by awakening my consciousness to my envy, to my delirious desire to possess, that I now had to produce the antidote within myself—the serum that could put an end to the putrefaction that had been unfolding within me for more than a decade. But I knew this method well! Back then, after my break-up with G., I'd repeated the magic formula, 'I am vile', to myself more than often enough.

When initially feeling my way around all this, I injected myself with the simple sentence, 'You are envy!' I was like a doctor who, being late in administering a rabies shot, resorts to an overdose. It seemed as if my vocabulary had effectively narrowed to this accursed adjective and this particular conjugation of the verb 'to be'. This is what I whispered to myself for hours on end, constantly effecting subtle alterations of pitch, volume, tone. I wanted these three words to suffuse not only my mind, my flow of consciousness, but also my lungs, my abdominal wall, my groin. And so in fact I just barely murmured them, taking care that they should leave my lips only in part; indeed, I tried stuffing these seven sounds—You-a-re-e-n-v-y—down my gullet, so I could then paste them, with seven seals, to my bones. I slipped these sounds onto the wounds under my skin, wounds that could never be detected with a microscope. There, as seven times seven thousand semitones a minute, these sounds would turn into antibodies to my sordid character trait; since it was envy that had gotten me to this point—envy that had produced in me a mendacious, unarticulated, pathological relationship with time and presented itself in the form of delirious thoughts—why then, it too had to come undone. By calling a spade a spade, I aimed to free a counterforce that would virtually nail me onto the words I'd pronounced, so I might become one with them. This is unconditional and perfect self-capitulation, meaning as it did my own condemnation, and it even held surprises in store for me. The more the weight of these two words bore down upon me, the more decisively I felt the magnetic effects of this bundle of meaning created by vowels and consonants—as if the two words were clamping down so as to suck out that which they'd evoked. Why should it be hard to believe that a feeling that has been turned into a concept undergoes the same attraction and repulsion as anything else in this world?!

I came up with other methods as well. On certain occasions I uttered the same sentence loudly: 'I am envy.' Retreating to a safe place, one where no one could disturb my lonely solitary exercise, I chanted these words, much like 'God is One' is chanted by a vigil-holding monk who believes that only through his prayer alone can this truth of the revelation be preserved. Many people believe that we can shout pain out of us. And so I also gave this a try. Once, after a prolonged breathing exercise, these two words erupted from within me, and at other times I was practically suffocating as I pressed them out, that's how little air I had. But no matter which ruse I opted for, the feeling that the shout should have banished still lurked within me. I'd bring my midriff and thickened vocal chords to my service in vain, I knew; for I'd feel genuine relief only for the duration of the shout, a few seconds at most. These acoustics belonged to my punishment. My lie had lasted too long for me to escape it so easily.

On other days I didn't even hide from people. True, on such occasions I couldn't shout but, rather, had to be content with normal intonation. At the same time, the proximity of others opened up completely new possibilities. For example, when I met up with one of my acquaintances, I smuggled the words 'I am envy' into my greeting. In the presence of others I never used the second person 'You are envy,' fearing that the pronouncement's destructive force might suddenly switch directions. My acquaintance presumably heard only my polite 'Hello' or my somewhat aloof 'How do you do?'—not suspecting the very different chord my greeting had so shrewdly concealed. Those with sensitive ears sometimes might have caught the words—say, on account of the dubious intonation. No, it is not a sensitive ear for music that helps the person being greeted to expose such an innocent trick, but a foolproof intuition that certain people are born with—those people who involuntarily perceive a subtle deviation in a greeting that has taken a polyphonic course. Most people think merely that the other has fulfilled his or her obligation in a greeting of this nature, and yet the greeting is in fact clearly directed at someone other than what the words themselves would suggest. Even without a detailed analysis of facial lineaments, these people are capable of determining that a greeting has eluded them not because it wasn't meant for them, but because the 'Hello' or 'How do you do?' has become estranged from the greeter, independent of his or her will. Presumably they know from personal experience that at given moments, a greeting is impossible. At such times they don't even reply, instead only giving a short nod or a flash or two of the eyes, and they forgo their usual practice of assessing the sounds arriving from the other. They would, however, have a thing or two to say; for example, that this 'Hello' is in fact dubious not due to its hesitant tone, and that this 'How do you do?' is revealing not on account of its deliberate coolness but, rather, owing to the contradictions of the sound quality; as if that impeccably articulated 'do?' kicks up a piece of dirt or trash into the air before it, as if a certain opaqueness whirls about that double *l* in 'Hello'.

For the most part, I didn't have to worry about being unmasked in this way. Besides, my technique was to whisper the 'I am envy' along with my sentences while inhaling. If, however, a conversation then unfolded, then I'd let these three words slip only on occasion, and imperceptibly so, thus ensuring the continuity of what I had to say. It wasn't hard at all for me to maintain this duality; after all, I'd long conversed with people in such a way that I simultaneously spoke to them and, more so, to myself. This also explained why it was so easy for me to steal this simple sentence as a binding agent injected into the flow of my longer sentences. It was onto these seven simple sounds that I lined up the meaning of my sentences, as if onto an imaginary board. Even the most everyday of my assertions had to remind me of my envy. If I concurred with a comment voiced by a friend of mine, this meant nothing other than double emphasis on these three murmured words. Of course, he could not have suspected that I required his sentences only insofar as they reinforced my adjective, my predicate; otherwise I'd let the sentence pass right by my ears. I took the same measures with his occasional questions. When I gave an affirmative albeit curt, slightly impolite reply to his query about whether I was in a bad mood, it wasn't weariness bordering on depression that I admitted to myself, but that loathsome attribute of mine—envy.

Often I had a greater need for this constant duplication of my words and sentences than a hospital patient does for a visitor, than a cat burglar does for being alone. It was with this rather dubious approach that I brought myself face to face with the tacit judgement of those around me. Rarely did an 'I am envy' pronounced while alone produce the same effect as when I did so in another person's presence; which is to say, my environment was perfectly suited to the challenge I'd posed myself. When I stole these seven sounds into a sentence during a pause intended as a rest, it invariably seemed to me that the other person had understood it, like a mind reader, but had simply winked at it. It was precisely this well-intentioned complicity that shamed me, this playing down of the obvious in so fawning a manner. What to them was a friendly gesture signified, for me, the untenable nature of the situation. And yet I'd been waiting precisely for these moments! Without undue risk I was able to awaken contempt towards me, the disdain concealed by a smile, which I could defend myself against only by expressing hatred for my accursed trait. The more often I'd feel this shame evoked on my face in so circuitous a manner, I figured, the greater my chances; for if I were to see my envy in every person's eyes, then perhaps that would mean I'd arrived at the final stage. Even a castrated man can endure others' suspicious gazes more easily than I received the stares of my given partner in conversation, whom I had promoted to be my judge.

The physical proximity of other people also had its dangers. Namely, I imagined that with a handshake, a pat on the shoulder, or an involuntary moment of brushing up against each other, I might infect the other with my contagion. Indeed I gave up handshakes altogether, extending my hand only when unavoidable. Naturally I took care so my older acquaintances in particular would by no means take this as an offence. In the colder months I cited my susceptibility to the flu, and at other times I mumbled a witty remark about my conspicuously sweaty palms. Introductions were easier: I gave a slight bow, as if I'd only grown up with the greeting customs of East Asia. In public places I always took a seat a proper distance from the person I was with, and if possible, I sat opposite him; for while speaking he might momentarily grip my arm or even nestle up against my torso, which I wanted to avoid by all means. If we met on the street, I was just as careful. With shuffling, seemingly absentminded steps I sought that point of ground closest to the other person, but that still afforded me security; that is, a point from where I'd be able to avert an approaching touch without offending him. With my gaze I tried counterbalancing the distance between us. If I managed to lure him into the centre of my vision, I didn't have to be concerned about his approach. He automatically accepted that it was precisely this distance that offered us the ideal condition for a one- or two-minute chat. If by chance I met up with some less-disciplined acquaintance, I was compelled to invite him for a walk, even if we happened to head in a direction opposite to the one I'd been going in. Along the way I was able to step out of his way as I pleased, keeping myself ostensibly busy either by avoiding passers-by in a wide arch, by slowing to allow hurrying pedestrians to pass me by, or by stopping momentarily now and again, as if only in one place could I ponder what we'd said.

These manoeuvres of mine, which could be seen as overcautious, weren't arbitrary in the least. This was how I protected my friends and acquaintances, who might otherwise have caught my disease. I was convinced that cells store not only pleasure and beauty, but also wickedness. One would think that the brain alone amasses our feelings, our thoughts, but I am of a different opinion. The sensation of envy must have been absorbed through my skin and into my mucous membranes over the years like the most cunning virus. And yet the former is far more dangerous than most infections, for it dissolves more insidiously in our blood and remains imperceptible for a long time. Invariably we recognize its presence only at an advanced stage, once it has us firmly in its grip. Even a superficial observer will immediately notice the differences presented by a face shining with pleasure and one racked by frustrations and failures. The former seems as if the tautness of its skin owes itself only in part to flawlessly breathing epidermal tissue; for we have the impression that there is something on this face that, for lack of a suitable word, we might call a glitter, especially because the gaze and the face seem to be winking at each other. In contrast, in examining the other face, even despite the smoothness of the skin we notice a certain slackness, as if the bitterness lying low in the epidermal tissue were clogging the pores. Our suspicions are further reinforced by the duplicity discernible in the gaze. The owner of this face wants constantly to deny that which shows on his expression. A keen observer can discern the sunken-in quality of the latter face, even though it seems to most people fuller than the other. This ostensible fullness is however but a superficial deception, a commonplace trick played by physiognomy. This visual fib on the part of bones and skin cannot make us forget our impression that this face is pulled inward by bitterness and dissatisfaction.

I thought that in my body—in this receptacle that collects and stores my feelings—the capsules of envy had dissolved just the same as had those of fear. This is why I had to keep others' bodies at a distance; for in the course of inadvertent or deliberate touching, they would have been subjected to the most varied of dangers. I regarded the human organism as a reactor brewing with well-intentioned and ill-intentioned forces; a reactor that gives off radiation constantly, even when in repose. This is easily confirmed by examining someone's gaze. At the same time, it is perhaps not without grounds that

I suspect the veil we call 'skin' of being unable to resist this continual current as it emanates from others. Sensitive souls know this
full well, keeping their distance from the proximity of certain people
or else fleeing altogether. At such times they are beset by an inexplicable tension, a sudden sense of alarm, and they need to be either
alone or else in the presence of a friend for a longer or shorter bit
of time. In these hours we hastily seek the company of our chosen
ones, wanting nothing other than to be near them. But touching
represents the real danger. A seemingly friendly gesture may exploit
our naiveté, and all at once we feel like an animal at the mercy of
a human being's carnivorous instinct. In the moment of the gesture
by which the other imposed his or her physical presence upon us,
we'd prepared for a caress, whereas our foe had been weighing the
opportunity for attack.

While our everyday touching naturally yields less extreme
cases, this does not mean that, for example, the deliberate or chance
meeting of two hands comes without consequences. I am not thinking
of open expressions of congeniality or disquietude, when we
mechanically touch our companion's hand, but of that hard-to-
prove effect which comes with a seemingly inadvertent rubbing of
fingers or the backs of the hands, or a momentary pause as they
rest against each other. In such cases the force that coheres a body
can erupt in wider rays from the fingertips, and this can serve up
surprises if either person is unprepared. Some men and women are
ever prepared to thrust their disquietude on those around them,
while others excel at provoking them to do so. Touching is an
exceptional opportunity and an even more suitable tool for both
character types.

Certain individuals are on occasion pitiably defenceless. Their
bodies are like a funnel that swallows everything unfiltered, as if
nature failed to provide them with a particular defence mechanism.

When an anguished man shakes their hand, they immediately take fright; when a hysterical woman touches them, they absorb her agitation at once; and if the one caressing their face is sad, soon enough dejection takes hold of them. Of course, the other swallows their pleasure or good mood with a similar finality. They are not unlike infants, who for months on end experience their mother's love or, perhaps, indifference shrouded in obligatory caring almost solely through their mouths, their skin. I may well be mistaken, but do these first months not decide the course of our lives? Either we've have pleasure and love verily ironed all over us, from our heads to our toes; or else, like so many others, we too have become the hope, so full of promise, of misery, which has been called the honour of life.

And so it was not by chance that I avoided the proximity and especially the touch not only of my friends and acquaintances but also of strangers. I sought to guard them against that invisible but possible chemical decomposition that bodies can evoke in each other. The more vulnerable among them might easily have contracted the free valences of my envy through a handshake or in friendly caresses, in a farewell hug, or in playful, bantering little punches. If, while talking to someone, I were to inadvertently touch him even once, this would not carry the effect of an intimate gesture. No, instead I would have shortened the path of the depravity that had been absorbed by the back of my hand, my palm, my fingers; for I could not know how well armoured he was against such assaults. It would be naïve to believe that the ennobling or perhaps degrading possibilities of sensuality are restricted solely to the realm of the erotic. The great variety of transitional experiences can be embodied by a handshake just as well as by a touch meant to emphasize a sentence voiced in the course of conversation, even if it happens to be wholly unintended. At such times it seems something has left us in the lurch. The time that passes between the lifting of a hand and its arrival in the grip of the other's hand is plenty for the motion to veer off its original path; and this is, in effect, an outrage against the intended objective. Some think of this as the snubbing of 'subconscious substances,' whereas I see it as the moment of inertia of the power amassed in the hands. That is why I crossed my envy-filled hands behind my back, why I sank those throbbing hot spits into my pockets.

At the same time, those persons in our proximity can also become instruments of detoxification. I imagine the human body as an independently mobile, open test-tube, on whose 96.8-degree walls all manner of visible and invisible materials precipitate, like light or shadows on the eyes. If, in the gaze of an elderly woman preparing for death, we notice that she is freeing herself of her final ties to life, then this liberation shows on her entire body. That which we believe to be a self-surrender akin to helplessness is in fact the mark of the mind and body's mutual wisdom, their fear of death. Fear and the will to depart now oozes out of this old woman's parched, wrinkled skin as did her life force through nine decades. If we were near this lady for very long, we would sense fragrances and odours that only those preparing for death can issue from within themselves.

In the case of young ladies, the workings of the body as an open laboratory are far easier to observe. Certain women needn't utter a word, for their fragrance gives them away at once. An unnameable material of some sort—which at times seems like a distillate of honey mixed with poison—disperses over their bodies. More cunning ladies can perhaps deliberately conjure up within themselves this inviting, gaseous chemical. Certain men could indeed even be suffocated with a concentrated form of this concoction. Sometimes I believe that this exceedingly strong fragrance of their bodies aims to counterbalance the scents that well up from their loins. Nature has rendered them vulnerable two times over in this reach of the body. No, I'm not thinking of that time of the month, when certain women would gladly shut themselves in their rooms for days on end, such is their shame, but of those odours often deemed unpleasant that accompany the fluctuations of desire. At such times the policewoman rises from her chair at the station and goes to the restroom to apply a bit more perfume; the secretary in the traffic-clogged big city opens the window, for she trusts in the smoggy draft to alleviate matters; and the businesswoman, citing urgent matters, flees from her office out onto the street.

The surface of these ladies' skin also functions as a sort of vacuuming mechanism, however. Their pores open up far wider than do those of men, and so these cavities must now be filled much faster. When we ponder the inexplicable friendliness of a certain woman toward us, we should remember that, whether consciously or not, she seeks to fill the unexpected gaps that have formed on her body. And so we won't find ourselves wondering why, after a few minutes in her company, we feel weaker; for we know that she has stolen our strength. In more fortunate cases we may feel quite the opposite: Certain women seem to specialize in sucking the anxieties out of us. And so we are not annoyed at their possible foolishness, for the relief we soon feel allows us to ascertain that their sentences served solely as an excuse; for only thus can their bodies fully express themselves. However, to assume that their bodies' intensifying attractive force is a practical matter intended to acquire us for themselves would be to misread the situation. In such moments, the most that can be said on this front is that the manifested intention is operating at the borders of the erotic. Perhaps we can even call this a 'subconscious selfishness', as the foresight of instinct—one that seeks to purify him who might indeed become hers. The structure of such women's cells and tissues is exceptional. They do not store away the foreign sensations arriving in minute, broken-down particles from out of the other's body but, rather, dissolve and neutralize them. These cells and tissues comprise that rare category of living beings which feed on poison. How else to explain the secret of those women who are capable of conquering the wickedness of certain men with their mere presence?!

This was one reason I always appreciated the proximity of young ladies. Like a well-practiced pickpocket, I often stole up beside them on buses and trams and subway cars. Not for the world would I have touched them, no, not even if the crowd would have allowed for this. If I could, I stood three or four steps away, but without looking at them, and I waited to see if something would happen. Sometimes I seemed to breathe easier for one or two stops, and at other times an inexplicable warmth took hold of me that only their presence could account for. I strictly prohibited myself from turning to a more furtive, internal sort of advance, for my despotism had transgressed the allowable border enough as it was. Of this they knew precious little, of course; but why would they have suspected that standing a few feet from them was a man awaiting their help? They had to open the channels between us subconsciously, and if in doing so they inhaled a helping of my envy, they still remained uninitiated. They could not understand why their throats bunched up between the two stops, why all at once their bodies seemed heavier; and if I didn't jump off at the next stop, why, they'd suspect that an illness was brewing within them. In fact, it is because of men and women like me that riding subway cars, half-filled trams, and trolleys feels so oppressive. Not only do we smear our bad moods onto seats and handholds, we also allow the defenceless to unsuspectingly inhale our depravity. We should voluntarily relinquish our right to use public transport; indeed, we ourselves would fare better with a good walk! Perhaps we'd even get special permission from our workplaces for being late every day.

In my own defence I can cite only my vigilance. I took care not to step beyond the limits, and the mere suggestion that I had caused me to disappear as soon as possible. Some meetings were of course exceptions: those in which I sensed that my presence, even despite the initiation of the usual secret communication, did not endanger the other's safety. One such occasion gave me a real scare.

I'd gone to a downtown cafe for tea. There I tried out the various chairs with my usual thoroughness before finally settling into an acceptable one. A few people had meanwhile eyed me distrustfully. Only on looking up did I notice that I'd taken my seat beside a table occupied by a young woman. Not attaching particular importance to this fact, I waved a hand to get the waiter's attention, and then placed my order. After a short time, however, I was overcome by a disquietude that I, who'd always clearly understood the various manifestations of my worries in an instant, couldn't make heads or tails of. But I didn't have to think for long. The waiter hadn't yet even brought out my tea when it struck me. The woman sitting at the adjacent table was exuding the same characteristic fragrance as L., and the more deeply I breathed it in, the more certain I became that this could not have come from a bottle! To be certain, I asked her if she was using perfume, but her smile only confirmed my suspicions. I was on the brink of closing the matter by determining that the two fragrances, hers and L.'s, were beyond a doubt the same, when all at once I began feeling that very same slackening of the body that only L.'s proximity evoked in me. It was as if the young woman's fragrance had now sprayed itself all over my body so that, like L., she too could worm her way close to me and free me of the strange substance of shame within me. Like some newly opened wound, my entire body was throbbing, and within moments

I was bathed in fine beads of sweat, as if my envy and cowardice had precipitated onto this salty fluid. All the while I felt that this chemical breakdown was occurring not only within myself but also between me and the young woman sitting practically beside me. Something was decisively pulling me toward it, in a manner strikingly similar to that in which light lures the leaves of plants. She was swallowing the strength dissipating from within me every bit as imperceptibly as a flower does water vapour from the air. This was a crime, I understood at once! And so I sprang up from my seat, paid the waiter at the counter, and ran right out of the cafe.

That is not to mention that it have been unfair to L. had I stayed. I would have violated our alliance if, beyond my experiments, I used strangers to detoxify my body, my imagination. I could count on the help of men and women I didn't know only while mapping the possibilities by which I might free myself of envy. That is how I came to realize that L. was immune to my illness not only due to her understanding, but also on account of the enigmatic biochemistry defining her cells, her tissues. Of course, it may well be that it was her love for me that produced within her the antibodies to resist the poison of my compulsive thoughts, that her unshakable love diminished the toxicity of my wretched feelings.

When, after some such episode, I went up to L. and, having plucked up my courage, embraced her, it seemed that that certain oppressive force I'd sensed during the day in my throat and around my heart had found a new road to traverse: her body. Suspiciously I watched to see if she could endure the weight of my anguish. But L. seemed not disturbed in the least; and indeed, if this was possible at all, she seemed to nestle up close to me with even greater devotion— as children do to their favourite toys when they are afraid, or when they share their secrets with these objects, which to them seem more alive than do adults. Then I extricated L. from my arms, stepped back and sized up her face. Though she seemed surprised, she also exuded warmth. The anguish that a moment before had clutched at my throat now seemed to appear in her eyes, but I felt absolutely sure that in the meantime it had turned to light. The dissolving of my anguish into beauty within her body must have transpired just as incomprehensibly to the naked eye as when plants squeeze toxic gases out of themselves through their leaves, so that these gases might quickly become fragrances. I thought of it as 'beauty', this light that spread out over L.'s entire face as fear does through the body of the condemned when their cell door opens for the last time as they head for execution.

I should have fled from L. at once, had I noticed her lineaments contorting amid my relief, or had I had even a moment's doubt as to the beauty of her eyes; for nothing is worth the sacrifice that occurs, albeit subconsciously, when someone breaks under pressure while lifting a burden from someone else. This is an age-old mis-calculation on the part of those who overestimate themselves—those who do not suspect that even intentions are subject to the law of secret harmonizing. L. must have been intuitively heeding this law when transforming my misery into the razor-sharp light on her eyes. This was an all-accepting glance, one that perhaps doesn't even see, only radiates. One time I saw this under the upturned eye-lid of a blind man, on the white of his eyes—as if every sheaf of light comprising his inner vision had adhered to this whiteness, to illuminate its sightlessness. Perhaps the light he carried around inside of him had found windows on those two moist orbs—a light that, on account of his blindness, he could never let out of himself, after all.

3

There were, however, also days when L. reinforced my sense of shame. I began observing her differently. No longer did I have to fear only my unexpected visions but also the alluvial deposits of the self-loathing I'd felt ever since becoming aware of my envy. No sooner did I notice the disquieting streaks on her hand left behind by others' caresses than I also discovered the visible evidence of self-loathing—as if the envy that stoked my compulsive ideas had assumed visual form on that thin wrist and on those fingers. At first, with an anguish I'd experienced a thousand times, I was able to trace the paths of those marks I knew so well. I closed my eyes, and on reopening them I saw her hand, which moments before had looked flawless, as a charred stump. Only my hatred, my disgust could have burnt it to a crisp!

Sometimes the vision I saw superimposed on L.'s face was succeeded by an image of decomposing skin. My own decay was opening up before me, I thought, and I'd have to keep watching it until the face would finally flake right off the bones. At such times I didn't even dare touch L.'s face, fearing as I did that a piece of skin would remain between my fingers. In vain I tried directing these hallucinations onto my own body instead, so they would dismember my own hand, devour my own face—the visions held firm to L still.

This infernal trial was part of my punishment. When, one night, I found the marks of my depravity even on L.'s naked body, I knew I'd arrived at the final limit. Had I had the courage, I could have sunk my fist into palm-sized, gaping lesions. L. lay motionless beside me, waiting patiently for me to initiate the first caress. For several long minutes I thought of the devastation my imagination had wreaked on this body. And all at once it hit me that the hatred and scorn I felt towards myself was casting its net over me far more shrewdly than I'd ever imagined. It seemed someone or something had cunningly seen to it that my desire for self-destruction would consume not only me but also someone outside myself; for only thus could a sin be perfect! If we ruin only ourselves, we could justly expect a lesser punishment! My envy demanded the strictest judgement, however, which is why I was fated to defile L.'s body. Only by doing so could I hope for a suitable chastisement myself.

And so I held this latest chapter in the flights of my imagination to be penance. While the fading of my erotic visions was a great relief, those that took their place, which were solely about bodily decomposition, alarmed me to no end. Sometimes it was some characteristic odour that signalled the coming of yet another phantasm— though not long before I'd brought home a bouquet of flowers, and a few minutes ago I'd opened the windows to air out the apartment. I defended myself in vain, for all at once my nose was hit by the scent of rotting flesh: the stink of the dead cat down in the cellar, which even the rats turned away from, and the sweet fermentation of corpses flung atop one another into a mass grave, which perhaps only survivors otherwise smell, on occasion, in their dreams. I tried thinking of a poor, hungry kid in the habit of asking for prices in a butcher shop only so he could illicitly inhale the scent of flamed sausage and smoked ham. Then I imagined someone gone mad from love, who has lost everything but for the smell of the rose he

THE PARASITE

bought on his last illumined day. But I endeavoured in vain: I could no longer sense even the actual stimuli around me. Perhaps these gases had bubbled forth from my guts or poured out of my throat, but wherever the source, from L.'s unperturbed expression I gathered that she'd perceived not a bit of this.

After a little while L.'s face changed all the same—as if the stink emanating from *my* body had targeted her face! In no time it had settled on her mouth, boring into the pores, closing off all remaining open entryways through the skin. Bluish-yellow fungal growths appeared, gradually turning her face into a single culture. Then buds began taking shape in a few places, bleeding little heaps projecting here and there, at first expanding and then collapsing sand hills of accelerated decomposition. The entire surface of L.'s face was by now soaked in indeterminately coloured fluids. What I saw before me was a gelatinized form with a furry surface, which had only my imagination to thank for not yet falling apart. It resembled the face of an embryo, one whose body has so far been mangled only as far as the neck.

I was just about to scream when the vision suddenly ceased. L.'s face seemed unperturbed, as it had a few seconds earlier.

Leaving her there, I went out to the bathroom and locked the door behind me. I was as disgusted with myself as the commander of a firing squad who, recovering from his drunkenness, discovers his own mother's body among the massacred. The insidiously transformed images had sobered me. The decay of L.'s face, the frightful charring of her hands, and the palm-sized gaping lesions on her belly and chest were a sign that the final warning was now behind me. It was now that I truly understood that if I didn't tear out of myself the roots of these visions, I would be lost for ever. Not only had these images broken the force of their relentless erotic forerunners but also my usual resistance to my madness. Until now I'd regarded myself as a hyena; but starting now I also held myself to be a murderer, one who must witness his victim's disintegration again and again. But this is precisely what I needed—this vileness, this depravity. From this sensation taken to the extremes there emerged a strength that nurtured in me an unfamiliar fear: the possibility of the other's irrevocable annihilation.

Although I knew full well that even this most extreme phase of my corrupted imagination did not endanger L.'s physical existence, I was nonetheless consumed by fear, as if she were now suffering an incurable illness. So it was now also in her defence that I had to conquer my accursed visions. Not for a moment could I be fooled by the fact that these hallucinations had so obscured the very images buttressing them mightily for years that those images had become virtually unrecognizable. Even the immediate prospect of my long-awaited liberation would entitle me to commit this insidious deed. If I threw L.'s body to my demon like some bone to a dog, then every previous attempt of mine would have been in vain. If only in my imagination, I would have allowed that very woman, who had revealed my torments before me, to be destroyed.

At the same time, these new phantasms of mine seemed to have nabbed my demon by the collar. They proved the routing of its strength, marking the borderline beyond which my demon could step only with my help; for without my assent it could not give me the *coup de grâce*. Only now had it become clear that in the final settling of accounts, my demon was just as dependent on me as I'd been dependent on it up until then. Nor could it count on me to assume the terrible lightness of the real murderer, whose body tenses up the moment he fires a gun or plunges his knife, so from that point on he is unable to ever free himself of this sensation. It was as if the vision projected onto L.'s face had verified a simple fact: my dictatorial master could no more undo the taboos hidden at the depths of my body than could I—at most, it could accompany them.

I was not deceiving myself when, deathly pale, I returned from the bathroom and lay down in bed beside L., who fearfully scrutinized my face. I had to sleep, I told her, although I knew that on this night some time would pass before I'd doze off. I understood all too well everything I'd thought through in the bathroom. Better to surrender myself to the compulsive ideas I'd had for years and that concerned solely the erotic, I decided, rather than again observe this decomposition, this insidious rotting that sprang from within myself but ran its course on L.'s body! It seemed—and I now turned towards L. with more suspicion than usual, fearing as I did that I'd once again see the decay—that my illness could be vanquished only with an even greater blow; like someone who, after losing his dearest loved one, immediately breathes a sigh of relief on being told by a doctor that he has an incurable disease.

Search L.'s face though I did, the marks I'd seen before were now nowhere to be found. At first I thought that this particular phantasm had retreated only to give way to L.'s former lovers. I waited in vain. All I could see was her anxious face, her frightened eyes fixed on me, the wrinkles between her brows, which now seemed solely to be physical manifestations of her concern for me. I was suspicious nonetheless. I'd had symptom-free days before, when my hallucinations could not assail L.'s face. Then, like someone who does not want to recognize a deception he's experienced so often before, I turned to a ruse. It was the successful erasure of the vision of decomposition from L.'s face that gave me the idea. Namely, it hit me that I had my own will to thank for this! Why couldn't I do the same thing with my long-time foes? Perhaps the two types of visions sprang from the same source, the difference being only one of intensity? The juxtaposition of my erotic visions with my imagined images of bodily decay left me in doubt. And yet the neutralization of those agonizing images of decay had filled me with a liberating sensation I cannot overestimate. If I'd been able to incinerate my visions of L.'s putrefying face and ulcerous hands, why would I not be capable over time of demolishing those of her lovemaking past?

But these visions I'd thought impossible to forget were late in coming. Had I outmanoeuvred them by voluntarily accepting them, or were they now *not* visiting me merely because they'd grown exhausted? Had I been rewarded by my readiness to undergo such torment? Had acknowledging my envy freed up the warriors within me—warriors who'd established a cordon around my obsessions? Or had maintaining the penitence I'd imposed on myself on account of my loathsome trait protected me? Perhaps it hadn't been in vain, after all, that for weeks I'd repeated those seven magical sounds, *You-a-re-e-n-v-y?*

Of course, there was certainly no guarantee that my pathological thoughts would not return with a vengeance in the days to come or, say, within a few minutes. Despite this, I felt that with my uncertain questions I'd definitively moved beyond the impasse. Something told me that I was less vulnerable than before. It seemed as if only now had that foreign matter which had planted itself in my body more than ten years earlier finally dissolved within me—that which until now had held me in its grip, from my throat to my belly. I was like a convalescent who, after a heart operation, believes he can feel the stitches every day that hold his capillaries together, all the way up to the point when the white thread dissolves in his blood.

At this moment, I would have been pleased to test my strength by wilfully evoking one of my dubious visions with the same reasoning with which a child might stick his finger into an electrical outlet: Will he really get a shock? Using my hesitation to my advantage, I even gave it a go—namely, by trying to steal onto L.'s face that certain smile of hers I'd suffered from so much. After fracturing the arch of her sealed lips ever so slightly, I took to searching her gaze for evidence of sensuality born of the attention of other men; for the seductress, for the woman seduced. To my great dismay, I could not tempt myself to delve too deep. Were my phantasms really so self-determining, the rules governing our behaviour so strict, that only my demon could decide the etiquette of the torture it inflicted? But I understood at once, before confusion might have set in anew, that these questions had long been ingrained in me. I could not associate the present failure of my imagination to produce at will with the usual scheming of my demon, its shrewd injection of breaks into the spans of my torture. Due to an intimation of sorts gathering force within me, I now saw it as beyond doubt that my freedom was near. Nothing could shake this feeling—not even my awareness that in the weeks, months and perhaps years to come, the visions might well visit me once again.

It was with this newfound lightness that I turned again towards L., who had, however, fallen asleep in the meantime. Previously, in such moments I would have taken advantage of her unconsciousness by robbing her dreams, but doing so didn't even occur to me, not any more. On her face I could still see the fear with which she'd received me on my return from the bathroom. That tell-tale wrinkle between her eyebrows had not smoothened out—as if even in her dreams she was concerned for me, as if she was inhaling my doubts. Not only in my belly and around my heart had the pressure ceased in the minutes that had just passed, but a cleansing of a sort had ensued within my mind. From now on, I knew, I would judge my situation far more lucidly. Dawn was breaking by the time I fell asleep.

4

The next morning it occurred to me that I'd be misinterpreting my situation were I to pin all the blame for my compulsion to compare myself with others only on my envy. All at once I had to give credence to a supposition I'd been formulating for years now—one that until then, in the absence of even a minimal distance from my situation, I'd been incapable of analysing clearly.

It often seemed to me that a portion of my self sometimes separated from me, that it withdrew from my control to live its own life. But even its high-handed propensity to do so didn't ensure it such independence that I couldn't keep track of its machinations. Still, it was constantly one step ahead of me. In vain I prohibited my imagination from veering into its delirious flights of fancy if the self that was one and the same with me, and yet distinct, nonetheless dredged up some phantasm before my eyes. In such moments, my role was thus limited to confronting the bare facts. If, however, I managed to undo the image by scratching it off my cell walls, I had to count on its aftereffects; say, that my optical nerve endings had become contaminated with radiation. Why couldn't the force that had held the images together be absorbed by my cells, why should the matter that was my body not receive into itself that light which makes the image possible in the first place?! Certain images give off substances even more dangerous than radiation, and there is no protection against them.

That portion of the self which slyly separates from a person resists all aggression. This too goes to explain why treatment with medications is so fateful a course of action, for by dismantling a self that's said to be ill with the aim of curing this or that constituent component, we unwittingly destroy even those of its territories that are still sound; for even a fragmented self possesses a vague oneness, and what happens to one territory affects the others. Perhaps this accounts for the anguish borne of that helpless sensation that one is simultaneously outside and inside oneself—that I am in fact superior to the force smirking at me. A tad profane though it may be, we might venture to say that God may be the exemplar of the exquisitely developed schizophrenic, who is reminded every minute of creation's mockery by human beings. Of course, believers equate this with the mystery of God's boundless understanding.

Had these 'selves' that had torn away from me and yet remained part and parcel of my Self been the hotbeds of my obsessions? Notwithstanding that I'd undeniably been the one who'd noticed the traces of earlier caresses on L.'s hands, it now seemed to me that the image could only have been so sharp because a portion of my Self had become one with it—as if I alone were taking care to ensure that the motion should become not a touch but a caress. It may sound absurd but I felt as if I myself were the caress. A normal person can rightly regard this as nonsense, but for me it was an everyday experience of a sort I wouldn't even wish upon my foes.

At such times I infiltrated L.'s personality, much as others work their way over years into a well-crafted role—a role without which it would be impossible to maintain their sense of self-identity. But how much more oppressive it is, despite all our trouble, to finally become one with that which we sought to identify with! The further I wished to be from the signs I discovered on L.'s hands, the more I had the feeling that it was the power seeping out of me—a force that necessarily seemed part of my Self—which now welded together those fingers so restless with desire. It would have struck me as imprecise to keep equating this state of consciousness with my phantasms. If imagining things force the person imagining them out of the shaping of the visions, why then, I must postulate the existence of a space within myself, one that might be called a void. Indeed, I always was one to liken even that something called the 'soul' with emptiness. If it were otherwise, how could even a single person receive the entire world into themselves? God scattered his emptiness every which way inside of us. Not only does this render his solitude more tolerable, it also makes us the instruments of his redemption. Perhaps one day it will be from within us that the being He'd wanted originally to send to Earth will be born.

The anguish that had regularly accompanied my visions must have emerged precisely from this emptiness. Sometimes it hit me even before I saw the image, at other times during the vision, and then there were occasions when it came a few seconds afterwards. This concurrence of the vision and the anguish or, as sometimes was the case, the opposite, gave me cause for further suppositions. If something suddenly began to oppress me while I was near L., I could not be certain that one of my obsessions was not about to visit me. Was it perhaps I who, after a little while, deliberately summoned forth some image, for doing so seemed more bearable than not knowing where my anguish sprang from? Could it be that what I was in fact trying to counterbalance the suffocating condition brought on by my separating self through images that were by all means dangerous to me—substituting the formless and inaccessible anguish with resolute self-torment? Never could I have overcome such moments by summoning pleasant memories, I'm certain of that. And substitution has its limits. In vain I would have thought of my oblivion that lasted from the moment we met to L.'s first confession.

Beyond the cheap lie, I would only have been able to sense the strangeness of my onetime rapture. While yesterday's rapture is all but incomprehensible, pain by contrast stakes an ever greater claim on us with the passing of time. Perhaps it was only my desperate desire for an explanation that gave rise to this self-contradictory supposition; for how could I possibly have deliberately chosen that which had tormented me so much in the past?

I remembered the day M. had found that stupid letter in my pocket. But even back then it wasn't by chance that I'd projected M.'s jealousy onto myself, I thought with a shudder, as if the meaning of my act only now became clear before me. What I'd believed to be my capacity for identifying with another's feelings—namely, M.'s jealousy—was in fact nothing other than an opening up of my self! The self-abandonment that had sealed my fate was not the sort that accompanies the most intense love affairs. If I too had been at risk of this blissful disintegration of the self, then as the passion waned I would have found my way back to myself. However, my tribulations had begun precisely when I'd finally broken up with M. And so it wasn't without reason that I believed myself to be showing symptoms of self-abandonment entirely different from those sometimes experienced by lovers. I'd tried conquering the hatred M. felt towards me by projecting her jealousy onto myself, believing that my decision to do so was the product of my free will, although I should have seen in this the first stirrings of my madness. I made as if I'd discovered the notion that a self can split in two. Indeed, I thought of myself as a talented magician, one who can imperceptibly influence the other's feelings and shift the very direction of the other's thinking. Amid my pride over my onetime successes, I did not notice that I was in fact busily building up within myself a schizophrenia that, at the outset, could perhaps have been termed only a peccadillo.

Never could I have figured this out if my demons hadn't clung to me so tenaciously; which is to say, I had to find an explanation, for my compulsion to compare myself with others had now begun to undermine even the self-identity I'd grown used to. If I were to determine the cause of my diseased imagination, I knew, it would be easier for me to surrender. I was grateful for my discovery demarcating the borders of my envy and my visions. My newest insight was even more of a relief. It was, indeed, a godsend; for it allowed me to understand the wild turns of my imagination as the necessary consequence of my ever-slackening Self. The visions had become the very counterexample of a unified Self! When some image so strange despite its familiarity spread out over L.'s body, that is, I became the observer of the self that had high-handedly broken free from within me. Were I a less extreme case, then this film would have played out solely within me. My advanced condition was such, however, that it projected the sensation of being pulled apart at the seams onto a human body outside myself, so I could see before my eyes everything that would otherwise unfold uncontrollably in the recesses of my mind. Of course, if my pathological thoughts hadn't been about the human body, I would not have had to be so ashamed. Hardly do we condemn those who go mad from a fear of God; indeed, we're more apt to view them with a sort of wonder, for the wild workings of their imaginations remind us of the distress we ourselves continually flee from. And do they deserve our scorn—those who evoke within themselves the images of their own death again and again with such alarming tenacity? And yet these same respectable fears become open to attack at once the moment they touch upon the erotic. Yes, a fear of God is mandatory, but a fear of the body, of corporeality, is an illness. With a clear conscience we can torment ourselves over our inability to ease suffering by explaining it, but if we turn our attention to our wretched sensuality, why then, we are seen as deviant. Still, with L. I now wasn't saddened, after all, to find myself classifying fear as respectable on the one hand and depraved on the other—perhaps because in the course of writing her story I came to understand that the most serious consequence of the fear that accompanies a heightened awareness of sensuality is not, in fact, our being branded as perverse by the outside world but, rather, the devastation the fear wreaks on our bodies.

Up until now I'd viewed myself as a character in a degenerate drama. I was simply a riverbed compelled to amass all the sediment that flowed its way from somewhere else. True, my demon was something I could at least cling to, something that simultaneously stirred in me the notion that it was somehow integral to my identity, yet discrete. On the one hand, I could not deny that I was the wicked one; on the other, there was no doubting that this force also existed outside myself. But never would I have suspected that which my most recent self-diagnosis had led me to discern. Many people would be terrified to perceive in their behaviour signs of a splitting of the Self. For my part, this realization was a bit heartening, for it gave meaning to that which, until now, had seemed incomprehensible. Finally I'd stumbled upon a sort of order behind the capricious assaults waged by my foes! That which for years I'd believed to be random torture had finally taken shape as law. I now saw my visions as a necessary function of my sense of self, as a part of me that had formed into images after separating from my Self; something that came from me but which I did not mould. In times of danger, perhaps everyone experiences this momentary interruption of the flow of the Self, or even an interruption of its rhythm. Depending on the degree of our shock or despair, we seek something with which to compensate for this sensation's evoking of non-existence.

This distancing and nearing of myself from myself and to myself, these seconds of breathing easy followed by tension—I experienced it all as if I were a substance sensitive to the slightest shifts in temperature, one that expands one moment and contracts the next. Neither my constitution nor what abilities I'd acquired over the years allowed me to determine the rhythm of this constant fluctuation. And so this was no more liberating for me than any freedom I might have earned to begin with. At the same time, the relative clarification of the relationship between my obsessions and my Self evoked in me a certain degree of satisfaction. My latest self-analysis had at least taken me a step further from where I'd been before. I'd managed to establish a distance between myself and the wild stirrings of my imagination without, however, absolving myself of responsibility. Being conscious of my illness on the one hand made me pitiable indeed, and yet it also brought me the very sort of peace I no longer hoped for.

I now suspected that my incessant compulsion to dredge up the past served merely to formally reinforce the slackness that so defined my Self—one in which present and past, indistinguishable from each other, held me in their mutual grip. Indeed, for me, summoning up the past was mandatory even if I'd already demolished all the lighthouses of memory. Once again I'd brought up some nonsense, I knew, but how could I even have hoped to validate my assertions with the approbation typical of schizophrenics with cases far more serious than mine? And yet it is so alarmingly simple. How often I'd tried ensuring that not a single wretched thought should take hold of my mind! Rarely indeed was I overcome by that sense of emptiness which perhaps only Buddhist monks who've meditated constantly can achieve towards the end of their lives. Mostly it was in vain that I repeated the incantation, 'I may think nothing, You may think nothing.' Even when they temporarily retreated for some reason, my compulsive notions, fears that words would free up in no time, constantly lurked near me. I was beset by the memory of memory, it seemed, and that the only reason some perilous scheme that could be born at any moment hadn't yet erupted from within me was that it was awaiting a more suitable moment to do so.

Had someone asked me what I was thinking at such times, I would not have been able to say. Besides numbness, I felt nothing in particular. As the minutes passed, something began sharpening within me, but without reaching the point where a thought could take shape. It wasn't a lack of strength that made me incapable of articulating words, but a slackness—as if I were simultaneously asserting and denying, approving and rejecting, whatever happened to be within me at the time. In this light, perhaps my simultaneous relationship to present and past is more understandable. I stood with one foot in each of two parallel tributaries of time, and could not take a single step in either in such a way that I would have left the other. Without *wanting* to remember, I was in the past, and when my obsession to dredge up its images took me in its grip, it was solely this condition that made itself felt. For me, the present, besides maintaining a sense of relative normality, had place value only to bring to light the past.

This duality played itself out in similar fashion in the course of conversations. Pronouncing a word or a sentence could not cease in me the sensation of past turned present, present turned past. This state of consciousness was given to strike me even in seemingly innocent situations. If, say, I wished to follow through on a line of thought with schoolbook logic, an arch of sorts flashed before my eyes that, while parallel to my sentences, ran in the opposite direction, and which thus undermined the validity of my assertions in no time. Starting then, I kept as much of an eye on this shadowy counter-arch as on the meaning of the sentences uttered in the course of the conversation. But the latter gradually faded into the distance, and often I myself knew least of all just what I might have asserted a moment before. Then, after a little while, I discerned the abiding presence of one of my harassing memory-borne images. So my thoughts served merely as an excuse for an enhanced sensation of the past.

Had I earlier recognized this slackness for what it was, perhaps I could have defended myself with more success; say, by voluntarily identifying with the selves estranged from my Self. In doing so I could have kept at bay that repugnant sensation, helplessness, that accompanied obligatory choices. I would not have been at the mercy of chance but, rather, of a personality I'd previously mapped out—one that, on the basis of suitable connivances, I could call my double. I suspect it is only after lengthy research that 'talented' schizophrenics happen upon the new personalities to substitute for their selves, personalities that ensure almost ideal conditions for the unencumbered functioning of their expanded consciousness. That which outsiders regard as the pitiable failure of a deranged mind can, for them, be the endless freedom they never would have hoped for, but which they can now experience every day. If it had been through my own will that I worked my way into stranger's lives, lives I could consequently replace at any time with others, why then, the danger would have diminished to a minimum of me being appropriated by L.'s past or the pasts of my former loves. After all, even the directed drifting and hiring out of the self has its limits! Perhaps it was not without foundation that I could have counted on my chosen doubles to satisfy my prowling self's thirst for adventure. Indeed, I could even have hoped that they would return to me voluntarily, giving up further infidelity.

By now I could explain the source of my manic thoughts even with formal logic. The visions were exposed as invitations mercilessly imposed upon me. Only a 'self-transplant' could have guaranteed unmitigated protection, but not even in my most vulnerable hours would I have undergone that. My newest insight brought with it the recognition of necessity. By this I mean acceptance, not resignation. The latter evades the despair that comes with resistance, a despair that prepares us for recognition of the irrevocable. The therapeutic effect of confession allowed that which until now had been inscrutable to take more definite form. It seemed as if this analysis of my illness had allowed my absolution; no, not by having the burden lifted from my shoulders, but simply because the meaning of my torture had been made clear before me.

I would illuminate my situation with the example of the possibility of freedom from evil. It sometimes seemed to me that evil which appropriates a self can be conquered only by evil. It is no coincidence that those who carry much evil around in themselves turn even more depraved in the proximity of so-called 'good'. But they find themselves in an entirely different gravitational field if they encounter their own brand of perfidy in themselves. The possibility emerges of a moment in which wickedness turns against itself, for its power has reached the point beyond which its neutralization would ensue. Presumably this is why Christian metaphysics created hell and purgatory. Only thus is it truly understandable why the direct attributes of God are missing from these realms. Never could forgiveness complete that work which expiation regularly does. Let us not forget that one self of God's otherwise indivisible Self also atoned for the sins of creation, even if we ascribe his sacrifice simply to our salvation. But it is possible that Christ's suffering serves only as an example of that which has played itself out in God from the beginning of the World. One step in the earthly realms of hell is confession. In doing so we come face to face with our own wretchedness like a flower staring upon the freshly mended sole of a boot before being trampled by it. The more vulnerable we become by confronting our own misdeeds, the greater our prospect of coming closer to the centrifugal force of despair, where an elevating force that functions in accord with unknown laws can create a new order within us. We tend to experience this as a shocking sense of emptiness, whereas only our wickedness has reached its limits.

Of course, all this analysis pointed far more to the vanquishing of my envy than to a newfound freedom born of my having brought my illness to the forefront of my consciousness. Nonetheless, I discovered similarities between the two. By understanding the underlying structure of my phantasms, I'd created the core condition for me to be the equal of my demon; for a subordinate relationship would not have allowed me to pass judgement. The judge can never truly punish the accused; only the guilty has the right and the power to do so. Helplessly, perhaps, but I did now stand before my foe as its equal. Not that I could rise to the level of my loathsome trait and scratch it out of my system with the strictest of methods, as I had envy. But simply knowing that I was its equal allowed me to set certain conditions. For example, I demanded abilities that would have allowed me to finally measure up to my tormenters' expectations—say, to accept suffering as natural, and so not to flee foolishly from before it, for it is as inseparable from our fate as gravity from a dropped stone. Not that I could wish for a change in the eternal order of things, by which I might have averted by failure altogether, but I could expect to be able to choose from among the modes of surrender. My new status demanded a dubious title as well: to develop as a talented victim, so read the call to action, as in a race without stakes, in which the struggle's goal need be defined only towards the finish line. My example might have been that person who, while receiving blows, pays at least as much attention to his tormenter as to his own pain, thus taking measure of the veiled alliance between aggression and defencelessness. Most of all, I claimed the right to have my obsessions confer on me the honorary degree of specialist in patience and perseverance.

With the slow realization of this condition, I noticed something in myself. Although my role in this realm was fundamentally passive compared to the above-analysed dramaturgy of looking things in the face, still I couldn't regard my acceptance of the forces charged with my torment as surrender. The relationship that emerged was the same as the one I achieved after proclaiming my envy. The precise parting of roles now seemed to be the manifestation of a certain freedom. While my demon's existence was synonymous with my torture, my fate, I understood, was all about enduring this. Some will call me a fatalist for saying so, whereas I am talking only about the whimsical curiosities of every distinct deal presumably offered to each of us. I call it 'freedom', the recognition of the law that consigns the tormenter to the side of him who awaits the torment. The liturgy of existence continues differently with this, since from now on, suffering can be a source of invigoration, much like its sibling, pleasure. A true captive wouldn't give up his guard even if the rules allowed for this, for he knows it takes both of them to realize the purpose of the punishment. The guard senses this, too, even if his presence is but a formal confirmation of the other's captivity.

The acceptance of suffering has enhanced the possibility of resistance. As a well-practised tormenter, I acquired those capabilities by which I could perfect the methods of conquering pain. After my cowardly flights of escape, I studied these much like some fakir, and I can say that over time I got pretty far. But the real surprise came when I realized that the positions of torturer and tortured are by no means definitive. Presumably this ensued from the dynamics of suffering, which must have been subject to the physics of power just as much as anything else on this Earth. I experienced this in my bitterest hours, when I had the sense that I had the upper hand over my foe. I thought I had my sense of dignity to thank for the tilting of the scale, after which, even as the vanquished, I was able to think of myself as stronger than my attacker. But then it seemed more precise to suppose that my unexpected respite stemmed from a gravitational force that ruled even over my torturer. Yes, I suspected that not even my torturer could escape its fate on completing my torture; that it, too, had to surrender itself to the force borne of my despair. In such moments it proved true that suffering and all its attendant perfidy served not to break me but, rather, to make me into a stiff-necked rebel. Our steadfast resistance can force our torturer to pass judgement against itself, from which it turns out that it is just as much at the mercy of the law that forms us as we ourselves inscrutably embody this law.

My explanation perhaps points to the purest form of schizophrenia. Instead of seeing in the suffering the evidence of a degenerate drama, I sensed in its acceptance the possibility of being free of suffering. I clung to my theory as a blind man might to the eyes of his true love, which for a while he'd seen more clearly prior to losing his sight. Never would I have believed that accepting the unacceptable would lead me back to that order we usually call the sense of hope. And yet this is a simple case of necessity, one in which everything embodies its opposite, exemplifying the law: the victor must go down in defeat, and the vanquished must triumph. This is a mercy the sad must feel when the sadness within them is exhausted, or which the body must know when, in the moment of death, it wrestles fear to the ground, so that the motionless can reign over motion.

5

While reviewing L.'s fictional story I realized that I could thank what I'd written for offering me the greatest help. I'd begun the project, after all, because I believed in the power of words. And I wasn't disappointed. In recent days I was less terrified by the thoughts that had long assailed me—in addition to the aforementioned reasons, perhaps also because I'd forced my pathological ideas into my sentences, adverbs and quotation marks. The imaginative venture that unfolded between the capital letter at the head of the sentence and the period at the end could never breathe as easily as in my mind. I could see that fears packaged neatly into grammatical form were less dangerous than their free counterparts, which neither punctuation nor rhythm could compel to obedience. When I managed to lure some utterly depraved thought into a sentence that took form before me on paper, then for a while afterwards it couldn't set upon me as it pleased, for it had to bring along the fruits of my discipline: word order, punctuation, stresses. Of course, it's not as if fear comes to heel on being conferred with an attribute, but—and I can prove this with more than one bit of evidence—it can wind up in a subordinate relationship. This is in part because it has been denoted, and in part because from now on it could appear before me only with this designation. I'd forced upon fear something that until now had been alien to it, something it now had to carry around as long as it laid claim to me.

I took the visions I'd seen on L.'s face and worked them into word collocations. In doing so, I not only fixed the image but simultaneously cast it to the words. The space between two words can continually tighten, so much so that it can redirect the meaning. I was not deceived by the spectacle of motionless letters typed beside each other, for I knew full well that words could pile up even if no external signal suggested this. And then I hadn't even figured into the equation the enigmatic chemistry of words that influence one another. Every single word has its own unique valence, which another word can either fix or else dissolve. In the case of certain word collocations and attributives we get the feeling that the meaning weighs down upon the sentences independent of our will, or, say, slips right off them, sometimes outright making a mockery of our original intent. Intended or perhaps unwelcome by-products of decay are released at such times from words placed directly beside one another.

I would be lying, were I to claim that I consciously exploited the chemical reactions of my written words. Only after many long months did I think of this laboratory procedure; namely, when I discovered the occasional weakening of those anxieties of mine that I'd managed to lure onto the islands of grammar. I had to give credence to my supposition that the fear linked by the paper clips of my sentences was also subject to the chemistry of the words. Perhaps the attributives inserted between subject and predicate began leaching the potency out of some pathological idea of mine, and well-chosen adverbs corroded certain of my manias, so that with time they might swallow them forever? Those who believe that sentences serve only to help us visualize are mistaken. Grammar sometimes assumes the role of a pander with embarrassing ingenuity, offering concessions to its creator. For example, with a simile we can inoculate the overpowering, nay, suffocating semantic content of a word, and we find it peculiar that we've calmed down even before reaching the full stop. These are the moments when a sentence lays claim on us, and not vice versa. In other cases exactly the opposite happens: we compel the sentence to cohere, a demand we often accentuate in a rather ostentatious manner by way of odd punctuation, as if in its absence we could not count on success. Besides its drawbacks, this method does carry advantages; for example, perhaps fear, too, will assume the sentence's exceptionally fragmented rhythm, and so we can't be discreet enough in applying it.

More than once I noticed that the anxiety that fled into my sentences donned the rules of grammar and then, wearing its new attire, fell back upon me. The image, once so sharp, now seemed fractured—as if its path was blocked by commas, semicolons and conjunctions meant to ensure either a pause for a breath or to introduce a subordinate clause. What is more, fixed meanings had to break through the moonlike halo around the sentence, which usually diminished their power. And if we think about it, this means even more energy loss, for by all means they had to subdue the gravitational force of the words. A well-formed idea on paper comes to us without resistance, so we would think. But the especially vigilant rightly suspect that not even the subtlest expressions can escape the pull of gravity. In certain cases, a thought seeks to escape the constraints of form without meanwhile losing its unity. Perhaps I am again talking nonsense, but if I think of the structure of our solar system, I cannot escape the fact that over billions of years stars expand and contract by turns. That which wants to break out is simultaneously advancing towards the midpoint.

In any case, this parallel, which is by no means spineless, renders more understandable that experience of mine which on rare occasions filled me with confidence. In exceptional moments I noticed that the meaning of a word was loathe to reveal itself; of course, by no means because I didn't grasp it but, rather, because despite the workings of cognition, something was ushering it back towards a certain borderline. I might also put it this way: the outward radiation of the word's meaning seems to have been broken by an invisible, prism-like force that was simultaneously in contact with the word and with me. One thing is certain: the fear that escaped the confines of the word did not find a direct path to me; instead, it was as if something or someone had ricocheted it off the wall of a billiard table my way, the decidedly perceptible effect being to diminish its force. Of course, I might have sought a simpler explanation for this perplexing phenomenon; say, that feeling formed into thought necessarily undergoes a miscarriage of sorts.

In the same fashion I held to my theory of silence—namely, that the quiet of my pages further ensured the protection of the sentences therein. Some believe that the lines we write engage in dialogue with one another, independently of us. Not only do I not cast doubt on this concept, which has gained considerable currency in certain circles, but I myself have much to thank for this hard to control, sometimes roguish, other times disheartening inclination of the written word. Only through our intuition can we determine: Is the good mood that unexpectedly strikes us as we stand near our written work the product of our sentences bantering with one another, or would we be best advised to suspect some other peculiar phenomenon? Likewise a matter of intuition is whether we should ascribe our sudden sorrow in the same circumstances to the meeting of two of our sentences that until now we've deliberately kept at bay from each other, or instead, as an ill omen, as a warning of a danger lying in wait? Nonetheless, there are cases when it is possible to determine beyond a doubt that sentences are secretly edging towards each other, a movement that can completely transform the typographic structure of a page—not that catching them in the act is ever quite possible, either.

At such times an utterly compounded sentence is dissatisfied with the services rendered by its counterpart in the same paragraph but placed at the bottom of the page—with its coddling or, say, being called to account—and, after a pause to gather up its will, heads off in its direction. The predicate of the main clause will dally about with the verbs of each and every clause or sentence in its way, and so too the modifiers, which especially like adventure, for the freedom to move forward opens up the opportunity for intimacy on par with fornication. On reaching the middle of the page, for example, they take to outright chatting up a mass of modifiers they happen upon, and if they manage to outwit the bleary-eyed guard, the noun, they might even copulate. The whole thing is over in a flash. The predicate of the main clause impishly turns a blind eye to their looseness, and indeed it commands them to hurry it up, for the verb of the simple sentence breathing at the bottom of the page is impatiently awaiting its arrival. The clauses and sentences standing in the way step warily to the side, as if they know they must not resist. If at that moment we were to take up the page, we'd be really surprised. We'd see a heap of piled up lines, and at the bottom of the page, a lone simple sentence. We'd be annoyed with ourselves for having typed so carelessly the previous day, and would not suspect that the preparations for the meeting of two sentences had yielded this change.

Only that this opportunity is never a given for us, which however does not mean that we can't subsequently discern this sometimes risqué, sometimes curious, and most often fruitful unity of sentences. I am talking of that unmistakable confluence of sentences' sundry aromas and flavours that takes shape over months, years or perhaps only hours. If in thought we follow only the path taken by this restless compound sentence, we come to realize that the fluids generated by the wedding of adjectives and adverbs don't dry out for quite a while. If the sentences were to persist in eking out their independence, never could that change ensue which, as I see it, imbues their existence with succulence. Thanks to this enigmatic chemistry of mixing and dissolving solutions, I could rest assured that lurking behind the bastions of my sentences, even my obsessions underwent a sort of decomposition. The first stirrings of fermentation are present even in the zesty flavours of overripe fruit; we need only put the fruit aside until the juicy fibres arrive at the point of decay. So it was that I awaited the slow decomposition of my maniacal thoughts, until finally they would dissolve.

In light of all this, on certain days I strove to ensure that my typed-up pages would enjoy undisturbed silence; for I held quiet to be superior to any sort of benevolent ruse. Although in a bit of a roundabout way, I did manage to secure silence for my pages. At first I placed thick, mostly coloured sheets of paper between them, thus hindering the pages' permeability. In doing so I tried choosing the most inhospitable colours—for example, a cheerless, railway worker's blue or a sickly, operating-room green—figuring that my sentences would perhaps be less enthused about penetrating them. Naturally I couldn't yet rest easy; after all, the possibility still existed of this or that page carrying on a dialogue with itself. Then I took up a pen and drew frames around sentences I felt to be particularly dangerous, taking care that my lines should be forbidding and, ideally, geometrically precise, depriving them of the warmth that comes from the disarray of irregular curves. Using a pencil was the furthest thing from my mind, for despite my best intentions, the graphite would no doubt have conspired with the recalcitrant sentences. In contrast, a pen's cold blue seemed to ensure a certain barrier, especially given that the utterly methodical lines didn't even allow the fenced-in bits of text room to take a breath.

In those instances when even these sixty-character-long, three-quarter-inch-wide frames proved incapable of restricting my sentences' freedom, I then proceeded to shade some word that seemed to be the ringleader, figuring that its shiftless companions would take this as a due warning. The paradoxical logic of this procedure must be familiar indeed to those who can summon forgotten thoughts only with the help of certain words, who anxiously carry on their search until they finally happen upon the single, bellwether verb. In vain they fling upon one another expressions related to the sought-after word, only that certain, spunky verb is snap open the lock of memory. I experimented exactly with the reverse in taking stricter than usual measures against singled-out words. Depriving them of their elegance, of that almost ostentatiously dark lustre which, right after typing, I was otherwise always fond of gazing upon, I gloated as my shading turned them bluish grey.

I had even shrewder techniques, however; namely, I subjected the most suspicious of sentences to a sort of musical aggressions. On certain days I put some Vivaldi concerto on the record player and arranged my pages in front of the speakers while I left the flat, trusting my sentences to the gaiety of the Venetian priest. After about half an hour I returned, repeating the exercise, but this time remaining in the room. On more fortunate occasions I scored a double success: for one thing, I figured that not only could my plants become stronger and lovelier from the luminosity of the baroque magician's music, but perhaps my sentences would also be seduced. Let us remember the netherworld melody that resurrected the dead. Surely my method sought much less—only that bitterness should receive into itself, for two times half an hour, a joke dressed in the garb of rhythm, the princely cheer streaming out of a minor key! That is not to mention my presumption that, having been permeated by the music, my lines would yearn for silence once and for all, voluntarily renouncing their customary scheming.

Of course, my sentences might already have taken as a good example the narrow but unbroken white of the margins and from the emptiness of the space between the lines. And yet not even the sternest reproof or the most wily of techniques could have silenced them had that original silence not been there to begin with, that which belongs even to those pages most inundated with text. People experience the same thing: they are capable of perceiving silence precisely because this phenomenon that seems separate from them is in fact a part of their own inner cacophony. Of course, noticing this silence in continuous talking, for example, is anything but easy. At most, we can count on getting signs from the silence that has moved to the margins of our hands, to the empty spaces between the lines of our bodies.

In more fruitful hours my endeavours hit their mark. Hushed sentences fell into silence undisturbed as this bright flow absorbed every single word, accent, and clause. Not a single adjective or conjunction could elude this muteness, which was which was heavier than a plummeting body the moment it hits the ground after a suicidal leap. This silence permeated each such sentence from the capital letter at its fore to the period at its end. My foe now found itself face to face with the most relentless interrogator, and only through its strength could it endure the memory of itself, for even an obsession that has ended up in the stocks of grammar has a self-identity.

Given their demonic nature, my foes of course withstood the interrogation, and yet I was unsure whether the silence hadn't undercut the strength of some among them, reminding them of their servitude; for they were my creations, too, no matter how wickedly they danced about in that territory in which the borders of my own self and the demon overlapped. Thus I could demand my sentences, which served as an abode for my compulsive ideas, that they should enforce the rights of their constituent parts that gave these ideas a home. For example, I could expect that a dependent clause should shake fear right out of itself; after all, it was serving only as a sort of temporary shelter, out of compassion for those ideas that had landed in trouble. I was however more calculating when it came to a subjective subordinating clause. From it I outright expected the annihilation of the specified thing or person, no less by expelling its contents while retaining its form. As for pulling off this ploy, I left that up to it; my responsibility was solely to verify: Had an obscure idea indeed separated with time from the distress linked to the person, the thing?

As a rule, I perceived the amassing silence I'd projected in imagination onto the manuscript only days later. On again picking up the pages I'd written, it seemed to me that my sentences had turned lighter, more weightless, and I ascribed this to the favourable effects of my silence therapy. I wasn't bothered one bit about the sort of absurd procedures and delirious thoughts with which I was leading myself on; the only thing that mattered was that I defeat my temptress, much as some man on Papua New Guinea who, while sucking the brain out of a dead relative's skull, knows that he has triumphed over death. Hardly can I imagine that anyone could stir doubts in this man over his rather outdated convictions. I, for example, am able to definitely assert that a sentence sheathed with fear can never be as oppressive as when that same fear passes through our bodies. There is no comparing the insidious pressure around our chest with its counterpart that we recognize in a verb or noun, even if the latter appears to be more impudent. I'd had plenty of time to get acquainted with the images that proceeded across L.'s face for this contradiction to be somewhat allayed.

It wasn't my seeking to escape the visions, but the desire to experiment, that led me when I placed my sentences—these sarcophagi that undulated sometimes evenly, other times irregularly—beside the image that happened to be before my eyes. With little effort, I achieved that which, if for no other reason, doesn't count as out of the ordinary because there are many who voluntarily visualize that which is written, the dead. I would have regarded it as cheating, had I taken these sentences which I'd ushered to the proximity of the vision to carry out a sort of incantation. Indeed, I now deliberately relinquished such sorcery, hoping that the sentences would support me regardless of my will. The moving letters spread out on L.'s face rather like a snooty person's bumptious smile, one that not even the most unexpected news can wipe away. On the one hand, I wouldn't wish it upon anyone to have their imagination type evidence of their treachery onto a living face in the form of sentences. On the other, sometimes I was outright grateful for these breathing page proofs, for this typographic technique that exploited the warmth of the facial skin; for at times I noticed that the horizontal and vertical axes of these undulating sentences, and the diagonals that crossed them, had begun to vibrate the vision on the face. What until now had appeared to be a relentlessly fixed image, an immutable reminder of the past, was all at once preparing to fall away, to disappear.

I arrived at a rather simple explanation—namely, that the concept trumps the image, much as a capable hunter who applies amateur methods does an animal less wary than him. Indeed, my sentences, dispersed as relief troops, were visually manifested only on the level of graphic signals, and so I had to solve their delicate meanings separately. But this pursuit was a relief compared to the image I'd seen just before, which was perhaps due to the fact that although a series of several hundred frames passed before my eyes while watching a single image, during that time only a few dozen foes of mine could smirk at me from the waves of meaning of this or that word or sentence. At the same time, my simultaneous observation of the image and the sentences came with the astounding observation that, just before, I'd called the 'vibration of meaning'. It was as if this or that connotation of the compulsion to draw associations, which had been made the servant of the sentence, had wormed its way into the image, which not long before had seemed one but now comprised frames turning almost impossibly fast, so as to extend the duration of the millionth-of-a-second cuts. This pulsation of the images convinced me that the vision was now one step away from blowing over.

That which I was unable to achieve through force and cunningly planned rituals, I did so with the help of magic, which I became conscious of only later. Of course, this too had its dangers. A method that had once proved to be a solution impertinently left me in the lurch on the next occasion with a cagey confidence, with a uniformity as if I'd never had support. But I still didn't see reason for a calling to account, and so I saw it as much smarter to study the anatomy of the momentary instances of relief, the temporary liberations; for example, the dialectics of punishment and reward on the axis of images, which had become fused with sentences. Never in my wildest dreams would I have thought that the sentences tasked with my torment could, if only for an exceptional moment or two, become the sentries of my peace.

For this I could thank the outside intermediary, which held my licentious imagination under increasingly strict supervision—as if I might have instinctively sensed even at the outset of my written work that delirious thoughts lured to a more or less neutral territory—and writing by all means fit the bill—would be sapped of strength. It had previously struck me that my foes, leading lives

of their own, required their own space and time, and I really understood this only now that they had gathered in packs on my
manuscript pages. It was up to me, how to turn the uncertainty surrounding the work to my advantage.

Undoubtedly I was the author of my work, but in no case could
it follow that I was one and the same with it. Sometimes I believed
that the pathological thinking in the sentences didn't even originate
in me. At such times I became suspicious. Had it really been I who
thought that villainy, or quite to the contrary, was it imagining me
in such lowly terms? Of course, I could not satisfactorily answer
the question, but the doubt that unexpectedly ran to my aid gave
me a bit of relief. I didn't want to slip out from under my responsibility, pulling before myself Platonic ideas or the Kantean thing
in itself, for I knew full well that I could not separate my treachery
from my will, into philosophical speculation existing independently
of my character. Still, the knowledge that a force in the guise of the
unfamiliar was in possession of my mind, which related to me in
my written work but was nonetheless separate, meant that I was
less vulnerable to danger than was the case from my unstructured
self spying on me. The latter was so threatening precisely because
there, the stage demarcating the border between 'I am' and 'I am
not' was missing from here, the space where drawing a distinction
would have become possible.

Distress given form, imagination forced into the vessel of syn-
tax, yielded a different sort of unfamiliarity than that into which
my demon had pulled me into. When rereading L.'s fictional confession or the preceding chapters of my own confession, I regarded
certain of my sentences to be newcomers, intruders unknown to
me. In places I would have sworn I couldn't have written such a
thing, and indeed I would have denied it outright, had my characteristic word usage and faltering style not given me away. It seemed

these sentences were bent on living separate lives, generously reminding me that with a period I'd sealed their fate. I might have thought of this unusual demeanour to be an unanticipated unity on their part, one born of their desire for independence. The vanity of the created had thus come face to face with the creator, their distrust in the creator. But I was glad about the self-confidence of this or that completed sentence, of its proud will to stand apart or, say, even of its open rebellion. I saw in this a guarantee of the distance they'd scratched out for themselves, a sign of the coming light, which I'd been excluded from before articulating my thoughts or even in the moment they found their way to paper. It wasn't in vain that I'd refined my customary method of self-duplication! After my loves, finally I'd come upon an intermediary outside myself whose crucible simultaneously safeguarded and dissolved my wretched imagination. I would have risen to the real challenge only if I'd been capable of staying silent; which is to say, if I'd renounce the magic of projecting my thoughts onto paper. But I had to admit that this stern expectation was completely unfounded, for I wanted not to be a hero, but a healthy human being.

All this by no means meant that each sentence and word I'd written had passed through every station of the secret path of self-alienation. I had some stubborn thoughts that, it seemed, could not count on the relief of metaphors, the balancing effect of modifiers, the help of particle words that served as a counterpoint to certitude—in a word, for the sympathy of form. Even in the garb of nominals, these thoughts remained naked, rather like a prostitute whose brazen nakedness only really surges forth when she dons her flashy fur coat. It was with heightened mockery that certain of my obsessions called my attention to the fact that the privative intended for it was much more of a mantle, a jewel received as a gift, than a shadow threatening its existence. Indeed, they must have found the open vessel of the sentence outright pleasant, for they kicked aside its closing period and the intimations of finalization it embodies as surely as a contract that, at the last moment, one party is struck to realize is to its disadvantage.

I devised special procedures to vanquish these sentences of mine, whose hard-headedness deprived them of the opportunity that would otherwise have been at hand to become quick-witted torturers. Without a shred of guilt I placed the more stubborn rebels among them beyond the law, trusting their fate to my ritual ceremonies. If one of them perchance began flaunting its existence, I'd look up the page at issue and seek out those sentences that best expressed my compulsiveness, and then I'd repeat them until the content neutered itself. In the first minutes it seemed I was summoning them into their own memory, but as time passed, constant repetition deprived them of meaning, and I increasingly had the feeling that a sort of magic was underway; for the row of notes that had lost its meaning had become an enchanted, charm-like word on my tongue—at least that's how I explained the calm that quickly descended upon me. Needless to say, this pleasant state lasted only long enough for me to be assured of my method's beneficial effect.

That is when I decided that I would acknowledge an unwelcome thought only if it appeared in a manner I'd devised. Not even then would I be willing to accept it, should it be missing even a single indefinite article or a seemingly trivial particle. I decided to relentlessly reject the terror of subject and predicate, which was putting on airs in its role of the vehicle of essential content. Unremittingly I punished the thought if its manifestation as a sentence substituted even a single adverbial phrase for a related alternative; and I did so by questioning its existence. I really wasn't asking it to do the impossible, only that if it wanted to torment me, it should at least do so in my 'language'. I did not allow it to deviate, not even to the tune of a comma; no, it had to repeat the same tempo I'd intended for it when articulating the sentence, and so it couldn't burst in on me with a loathsome free rhythm, but instead had to inject a short pause ornamented with an accumulation of attributives and clauses whose effect was similar to that of commas. It could not outwit my inner ear. On those occasions when it underestimated me, surging ahead in an effort to gain an advantage, it always paid the price. A moment later I effortlessly pressed it back onto the page, making as if nothing had crossed my mind a moment before.

It didn't surprise me much that my foes got used to my ostensibly strict rules more quickly than a plant to its new circumstances after being dug up and replanted in a relatively disadvantageous place. Indeed, I noticed that my operation intended to imperil their existence was wholly to their benefit, similar to those flora that can most saliently prove their viability amid dire circumstances. That is when I devised a newer technique. From now on I didn't stop at insisting that the given sentence be impeccably dressed; I didn't sit back and relax on seeing it live up to my expectations. It now had to carry the words around it, too, if it wanted to count on a worthy welcome from me. I made it its own prompter, much as first contracts render aspiring actors behind-the-scenes experts. I gladly applied this ruse, for although context could not chip away at a sentence's provocative edge, it did break its momentum. For me, these dynamics meant the prospect of protection. That is why I sought to make sure that those standing guard in and about a sentence—word endings every bit as much as adverbial phrases starting off new clauses—would hold my foe captive for as long as possible. I acted brazenly towards my rival, which boasted of its firmness even while voluntarily accepting the supervision of its warders. I meanwhile paid attention not to it but to the latter, to the context, much as a depraved person who, in the presence of a king, might stare at the servants. By the time only adverbials or auxiliary verbs, which posed no danger on their own, were going through my head, I noticed that the thought lurking near me despite all this was slowly surrendering, edging back to the fortification being built up on the pages before me. Knowing its cunning nature, I still couldn't decide whether its retreat was a newer sign of machinations on its part or a singular loyalty; for, after all, I had just as much reason to suppose the latter as the former.

To be on the safe side, I then took the necessary precautionary measure—namely, if the thought would insidiously venture back despite adhering to all the rules up to now, I would play a trick on it. For example, I would transpose the particularly important words into related forms, where, owing to shifts in emphasis and mood, a once-dangerous pronouncement underwent a change in meaning beneficial to me. I would be a shrewd as a composer out for revenge, one who modulates a colleague's all-too-successful piece from a minor to a major key, so as to make a mockery of its manly, resolute firmness. When the sentence then really did appear, I was the most surprised of all to find that I didn't stick to my original plan. I replaced dangerous words not with related words, but with their opposites, which not even in the freest interpretation could I regard as the linguistic counterpart of retrograde in music. But the dubiousness of the method caused me no more disquiet than the suspicious nature of the parallel I drew between my technique and musical composition. It was clear to me that my procedure made me similar to those fools who think they can nullify the effects of verbal humiliation with a negative particle, a slap on the face by covering their face. Nonetheless, I kept up the game.

I thought this childish ruse would allow me to accelerate my sentence's self-alienation. If they were unwilling to deny themselves, I had to do it for them. Criticism reminiscent of open contradiction does not get to me; first of all, because we all know situations where even the most sincere assertion is exposed in us as a denial; and second, because by its very nature, every single word is also its own confutation. He who does not want to acknowledge this will resemble that experimenter who, rejecting the notion that breathing is fundamentally a two-directional process, constantly inhales—until, that is, he suffocates.

Just why certain thoughts take hold of the tongue is among the great mysteries of life, even if scientists a bit injudiciously draw an equal sign between them. Perhaps I should be more understanding of them, however, for it could easily be that we, the lay, identify some menacing feeling with a thought, a feeling that otherwise could not have the right to this. And yet our mistake is also understandable, for we haven't even had the time for a bit of savoury distress when a thought that satisfies even the experts takes to spying upon us.

My rather arbitrarily applied negation technique set its sights on an uncertain target. Perhaps I could have led my delinquent sentences back to the point where the thoughts behind them had once been borne of a feeling, an obscure idea. Only in part was I thinking here of the moment when, a few weeks or months before, I'd articulated the thoughts in writing, for then they'd gotten only custommade clothes, as it were. No. I sought to place the case strictly on the foundation of that first metamorphosis, onto that fusion even more mischievous than a meeting of cells, when a thought took shape out of some feeling of mine, a thought that then became an idea with time. My venture was a bit similar to that practice method well known among musicians, which aims to change the metabolism of the appropriate nerve fibres by way of motions repeated a thousand times and a thousand times again, thus correcting a technical error committed the first time and then stubbornly recurring ever since. What I hoped to achieve by ushering back into the past some obsessive thought I'd earlier stowed away in a sentence was this: By renewing the exchange of feelings and thoughts that had occurred at the beginning, to have this thought repeat the moment of its transformation. Of course, my foolishness was not so extreme that I thought this could be verified. But why couldn't I regard this nonsense as a door left open, one that perhaps the very absurdity of our existence would leave wide open even independently of us! A more precise measure of the irrevocable, the irreparable, was especially important in my case. A person who goes mute as an adult will not feel relief at their diagnosis, I suspect, just because a doctor shows that which was unavoidably in his genes. To me, however, thoroughly investigating the nature of the irrevocable became a compulsion! So it happened that as my sentences approached the boundary of feelings and thoughts, sometimes surprises were in store.

It sometimes seemed to me that in the course of this descent, a particular obsessive thought of mine had reached all the way back to the realm of that feeling first experienced, dissolving there again and again. This was a risky mingling indeed, for all my efforts to that point had now unexpectedly come into danger. In these sudden flashes of light, neither fear nor distress could count on the sutures of verbal articulation; indeed, by demolishing the thought I'd opened up the half-healed wound. Unbridled distress could once again take hold of me.

Those who suspect some sort of perversity or masochism behind this forget my shrewdness; for this was how I sought to step beyond the distress I'd neutralized only in part by articulating it in writing, by transforming it into words. I allowed it to grow massive within me, as by doing so I could guide it back to its origin. I acted as does that doctor who deprives his patient of a medication because only his patient's unrestrained pain can lead the doctor to the correct diagnosis. Though I knew this condition well, still I noticed something in myself that was new compared to my bouts of distress up to that point, something I can best describe as a presentiment of sorts. The unique dynamics of the strengthened pain may have gone to explain why I sensed a space akin to a person in the unexplorable territory separating feeling and thought. The longer my voluntary distress lasted, the more unequivocal this unnameable hiatus became. Most surprising of all was the fact that this remained in me even when, with the easing of the distress, my sentence once again led the flow of my consciousness. I had proof of this, too; and nothing less than the further weakening of the fear locked within the sentence. No longer was this just about the beneficial effect of abstraction, I felt, but my distress had begun to head towards this strange space—as if, starting now, someone or something else had also assumed a role in my struggle.

6

There was no further delaying the hour of confrontation. Within days, I knew, I would give L. the story of her fictional confession. In the meantime I'd decided that she would get the whole of my manuscript, for if I wanted her judgement, why then, my shame should be complete. By now, I was writing only in my dreams. On waking up, all I could remember was that I'd been pondering the structure of some sentence, but there was no recalling the thought I was hoping to write in the first place. In this I saw yet newer evidence of my recovery.

How wise I'd been—I, the connoisseur of hospitals—to have kept my distance from doctors all these years! To establish their diagnoses they would first have medicated me into a vegetable, and then as a sign of their compensatory care they might have experimented on me with sincere empathy. Had I entrusted my powerless psyche to their expertise, today I would be lying strapped down in a godforsaken room, and at most I could be entertaining my attendants and roommates. My one merit is that I didn't take advantage of those budget allocations of psychiatric institutions that might have been allotted to me. True, even this perspective, a bit practical but that much harder to dismiss, was not enough to make me forget the instances of perfidy I'd committed against L. and other women I'd been close to. Although I'd atoned for that, but the true calling to task had still been postponed to a later date. Still, I was certain that *then* I'd regard even the heaviest sentence as more endurable than that which my compulsive ideas had tortured me with for years. Or was I just consoling myself—I, who might have had more than a vague notion of this certain dispensing of justice? On the night I wrote these lines, I had a dream.

I was standing in the bathroom in front of the mirror, washing up after shaving. As soon as I finished drying my face, I noticed I'd cut my chin. I took a Kleenex off the shelf, and would have soaked up the blood in no time, but then I had a second thought. Having put back the Kleenex, I pinched my skin by the wound, and as if I wanted only to tear off a Band-Aid, with a sudden motion I tore the skin off my face. A strip of skin three or four inches long stayed between my fingers, and I put that on the shelf. Then, with barely a thought I again lifted my right hand, tapped around for the widest bit of stripped-off skin, and, now with a firm grip, I tried ripping the skin off one side of my face and then the other with the same confidence of the women I'd seen a while back at a rabbit-processing plant as they skinned the creatures hanging from hooks. As easy as it was to get the skin off the area under my chin, which was still blanketed by stray hairs here and there, I had no little trouble with my forehead, from which I couldn't tear off the skin even after several tries. Not that this surprised me, and I was even less surprised to see not a single splotch of blood on the three-fourths of my face I'd skinned. I felt no pain, if I don't count the recognition that struck me while standing in front of the mirror that never again could I appear before other people. I was just about to begin setting the various other larger and smaller shreds of skin into order when I awoke.

Though I barred myself from ascribing more importance than necessary to this dream, over the course of the day it nonetheless caused me more and more distress. But even psychological pain has its stages that smooth out pain. Gradual possession occurs here, too, much as in the case of physical suffering. Compared with the latter, this of course is hopeless in that we can't escape so conspicuously from the burden of that which has insidiously descended upon us. In the case of pain that happens to take hold of a single part of our bodies, after a particular barrage we can catch our breath for a shorter or longer time, preparing to endure the next round. Indeed, by experiencing the rhythms and pace of the pain, we come to enjoy a sort of protection, too, for we know that once it reaches the peak, our foe will retreat, and in fortunate moments it might even dull our senses. Perhaps this is precisely why certain people escape to 'concrete' illnesses, for at least shooting, stinging pain doesn't go about malingering. It attacks the ailing part of the body openly, in a somewhat aboveboard sort of way, and its arc can be calculated with a suitable discipline. This unspoken agreement might also be called the alliance of body and pain, under which unendurable torment yields a loss of consciousness, while tolerating a lesser pain for a few minutes or perhaps hours soon results in an incomparable calm. It is precisely that pain which has already escalated to the utmost degree that guarantees the attacked reaches of the body a momentary calm, one that psychological torment, which feels immaterial, without foundation in the physical world, can never partake of. Distress, continually indefinable in different ways, can wound the body's nerve tracts not even once! Insidiously sprawling fear can never turn into a painful stimulus, so we might subdue it even temporarily with cunning medications!

While tearing the skin off my face with the expertise of a pig-slaughterer, I felt no physical pain. As for the dread that took hold of me not long after, however, there was no shaking it off even into the morning. In vain I turned to various, previously successful techniques to forget the yellowish-white surfaces of flesh; the bulging, denuded cheekbones underneath the eyes; the zigzagging strips of skin left on my forehead—I could not free myself of the thought of my temptation. As if by staging a preliminary display of the punishment awaiting me, the image from the dream sought to prevent me from handing over my manuscript to L. True, my hand did merely what my entire body desired. After all, I was the one who, if a bit clumsily, carried out the ritual as an instrument of the involuntary desire for transformation. I tore even the final vestige of humanness off my face, and saw before me a being that had previously shown itself only in my phantasms.

The sharper the image became over the course of the morning, the more distant the original meaning of the act I'd committed in my dream became, and increasingly I saw only L.'s expression of disgust and disdain—the moments when, after reading the last line of my manuscript, she steps before me, and I, as if again standing in front of the bathroom mirror, raise my hand in a defensive motion before my face. But L.'s gaze penetrates my palm. I then lower my eyes and feel my skin peeling off me in a single, gauzelike sheet, from my hairline all the way to the bottom of my neck. When I look back up, I want to say something to L., but I have no mouth. Now I lean down to pick up from before my feet the skin that has fallen from my face and set it back in place, but without first sweeping away the salt of the hatred that has been deposited on the open flesh, without first disinfecting the cartilage, the jawbone.

Soon the image ceased. But by then it seemed impossible to determine whether perhaps in fact I'd dreamt the latter, only that I didn't notice L. in the bathroom by the mirror. Was I remembering incorrectly? Had I not even wounded my skin while shaving? Was it not even I who'd ripped off that narrow strip of skin? Had her invisible gaze done the flaying instead of my hands, or had my fingers complied with her disgust? I recalled the visions that had eaten away at her face. How unattainable it had seemed then that I could project the signs of decay, of slow disintegration onto my own body! Finally it was my turn, even if I had to regard this as a different sort of temptation; for the admonition of this muddled dream told me I'd arrived as a final choice: either I'd show L. my manuscript, and with this accept the consequences, disgust, disdain, and all, or else I'd relinquish the illusion of my freedom. I could not imagine a third possibility, after all. But I knew the nature of my tempter too well to suspect a sidelong deception in the contract on offer. Even less apt to deceive me was my awareness that the dream was in fact unrepeatable, for I sensed that in the hour of my exposure, a different sort of sentence would await me.

Perhaps for weeks or months I would not be able to look upon her, insofar as I would have the opportunity at all. She'd open the door upon me with a wordless motion, for example, enveloping me with a silence plants must know when their sap runs dry in the fall. And could I ever forget the arch of her hand, that bridge linking the shores of our now mutual disdain? Or would I from now on always see the angle of inflection of hand and paper, the shadow cast by her thin fingers as they come down upon the title page?

But perhaps after showing my true colours for the first time L. would remain indifferent, waiting for me to pass sentence. Such strength was not beyond her, I knew, and so I could not discount the possibility that my punishment would take this form. Why should she not have trusted in the inventiveness of the master of dissimulation—namely, me? Outlining the content of my work would be just enough to reassure her that she'd gotten beyond the shameful matter herself, and with my kind permission she could then leave the rest to me. I would have to measure the degree of disgust behind her unnatural indifference, hear in her silence my vileness.

I would be in a state of constant doubt relative to my suspicion thus far, for I could never be certain when our eyes chanced to meet, that in her eyes I wouldn't discern the same gravitation that had always characterized my own gaze. Perhaps now she'd deliberately slip into her glance that equivocation that until now I'd only imagined. Perhaps she'd voluntarily accept the role my perversity had assigned her, for she could avenge herself with this uncertainly certain game. For me, the indifference accompanying all this would be the least endurable, and that would raise a heavier shield between us than any punishment inflicted upon me possibly could. My face would turn as white during these exchanged glances as that of a traitor who, knowing he has been unmasked, carries out one last mission. Would her touches not feel like provocations when, stepping up beside me, she'd take my hand and pass my fingers over her face? Perhaps I would see this as merely deception, as her perambulation of my deliriums, both those that had been hidden in the paragraphs of my manuscript and also those she'd earlier exposed. Of course, I still wouldn't be able to decide whether I should see in her a lover, an accomplice, or both at the same time.

No matter how harsh I believed the modes of punishment that would accompany my self-revelation to be, I did not give up the illusion of freedom, which my tempter sought to deprive me of by way of the unavoidability of the humiliations awaiting me.

I'd always doubted the supposition that we human beings had been born to be clear-sighted. When an observer's attentive gaze arrives at reality without illusions, he must necessarily realize that his new state of illumination differs in practice not at all from the fog of the preceding conditions. Does not the most brilliant observer of all, God, not experience this same bleakness? What force of inertia gets him past the deadlock? Or am I misunderstanding him? Should I see him not as he who embodies the law but, rather, as the chief dispenser of appearances, the inexhaustible grantor of illusions? After all, it is not us who maintain the illusion, but vice versa: the illusion keeps us alive. Those know this full well who pass their hands over their foreheads at least once a day while contemplating the most populous class of living beings, who would soon be staking out fifty-lane thoroughfares on their skulls. But not one is racked by doubt; indeed, if someone happens to be digging a cesspool, he'd press the shovel even harder into the ground, smiling upon the increasingly desirable figure when she appears at the other end of the yard with beer bottles in her hands. This smile shares something in common with the way a hog about to be butchered nestles up against his owner. For how else to characterize the blind trust that fills this creature even on the day the pig-killer is to arrive, even as his final corncobs are thrown before him?

Those deprived by their fate of all the good works of appearances won't be able to take a single step without recalling the lie that still makes their walking possible at all. But it would be foolish to think that this is the will of our creator. His aims for us are different; perhaps to make us the instruments of his illusion. Perhaps because he himself is dependent on our happiness. Acceptance of the illusion is a lure that, while it makes us blind, can free us from the feeling that we are being bilked. He who rejects it says no to the point of existing at all, while by choosing it he swells the numbers of dilettantes, although it is true that the real illusionist invited him for a far merrier adventure. Perhaps those errant souls seasoned by pleasure have the most to say about this falsity, those who finally give in with incomparably lighter hearts than their cheerless counterparts, incorrigible deniers of appearances.

In my wretched hallucinations I'd seen before me two bodies resting calmly after lovemaking often enough to suspect that their embraces had trounced the meaninglessness of existence more assuredly than all the sterile rationalizations of the clear-sighted; for those two bodies had taken for themselves that which knowledge that winds up behind appearances can never know. The rest is the secret of the hope built into cells.

In contrast with my tempter, I held as firmly to illusion—illusion flirting with pleasure and meaninglessness—as someone condemned to hang does with the most congenial executioner, from whom he hopes for a quick and expert death. My comparison is imprecise. What I awaited from this was my liberation, trusting that, with the acceptance of the punishment awaiting me, I could finally study that most precious art of illusion. If need be, I would tear the skin off my face from dream to dream, or else I would allow L. to shame me from day to day, hour to hour, for I would endure even the most skilfully planned humiliation better than my accursed deliriums, which had torn me from the world of appearances.

How could I have ever compared L.'s demon with my own?! Fear and jealousy had laid out the boundary which, from out of the worlds of appearances, had showed me only hell; for depending on our capacity for happiness, the distance between the two is shorter than even a step. But even as a child, when I was drawn to rundown hospitals, I was bent on noticing only a certain type of illusion. I narrowed down what could not be previously eliminated and had rendered unidirectional that which had always been flowing in several directions.

With the perennial faith of the foolish I prepared for the day when I would hand over my work to L. This is what I expected would change my relationship with appearances. This became an obsession I might have called my newest compulsive idea, one I defended like certain girls do their honour. It seemed possible that from the very moment in which I'd hand over my manuscript, I would feel relief. Why should I not have thought that by disclosing the illness of mine I'd kept a secret for years, I too would be visited by the calm of those who confess? If this is how it would be, then not even the judgement would count. Nor did I think it inconceivable that over the course of those few days during which L. would read my pages, something would strengthen in me, something I can at most call a realization beyond despair. I thought of the pitiable strength of a man who recognizes over the bodies of his loved ones that from now on, nothing more can be taken from him.

On a rainy, early Thursday afternoon I gave L. my confession. I wasn't afraid, though I would have had reason to be. Perhaps my courage stemmed from the same determination that moves a criminal to surrender after a long time in hiding, for he secretly hopes his decision will bring him relief. As soon as L. reached towards the manuscript I'd placed on the table, it occurred to me that not even my unhappiness could have forced me into this, and perhaps indeed I would have been wiser if, instead of a pathetically writing it all down, which might make me seem a monster in her eyes, I'd turned to a psychiatrist. Only a bit later did I notice that her fingers had formed a slightly curved triangle against the pages.

AUTHOR'S ACKNOWLEDGMENT

With gratitude to Paul Olchváry, who in the past twenty years has done a great deal to ensure this novel's publication.

Jakarta

TRANSLATOR'S ACKNOWLEDGMENT

This translation would have been impossible to realize fully in the absence of Ferenc Barnás's enduring friendship and close collaboration over so many years.

Williamstown, Massachusetts